Paula Boer has been passionate about horses since an early age and is particularly interested in natural horsemanship. She lives on 500 acres in the Snowy Mountains of Australia, with two retired endurance horses and a stick loving dog. Inspiration for her stories comes from walking through the forest, listening to the birds, and watching wildlife.

Paula has been a regular contributor to horse magazines and has had many animal short stories published. Her best-selling *Brumbies* series of novels for middle grade readers follows the adventures of two teen-agers catching and breaking in the wild horses of Australia.

For more information about Paula and her books, visit paulaboer.com.

T0288791

THE BLOODWOLF WAR

THE EQUINORA CHRONICLES: BOOK 1

BY

PAULA BOER

The Bloodwolf War

ISBN-13: 978-1-925956-16-0

V1.0

Printed in Palatino Linotype and Badloc ICG.

IFWG Publishing International
Melbourne

www.ifwgpublishing.com

For my beloved Pete, without whose support I would never have become a writer.

Acknowledgements

It is impossible to list everyone who has helped and supported me through my writing journey, but I especially wish to thank fellow writers Mike Murphy and Michael B Fletcher for their early feedback; beta readers Megan Matters and Suzy Butz for reading many sections, if not all, many times; and Rob Porteous, whose critique resulted in me turning the manuscript on its head. Thanks also to Gerry Huntman, my wonderful publisher, not least of all for the terrific maps; Steve Santiago for the fabulous cover; and Noel Osualdini for being the easiest editor I have ever worked with.

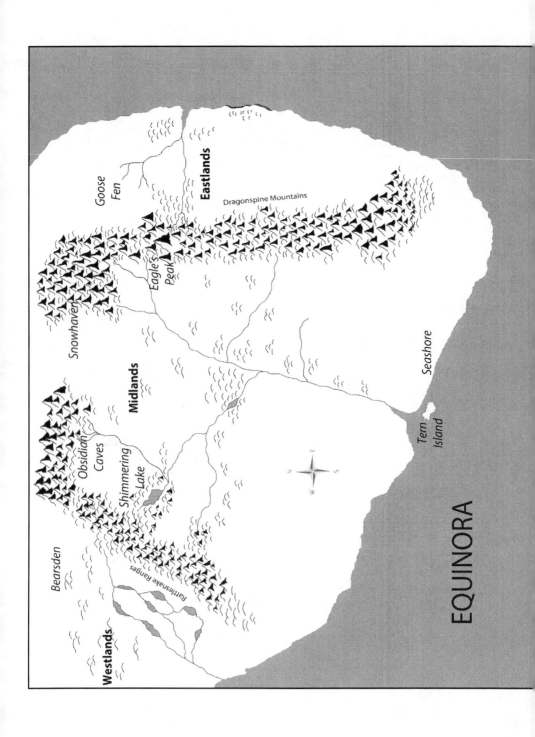

EQUINORA

Westlands

Bearsden

Rattlesnake Ranges

Obsidian Caves

Shimmering Lake

Midlands

Snowhaven

Eagle's Peak

Goose Fen

Eastlands

Dragonspine Mountains

Tern Island

Seashore

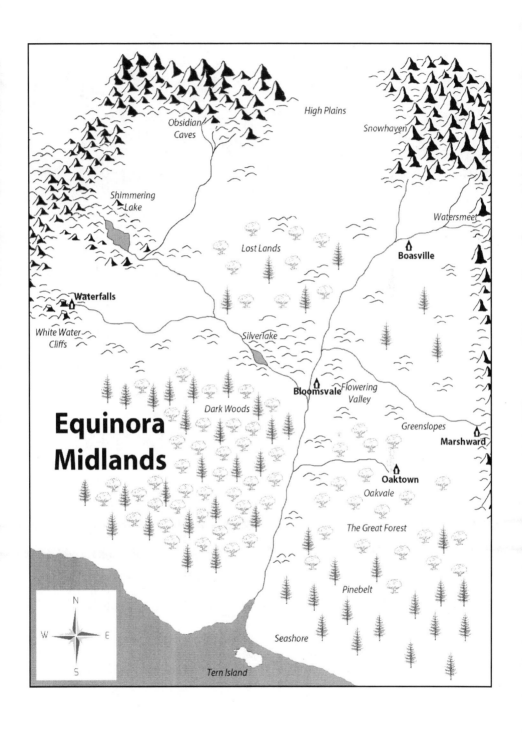

Prologue

Aureana trotted through the meadow, proud of the land she had created, yet a hollowness remained in her soul. Her hooves thrummed as she broke into a canter, trailing the golden feathers of her wingtips amid yellow and orange marigolds. She breathed in the delicate bouquet with flared nostrils and soaked in the warmth of the sun. Clouds of pollen dusted her in sparkling flecks, but the beauty failed to delight her.

Loneliness gnawed at her heart.

She halted on a knoll and surveyed the herds of horses grazing in contentment in the valleys. A mare nuzzled a newborn foal reluctant to drink. A pair of yearlings reared in play, squealing and nipping in a mock fight. The stallion king remained apart, his neck arched and tail high, keeping a watchful eye on his boundary for intruders. Even people busied about hunting game and gathering fruit, each clan living near a herd of horses to take care of them.

But she was alone. As alone as when she had lived in the spirit world. Whenever she approached the horses, her favourite creatures, they fled, dazzled by the power radiating from her in golden light. What was the point of having created this idyllic world if she didn't participate in its pleasures? She wanted a partner, and not the short-lived horses who graced her land, living and dying in the natural cycle of life. Could she create an equal to fulfil her need for companionship and help her manage this physical world she had named Equinora?

Filled with fresh enthusiasm, Aureana considered her options. She wanted someone to complement her powers, not match them. She wanted someone who would challenge her thinking and inspire her to greater deeds. She wanted someone who would live for millennia.

Standing four-square, she drew power from the sun and wove the threads of energy into life, waving the golden horn on her forehead to outline the shape she desired. As the unicorn formed, she opened her heart and let her essence flow into the new being, a mate of her spirit.

A snort broke Aureana's trance.

A snow-white mare with golden mane, tail, hooves, and horn stood before her, the unicorn's sapphire eyes glinting like a deep lake. What had gone wrong? She'd wanted a stallion!

Aureana trotted around the newcomer, admiring her beauty even if she wasn't what Aureana had intended. "You're the moon to my sun, glowing with my spirit. I name you Moonglow, and grant you the power to see the future." She opened her wings and ran her feathers from the tip of the Spirit Unicorn's ears to the end of her tail.

Moonglow sniffed the ground and took a tentative step forward. Her skin twitched as if assailed by insects. Her eyes glazed over. Her lips trembled.

> "Three from spirit, earth, and water
> Three from light, air, and fire
> Impart your soul to unicorns
> So you never tire"

Aureana wandered the glade, deep in thought. "Create six unicorns? Yes, there's much to do in managing a world."

Using her golden hooves, she dug moist earth from the riverbank and created Echo, his body the colour of loam, his mane, tail, horn, and hooves bright emerald like new shoots in spring. Using her wings, she granted the Earth Unicorn the ability to transform wood and stone into food and medication for all the animals.

Moonglow and Echo greeted each other with whickers of delight, snuffling noses, and thanked Aureana for their creation. They pranced and snorted before galloping along the creek and jumping rocks, kicking up clods of soil in their exuberance. Leaving her alone. But there were four more to create. One of them would be her mate.

She stepped into the river and drew up water to create Tempest, his coat ocean-blue, his mane, tail, and horn the white froth of waves, and his hooves the black of tar. She gifted the Water Unicorn power over the weather, the rivers, and the seas. He emerged in a rainbow spray and chased off after the others.

Aureana stamped a hoof. Three more to go. The sun shone strong overhead. She captured its beams and absorbed the light to create Diamond, empowering her to traverse the land without the need to run. Like Moonglow, her body shone snow-white, but her mane, tail, and horn glistened silver, her eyes crystal, and her hooves black onyx. The Light Unicorn also galloped away to stretch her legs.

Aureana didn't join them. Their creation had exhausted her. No matter, she must fulfil the prophecy, or else what had been the point of creating a Spirit Unicorn to see the future. And she still didn't have a partner.

Holding her head high, she tamed the breeze teasing the grasses, called the winds ruffling the treetops, and sucked down the currents driving the clouds. Moisture beaded on her muzzle hairs and dripped to her hooves, forming a pool. The water shimmered and changed form into a dappled mare. She lay prone, tiny and delicate, as fragile as moth antennae.

Aureana lowered her wings and swept them over Dewdrop, from the tips of her black horn and hooves, over each rosette of grey on her body, and along the white wisps of hair of her mane and tail.

She nuzzled the mare's shoulder. "Can you stand?"

Dewdrop opened her eyes and blinked. She sat up with her forelegs thrust in front of her and staggered to her feet like a newborn foal. After shaking in a spray of mist she coughed, tears seeping from the corners of her black eyes.

Concern flooded Aureana. "I will grant you the power of healing so you can mend whatever ails you." She stepped around the Air Unicorn, stroking her with her wings, enveloping her in love.

Dewdrop staggered on wobbly legs.

Aureana led her to drink and guzzled the snowmelt too, chilling her insides to match the fear in her heart. Why was Dewdrop so small? Why wasn't she strong like the others? Maybe her physique represented her element, light as air. Perhaps time would aid her.

Aureana must ensure the final unicorn was strong—a worthy mate.

Taking care to gather dry firewood from beneath the nearby aspens, she built a bonfire as high as her withers from sturdy boughs. She placed flints and dry grasses at the edge of the tangled branches and struck a spark with her hoof. A lick of flame tickled the kindling, sending up a spiral of smoke. The fire spread and caught the remainder of the pile, crackling and roaring in its own wind. She jabbed her horn into the raging flames and concentrated on the minerals of the world, inviolable, immutable.

The fire died down and the air stilled. Instead of a pile of ash, a unicorn stallion formed from the embers, his body glowing like hot coals, his mane, tail, and hooves as black as wet ash. Jasper, the Fire Unicorn, leapt to his feet, whinnying in challenge.

Aureana answered in welcome. He was magnificent! "Remain still while I add your power."

"Power? Rid me of this pain!" Jasper trotted in circles, his head lowered with froth blowing from his mouth. Sweat lathered his chest and flanks.

Stunned, Aureana hastened to keep up with his agonised pace. Running beside him, she wrapped a wing over his back and caressed his rump. She raced in front of him and smothered his neck and head with her other wing, passing on the ability to shape earth and rock. As her wing slid from his face she stumbled in horror; instead of a smooth straight horn, the protrusion from his forehead twisted and curled like an ancient pine, mottled brown, knobbly and rough.

Had the fire been too hot? He was strong, there was no doubt about that, but aggression erupted from his every step, anger pulsed in his throat. She sent him love, cantering beside him as he tried to outrun his torment, galloping when he attempted to flee her help.

Nothing worked. She let him go.

Dejected, Aureana wandered off to be alone, scuffing up a cloud of dust that trailed her like a wake of inadequacy. Cresting a hill, she surveyed the land rolling before her: vast forests of pine and oak stretched to the horizon, sparkling waterfalls tumbled into rivers, and furred and feathered creatures went about their lives.

They gave her no joy. Her hope for an equal dissipated like mist.

Aureana introduced the unicorns to the regions she had made, teaching them to draw strength from the sun, the wind, and the earth. They invented challenges to test their powers and raced over the toughest terrain to strengthen their bodies. She didn't join them. They developed the ability to communicate by mind from afar and block their own and others' thoughts when necessary, but she didn't share their thrills of discovery.

Aureana remained alone. Instead of creating a partner, she had six helpers to rule the world. They had taken to their roles so easily she had little to do. That had never been her intent.

Still she desired a stallion to fly by her side, someone to share her joys and worries, to dream with, and to build new creations. Someone like her. But how could she create him? She had used all the elements. The sun crossed the sky as she pondered her problem, her shadow moving around her as if it had a life of its own. Her shadow. That was how she could make a true equal of herself.

She located a high platform of stone and stood side-on to maximise the light she blocked. Absorbing the sunshine into her golden body, she pulled life from the rock, drew in the force of the wind, and threw all her power into her shadow. She poured more of her spirit into this creation than she had used for all six unicorns together.

Shadow came to life. As tall as her, he rippled with muscle, oozing power. His crimson mane and tail spewed like a volcano above his obsidian body. He was stupendous!

Then disappointment hit Aureana. Like the unicorns, he was wingless. She must have left her wings pinned to her sides while she worked. How could he join her in the delights of soaring among the clouds? As he finished forming, his forehead failed to sprout a long straight horn, his symbol of power. Instead, two horns curled around his ears like those of a ram, black and warped. How would he wield those? What power could she give him?

Shadow didn't wait for her touch. He bolted from the ledge and galloped down to the valley.

She flew after him, desperate not to lose her partner.

Power cracked from the duocorn's horns like lightning, searing the ground and bursting shrubs into splinters. Coneys and weasels scurried beneath his hooves, expanding as his force hit them and exploding in a mess of flesh and bone. Shadow didn't need Aureana to grant him power from her wings—he already burst with more than she could give. Instead of the perfect partner, she had created a monster.

He upset the horse herds, killing the lead stallions and raping the mares. Landscapes Aureana had carved crumbled into dust at his touch. Plants she'd created withered and died in his wake. Animals she'd nurtured with love and care became malformed or riddled with disease. Aureana couldn't keep up with the destruction. Shadow even harried the unicorns, mocking them as weak and ineffectual, destroying their unity.

Pain pierced Aureana's skull. Gold flashed behind her eyes. She reared, screaming, and leapt into the air. She flew to the source of her agony and landed at a run, wings still outspread, horn pointed forward in a charge.

Shadow and Jasper fought, their chests crashing together with thunder.

Aureana smashed into them. "I demand you stop!"

As soon as they parted, she galloped to where Dewdrop lay on her side, covered in bleeding gashes, skin hanging from her in ribbons.

Dead.

Jasper raced over. "Shadow—"

Aureana heard none of his babbling. She blew into Dewdrop's face, licked her muzzle, and nipped her ear.

No response.

She sucked in all the power she could hold from the sun, the wind, and the earth, and swept her wings over Dewdrop's mangled body. Blood stained her feathers, clogging them in useless mats.

Dewdrop remained dead.

Aureana grabbed one of her own wings in her teeth and tore at the feathers. One came free. She spat it out and stamped on the useless plume. She pulled out another, and another. What good was her power if she created corruption and couldn't even save Dewdrop? She snatched at her other wing and ripped out two more feathers.

"Stop!" Jasper lunged at her neck with bared teeth. "You won't be able to fly!"

"Don't give me orders!" Trembling, she stood over Dewdrop and hung her head as the world spun beneath her.

The other unicorns crept up, reaching out their noses and uttering words of consolation.

She ignored them. She had failed Equinora, her strength gone. "I must return to the spirit world."

Moonglow whinnied in dismay. "You can't leave! There are only five of us now. You must create another unicorn. It's the prophecy."

"No, I won't create another. I will choose a strong foal and make each generation stronger. You are now the guardians of Equinora. Take especial care of the horses." She cantered away, ignoring their pleas for her to remain.

Jasper raced in front of her, blocking her path. "What about Shadow?"

Aureana halted and looked around. "Where is he?"

Jasper snorted. "He's gone."

"I will deal with him." Aureana resumed her gallop up the hillside. Once on higher ground, she straightened her remaining flight feathers and took to the air, struggling to stay straight and unable to gain height with her unbalanced wings. She sought Shadow, ranging in circles until she spotted his dark form. He galloped faster than she had imagined possible, leaving a wake of destruction, trees torn up by their roots and the earth churned to a quagmire. Herds of horses and deer fled in panic.

Swooping low, Aureana prodded him with her horn, driving him hard until they reached a valley of bubbling lava and steaming pools hidden among mountains of rock where nothing grew. He galloped between two pillars of obsidian into a narrow gorge.

She streamed power from the sun to block the gateway and flew in a wide circle, using thermals to aid her flight around the mountains. She lapped every entrance into the valley, building a barrier of power, adding layer after layer to hold Shadow forever in its embrace.

With barely enough strength left to fly, she sought solace at the far southern ocean. Her heart broke at having to leave the unicorns to protect Equinora. But she couldn't remain.

She plunged into the surf. Leafy sea dragons and potbellied seahorses milled around her, their camouflage blending with the kelp wafting with the tide. They blew bubbles at her, tugged on her mane and tail, and tickled her face to cheer her up.

If she couldn't stay on Equinora, at least she could give the unicorns companions to lessen their burden of guardianship. Blowing over the sea dragons, she granted them the freedom to roam salt and fresh water, gave them long lives and the ability to communicate with other species. The aquadragons thanked her, shining aquamarine and turquoise from her love as they darted and dived in trails of phosphorescence.

With Aureana's encouragement, the seahorses left the water, wriggling up the sandy beach. She followed and enabled them to breathe through their long snouts. As she bequeathed them her remaining power, their dorsal fins split into wings and other fins transformed to pairs of legs like those of birds. Their skin hardened and grew protective scales of emeralds and rubies, diamonds and sapphires.

The brighter the dragons' scales grew, the more Aureana dimmed, until her body became translucent. "Befriend the unicorns in my place."

With a flash of golden light, she returned to the spirit world.

Shadow charged up and down the jagged peaks of savage stone that formed his prison. He explored every path, every niche of rock, every gorge. There was no escape. Damn Aureana! Why had she granted him so much power without the skill to control it? No matter what he did, nothing turned out the way he planned.

He must have his freedom! He must learn to control his powers.

With few creatures living at Obsidian Caves, Shadow practiced on spiders and insects, lizards and newts. Most died. When a few survived, albeit with disfiguring abnormalities or shortened lifespans, he moved on to bats and birds. But the colonies and flocks moved away, scared of his interfering. They wouldn't be able to help him escape anyway. Emboldened by his power, he created storms and froze waterfalls, shaped valleys and redirected rivers—anything that might break down the barrier that contained him. Nothing worked.

A wolf pack sought shelter from the northerly winds, their ribs protruding and their fur falling off in clumps. They limped on bleeding paws, their toenails worn to nothing. They barely had strength to pant, let alone hold up their heads.

Shadow welcomed them into his cavern. "Warm yourselves near the lava."

This time he would attempt something different. Exhaling over a pile of obsidian fragments, he transformed the rock into sustenance for the wolves. The molten pile steamed, exuding the ammonia tartness of raw flesh. The pack pounced, tossing their heads back and devouring the chunks whole. Their eyes brightened.

Shadow created more food. And more, until the wolves' bellies swelled close to bursting and their movements slowed. They lay down, heads on paws, and slept. Their bodies grew and their coats thickened, their bones hardened and their muscles strengthened. Streaks of crimson threaded their fur and their canines lengthened into great hooks.

Delighted with his success, Shadow pranced around the cavern, anxious for them to wake.

The leader stirred. "That's the best meal we've had in a long while. What can we do to thank you?"

Shadow didn't hesitate. "Travel the whole of Equinora. Send all wolves to me. And annihilate every one of Aureana's precious horses."

Chapter 1

Fleet picked at the little grass remaining in the clearing, a wedge of sky teasing him with its sense of space. His legs itched to run, to gallop until he couldn't breathe, to pound the earth so the world passed by in blur. He never had. He'd spent all his two years of life locked in this dense forest of giant oaks, horse chestnuts, and elms.

He wandered over to where Sapphire, his dam, dozed. "Tell me again about racing with the wind."

Sapphire opened her eyes and shifted her weight. "Why? We must stay here."

"I want to see the wide open spaces you've told me about. I can't imagine grasses like you say, as high as our chests. How can water rush in streams?" He nibbled her rump and swished his tail to keep the flies off her face.

She didn't reciprocate. "Leave me be. I'm tired. Something's not right, but I don't know what."

Fleet flicked his ears. He couldn't detect anything untoward. With a heavy sigh, he left Sapphire to her worries, and snuck out of the clearing as she closed her eyes again. She was old and rarely wanted to explore, only ever moving to find fresh grazing.

Following the trail back the way they had come the previous day, Fleet broke into a trot. Darkness enveloped him under the dense canopy. The hairs down his spine prickled. A heavy lump churned his guts. He could go no further. Sapphire was right—something threatened. He broke into a canter and hurried back to the clearing.

A huge wolf slunk across his vision, heading for the oak where Sapphire grazed. He neighed to warn her and galloped over. Pain seared his rump. Sharp claws gouged his hide. The stench of rank

11

breath accompanied a deep growl. Fleet lashed out with his hind legs, spun around, and thrashed his forelegs on the wolf's back.

It ducked beneath him and leapt at Sapphire. Its curved fangs closed on her neck. She reared and struck out with her front hooves. The wolf smashed against her chest, knocking her over. The air filled with the metallic smell of blood as her flesh was rent by its fangs. "Run!"

He ignored her command and charged, neck stretched forward, teeth bared. His hooves skidded on the wet grass as he neared the wolf.

The beast spun on sturdy legs. As tall as Fleet's shoulder, its maw opened wide, its tongue slick with gore.

Fleet raced into the trees, trying to draw the wolf away from Sapphire.

Neither of them followed.

He slowed and listened. Nothing. Not even the birds raised a warning. He returned to the clearing, every hair on end, nostrils wide, and blood streaming from the gouges in his hindquarters.

Sapphire lay on the far side, her sides heaving.

The wolf streaked out of the shadows on silent paws, drool dribbling from its gaping jaws, straight at him. It leapt.

Fleet reared in defence. Before the wolf reached him, it fell across Sapphire's body, a wooden shaft protruding from its throat.

Dead.

Fleet skidded to a halt and dragged the corpse off Sapphire, gagging on the foul taste of the fur. "We must flee! There might be another one!"

Sapphire peered at him through slitted eyes. "I told you to go. Why did you come back?"

Fleet blew into her nostrils. "To save you."

Her head slumped to the ground. "A man shot it. You can trust people. They help horses."

"Who?"

Her breath came in shallow, rapid rasps. "Upright beings. One saved your life. You must thank him. There's so much I haven't taught you."

She thrashed and groaned. She writhed and gasped. Her body shuddered.

Then she went limp. Her eyes opened, their vivid blue dimmed to smoky grey. She struggled to breathe. "A vision…so terrible…a black and red horse…with twisted horns…an army…of bloodwolves… Save horses…from destruction… All horses… You."

"Me? What can I do? I don't even know any other horses." Fleet trembled and sweat trickled down his legs.

Bloody froth bubbled from her lips. "The unicorns…are meant to protect us… Find them… Warn King Streak… Promise me!"

Fleet lowered his head to hear better. "What am I meant to do?"

"Go east… Streak must know… Promise."

Fleet shook his mane in confusion. "I promise to do whatever is necessary to save the herds. But I need to know more. Who are the unicorns?"

There was no reply.

Sapphire's final words rang in Fleet's ears, nagging him to move, yet he couldn't leave her. Sorrow swamped him like a winter fog, chilling his heart. He'd known no horse other than his dam. He had never met his sire or any of his siblings. But instinct ran deep— he desired to run with his kind. He wanted to be part of a family, dreamt of mock battles with other stallions and showing off for the fillies. Instead, he was alone with no idea how to find other horses, let alone unicorns.

And Sapphire's words confused him. How did people help horses? Who was King Streak? The only stories he had heard were of King Thunder, his sire. When he was a foal, Sapphire's eyes would glaze over as she mentioned the stallion's name. Then with a snort she would mumble something about needing to find thistles or dandelions and trot off without finishing the story.

How can a horse have horns?

The wolf's carcass lay where he had dragged it, its neck sagging on the ground, its legs and tail sunken into the leaf litter. The taste of the putrid coat lingered on Fleet's tongue. No amount of water washed away the taint. A sense of being watched made the hairs on his back prickle, every nerve afire with the impulsion to flee. He needed to get far from this place of death. The smell would attract other wolves.

He tottered forward, his hindquarters stiff and sore from the wolf's claws. North was wolf territory. To the west lay the country

13

Sapphire had fled. A desolate wasteland of bogs and marshes border-ed the southern lands. A dense thicket of blackberries barred the way east. But Sapphire had said east. With a last glance at her corpse, he nickered a farewell, and used his broad chest to force his way through the prickly bushes.

With each step away from the carnage, the air smelled cleaner. In stark contrast, his sense of isolation grew. His hooves made no sound on the soft moss and leaves that carpeted the ground. Only the chirruping of robins and chats reached his swivelling ears; no slow breath of his dam, no reassuring tread of her hoof falls.

A twig cracked.

Fleet shot into a gallop, fearing another wolf. Branches slashed his face and tangled his mane. A fallen tree blocked his way, too high to jump. Spinning to face the threat, he smashed his head against an overhanging limb. He backed up and reared in frustration, tearing open the wound in his rump. He pawed the air against an invisible enemy, sending fire searing down his hind legs from his injuries.

The air remained free of wolf scent. He couldn't even detect a hog. Or could he? A faint whiff of long-dead hogskin drifted from above. But hogs didn't climb trees. Looking up, Fleet shied.

A strange creature with wooden shafts slung on its back crawled along a branch, the scent of hog emanating from its coverings. A meat-eater!

He bolted south.

Yuma slumped as he watched the horse gallop away. "Don't go into the bog, my beauty." In his years of being surrounded by horses, he had never seen such a magnificent specimen. The stallion didn't appear to have a single white hair on him, not even a tiny star on his forehead. Only the festering wounds from the wolf marred the black coat. His neck and rump were thick with muscle, belying the youth evident from his narrow muzzle.

After hefting his pack and quiver onto his back, Yuma swung his rope over his shoulder. Should he continue to follow the horse or not? Already his laced boots squelched and the late summer sun warmed his jerkin and leggings. He daren't remove the hogskins as they prevented chaffing and would only be more to carry.

When he had first encountered the two horses, he had recognised the chestnut by her deep blue eyes. She had been the boss mare near his home until the lead stallion had been killed and the herd dispersed. By the way in which the old mare chivvied the black horse, he was her colt, not a bachelor keen on establishing a herd. Surprised to find the pair so deep in the woods, Yuma had followed them from his vantage point in the trees, curious to see where they led.

He'd been startled to encounter a lone wolf. The creatures rarely ventured to the warm south and he had never seen one on its own. It had been a lucky shot that found its throat and killed it. He'd loosed his arrow without thinking, wanting to protect the horses that usually helped his clan. The flint tips were suitable for coneys and squirrels, and, when he could get close enough, hogs. He'd never hunted wolves—they were far too large for people to tackle, especially with such thick coats.

Although Yuma had been tempted to skin the beast for a bedroll, the stench of the fur had made him gag. The wolf had probably been sick, which was why its pack had pushed it out. Or maybe the wolf's deformity was the reason it was on its own. It was unusually large with humped shoulders and peculiar teeth, and streaked red instead of grey. He had extracted two of the overgrown incisors as a gift for any potential lifemate. The enormous fangs would look good on any piece of jewellery, even better than hog tusks. He doubted he'd ever see another pair like them.

Yuma had travelled east before, often attending the annual summer gathering of the clans at Oaktown to trade his flints for hog products, though usually he took the easier route along the river. This time he hadn't been able to resist following the horses.

He had been angry when his father, Tyee Valiant, had demanded he remain at home this year to care for those too sick, old, or young to make the arduous journey. Yuma suspected Tyee wanted to instil responsibility into him, knowing eventually he must take over as leader. Against tradition, Yuma had no interest in taking his place as Chief of Waterfalls clan.

Returning from Oaktown a moon ago, Tyee had finally agreed to let Yuma travel. "You're twenty-five. Don't come back without a partner. I need grandchildren raised here to learn our ways, not those you've probably sired all over the country who I'll never meet."

Many a woman would have accompanied Yuma back to Waterfalls. Instead, each year after the gathering, he wandered off to explore the world, collecting anything of interest and visiting other clans. He revelled in playing his pipe, swapping tales over a few ales, and carving figures. And every winter he returned to his village alone.

Alone like the stallion. The horse acted as if he had never seen a person before, nervous at Yuma's approach and ignoring the signals people used to communicate with the herds. How could that be? The horses he knew relied on people to feed them through the winter as much as the clans relied on the horses to chase hogs during hunts. Deciding the mystery was worth wet feet, he trudged in the handsome stallion's hoof prints, each filled with water to Yuma's knees. At least the heavy going would slow the horse down, too.

Tired from wading through thick mud, Yuma stopped for a break. The last camp had provided a plentiful supply of nuts and fungi to eat as he walked, so he wasn't hungry, but his legs ached. Swigging from his bladderflask, he relished a few mouthfuls of precious creek water before setting off again. He didn't want to stiffen up and needed to be out of the wetlands before camping that night. He'd be glad of a longer rest. Biting insects swarmed and buzzed around his face, attracted by his sweat. The foetid air, humid with rotting peat, and his lank hair hanging down his neck, added to his discomfort. He extracted a twine from a pouch on his waist and tied the red mass into a horsetail that hung halfway down his back—another feature that made him different from the other men of the clan.

He hoped he'd reach a river soon. A wash would be welcome. "You'd better be worth this, my beauty."

By the time the sun shone overhead, Yuma was exhausted. His muscles cramped and his arms hung like pieces of firewood. Salt crusted his face. He regretted shaving that morning, a habit he had formed to advertise the sharpness of the flints he traded. At least a beard, even his ginger one, would give him protection from the harsh rays. He adjusted his pack and scanned the horizon for somewhere shady to rest.

A dark mound in the same direction as the horse's hoof prints caught his eye. It was an odd shape for a shrub. Curiosity spurred Yuma on.

The shape grew larger.

And moved.

"You're not a shrub! Hold on, my beauty, I'm coming!" Yuma struggled through the quagmire, flapping his arms to keep his balance as the sucking mud threatened to trip him.

The horse was buried to the chest. Not wanting to end up in the same predicament, Yuma tested each step before advancing. He circled the stricken horse to approach from his head, cooing to him as he crouched low.

The ground gave way beneath his left foot. He floundered, cursing.

If he were still in the woods, he could find green saplings to weave into a mat. Nothing useful lay nearby; he had only what he carried. After removing his pack and quiver, he stripped off his jerkin. Sliding two of his arrows through the arm-holes, he made the leather as rigid as he could and spread it across the soaked ground. He sprawled across the makeshift base. Only his torso fit, leaving his legs dragging in the mud as he used his elbows to advance, dreading the onward journey wearing a mud-stiffened coat.

He squirmed forward. Having neared as close to the stricken horse as he dared, he rolled on his side to slip the rope off his shoulder, made a loop, and gestured in the hope the horse understood his intention.

The horse thrust his muzzle in the air and whinnied. He writhed to free himself. Instead, his body sank lower with each struggle.

Yuma's first throw fell short. He couldn't risk standing up to make his cast more accurate. He tried again.

The rope smacked across the horse's face. The stallion fought to turn away, thrashing his forelegs and tangling his hooves over the rope. His ears flattened to his neck and he showed the whites of his eyes as he sank deeper. Noxious gases burst from the bog, sounding like a great beast sucking the marrow from a bone.

"Come on, my beauty, you can do it!"

Caught under the horse's front legs, the rope pressed down on either side of his withers and snagged behind his elbows.

Yuma hung on as the stallion lunged against the restraint.

The horse's chest raised a hand's width. He lashed out again. The rope pulled taught between his forelegs. He heaved and lurched, and moved against the tug of the bog.

Yuma increased his efforts, taking the strain on the rope as he squirmed backwards like a lizard.

With each lunge the horse made more ground. Exhaling a mighty groan, he surged to his feet, his skin quivering as great gobs of muck slid from his body. His head hung to the rank earth.

Yuma flicked the rope free.

Fleet's tongue stuck to the roof of his mouth, his lips parched. He must get away from this bog, back to the safety of the forest that offered shelter, grass, and water. He was mad to think he could travel on his own. He scrambled clear of the squelching ooze and staggered back the way he had come, dragging his hooves over the uneven ground.

The upright beast trailed him from a distance. This must be a man. Sapphire had said he could trust people, and this one had saved him.

Scenting a pool, Fleet stumbled to the edge and nosed away the algae that swilled on its surface. He sipped through rank weeds but couldn't drink enough to satisfy his thirst. He needed to find a better place. First he had to ease his aching body. Underneath the dried mud, the wounds on his rump throbbed. He located a patch of moss and rolled to remove the crust from his coat. Squirming on his back reminded him of happier days with Sapphire.

Sapphire!

His promise forced him to his feet. Dust flew as he shook from head to tail.

He must go on.

He would have to head northeast to get back on track. With a slight limp in his off hind, he followed the tree line, grazing as he went to rebuild his strength, keeping well ahead of the man.

Too slow. Other bloodwolves might be threatening horses as he dawdled along. He must locate King Streak. He broke into a shuffling trot. Almost immediately, the throbbing in his heavy legs dragged him back to a walk. The pain in his hindquarters built with every step.

The scent of water drew him on, his mind numb to all else. He focused on placing one hoof at a time, stumbling over miniscule stones or grass tussocks. His head hung low and his ears lolled as he staggered towards a steep bank. A vast river swept by. He had never imagined so much water could be in one place and move so fast.

Pain shrieked through his wounds. His head swam. He slipped down the crumbling slope and collapsed at the water's edge.

Chapter 2

Wetness dribbled onto Fleet's tongue. The water tasted sweet with a bitter aftertaste unlike any he had experienced before. A tuft of clover was stuffed into his mouth. He chewed. As his head started to clear, the man offered him water from a hollowed piece of wood. Fleet guzzled, half the contents dribbling from his swollen lips. He swallowed. His head sank back into the sand. He was so tired.

No! He should flee! Unable to stand, he kicked out with his hind legs, their feeble twitching the only result.

The man brought him armfuls of ryegrass and tempted him with the rich seed-heads. He ate and drank more before feeling a new dizziness. Drifting in a daze, as if he'd eaten the forbidden fungi he'd tasted as a foal, he no longer wanted to fight. The man massaged Fleet's stiff muscles and creamed a salve into the raw gashes. Fingers teased out the tangles of his mane and tail. Still he couldn't rise, the pain and exhaustion too much. The grooming lulled him like Sapphire's lips.

Sapphire… He should move…

Instead, he slept.

Fleet woke with a start. Where was he? The sun glared in his eyes. Memories came back as he sighted the man through blinding patches that drifted across his eyes. Fleet winced, his head thick and fuzzy, and his hindquarters as sore as if a tree had fallen on them in the night.

But he had promised. And he would do all he could to prevent another awful death like Sapphire's. The pain in his rump had subsided. He thrust his forelegs out and tried to stand before thudding back to the ground. He struggled again. This time he managed to rise, legs akimbo and panting hard. He tottered to the river and savoured deep swallows. His thirst satisfied, he needed to eat.

As much as he yearned to fulfil his promise, and belong to a herd, Fleet feared the encounter with King Streak. Would the stallion accept him, another king's offspring? Would Streak heed Sapphire's warning? She had always avoided other horses, so he had seen them only from a distance. For a moment he considered not searching for the stallion. It would be easier to stay here and rest his injuries. Loneliness built like his pain; Sapphire wasn't there to tell him what herbs would ease his wounds.

Fleet ambled along the base of the bank until he found a gentle rise. Climbing the shifting sands took more effort than he'd expected. He finally reached the top and picked at the coarse grass. He chewed and swallowed, chewed and swallowed the sourness, needing to recover.

Sapphire's words continued to chase around his head like annoying insects. He must be on his way soon.

The man arrived with an armful of sticks and lit a small fire within a ring of stones. After eating, the man wandered over, holding out his arms smelling of the salve that had eased Fleet's pain. The man slowed and signed with his hands towards Fleet's rump. Not detecting any threat, Fleet remained motionless, his heart racing, every hair on his body alert.

The man approached and rubbed Fleet's neck.

He should run! But his legs refused to work. Hunger overcame his need to remain vigilant. He resumed grazing, the man following his steps to work on Fleet's body. The man continued the massage before running his hands along Fleet's back to the wounds. With tender fingertips, he rubbed the ointment into the scabs, softening the edges. With a firmer motion, he rubbed the large muscles. Blood flowed through Fleet's legs, warming his hooves.

With every moment, Fleet relaxed more and his energy returned, remembering again that Sapphire had said to trust people. He accepted the ministrations and started to plan. If he were to keep heading east, he'd need to cross the river, a challenge he dreaded. He'd never encountered such a deep and wide body of water. He should go back. He could survive in Dark Woods.

No. He had to go east and find King Streak. Feeling stronger, he meandered down to the river and sniffed the water's edge. Gravel washed away beneath his hooves, sucking his feet deeper. He peered across the expanse of water. Nothing indicated how fast the river flowed; no sticks spun by, and no rocks protruded, washed by the current. He waded in to his knees, the cool water dragging at his legs. As he ventured further, the force against his body became stronger than a storm.

Fleet plunged, throwing up his head as the cold force hit his chest.

Out of one eye, he saw the man hesitate before following him. The man had strapped his pack onto his back and now the river tugged at the hogskin, the rope around his shoulders floating in loose loops along the surface of the water.

Fleet ploughed on, cutting across the powerful current.

A yell rent the air. The man thrashed his arms, torn off his feet. His head bobbed and gasped between dunkings. The river swept him downstream.

Fleet leapt after the sinking figure, his only companion. In moments, his hooves left the security of the river bottom. Instinctively, he swam. He overtook the floundering man and blocked him with his chest. Fingers grasped his mane. The river sucked at his legs and buffeted his body, ripping away his strength. Swimming for his life, Fleet paddled hard, carried along like a limb torn from a tree, the man limp across his back.

As Fleet's hooves found firm gravel, he lurched forwards. The man had one leg on either side of his barrel. Before Fleet could think about being straddled, the ground disappeared, demanding he swim again.

He reached the far side and struggled up the slippery bank, the effort draining him. He staggered. He dropped to his knees and deposited the man on the grass, having no idea why he'd risked his life to save him, only knowing it felt right.

Coughing and spluttering, the man came to with a heave. He rolled onto his hands and knees, and vomited before collapsing.

Fleet studied the land on this side of the river. Maybe these were the open plains Sapphire had described. The sky stretched forever, unmarred by clouds or trees, far more welcoming than the marshland. Grass was plentiful but it was drying off. All the flowers had long since shed their seeds. Summer was ending and food would become hard to find. He needed to learn the whereabouts of King Streak soon. But the man was in no condition to run and Fleet couldn't bring himself to leave him behind.

If he could carry him like the man did his pack, they could go faster. The man had straddled him in the river. Perhaps in time he could teach the man to speak, or at least understand language. Sapphire had said people and horses had been friends, so they must have communicated. In reference to the colour of the hair hanging down the man's shoulders, and the fact he was always gathering food, Fleet named him Squirrel.

As Squirrel staggered to his feet, Fleet attempted to strike up a conversation. "If you mount, I can save you from running."

No response.

He poked the man with his nose.

Squirrel moved away, mumbling.

Fleet tried again, shoving the man in his back. Almost knocked from his feet, Squirrel grabbed at Fleet's mane.

Shocked by the sudden movement, Fleet dodged sideways.

The man remained still.

He can't have meant any harm. Fleet returned. Squirrel was too short to lean across his back as he had in the water. Bracing himself against all his instincts, Fleet dropped a shoulder to lower himself beside the man and nudged him closer.

Squirrel raised his eyebrows before wriggling over Fleet's back, his legs dangling on one side and his arms over the other.

Fleet straightened his foreleg and took a step forward. Unaccustomed to the weight, he hesitated, the sensation all wrong. He backed up and spun in a tight circle, causing the man to swing one leg across his rump and sit astride, his arms around Fleet's neck.

Feeling more secure, Fleet walked forward. Gaining confidence, he broke into a trot.

Squirrel bounced for a couple of strides before sitting up. His head rose above the level of Fleet's ears, his forward-facing eyes like a predator clinging to Fleet's mane.

Fleet surged off at a gallop, blinded in panic by visions of wolves attacking horses.

The wind tore tears from Yuma's eyes and whistled in his ears. Sweat stuck his leggings to his thighs and the smell of hot horse wafted around him. He didn't care. Astride! He had never dreamt such a thing was possible. Never once had it occurred to him to try to mount a horse. He couldn't imagine the young stallions living on the outskirts of his home valley permitting anyone on their backs. Those bachelors had never shown any inclination for a closer relationship with people other than driving hogs in return for feeding. "You're certainly special, my beauty."

When he had first sat upright, the stallion had bolted from the river as if a pack of wolves chased him. Not daring to release his hold on the thick mane, Yuma had clung with his knees, bouncing to the extent he feared he would be flung to the ground.

"Thank the Mother you don't buck!" He had never known a horse to cover ground like this. Or maybe it was only his new perspective from being astride.

Whether from tiredness or because he detected nothing to fear, the horse slowed. Yuma tried to calm the trembling stallion with soft words while stroking the slick sweat on his neck. As the horse dropped to a trot, Yuma became unbalanced and precarious, the jolting pace threatening to unseat him. Sitting deep, he squeezed with his calves to get a better hold, not wanting the experience to end.

The horse rolled into a canter. Was that coincidence or had he signalled for a change of stride? Trying to keep his legs still in case the horse bolted again, Yuma released the tension in his back, letting his body merge with the horse and going with his motion— much more comfortable. As he became accustomed to the rhythm, he rode without conscious effort and revelled in the faster pace.

They came to a creek small enough to wade through. Instead, the horse dropped his nose to drink, sending ripples across the clear water and tiny silver fish into the reeds. Yuma slid to the ground. His legs threatened to buckle beneath him as he patted the heavy neck. "Thank you, my beauty. That's been the best morning of my life. I've never heard of anyone travelling on a horse's back."

The stallion walked deeper into the creek, splashing with his forelegs.

Yuma stretched and staggered forward. "Do you want a bath? Me too." After placing his pack on a rock, Yuma removed his clothes and boots, paddled into the cool water, and cupped his hands to throw water at the horse's belly.

The stallion shied and bounded downstream, tossing his head, and rolling his eyes.

Yuma approached with careful steps. Crouched low, he played his hands in the water before flicking drops onto the horse's lower legs. Taking his time, he worked above the knees until he touched the horse's shoulder, the muscles tight beneath his fingers. Keeping one hand on the horse, he used the other to scoop water over the stallion's chest.

The horse's muscles softened and his neck lowered, his tail no longer clamped between his buttocks.

Yuma moved to his neck, gradually working along his back, scraping off grime and sweat with each handful. When he reached the rump, he investigated the wounds. The hard work of the morning had split the scabs. Pus oozed from the gashes. "These need more than water and light salve. They'll have to wait until we get to a village."

Yuma retrieved his possessions and splashed to the opposite side of the creek. After dressing, he perched on a moss-covered boulder and chewed on a strip of dried meat.

The horse drifted out of the water and searched the ground, sniffing as he went.

"Looking for a good spot to roll?"

The horse bent at the knees and dropped on his side. He grunted as he wriggled his legs in the air, and then stood and shook in a cloud of water, hair, and earth. Then he picked at the short grass, step by step along the creek bank, ears swivelling to detect any threat.

Yuma extracted his pipe from his pack and trilled a few notes.

The horse lifted his head before returning to his grazing.

Yuma played on, mimicking songs of thrushes, blackbirds, and robins. The ribald songs and ballads of lovesick maidens his people usually played were not to his liking. Nature provided the best music as well as helping him hunt. Copying the sounds of a coney in distress could be used to attract a wolverine, or he could call ducks to water from where he hid in nearby reeds. Such bush skills meant he never went hungry no matter where he roamed, though he played mainly for pleasure.

Carving was his other passion, transforming bone or wood into creatures. They made popular items for trade. Some said they were charms for good hunting or fertility, depending on how the animal was depicted. He didn't believe in magic, merely delighted in their creation. Or perhaps that *was* magic, transforming one thing into another?

The horse whickered.

Yuma slung on his pack. "You should be resting those wounds. What drives you? Not the need for a mate, like me, not at this time of year."

The horse seemed content to go at a slower pace. Yuma jogged at his side to loosen his stiff muscles as they continued east towards Oaktown. Glad he didn't have to choose between following the horse and obeying his father, he looked forward to catching up with friends, even though he didn't relish selecting a partner from one of the young women. They wearied him with their limited conversation of children and food.

Imagine if he rode in on the black stallion! That would make tongues wag.

By mid-afternoon, unused to keeping up the hard pace, Yuma stumbled and almost fell, the pack dragging on his shoulders.

The horse trotted back to him, bobbing his head, and pawing at the ground.

"Are you inviting me to get on again?"

The horse bobbed its head again, as if in agreement. As if it understood him.

Grateful, Yuma grabbed a handful of mane. The horse didn't offer to lower his leg as before. Not sure if he would end up on his rear, Yuma sprang so he lay across the horse's back and wriggled to slide his leg across the rump, taking care not to touch the raw wounds.

Before he had a chance to straighten up, the horse trotted off.

"Steady there! I'm still getting the hang of this." Remembering how he squeezed with his legs before, Yuma encouraged the horse into a more comfortable canter.

Yuma chatted aloud, regaling the stallion with stories of his family and adventures. "I know you can't understand me, but it's nice to have someone to talk to. Did I tell you I have a sister? She's training to be a healer like our mother. She made the salve I've been using on your wounds. She'd know something better to stop the infection."

The more he relaxed, the more secure he felt on the horse's back. Even trotting became easier. Riding not only saved him effort, it gave him time to enjoy the scenery. When on foot, he kept an eye out for food or useful items such as flints and interesting shapes of wood. Now he could study the country they passed through. Shrubs and small trees started to dot the grasslands, becoming thicker and turning to forest the further east they went.

The horse slowed to a walk along a narrow twisting game trail. Yuma slid to the ground and wandered along, savouring crunchy huckleberries. The horse tore at pockets of lush grass in the small clearings and nibbled the wide variety of herbage growing in the dappled shade.

After a while, the stallion signalled for Yuma to remount. He didn't complain. This was the most fun he'd had since climbing the peaks above Waterfalls as a boy—the same mix of thrill and danger as when an eagle swooped him on a rocky ledge. He'd saved himself only by grabbing a tree jutting from the rock. Hopefully he wouldn't fall from the horse. The prospect of hitting the ground at speed held no appeal.

The horse propped to a sudden halt.

Pain exploded in Yuma's crotch as he slid forward onto the withers. He used both hands to push himself back, sweat beading his forehead.

The stallion raised his head to scent the air. He whinnied, loud and long, the call echoing through the trees.

A shrill neigh reverberated back.

A bay stallion emerged onto the track from the forest, prancing with forelegs striking the air and tossing his heavy-boned head. He stood taller than Fleet, his crest thick with muscle. "Who are you? What do you want?"

Fleet held his ground on trembling legs. He'd be no match against the older horse and the stallion appeared ready to fight. "Are you King Streak? I have a message for him."

The stallion reared to his full height, ignoring the branches that snapped around his ears. "How dare you speak to me like that?

Introduce yourself properly. I'll ask only once more. Who are you and what do you want? And why are you carrying a man? No-one here would do that."

Backing up a step, Fleet lowered his head in respect. "I'm Fleet. Do you know King Streak?"

Without warning, the stallion charged forward, teeth snapping. He hit Fleet with his full weight, knocking him to his knees.

Squirrel grabbed an overhead branch and swung to safety.

Good. He couldn't think about the man now.

Gasping for air, Fleet staggered up. The close confines of the woods prevented him from turning around and fleeing. He had hoped to meet other horses and enjoy conversation and mutual grooming. Nothing had prepared him for this assault.

"My patience is running out. State your full name and business. You're too young to be a delegate."

Other horses emerged among the trees, mainly bays and chestnuts with a couple of buckskins. They ranged in age from colts to older stallions marked with scars, with no mares or fillies, standing rigid behind the challenger's position, staring in silence.

Fleet's mind whirled. What had he done wrong? "I'm Fleet of Foot. Sapphire, my dam, had a terrible vision of unnatural wolves with crimson-streaked fur and humped backs, destroying horses. One of these bloodwolves attacked us. Now she's dead. I've got to find King Streak."

"Sapphire? The only one I know is old Queen Sapphire of White Water Cliffs. She'd never raise a colt with such appalling manners even if she could still conceive. And I've never heard of Foot. Where's that?" The stallion remained standing with his neck arched and tail up, every muscle bulging.

Fleet shook his mane as if he could untangle his thoughts. "No. Foot is part of my name, *Fleet of Foot*. My dam used to be from White Water Cliffs, but I was born in Dark Woods. She fled after King Thunder, my sire, was killed."

A loud snort erupted from the bay. "So, Prince Fleet of Foot of Dark Woods, you think to trick me? I presume you're after King Flash's mares. Get lost before I teach you a lesson you won't forget."

The other horses edged closer, whispering and whickering to each other.

Fleet took a few more paces back. "It's no trick. I'd love to be part of a herd, but I must find King Streak and warn him of the danger."

The stallion advanced and struck out with his front hooves. "I'm Wolfbane of Oakvale, Head of Warriors. This is King Flash's territory. We don't need your warning. If you really want to find King Streak, go back to the river and follow it north to where it forks, then head east to Flowering Valley. If you try to cut through Oakvale, we'll kill you."

Seeing in Wolfbane's eyes he meant what he said, Fleet bent himself double in an attempt to turn around. A branch snapped off on his rump. The sting against his wounds drove him to panic. He fled through the trees along a narrow trail, crashing through the undergrowth.

Wolfbane's neigh rang out behind him.

Fleet broke out of the tight copse into clearer ground that allowed him to travel faster. Unlike Dark Woods, here the trees had spacious clearings, and tracks dotted with low shrubs he could jump. He raced on.

Why was he running? He had sought other horses and now he fled like a foal from a swarm of insects. He slowed and tried to gather his wits. By the time he reached the edge of the forest, he dripped with sweat and his rump throbbed in pain, but he was no nearer to deciding what to do next.

He'd love Squirrel to wash him. With a jolt, he remembered the man had retreated to the trees. He was on his own, alone again. The man's absence saddened him.

Should he go back to the river as Wolfbane had ordered, or risk heading due north to find King Streak and save covering old ground? How far away was Flowering Valley? He couldn't afford to delay. But if he stayed in King Flash's territory, he ran the risk of being attacked.

Flashes of crimson wolves leapt through his mind, leaving him nauseous. Dizzy spells had haunted him ever since the wolf attack. In these moments, all he wanted to do was lie down and give up. Only his promise and loneliness kept him going. But finding other horses had brought no relief.

He rested until the pain numbed and the dizziness receded. But he must locate King Streak, pass on Sapphire's warning, and learn about unicorns and the horse with twisted horns.

He walked on.

Heat from the overhead sun added to his exhaustion. Blood seeped from his reopened wounds. He ignored it. He didn't have the luxury of resting to let the gashes heal. He glanced at the trees and made up his mind, heading back to their shade, north.

A movement in the forest halted him.

Squirrel emerged with outstretched hands.

Nickering, Fleet strode across. No smell of other horses lingered on the air. He rubbed his itchy head on the man's shoulder, relieved Wolfbane hadn't followed him.

Squirrel grabbed handfuls of grass and rubbed away Fleet's sweat. Lightening his touch, he checked the wounds before rummaging in his pack and applying the salve.

Forbidding himself to be lulled by comfort, Fleet nudged Squirrel to mount; having found him, he didn't want to leave him behind again. After the man scrambled onboard, Fleet trotted along a leaf-strewn track, glad to have company, albeit not a horse.

The ground trembled. Snorting accompanied the growing pounding. The smell of horse drifted on the air.

A buckskin stallion appeared at full gallop, teeth bared and front legs thrashing as he churned the earth.

This must be King Flash!

Fleet shot into a gallop. He considered Squirrel only when the man grasped his mane and clung tighter with his legs, but he couldn't slow. At least his youth and speed offset the buckskin's stamina and knowledge of the country. He galloped on, ducking branches, jumping logs, and swerving around others. This wasn't what he'd had in mind when he'd dreamt of racing across open grasslands.

On and on he rushed until he encountered piles of dung, their scent demarking the end of King Flash's territory. He slowed to a canter, then a trot. Dripping in sweat, he dropped to a walk.

A fresh set of dung piles steamed and swarmed with flies. He sniffed them. These belonged to a different stallion. This must be Flowering Valley. He drew warm air deep into his lungs. What reception would he get from King Streak?

Chapter 3

Morning sunshine glistened through the spider webs at Flowering Valley, their threads heavy with dew, a sign the long days of warmth would soon end. Tress nibbled at the damp grass and picked at the remaining clover heads. Switching her tail at a fly, she wandered closer to Breeze, her best friend. "Let's go to the camp. I need a brush."

Breeze, a dark palomino, agreed. "My winter coat coming through is making me itchy already."

Having been born the same day the previous year, at eighteen moons old Tress and Breeze had filled out with the promise of the grand mares they would become. Their once lanky legs had strengthened, their necks crested, and rumps rounded. Although they had both been sired by King Streak, Tress always made the decisions as her dam, Queen Starburst, was the lead mare.

Tress broke into a trot. Going for a groom was a distraction as well as a pleasure. Since yesterday her mind had spun from the news her sire had shared. "I'm expecting the delegates from other herds soon to negotiate for mares and fillies. I need you looking beautiful and on your best behaviour. No nipping or kicking when we have visitors."

Her dam also had instructions. "Watch out for the bachelors, both our warriors and lone travellers. Stay within the confines of the other mares. You're too great a prize to risk being stolen by an inexperienced stallion with no territory."

Streak had high hopes of a making a good trade for Tress due to her special colouring, as well as her bloodlines. Many stallions had expressed an interest and admired her beauty, her white mane and tail a stark contrast to her unusual black. Streak would bargain hard to expand his territory or gain more mares.

Tress grumbled as Breeze caught up with her. "Why can't we choose our own mates? I don't want to leave home."

Breeze swung her flaxen tail in a jaunty manner. "You know you can't have a foal by your sire. You'd probably end up with an ugly colt with a big nose. I think it would be good to get away from here as long as we can stay together."

Being separated had never occurred to Tress. "If they try to split us up we should run away and find a handsome bachelor."

Breeze snorted. "Dream on. Where would we go? There wouldn't be anyone to groom us or provide feed through winter. And what about wolves?"

They reached the collection of mud huts where the people lived. The dwellings nestled next to a copse of firs that provided shelter from northern winds. Smoke twisted from an opening in the roof of the open-sided shelter that dominated the central clearing. Women sat cross-legged under the shade of the trees and wove baskets from willow saplings, nattering and laughing as they worked. A girl hummed as she stirred a clay pot over the fire while other young women pounded grain. The men would be down near the river gathering hay. It was too early for the oat harvest. Then the horses would gather too, gorging on the fallen grains and chaff.

Breeze ambled alongside Tress as they entered a swept area on the outskirts of the village. Tress nickered, causing two women to emerge from a nearby hut bearing hog bristle brushes. They commenced grooming the fillies, teasing tangles from their manes and tails and massaging their coats. Every handful of hair went into a basket to later strengthen the walls of their mud huts or to stuff their bedding. The long mane and tail hairs would make twine or jewellery.

Breeze faced Tress without moving from the woman grooming her. "Did you see Blackfoot staring at us yesterday? It would never surprise me if he made a challenge for us before spring."

"He wouldn't!" Tress stamped a hoof, shocked the stallion would deign to consider mating with one of Streak's mares. Breeze must be wrong—she was always imagining things like that.

"Why not? He's been Head of Warriors for several years."

Tress denied the possibility. "More likely he'll die of old age, or chasing hogs. He'd only take over if Streak dies."

The fillies gossiped on, luxuriating in the attention and the warmth of the sun. As the woman caring for Tress picked burs out of the long hairs around her lower legs, she lifted each hoof in turn to be checked for stones.

Breeze crept closer to her friend. "Did you hear Acorn thinks Blue Eye was sired by Blackfoot? She reckons Heather disappeared into the trees with him when she was in season."

Tress tossed her head. "How can you spread rumours like that? You know it can't be true. Streak would run Blackfoot away if he had any suspicions."

"Blackfoot has a blue eye. And they both have one black hoof. Anyone can see Blue Eye will go grey in a few years." Breeze stepped across as her groomer changed sides.

Tress defended her sire. "Streak is grey too, so that's no proof."

"You would say that, wouldn't you, being the princess? I don't see how being foaled by the queen makes you any more special than the rest of us."

Stung by the old argument, Tress snapped at her friend. "And you still think you're special because of your golden coat. Maybe it was you who was sired by an outsider."

The palomino shrank back. "That's mean. If Streak thought I wasn't his bloodline he wouldn't trade me next spring."

"He probably wants to get rid of you because you're such a mouse."

Breeze didn't reply. She nuzzled the woman to thank her and accepted a handful of oats. "I'm finished here. Let's get a drink."

As Breeze walked away, Tress hesitated, still annoyed at the argument. Another woman brought out an empty sack to show her. Tress signed her understanding with a few bobs of her head and called after Breeze. "You go. I need to speak with Starburst first."

Still in a huff, she trotted off to find the queen who had been the herd's lead mare for ten years. Tress found her disciplining one of this season's colts who had strayed outside the boundaries the queen declared safe. She always wanted to know where all her subjects were. Teeth bared, Starburst chased the recalcitrant youngster back to his mother's side. Tress waited for her dam to notice her and come over.

"I saw you and Breeze go down to the village. Where is she now?"

"She went to the river. I came to let you know the people want a hog hunt. Do you want me to take a message to Blackfoot?"

Starburst gave a loud snort. "Absolutely not. I'll let Streak know and he can organise the bachelors."

"But if I'm training to be a lead mare I should learn to communicate with the stallions."

Her dam switched her tail in annoyance. "You don't need to go flirting with bachelors to learn how to communicate. Why didn't Breeze come here with you before going to drink? That's your normal routine."

Tress lowered her head. "We had a bit of a disagreement."

The mare nipped at her filly. "I assumed it was something like that. Go and make it up to her. I don't want anything disrupting the harmony among the herd."

"What makes you think it was my fault? She was the one spreading rumours."

The queen stamped a front hoof. "Don't argue with me. I don't know what's got into everyone lately. I'd normally think it was hormones playing tricks with you young ones, but spring is far away. Something's not right."

Chapter 4

Fleet picked at grasses and sipped at creeks, drifting from one patch of feed to the next between small clusters of paper birches, eating only because he must. His stomach churned and his muddled thoughts added to his dizziness. The sores on his rump pulled tight at every step, never letting him forget the bloodwolf. And he'd seen only one! What would an army be like?

How could he safely approach King Streak to pass on Sapphire's warning? And he wanted to join the herd. Maybe other bachelors could tell him more about unicorns. If they pushed him away, he'd have to try to steal a mare and start his own herd. But how? And where? Were there any vacant territories? What else hadn't Sapphire taught him? The last thing he wanted was to return to Dark Woods and his memories, despite the security the thick forest offered.

It didn't help his mood that Squirrel had wandered off to gather berries and nuts. Fleet hated being alone. Would Squirrel leave him to be with his own kind? Did people always wander by themselves? How many were there? He had learnt nothing of them other than that the man ate plants as well as animals. Was he a threat, waiting for Fleet to recover from his wounds before shooting him? It was all too confusing. He needed to find King Streak and learn all he could—if the stallion didn't try to kill him.

Fleet crested a ridge and halted, every muscle alert, every sound and scent accentuated.

Horses milled in the meadow below, two greys in conversation while the remainder hung together in loose formation. None of them grazed.

He had no chance of outrunning such a large mob in the open.

Remaining among the trees, he announced his presence with a low whinny. "Hello! I'm Fleet of Foot of Dark Woods with a message for King Streak!"

The larger of the two grey stallions regarded him with pricked ears and called a greeting. "Come down. I'm King Streak of Flowering Valley."

Relieved at the positive reply, Fleet strode down the hillside, ready to turn and flee if it was a trick. At least twenty stallions watched every move he made. Taking care not to slip on the steep stony slope, he held himself erect, tail high and neck arched, to appear older and experienced. As he neared, the grey who had spoken strutted out to meet him. Fleet halted and extended his nose.

The grey ignored his greeting and stood firm. "I don't recognise you. What's this about a message? Who from?"

With his heart thumping and blood running hot, Fleet met the king's eyes. "I've travelled a long way to pass on the dying vision of my dam, Sapphire of White Water Cliffs."

"Queen Sapphire? Dead, you say. That's very sad news, but hardly surprising. She was a fine mare in her day, but ancient. And King Thunder, what of him? I assume he's your sire, Prince Fleet of Foot."

The title Wolfbane had also named him confused Fleet. "I'm not a prince, at least I don't think so, but yes, King Thunder was my sire. He's also dead."

Streak threw his head up in alarm before inviting Fleet to join the other horses. "I think we all need to hear what you have to say. I thought you were too young to be an emissary or seeking your own mares."

After he was introduced, Fleet told of being born in Dark Woods. The stallions listened with politeness. Enjoying their presence, Fleet relaxed for the first time in the company of horses other than his dam. He explained how he and Sapphire had wandered in fear of the stallion pursuing them, avoiding contact with anyone, and finally the attack by the unnatural wolf. "Sapphire's final words were about her vision of a horse with twisted horns and an army of bloodwolves intent on destroying all horses! She sent me to you."

The grey stallion stepped back as if to avoid the devastating news. The other horses muttered among themselves and shuffled their feet.

Streak looked around as if seeking answers. "Queen Sapphire is famous for her visions. She foresaw the collapse of a cliff that flooded a valley, and knew about a great fire that destroyed all the grasslands far to the east, over Dragonspine Mountains. We must take her words seriously."

Fleet had never heard either of these stories. "What about unicorns? Sapphire said they are supposed to protect horses."

Streak blew through fluttering nostrils. "Some say they're no more than a myth, others claim to have seen one. I haven't. I can't rely on them. We'll need to provide our own defence."

Not understanding what that might entail, Fleet trembled. "Can I join your herd?"

The king licked his lips and flicked his ears. "Perhaps, if Blackfoot agrees, you can run with my bachelors."

The other grey stallion walked closer. "I'm Blackfoot of Flowering Valley, Head of Warriors. We're organising a hog hunt. That'll give you a chance to prove yourself."

Streak bobbed his head. "Good. Meanwhile, stay away from my mares. I need to think about this warning. I suspected something wasn't right from the birds migrating early."

Yuma wiped the sweat from his face, and retied his hair after straightening the tangles from galloping in the wind. Would he ever see the black stallion again? Not that he could complain—riding here had been the thrill of his life. But when they'd neared the approaches to Bloomsvale, the horse made it clear the time had come for them to part. And unlike the previous encounters, the stallions here welcomed him rather than chase him away. This must have been his destination all along.

Yuma wished him well, concerned the wolf wounds hadn't healed sufficiently to remain untended. He'd hoped to ask the Bloomsvale healers for stronger liniments. Now there was little point. He should probably have left the horse when they reached the small river that ran from Oaktown, but going this far out of his way meant he could catch up with friends while he replenished his stores and conducted a bit of trading.

Settling his pack on his shoulders, he headed towards the rolling pastures of rippling hay, the sweet scent of mowing drifting from where men worked to build stacks to feed the herd through winter.

He strode up to a man tying bundles and stacking them to dry. "Don't tell me you're working, Chaytan Strong!"

The stocky man turned around, his mouth open and eyebrows raised. After a brief pause he opened his arms wide. "Yuma Squirrel! I thought you must be dead, or you ran away to join the Westlanders. We missed you at the gathering."

The two men hugged with much back slapping. Yuma peeled away and held his friend at arm's length. "Dead of boredom, perhaps. Father insisted I stay behind and care for the old and sick until he returned."

"You've managed to escape, then? Have you come to entice away our young women?" Grinning, Chaytan scooped up another armful of hay and twisted strands to hold them together.

After dropping his pack to the ground, Yuma helped with the work. "That's what father thinks, but unless any new families have arrived since last year, I doubt there'll be anyone to attract me."

Giving a short laugh, Chaytan continued to work. "No, no new families. And when did only one young woman satisfy you? A dozen maybe!"

Yuma cocked his head. "Who said they have to be young? Give me an experienced woman any day."

The men continued their banter as they worked along the windrow, the sun warming them as much as their labours. Yuma enjoyed the fragrance of drying grass and trampled clover along with the conversation. Mice and lizards scurried away as he stacked the feed, amazing him as always with how much life the rich meadows sustained.

As they completed the row, Chaytan called a break. "I've bread and dripping under the old oak. I even have a skin of ale. Let's celebrate your health."

Other workers joined them in the shade, all of them greeting Yuma with the same surprise though not always the same welcome.

Chaytan squatted and tucked into his meal. "You must have left Waterfalls before your father returned from the gathering. It's too soon for you to have arrived here so quickly otherwise. Did you meet him on the way?"

Yuma swigged from the bladderflask before answering. "He was home long before I left. I came here on the back of a horse, much faster than travelling on foot."

A guffaw erupted from one of the men. "In your dreams, Water-falls man. We know the bachelors from other territories will be visiting soon. If you did arrive with a horse, no doubt you encountered one and happened to arrive at the same time. You might charm the women with your fantasies, but don't try them on us."

Not even Chaytan gave any credit to the tale. "Steady on, Jolon, I'm sure Yuma is only being funny. We know he can charm animals with his music, but he doesn't really expect us to believe he can convince a horse to carry him." He turned back to Yuma. "What's really behind this trip of yours? Perhaps you're after some bumblebee nectar to heal an elder? You'll be out of luck I'm afraid. It was all traded at the gathering."

Although it had occurred to Yuma people might find it strange he had ridden a horse, as a trusted trader he hadn't expected outright disbelief. "No, it's true. I did ride here on a magnificent black stallion. We separated earlier. I saw him meet your herd's lead stallion, the grey, who was with a bunch of bachelors."

Jolon Fist grunted. "I'm not listening to this nonsense. There's hay to be gathered." He rose and left, the other men with him.

Chaytan stayed and ate another mouthful of bread. "We need more meat. Aponi asked one of the fillies this morning. That grey horse will let us know when they're ready."

Delighted he had arrived in time for a hunt, Yuma hoped the black stallion would remain. What drove a young horse to travel so far from his territory? No matter what Jolon and his followers thought, the stallion acted as if he was on a mission other than looking for mares.

Yuma shielded his eyes with one hand and scanned the nearby copses for birch or hickory trees. "Most of my arrows are for small game. I've plenty of flint tips but only a few suitable shafts for hogs. I had to use one on a wolf. That's how I came to meet the horse. I was heading to Oaktown in the hope Eastlanders still lingered, but before we reached the village, the herd stallion chased us off."

He told Chaytan how he came to rescue the stallion. "After he saved my life in the river, we just kept going. Then he encouraged me to mount. I wouldn't have thought to get on if he hadn't signalled me."

"No, you'd be more likely to end up trampled. Do you think he'll let any of us sit on him?"

Yuma recoiled. It hadn't occurred to him other men might want to try. The notion of someone else straddling his beauty made his blood surge. He considered the horse his. Of course that was stupid. No one could own a horse. Still, he'd be disappointed if the stallion permitted other people on his back. "I don't know what he'll allow. He might not even let me on him again. Perhaps he's come to barter for mares. I don't even know if he'll stay. He's been pushing hard to get wherever he's going."

Having finished their lunch, they returned to work. Yuma continued to help for the rest of the day. As he wandered back to the central hut, an enticing aroma of cooking hog and roots drifted on the breeze. Children ran and played around the clearing, their chores of gathering mushrooms, berries, and firewood done.

After greeting the remainder of the Bloomsvale clan, Yuma enjoyed the meal, the fatty hog meat a tasty change from the small game he'd been catching. He thanked his hosts by playing his pipe and telling stories while the women sat and braided twine and men worked leather. The glowing coals of the fire darkened. A young woman, her raven hair hanging in braids to her waist, placed a few more sticks on the embers. Sparks reflected in her green eyes as she turned away from the flames curling around the fuel.

As she met his eyes, he recognised her. He'd met Jolon's daughter on previous visits. She was a loner and rarely said more than a few words. "Thanks, Laila, my fingers were getting numb."

With a nod of acknowledgement, the slim figure retreated to the back of the hut and sat near her father and two young men. So she hadn't been given her second name yet. After her womanhood ceremony she would sit with the unpartnered women. Yuma's glance swung to her brothers. Neither of them smiled or looked across the fire towards him. The last time he'd seen the boys, Bly and Delsin, they had been playing at hunting. In the intervening years Bly had grown tall, his body heavy like his father's. Delsin's lean face gazed with pale blue eyes into nothingness, his bowed legs stuck out awkwardly in front of him. Yuma liked the boy though feared for him; Jolon could be an overbearing and unforgiving parent.

Before Yuma could ponder further, the children at his feet begged him to retell the tale of riding a horse, their eyes as big as full moons. He obliged, following on with his tell-tale mimicry of birdsong and animal calls, meeting all his audience's demands for encores. Sleep had his eyelids in its claws well before he unfurled his bedroll.

Yuma awoke to the sounds of people stirring around him. Someone snapped twigs to reawaken the fire. A woman clattered pottery as she added dry leaves to cups.

A man coughed near his ear. "You'd better get up. Your horse is outside."

Covering his mouth with his hand, Yuma yawned. "What?"

Chaytan toed his friend's elbow. "Wake up, sleepy head. It's the hog hunt today, remember?

Yuma stretched his legs as he kicked off his furs. "I didn't think we were heading out until after sunup."

"We aren't. It'll be awhile before the hogs reach the killing grounds. But that horse you've been talking about is here. I've never seen one like it."

Fully awake now, Yuma scrambled to his feet and tidied away his bedding. He shook his head to clear his mind of last night's ale. It was unusual for him to have slept in the communal shelter like most visitors. In the past there had always been a woman willing to invite him to her hut. As memories of the previous evening returned, he recalled the wariness of the clan. At the same time as showing fascination with his stories of the horse, their disbelief made them draw away.

That was *their* problem. He didn't care what they thought.

After tying his hair in a hunter's braid, Yuma slung his quiver over his shoulder. He didn't feel dressed without his bow and arrows, never knowing when he might spring a hare or porcupine. He wandered out to the clearing. Most of the clan was up and about, keeping a wary distance from where the black stallion pawed at the ground nearby. "Good morning, my beauty. I didn't expect you to come to the village."

Approaching the horse with his hand outstretched, Yuma took in the horse's appearance. The wounds on his rump had started to heal. His coat glistened with vigour. As Yuma ran his hands down each leg, the horse lifted his hoof. Yuma flicked a stone out of one before standing upright and stroking the horse's neck. "Are you going to hunt with the others?"

Stamping his near fore, the stallion tossed his head before nudging Yuma, the sign he wanted him to mount. Yuma grabbed a twist of mane and leapt to the horse's back.

Gleeful children ran over, waving their arms and shouting in excitement.

The stallion spun on his hindquarters and bolted.

Yuma hung on. He hadn't expected such a swift departure. Not knowing what the horse had in store, he let the wind freshen his crusty eyes and clear his head. Had he been right to mount up? If the horse was leaving, he didn't have his pack, nor had he said goodbye. Should he try to slide off? The stallion hadn't slowed. He looked down. The ground blurred, dashing away further thought of that option. He clung tight, hoping the horse was only heading to the hunt.

The lead stallion congregated with the mare herd at the opposite end of the valley, keeping the youngsters close by. They wouldn't take part in the hunt. The bachelor herd waited near a copse of trees. As his mount approached them, the stallions ceased grazing and gathered. The black stallion slowed to a halt a short distance from the others. A striking grey with one blue eye stood apart.

Yuma sat still, not daring to disrupt whatever was going on, keen for this rare chance to be close to the aloof males of the herd.

A couple of horses snorted as they looked his way before backing up and turning their tails. The grey stallion approached and eyed him. Taking a step closer, he swapped breath with the black stallion, their foreheads together and nostrils flared.

Were they conversing?

Some accord appeared to have been reached. The mob turned as one and headed through the trees, fanning out wide. Yuma's stallion remained a short distance behind the other horses. They trotted along well-used trails, moss and leaf mould muffling their tread. Startled birds flitted among the branches, twittering a warning.

Yuma's stomach rumbled. "If I'd known we were leaving I would've grabbed some breakfast. You've probably been eating all night, my beauty. Still, I wouldn't miss this for a chunk of bread."

The bachelors stayed parallel an equal distance from each other, making more noise once in position. Yuma had known the horses drove the hogs out of the forest, but hadn't realised they were so organised. Although he had participated in many hog hunts over the years, he had waited with the men at the killing grounds to shoot arrows as the beasts raced towards them.

Sudden squeals identified a family of startled hogs. They scampered ahead with their tails in the air, dodging this way and that as they fled through the trees. An old sow with a large litter of hoglets tried to retreat between the stallions. Two converged on her with snaking necks, teeth bared and heads lowered. The hog scrambled in the soft ground before fleeing along with the rest. One hoglet stood transfixed by the mayhem. A small bay horse came down on it with both forefeet, killing the animal before returning to the chase.

Yuma used his knees to stay mounted as he fought branches off his face. If he ducked underneath, he lost his balance and his legs threatened to tip him off. With both hands busy, he was unable to hang on to the mane. "Steady there, my beauty, I'll get dragged off."

His heart thudded. In the excitement he lost sight of the other horses. Bushes snapped and hogs squealed. The stallion picked up speed as the trees thinned. Coming out into the open, Yuma recognised they had travelled in a large loop and were now headed back towards the village. Hogs raced ahead as they cantered up to the bachelor mob.

They had almost reached the rocky gorge of the Bloomsvale killing ground. What should he do? The horses would stop in order not to be harmed by the flying arrows. However, he was expected to help with the kill. After all, he would be eating his share over the coming moons if he decided to stay. With no way of dismounting without injuring himself, Yuma worried his desire to ride would have a negative effect on the clan. Rather than making him a worthy lifemate, he would be shirking his responsibilities.

He couldn't help that. Let the elders think what they would. The thrill of this horse outweighed his duty to find a suitable partner. Tonight he could at least tell tales of how the horses rounded up the hogs and drove them, a feat no-one had witnessed before to his knowledge.

The bachelor mob slowed and veered away to seek water. The horse beneath him dropped to a walk. Squeals from ahead told Yuma the slaughter had begun. Most of the hogs would run free.

Hopefully, a plentiful kill would put the clan in a good enough mood to forgive his absence. He could return to the village to help with the skinning and butchering, but women usually did that and they might think he was interfering.

Before he could decide what to do, two hogs raced back the way they had come, running close to his mount. The horse took chase. Yuma had no choice except to stay aboard as the stallion attempted to turn the hogs. He had no chance alone—the wiry hogs darted all over the place. Accustomed to the erratic movement from dodging in the trees, Yuma risked freeing his hands to retrieve his bow. He extracted an arrow and took aim. The horse galloped alongside a small boar. Yuma let fly. Although the weapon had only a small flint, the close range meant the point penetrated the neck, felling the beast.

The horse raced after the second hog, clods of grass and earth flying from his hooves. Again Yuma aimed and shot close, the animal falling on its side, dead, the arrow erect from the base of its skull. With no more hogs to chase, the stallion puffed to a halt and tore up mouthfuls of grass.

Yuma slid to the ground and patted the slick neck. "At least I can't be scolded for not doing my bit."

The hogs weighed half as much as a man, if not more. Yuma retrieved his arrow from the nearest one. Now what? The smell of blood from the killing grounds would attract the crows and foxes. If he dragged the beast he would damage the hide and bruise the flesh. If he left it, scavengers might find it before he could return with help. Besides, everybody would be busy.

Yuma considered butchering and lugging the best parts on his own. A low whicker distracted him. "No, my beauty. I can't leave these hogs to waste."

The horse nudged him hard.

Yuma scratched his head. "Would you carry them?"

The stallion continued to stare at him. Deciding it was worth a try, Yuma dragged the nearest carcass to the horse's side. He didn't move. Encouraged, Yuma lifted the front legs to the horse's shoulder. Although his breathing quickened, he remained motionless. Taking great care not to spook him, Yuma hefted the hog onto the stallion's back.

The horse trembled, his neck muscles tight. He bent his head to the burden on his back and snorted at the blood running down his sides.

"There, my beauty, steady there." Yuma walked towards the other dead hog. The horse followed, his breath warm on Yuma's neck. When they reached the second body, he again hefted the corpse onto the horse's back.

Amazed the horse would carry such a load, Yuma offered him handfuls of clover. Soft lips teased the treat from his fingers. He gathered more and fed it to the stallion as he headed back towards the village. By the time he reached the central hut, the women were cleaning the first hogs brought in from the killing grounds.

Children saw them coming and rushed out to greet them. At the approach of the screaming youngsters, the stallion bucked, dumping the hogs from his back before bolting.

Chapter 5

Fleet's instinct at the noise and flailing limbs drove him to flee. He galloped with rolled eyes and flared nostrils. Dried blood crusted his sides. As he reached a safer distance, he dropped to a trot and veered towards two fillies on the hillside.

Both turned to stare.

The black one greeted him with a trembling whicker. "Are you lost? The hog trap is at the other end of the valley."

Fleet halted a few strides away, blowing hard. "No, I was at the village. Lots of tiny people ran out. I thought they were going to attack."

The filly snickered and quivered her upper lip. "Oh, those. They're only youngsters. They can be very noisy but they won't hurt you. Haven't you any babies in your territory?"

Fleet inhaled a deep breath and licked his lips, overwhelmed by the beauty of both young mares. "I don't have a territory. My dam was in hiding when I was born. When she was killed I came to find King Streak."

The palomino stretched forward her nose. "You haven't introduced yourself. I'm Golden Breeze."

The black filly marched up and pushed between them. "I'm Princess Silken Tresses of Flowering Valley. Did you get injured in the hog hunt?"

Fleet arched his neck and held his tail high. "It's not my blood. I was carrying hogs. I'm Fleet of Foot of Dark Woods."

"Carrying hogs? How disgusting." The black filly withdrew.

Golden Breeze sniffed his neck. "I've never seen another horse as black as Tress."

Fleet tossed his head. "I've never seen a golden horse. You're both beautiful."

Tress snorted. "Breeze thinks the goddess is her ancestor, but her dam was chestnut."

Fleet glanced from one filly to the other. "Sapphire, my dam, was chestnut. So I guess the colour of our dams doesn't matter. Who's the goddess?"

"Surely you know the creation story?" Tress edged away.

Fleet followed her. "Sapphire only taught me how to survive. Will you tell me?"

Tress stepped forward and reached out her nose. "Do you really not know it?"

"No. Please. I've never had contact with anyone other than my dam."

The black filly glanced at her friend. "Well, in that case…"

Delighted she agreed to recount the tale, Fleet listened with pricked ears.

"…the goddess is a mighty golden horse with wings." Acting out her story, Tress raced in a circle, calling out how the goddess wanted a playground, galloping across the skies to create the lands. After circling back to Fleet and Breeze, she stamped a hoof. "Lakes formed where her hooves touched the ground. The trail of her tail gouged out rivers. Where she jumped, a hill formed."

The filly sprinted off again, rearing and bucking before returning to continue her story. "When the goddess reared in joy, a mountain grew. She blew life from her nostrils into the rocks to make all the plants and animals. To complete Equinora she made horses, people to care for them, and unicorns to protect them."

"Unicorns? Can you tell me about them?" Fleet listened intently, admiring the filly. Her coat glistened and her tail flowed like a sparkling stream under a full moon.

Breeze stepped closer. "They're a myth, that's what. Supposedly horned horses with magic powers."

Tress ignored her friend and continued to prance. "All the unicorns are different colours of the rainbow."

Fleet had never heard such a tale. He glanced between the two fillies. "So unicorns are real? They're truly magical?"

Tress struck out with a foreleg and glared at Breeze. "Of course they are."

The palomino snickered. "So magical no-one has ever seen one."

Tress stamped again. "Let me finish. Every unicorn uses their horn for a different magic, and there must always be six to represent air, earth, water, fire, light, and spirit."

Breeze mumbled through a mouthful of grass. "All the stallions talk about finding a unicorn mare. Idiots. As if a unicorn, if it existed, would be interested in mating with a normal horse. It's just a story, maybe to coax bachelors to leave the king's territory."

A loud whinny prevented Fleet from asking more questions.

Streak galloped up, his mane and tail flying. He skidded to a halt between Fleet and Tress, teeth snapping. Clods erupted from the ground. "What are you doing here? You should be with Blackfoot."

Fleet yawned in submission. "I fled the village when I was spooked. I didn't mean any harm."

Tress came to his rescue. "It's true, sire. The way he ran, he had no idea where he was going, and he doesn't know anything."

The lead stallion kicked out at his daughter. "Be quiet. You and Breeze had better get back to the herd."

He barged Fleet backwards. "I told you to keep away from my mares. Tress and Breeze have destinies greater than running off with a disobedient colt from Dark Woods."

Streak struck the ground with his front hoof. "Finding you here makes my decision easy. I've considered Sapphire's warning and discussed it with my warriors. Someone needs to seek help from the unicorns, and you're used to travelling alone. You will leave tomorrow."

"So they're not a myth. How do I find one?"

The king snorted. "All I've heard is you need to cross River Lifeflow and follow Silverstream. One of the female unicorns is rumoured to live in the hills that surround a shining lake. I don't know about the others."

That all sounded very vague. Fleet shuffled sideways and twitched off biting midges. Or did he only imagine them? His skin crawled with fear. "What do I say when…if…I do find a unicorn?"

Streak tossed his head. "You'll have to follow your instincts. Tonight you can stay with the bachelors. Keep away from my mares, or I won't even allow you that respite. You must leave at dawn. If I see you in my territory after that, I'll kill you."

As the evening cooled, Fleet sought shelter under a stand of willows near the river. Despite his exertions, he had no appetite. He'd finally found King Streak and a herd of horses. Instead of being welcomed and gaining their help, he had been shunned by the other stallions, been looked down on by two gorgeous fillies, and upset the king. Rather than joining the herd, he must continue on his own.

His head spun from all that had happened that day—the hog chase, learning the creation story, and the reprimand from Streak. Although he had spoken in a matter-of-fact manner, Fleet had no doubt the king meant what he said. But did unicorns really exist? Maybe the king didn't believe in the threat Sapphire had foreseen and was just trying to get rid of him.

Hoping to gain more knowledge, Fleet sought out Blackfoot. He found the Head of Warriors grazing where the men had mown hay. "You must travel further than most horses. Can you tell me how to find the unicorn who lives near a bright lake?"

The stallion looked at him as if he were a rotting hog. "I never go west of River Lifeflow. What do you think would happen if I deserted my post?"

How could the big grey be satisfied with running with the bachelors all his life? He was strong and more than able to attract mares. "Don't you ever dream of starting a herd of your own?"

Blackfoot flicked his tail in annoyance. "Not that it's any of your business, but as soon as Breeze is of age she'll be mine. Streak and I have an arrangement. There's empty territory far to the east where I'll start my herd."

Fleet asked a few more questions and discovered the herd hierarchy was more complex than Sapphire had led him to believe. Even Starburst had to fight to remain as lead mare to decide when and where the herd would graze, when foals would be weaned, and who would interact with people.

Thinking of the queen reminded him of Tress. Who would win the beautiful princess? He had never imagined a creature so gorgeous, even if she found him uneducated. He could learn if given a chance. Golden Breeze was lovely too, but somehow the black filly pulled on his heart like he'd never experienced. What a couple he and Tress would make! He could imagine their offspring gambolling in lush meadows or snoozing under the oaks.

Blackfoot interrupted his thoughts as if he'd read them. "You'll need to do more than find a unicorn to win Princess Tress; you'll need a miracle." He strutted away, making it clear the discussion was over.

Despondent, Fleet looked for someone else to talk to. A pair of bays stood nose to tail under a broad maple tree. The leaves had started to turn deep orange, the smell of damp vegetation drifting up as he trod on the mulch, toadstools sprouting in the shade. He'd met the stallions earlier when Blackfoot gave out instructions prior to the hunt. Having been snubbed by Blackfoot, he re-introduced himself from a distance, unsure of the etiquette. "Did the people get many hogs today?"

The nearest horse twitched an ear his way. "You'd have known if you'd done your bit instead of racing off with your man. How can you bear anything on your back? Think you're special, don't you? Well, you won't find a welcome here. We all heard about you chatting up Tress and Breeze."

Fleet didn't approach any closer. "I wasn't looking for fillies. I was fleeing the village. The little people spooked me."

"So you can carry a man and hogs but you're scared of babies?" The bachelor refused to enter into any more conversation.

After trying in vain to engage with a few other stallions, Fleet drifted to the river. He had dreamt of racing with other horses or chatting in the shade. Now he was surrounded by his kind yet had never felt so lonely. Perhaps he shouldn't have invited the man to ride him.

Bachelors stood in twos and threes nearby, some alone on the perimeter keeping guard. Seeking the presence of another horse, even if he wouldn't chat, Fleet wandered over to a stocky skewbald. At least this stallion didn't flatten his ears as Fleet joined him. "What are you watching for? Can I help?"

The guard introduced himself as Rocky and shifted to make room on a level patch of bank. "The number of wolves has increased this year. Normally we wouldn't see any until winter. There've already been pad marks in the mud."

Quivering at hearing about wolves, Fleet pushed away visions from his nightmares. He sniffed the ground. "Are the wolves here red? The ones from home are grey."

"The ones that come out of Lost Lands are grey too. I've never heard of a red wolf." The guard pricked his ears and gazed into the night, his nostrils distended.

Pleased this stallion seemed content to talk as equals, rather than the patronising talk of the fillies or the aggressive attitude of the other bachelors, Fleet ambled closer. "I expect the smell of blood from the hunt will bring wolves in. How can people eat animals?"

Without turning away from his duty, Rocky explained. "Their bodies need meat. And as they don't have hair like us, they need the skins too."

"I've never encountered people before." Fleet nibbled at a few low hanging willow leaves hoping they would alleviate the pain in his hindquarters. His wounds had stiffened from all the galloping. He wished Squirrel were here to massage him and apply the salve.

Rocky shifted his stance, still keeping his vigil across the river. "I heard you had a man with you when you arrived, and I saw him on your back during the hunt."

Fleet acknowledged carrying Squirrel. "He's the first one I've ever met. He saved my life. I liked his company and my dam told me I could trust people. He couldn't travel as fast as me, so I thought it'd be easier to carry him. He brushed me and tended my wounds."

Rocky explained the bachelors didn't go to the village like the mares and youngsters for grooming. Although the men put out hay and oats in winter for them, the stallions had little to do with the village. None had ever allowed anyone on their backs.

Glad the guard was happy to chat, Fleet sought more answers. "How do you communicate with them? I don't understand Squirrel's mutterings, and it would be great to tell him what I want."

Fleet listened with new respect as Rocky described the various signals they used. So Squirrel had been offering to help him when they first met. A flash of annoyance at his dam's lack of explanation accompanied the revelation. She hadn't taught him anything of use for his new life alone or, for that matter, anything about life in a herd.

It was too late to worry about that now. He wasn't allowed to stay with the herd anyway, not unless he found a unicorn to save the herds from the bloodwolves. And who was the horse with twisted horns? Why did it have to be him to go in search of help? Many of these stallions were far stronger and wiser. He hadn't set out to talk to Tress and Breeze. He could learn to fit in if Streak gave him a chance.

And what if unicorns were a myth like Breeze believed? Was Streak sending him to his doom? Was there even a shining lake? Maybe it was poisoned.

But he had no choice. He had to leave at first light, and had nowhere else to go. And he had promised Sapphire he'd do whatever was necessary to avenge her death and save the herds.

Yuma rolled up his sleeping furs and stuffed his bag. Kneeling on the pack, he pulled the drawstrings tight before deftly tying a slipknot. He'd packed rations for a few days but hadn't had breakfast. Hogs' liver sizzling on the fire made him salivate.

"Are you leaving already?" The quiet voice sounded disappointed.

"I need more flint if I'm to hunt hogs again. I only brought heads for small game." Yuma accepted the bread Laila handed him, thanking her for her thoughtfulness, the thick crust smeared with fat from the stone plate used to cook the fresh belly flap.

The girl squatted next to Yuma as he ate. "I wish I could travel like you. I love going to the forest to gather nuts and mushrooms. It's so different from here, cool and calm. The birds are interesting too, like the crazy woodpeckers."

Yuma raised his eyebrows as he wiped grease from his lips. "I guess I'm used to them. I prefer your open grasslands. Especially the grouse! We don't get them where I live. They're delicious."

Laila twirled her braid. "The golden eagles think so too. I wish I could fly and see what they can."

Yuma had experienced the same desire. "I use the birds as my guides. If I see vultures circling there's a good chance there'll be something for me, even if it's only bones for needles. The swifts heading south tell me winter's on the way."

"I've seen them already. I think it'll be a bad season." The girl poked the fire. "Thank you for playing the songs last night. I prefer your animal music to Mojag's ballads. He always sings of brave men and weak women."

Yuma laughed. "Would you rather the ballads told of weak men and brave women?"

The girl shrugged. "That's how I see the world. I'd better go. Mum will expect me to help with the grinding."

Yuma finished his meal and relaced his boots. Looking for flints was really an excuse. He wanted to check on the black stallion, concerned other men might try to ride him. It could take him days to find the bachelor herd. They had dispersed after the hunt and he didn't know their territory. Of course there was no guarantee the horse would be with them. Yuma still didn't understand why the young stallion had travelled so far on his own. He could be anywhere by now. That saddened him. He'd enjoyed being with the horse, and had already tired of being back in a village.

Everyone had been hearty around the fire last night. Even Jolon had muttered Yuma had done well bringing in two hogs with the horse. Ale had flowed beyond their normal sleep time. Although he enjoyed playing his pipe to an appreciative audience, the same banter and age-old rivalries wearied him. He preferred being on his own. The thought of settling back at Waterfalls to take over as chief and raise a family made him shudder.

Yuma hefted his pack and quiver onto his shoulders and left the communal hut. He crossed to where Chaytan sat under a tree, stripping flesh from one of the hog hides, and asked where the bachelors might be.

His friend grimaced and gave rough directions. "And don't talk so loud. My head is threatening to split like an overfull hog's bladder."

Yuma slapped the young man on the shoulder. "Try some mint tea. It's good for clearing away the cobwebs. It sounds like I might be gone a few days. Will you keep a few marrow bones for me?"

"Huh. Don't be gone too long. People from Boasville have taken the best camps the last couple of years. Living so far north, they come whenever a severe winter threatens." He bowed his head to his work, sliding a broad flint in regular strokes along the inside of the hide.

fresh droppings confirmed Chaytan's suggestion that the bachelor herd was near the river. Yuma soon located the grey stallion that led the males and handed him a handful of oats. Horses of all sizes and colours dotted the pasture, all eating with gusto, another sign a hard winter was on the way.

He spotted the black stallion standing at the river's edge, splashing water over his shoulders and neck. Yuma whistled, and flushed with pleasure when the stallion whinnied back.

On joining him at the river, Yuma washed his hands and face, the coldness refreshing him more than the walk, dispelling last night's over-indulgence. He twisted ryegrass into a wisp to rub down the horse. The stallion's bottom lip quivered as Yuma scratched along his spine. Concerned to see the wolf wounds reopened, he massaged the horse's hindquarters. The underlying tissue must still be damaged. He probed deeper. The stallion flinched and lifted a leg. "Sorry, my beauty, I didn't mean to hurt you."

Working on the horse's other side, Yuma hummed in rhythm with the stroke of his hands, the horse softening beneath his ministrations, his head drooping as he relaxed.

A shrill neigh carried across the grasslands.

The horse threw up his head and trembled.

Yuma recognised the lead stallion galloping towards them, ears flat back, and teeth protruding from curled lips.

The black stallion shoved Yuma with his nose.

Yuma sprang aboard, relieved he hadn't removed his pack, slinging his leg over the horse's flank as they plunged into the river. Even with the wide and shallow crossing, Yuma had to lift his feet to keep his boots dry. On reaching the far bank, the horse scrambled ashore and set off at a gallop, his eyes rolled back to check for pursuers.

The grey stallion remained on the eastern bank, rearing and pawing the air. He continued to scream until they were out of sight.

They galloped on. Yuma doubted the stallion had any intention of returning. He didn't care.

Chapter 6

Fleet wound his way through the valleys, following Rocky's advice, until he reached what must be Silverstream. Narrower than River Lifeflow, the waterway surged and tumbled over black, white, and grey rocks glinting through the shallows. The pebble-strewn bank made the going uneven. After a quick drink, he retreated to higher ground and made speed over the short, coarse vegetation. Squirrel rode, whistling birdsongs, his legs dangling softly on Fleet's sides. He had been sure the man would have abandoned him once he found his own kind. Maybe he hadn't been lost. Why had he come?

At least Fleet wasn't alone. Having spent the night with Rocky, he had hoped Streak would change his mind about banishing him. But no. Once again, he was on the trail with no other horses for company. He had learned little from the Flowering Valley herd other than how ignorant he was. Did unicorns exist? Would he be able to find one if they did? The further he travelled, the more unlikely either possibility seemed.

The river straightened and the hills retreated, leaving a floodplain where the grass smelled sweeter. Fleet slowed and cropped mouthfuls as he dawdled along. When he halted to savour a rich patch, Squirrel slid off and unslung his weapon. Fleet had become accustomed to him hunting for his dinner, and no longer worried when he shot a coney or duck.

How far must he travel? He didn't want to be alone. Perhaps it would be safe to return to King Streak in winter, when the mares would be safely in foal. His life stretched before him, lonely and lost, searching for he knew not what.

The pain in his rump lingered like fog on a winter's morning, wrapping him in misery and dampening his spirits. At night, whenever he dozed, visions of bloodwolves tearing out mares' throats and slaughtering their foals smothered him. During the day, black spells swarmed him like a plague of bugs buzzing around his ears, dizziness disorienting him and nausea rising in his throat. So much for his brave words to avenge Sapphire's death! He couldn't save the herds from annihilation.

The smell of stallions teased his nostrils.

He swivelled his ears and picked up the sound of two horses trotting. While he dithered whether to run or stay, a welcoming whinny carried on the breeze. Excited, Fleet trotted to meet them, his pain and misery forgotten, tail over his back and neck arched as he pranced.

The older of the stallions swapped breath with him and squealed, striking out with one foreleg before introducing himself. "Where have you come from? It's an odd time of year to be driven from the herd."

Fleet briefly shared his background. "Can you tell me how to reach a shining lake?"

The younger stallion trotted in a circle around them, flicking out his toes and swishing his tail as his powerful hindquarters thrust him into the air, hovering between strides. "You're here. This is Silverlake, home of the homeless, territory of kings in the never-making. Come on, race me, let's see how fast you are."

The older stallion nipped the younger one as he passed by. "Leave him alone. We'll challenge him soon enough. Can't you see he's injured? What sort of defeat would that be, beating him when he's ill?"

Fleet didn't intend to get into battle with these stallions. "Are there many of you here? Does the unicorn live here?"

"Unicorn?" The younger stallion halted and rolled his eyes. "You're not looking for her, are you? I thought you'd come to live a life of celibacy with the rest of us no-hopers. Stop dreaming. Stay and fight, build your strength, and maybe one day you'll be able to challenge one of the kings and end your life of freedom."

Three more stallions cantered over, showing off their speed and agility as they dodged and weaved around each other. A stocky bay charged at Fleet and bit his neck, ducking out of reach before Fleet could retaliate.

He reared and screamed, pain and frustration driving him. He bit back at another stallion nipping him on the rump. Another flicked his heels towards Fleet's ribs. He kicked back and connected with hard muscle. The impact sent shudders up his hind end. "Stop! I'll go! I only want—"

The older stallion who had first introduced himself drove the others back. "Give him a chance. I want to hear why he's searching for a unicorn. I thought that myth had died out years ago."

Fleet puffed, the reprieve confusing him almost as much as the attack. "My dam was killed by a bloodwolf. An army of them is threatening the herds. She had a vision and told me to warn King Streak."

The stallions settled, standing close, their curiosity roused. "Did Streak send you here?" "What's a bloodwolf?" "Why do you need to find a unicorn?"

Gathering his wits, Fleet held his ground, determined to be strong. "Aren't the unicorns supposed to protect us?"

Once again, it was the older stallion who maintained calm. "That's a legend, but you could try talking to Cirrus. He's always muttering about a unicorn, though I warn you, he's quite mad."

"Mad? He should have been feeding the vultures years ago." One of the younger stallions sneered and muttered something to his neighbour.

Mad or not, Fleet needed to talk to him. "Where will I find him?"

Fleet continued along the river as directed, whickering to small bands of stallions as he passed. No more came to challenge him, presumably because the older stallion had admitted him into the territory. He trotted around the base of a hill and came to an abrupt halt.

A vast body of water glistened in the sun, surrounded by rich green reed beds. Fleet had never imagined a lake would be so big, stretching so far he couldn't see its full size. Geese grazed on the banks and flew overhead, their honking bringing the scene alive. He squelched through the soaked ground, in awe of the expanse. No wonder the bachelors congregated here where they'd never go thirsty or hungry.

Frog song hushed as he waded deeper, their croaking resuming as he moved on. Midges tickled his eyes and climbed in his ears. He shook his head to rid himself of the pests and clambered back onto firm ground. Squirrel dismounted and crept away, crouched low, brushing rushes aside with his hands.

Still taking in the wonders, Fleet searched for Cirrus. As predicted, he found the old stallion under a solitary willow near the lake's edge. He introduced himself and expressed amazement at the lush feed and plentiful water.

The old stallion rested a hind leg, his wispy tail swishing in lazy rhythm over his hocks. Scabs and scars marred the grey's coat, his lanky frame barely covered in flesh. "Can't go far. Wonky legs. No teeth."

Fleet understood why Cirrus remained where he did. He explained his dam's vision. "The others said you might know where I can find a unicorn."

Cirrus's head jerked up. "Emerald and opal! Sapphire and ruby!"

Although he had been warned Cirrus was mad, Fleet hadn't expected nonsense. "Sorry, I meant a horned horse, the ones who are supposed to protect us. Do you know where they live?"

The old stallion lowered his head and blew a stream of mucus from his nose. "Gemstone, gemstone, gemstone. Beauty, beauty, beauty."

Fleet shuffled his hooves. "An army of bloodwolves is attacking horses! We need to get help. Can you remember anything?"

Cirrus stared at him through cloudy eyes. "Shimmering lake… warm and lush…predator and prey."

Fleet could make little sense of the rambling old stallion who muttered the same phrases repeatedly. "Yes, the lake is beautiful. Do you mean the unicorns live here? How do I find one?"

"Follow the silver. Warm and lush…predator and prey… emerald and ruby."

Fleet decided on a different method. Maybe if he chatted about other things, he could bring the conversation back to unicorns. He regaled Cirrus with his life in Dark Woods. "I don't know what killed King Thunder, but I never met my sire."

"Thunder! Lightning! Mist! I knew them all!" Cirrus stirred and walked around the tree.

Fleet wandered after him, not needing a discussion on the weather. "Have you always lived here? What is this place called?"

Cirrus halted and stared at the water. "Silver...lake. White...water."

This was getting him nowhere. "Yes, it's beautiful. My dam was queen of a place called White Water Cliffs."

"I was king! Thunder came back. I came here."

Fleet stopped. "Are you saying you knew King Thunder? You were at White Water Cliffs?"

"My strongest colt. He usurped me. Good horse. I was tired." Cirrus sniffed the ground in a circle and dropped like a ripe fruit, landing in a puff of dust, stretching his legs out as he rolled onto his side. "Tired...so tired."

"Wait! If you fathered Thunder, you're my grandsire! I've never met any of my family. Don't sleep now, please. Tell me about my sire. Tell me about White Water Cliffs. Please."

No answer. Cirrus lay still, his ribs no longer rising and falling. Flies settled around his eyes and mouth. No breath fluttered his nostrils. He could say no more.

The further north Fleet travelled, the more visions of crimson wolves tore into his sleep, leaving him shivering under a sheet of sweat. Although Squirrel scrubbed at his crusted hair and untangled his mane when he woke, Fleet failed to shake the fear hovering like a flapping raven around his head. The wounds in his rump throbbed despite the salve.

To lose his grandsire after only just finding him! Having replayed the conversation in his mind, Fleet decided "follow the silver" must mean for him to keep following Silverstream. He didn't believe Cirrus had been as mad as the other stallions made out.

This must be where Streak had meant him to come. But was he only sending him to live with the bachelors, or were there truly rumours a unicorn lived at a silver lake? Living with the herdless stallions held some appeal, though not as much as having a chance to gain a mare or two. If he hadn't found a unicorn by winter, he'd return here until spring and then revisit Streak.

Fleet pushed his nightmares away with visions of Tress. The further behind he left Flowering Valley, the more he cursed himself for being a weakling. He should have fought to remain with Blackfoot's warriors and worked to convince the princess to gallop away. He envisioned the two of them, matching blacks, sharing rich pastures and watching their foals grow big and strong. Surely, with his youth and speed, he could have outsmarted Streak. Anger at the king for not providing more support competed with his dread of what lay ahead.

In contrast to the territory of his dreams, the hills edging the river became more rugged. Dung piles at the side of the track had weathered into anonymity. As the mountain paths ascended, Fleet watched each step to prevent slipping over the edge. On steep descents, Squirrel dismounted and scrambled down the track behind him. On difficult climbs, the man grasped Fleet's tail to be towed.

They descended into another gully where the river forked. Squirrel mumbled something, pointing at the river.

Fleet assumed the man wanted to rest. "I agree. There's good grazing, and food for you."

He nibbled at the duckweed along the bank. Even this treat failed to invigorate him. Maybe he should turn back. Winter was close and feed would become scarce in these northern ranges. Perhaps his nightmares would lessen, too. They hadn't been as bad with other horses nearby.

As he picked at thistle heads, his appetite returned, the meal the sweetest he had enjoyed for many moons. After eating he dozed, only stirring to shift his weight to ease his stiffness. Sapphire whinnied to him in his sleep. "Don't let my death have been in vain. You must save the herds!"

Waking with a jolt, Fleet expected to see the chestnut mare grazing nearby, her deep blue eyes watching his every move. But no horse stood guard, only Squirrel lazed under a tree. The smell of cooked trout hung in the air. No scent of horse came to him. Fleet wandered to the river, wading in to his knees to drink. Yearning for his own kind seeped through his bones like rainwater through the limestone cliffs they had passed, wearing away his will cell by cell, leaving him hollow and fragile.

But he must go on.

To the northeast, one branch of the river disappeared between two peaks. A sense of doom loomed in his heart as he sensed the cold wind from the mountains. The stream and the breeze from the left were warm. Was this what Cirrus had been trying to tell him? Warm and lush.

He backed out of the water and signalled Squirrel to mount. The man didn't like to get his hogskins wet. Once on the other bank, Fleet broke into a trot. The further he followed the stream, the warmer the air became, and the more lush the feed. Robins and thrushes filled the air with music. Squirrel matched their tunes, playing his pipe while he rode. Mixed deciduous and coniferous trees cloaked the slopes, filling the air with the sharp smell of pine and pollen. Flowers that should have turned to seed long ago still bloomed in abundance.

Hope raised his spirits. He broke into a canter, keen to explore further up the twisting valleys. "I could bring Tress here. It'd be a great place to raise foals."

Reaching a broad meadow, he stopped to eat, the urgency to find a unicorn dissipated. This place was too beautiful to worry about bloodwolves and death. He alternated feasting on lush grasses and resting in the shade of the drooping willows lining the river bank. Purple lupins welcomed hummingbirds, and bumblebees busied themselves among the sweet pink and white valerian flowers. He picked at the herbs Sapphire had instructed him to select, recalling the goodness of each plant from her teaching.

Sapphire. Was this country like the territory she had called home? Why had she fled? His good mood disappeared as if the stream washed it away. Memories of the bloodwolf attack flashed before his eyes. He could even smell the rank beasts.

The scent became stronger. Birds disappeared. Cicadas ceased rattling.

Fleet's wounds burned as if spiked with splinters. His head shrieked and his vision blurred. He cantered to Squirrel, shoved him with his nose, and set off before the man had settled on his back.

A grey form streaked from the forest, closely followed by another. Another wolf erupted from the forest, joining the chase. And another. One leapt for his shoulder, claws extended.

Fleet sprinted along the riverbank, throwing up clods of earth and small stones.

A larger beast surged to the front of the pack, its fur streaked crimson, its tongue hanging with black drool, canines bared. The bloodwolf bounded on silent paws after him, its stench wrapping his body.

He spurted faster.

Fleet poured all his energy into racing, neck stretched low, ears pinned back. Every muscle screamed for him to stop, every instinct drove him harder. His strength wavered, his legs moving as if they swam rather than galloped.

Then his hooves struck hard ground and he galloped on.

The wolves howled.

He slowed, spent. He cast a glance behind him, expecting to see death pounce.

His pursuers thrashed at an invisible barrier, thwarted, clawing the empty air in frustration, their angry yips and gnashing teeth receding as he made distance.

Chapter 7

The sun warmed Gemstone's emerald coat. Her ruby forelock shielded her eyes as she dozed lightly, half listening to the hummingbirds feasting around her. Something troubled them. Normally they rested at midday, preferring to suck nectar in the early mornings and late afternoons. Now they seemed to be storing reserves for a cold winter. Not that they needed to. Winter never came to Shimmering Lake. The plants and trees bore flowers and fruits all year round, often having both on their stems at the same time. The deciduous trees dropped their leaves at will, regrowing buds the next day.

She had been sensing trouble for ages. The dragons, usually so bright and playful, appeared dull and sombre. Their rainbow scales only lit up in flashes when she sent them love. Something drained their vigour. Should she contact the other unicorns? No. What would she say? Her dam had called her for years after her horn grew, but she'd never responded. Sometimes she caught mind messages between the others. She never joined in—better they thought her dead.

Gemstone's horn emerged when she was six moons old, a glorious opal like her hooves. But instead of being smooth, spiral ridges wound around the stem like a vine around a tree. Fearing she was tainted like Jasper and Shadow, Gemstone fled and settled in this valley far from all other unicorns. She didn't feel evil. She didn't harbour bad thoughts about anyone or anything. In fact, she dedicated her life to helping others. Her home was filled with creatures who found life too difficult or dangerous outside her territory.

But something was wrong.

She trotted down to the lake, swam out to its deepest part, and dived to where the aquadragons lived in the narrow channels carved by meandering currents. Like them, she could swim under water for as long as she wished. Her powerful legs drove her deeper, the aquamarine and turquoise aquadragons cavorting alongside, their kelp-like appendages pinned tight to streamline their pulsing bodies, their tails unfurled and swishing behind. Down here, the troubles that engulfed Gemstone above the surface disappeared. She blew bubbles for her friends to ride and towed them with her ruby tail. They expelled jets of water through their thin snouts, their ridged faces creating twinkling whirls of turbulence as they zoomed through the effervescence. Their giggles and the silky flow of water cheered her more than a feast of the lushest clover.

Renewed, she emerged from the lake and rolled on the sunny bank, wriggling in the short grass. A nip on her exposed belly made her squeal. "Stop that! You're too cheeky for your own good." She righted herself and stood up, shaking from head to tail in a glittering spray.

The dragon, similar in size to a fruit bat, though covered in scales of precious stones rather than fur, flitted above her. "It's good to see you in better spirits. I was starting to feel very pale."

Remorse swamped Gemstone. "I'm sorry. I can't stop worrying. I don't know what to do, Tatuk."

Tatuk was her favourite of all the dragons. He had been one of the first to join her when she discovered the valley. His rainbow scales glimmered as he alighted on her crest, his claws clinging to her mane, and his tail coiled tight. He arched his neck, serrated spines flickering as his body pulsed with many colours. "You should contact the other unicorns. They may know what's going on."

Gemstone slumped. "So you keep telling me. Sometimes I think you're right, but what if they don't answer? Or what if they think I'm stirring trouble? It might even be me causing the problems."

Her friend flitted to the ground and scratched at the soil. "Even the worms are dying. Something is amiss with Equinora's energy. The only way you're affecting them is by being so miserable."

Gemstone nibbled at the varied grasses around her. They didn't taste as sweet as usual. "Who do you think I should contact? Moonglow is Spirit Unicorn, but she's so peculiar. And from what I've overheard, she's getting frail and forgetful."

Tatuk folded his wings against his side with a clap, making his potbelly wobble. He trembled in agitation. "Why are we having this discussion again? It must be Diamond. She'll be thrilled to hear from you."

Gemstone quivered as if a fly had alighted on her. "She hasn't called me for years. She'll more likely be cross I haven't responded before."

The dragon's colour paled. "I can't stay here with you in this mood."

Before Gemstone could send love to him, he disappeared. She'd never worked out whether he truly vanished or whether he could fly so fast she didn't see him go. He was the only dragon she knew who could perform that trick.

Wandering down to drink, she was surprised how many fish congregated in the lake, large and small schooling together, and enemies among their quarry. She had to act. She couldn't continue upsetting her charges and not doing anything about her worries.

With firm resolution, she trotted to her favourite tree. The low branches of the mighty oak gave shade as well as providing a perch for birds and dragons. The earth was packed hard from her standing in the same place. She concentrated and tried to send out a mind message. Instead, the whistling of the blue jays squabbling over acorns distracted her.

She needed to find a more secluded place. She headed away from the lake, across meadows where flowers bobbed heavy heads, over the forested foothills where leaves rustled, and along trails where animals scurried in panic, all driving her on. She climbed a winding track high into the gorse and scrambled onto a granite ledge. A cool breeze teased her mane and tail.

Shivering, she sought shelter against a low cliff. Far to the northeast, turbulent clouds built into thunderheads, a sight she wasn't accustomed to. Shimmering Lake usually only received gentle showers, enhancing its colours with prisms of light, every droplet transformed into a rainbow.

She shook off her worries and focused on her task. She had never sought out the other unicorns before. Whenever she heard their communication it had been when she was dozing, unable to shield her mind from their calls. She shut her eyes to picture her dam. *Diamond, are you there?*

Afraid of a response at the same time as wishing to hear an

69

acknowledgement, Gemstone attempted to visualise where her dam might be. The Light Unicorn had the power to translocate across vast distances, moving from one place to another in an instant. She could be anywhere. The further away she was, the less likely she would hear Gemstone's call.

She waited.

No answer.

She tried again, several more times.

Still no response.

Now she had decided to send a message, Gemstone determined to contact someone. She widened her communication to include all unicorns. *Can anyone hear me?*

I can hear you, daughter.

The deep voice jolted her. She shied and slipped on the rock. *Echo, is that you?*

How many sires do you have?

Although thrilled at making contact, Gemstone froze with surprise.

Won't you speak to me? You must have something important to say for you to break silence after all these years. Are you in trouble?

Gemstone had never met Echo. Diamond had told her he was a generous and loving soul. All else she knew was that his coat was the rich colour of loam, and his mane and tail were a brilliant emerald like her own coat. She tried to imagine him as she thought of what to say.

Don't worry about what I look like. How can I help?

She had to share her concerns no matter how strange they sounded. *I'm disturbed by a change in the energy. Animals and birds in my territory are preparing for a hard winter even though Shimmering Lake never gets cold. I suffer from bouts of despair like I've never experienced. The dragons pale and sicken.*

Yes, I've sensed it too, though not perhaps as strongly as you. My own dragons are unaffected as yet. It feels like a storm brewing over the land.

Yes! That's it. Yet I can't place what's wrong. Sharing her worries lifted a weight from Gemstone's mind. She hadn't been imagining the trouble. Glad she had overcome her fears of contacting the other unicorns, she became eager to talk more.

Her sire interrupted before she could ask what to do. *It must be Shadow. I don't know how or what he's doing, but he's a threat to all life.*

Diamond had told her of a hotblood with two horns who lived

at Obsidian Caves. She shuddered at the image of the black beast thriving on pain and terror. What Echo said made sense. The duocorn must be the source of the cold and darkness. *Should we be talking with our minds like this? Won't he hear us?*

No, he can't communicate like other hotbloods. There's no need to block.

Only slightly reassured, Gemstone sent a mere thread of thought. *So what can we do?*

I don't know the nature of the threat as yet. Now you've experienced feelings similar to mine, I'll try to contact the others. Meanwhile, build up your power reserves.

It was a relief to share her concerns, no longer alone in her distress. Her self-imposed exile had made her lonely. Now she had broken her silence, she buzzed with questions. *What do you mean? What power? How do I build reserves?*

No answer.

The quiet in her mind left Gemstone as bereft as if she had lost a lover. She occasionally allowed a handsome stallion through the shields of confusion that protected her valley, always ensuring she ate contraceptive herbs to prevent producing a warmblood. Then she grew bored at having to translate for her mate with the other creatures who shared her home, and found their conversations dull. Her sexual desires met, she sent them on their way only to miss them as soon as they left. Now she could communicate with the other unicorns, she need never be lonely again.

She returned to the lake and searched for Tatuk to share her excitement. He would be surprised at who answered her call and keen to hear the news. He might also be able to tell her more about the duocorn. All she had learnt as a foal was that Shadow stank of evil and was as black as the tar seeping from the shales in the far east.

A wide valley spread before Fleet, the glint of water drawing him on. He had never seen anything like this lake before. Although he had seen rainbows, he had never seen water shimmering the same way, every ripple twinkling in bands of red, orange, yellow, green, blue, indigo, and violet. Following a well-worn track, he tested the ground with each step in case this was a hallucination. Had his nightmares become fantastical dreams? But he could sense each pebble beneath his hooves and smell the sweet fragrance of blooms. So many birds sang he couldn't differentiate their songs.

Foxes played hide and seek with coneys in their burrows. A golden eagle perched above them in a giant spruce, ignoring the potential meal. A bushy-tailed wood rat scampered among the leatherleaf near a sleeping bobcat. How could such harmony exist between predators and prey? He must be dreaming.

As he approached the vast expanse of water, fish of all sizes splashed in the shallows, throwing up a dazzling spray. He sauntered onto the sandy beach, which glistened like wet crystal. The firm footing massaged his tired soles and sent blood coursing through his body, invigorating him. He halted, content to stand and breathe the clean air as he watched the goings-on around him.

Squirrel dismounted and wandered along the lake edge, singing to grebes and loons where reeds replaced the sandy beach.

Splash!

The surface of the water shattered in myriad sparkling drops, pierced by a glittering opal horn.

Fleet jumped sideways, blowing through flared nostrils.

An emerald head and neck appeared with a ruby forelock and mane. Sapphire eyes exactly like his dam's gleamed from a broad forehead with a spiral horn.

Fleet stepped back and snorted. Dream or no dream, he'd expected a unicorn to be gentle and loving, not steaming in anger.

The apparition glided ashore, eyes blazing. As her hooves hit firm ground, she lowered her head and aimed her horn straight at Fleet's chest.

Gemstone charged.

The black horse spun and fled.

Surprised he didn't fight, she backed off and came to a halt. Maybe this wasn't Shadow, as she'd feared. He didn't have horns. But no normal horse could enter her valley through the protective veil without permission. *Who are you?*

Not even the twitch of an ear showed the horse heard her. She trembled in fear, the lack of response and the emanating stench reaffirming this *must* be Shadow. Why had he run? Perhaps he meant to lure her away from the safety of the lake, not realising the water only provided sustenance and healing. She couldn't instruct the waves to defend her like Tempest could control the sea.

She held her position, every muscle taut, fighting the urge to flee to the depths of the lake. "This valley is sacrosanct. Why are you here?"

The horse turned around where he had stopped at the edge of the trees and lowered his head in submission. "I didn't mean to trespass. I've come for help."

The apology confused Gemstone further. The horse appeared normal, smaller than herself and with no horn. She tested the barrier around her territory with her senses. It remained intact.

Her fear heightened.

"Who are you?" Her voice tinkled like a creek burbling over stones, though inside her a river roared over a waterfall.

The horse took a tentative step towards her, his head lowered. "I'm Fleet. King Streak sent me. We, that is, horses, need your help."

Gemstone remained tense. "How have you hidden your horns?"

"My horns?" The horse glanced at her before averting his eyes again, and shuffled his feet.

Trying not to take her gaze from the threat, Gemstone spotted a figure crouched near a shrub, his eyes large under raised eyebrows. "You have a man with you. I would have detected his meat-eating stink and your foulness before you got here if I hadn't been swimming. People have never entered my territory before."

Stretching every skill to detect any evil, Gemstone sensed no power. She waited for an explanation.

The horse bowed. "I've come for help because my dam had a vision showing a horse with twisted horns is threatening every-thing."

Gemstone stamped her hoof and tossed her head. "Shadow, the duocorn! If you're not he, you must be of his creation. I won't be tricked. Go away and leave me in peace. Tell your master the unicorns will not permit him to despoil Equinora."

Song unlike any she had ever heard distracted her. The beautiful tunes came from the man's pipe. She strode nearer to him. "Who are you to travel with this beast?"

The man leapt to his feet, held out one hand, and approached with caution. "You're real! I couldn't help but capture your beauty in music. And you can talk my language! The legends don't mention that. Can you understand me?"

Gemstone stamped in agitation. "Of course I can. I can communicate with all creatures, even people. Unicorn power translates for those we talk to. Explain who you are and why you're here."

The young man stopped a short distance from her. "I'm Yuma Squirrel of Waterfalls. My father sent me to find a lifemate, but instead I saved this horse from a wolf and have been travelling with him ever since."

"Squirrel! So you're a messenger of danger. This companion of yours can't be a normal horse. The pair of you would never have been able to enter my valley if that were the case. Yet I sense no duplicity in you. Where did you encounter him?"

Expecting to hear the man had met Shadow's minion to the northeast, where Obsidian Caves loomed, Gemstone was surprised to hear the tale of their journey.

The man summed up: "So we followed the river until we came to a fork. The going was much better this way. We were chased by a pack of unnatural wolves, but something stopped them. I've never seen such beautiful country."

Gemstone tossed her mane in a flash of red. "That must be why I didn't detect you entering my sanctuary. I felt the evil rebuffed but you made it through."

The horse stepped closer and stretched his nose towards her. "Can you understand his mumble?"

So, the horse hadn't followed their conversation. Maybe he wasn't Shadow's tool. The duocorn surely wouldn't send out one of his warriors so ill-equipped. She cocked one ear as she inspected him closer. He certainly appeared to be a normal horse. "I gather you can't talk with him, as he has no idea why you're here."

Staying on guard, she invited the horse to approach. "Tell me how you came to be travelling with a man rather than both of you staying in your respective herds."

Before he could answer, Tatuk arrived with outspread wings. "Who's got a new lover, then? He certainly has the hots for you! Stinky, though." His colours brightened and pulsed as he alighted on her crest in a flutter, his cheeky laughter filling her ears.

The horse threw back his head in alarm. "What's that? I've never seen a creature of so many colours."

Surprised that, unlike the man, the horse could see the dragon, Gemstone thrilled that Tatuk's reaction proved Fleet was no threat. Understanding dawned on her. "You're a noncorn."

"A what?"

"Corns, horses with horns, are hotbloods. Normal horses are coldbloods. When the two cross the result is a warmblood. Warmbloods don't have horns, so are called noncorns." She studied him further. "Who was your dam?"

"Sapphire, formerly Queen Sapphire of White Water Cliffs, and my sire was King Thunder." The horse told of Thunder being killed, driving Sapphire into hiding, the bloodwolf attack that killed his dam, and her dying vision.

Gemstone sighed in relief. "It's your wounds I smell. Come closer and let me heal you. Wounds from wolves get easily infected, particularly if they've been scavenging carrion."

The man rummaged in his pack and extracted the wolf's incisors. "These are the wolf's fangs."

She examined the remains and snorted in disgust. "They're not just rotten, they're venomous."

Squirrel looked at the curved teeth with distaste. "Maybe I should get rid of them. Hardly a worthy gift for a partner, after all."

"Not in my valley. Wrap them up and hide them until you go. Use anise hyssop and maple leaves."

She turned back to the horse and glided her nostrils over the length of his back, confirming the stench rose from his sores. Sparks spat like pine sap in a fire as she stroked the wounds with her horn. The gashes closed over. "There's still poison in your veins. It'll take time for you to fully recover."

"Could that be the cause of my nightmares?"

Considering it likely, Gemstone touched her muzzle to his. "Come and drink from Shimmering Lake and see if that helps."

With a spring in her step, she anticipated the pleasure of communicating with the other unicorns again. "I'll contact Echo and see if he's learnt more. These are worrying times. I don't want my charges at risk."

Fleet bounded up the hillside, leaping from boulder to rock shelf. Feeling stronger than any time in his life, he whinnied as he spotted Gemstone ahead. He caught up with her and blew a greeting. "Any more news?"

Gemstone sparkled in the sun. "Echo has spoken with Tempest, but he hasn't felt any threat at Seashore. Neither of them knows what we should do."

Fleet tingled from her close proximity, still stunned by her beauty and the existence of a unicorn. Meeting Tress seemed a lifetime ago. The black filly seemed arrogant, naïve, and plain in comparison to Gemstone. Streak had done him a favour by driving him away.

In Gemstone's territory, forgetting the threat of bloodwolves was easy—until he thought of Sapphire. Terrifying wolves continued to fill his nightmares, despite his dark moods lifting when he woke. Staring north, he shivered. Ominous clouds billowed. Thunder rumbled like a herd of galloping horses. "The winter has a strong hold outside Shimmering Lake."

Gemstone agreed. "I doubt it'll be easy with Shadow stirring trouble. A fox arrived yesterday and spoke of fires raging through Dark Woods, even though snow lay thick on the ground. More creatures than ever seek sanctuary."

Sombred by the reality of suffering animals, they wandered down the mountain. As they reached the grasslands, Tatuk flitted around their heads. Fleet shied, still unaccustomed to the flying rainbow arriving out of nowhere.

After conversing with the cheeky creature, Gemstone changed direction. "Tatuk wants my help in feeding the foxes. A new one still feels the need to eat meat. Come with me if you like."

Curious how the carnivores fed themselves where no animals were permitted to kill, Fleet trotted along behind. The colours of the dragon intensified as Gemstone sent him love. By the time they reached the vixen's lair in a hollow under a tree, Tatuk shone as bright as the rainbow surface of the lake in full sun.

The vixen had gathered a small pile of stones. Gemstone explained Tatuk would have implanted the idea in the fox's mind, as animals without power couldn't see dragons. Tatuk settled on the rocks and breathed deeply. With Gemstone sending him energy, the magenta of his legs crept up and over his body. When his whole form had taken on the purple hue, he huffed out his breath, enveloping himself in a cloud of steam. Beneath him, the rocks softened and became a reddish brown.

The vixen pounced on the meat, swallowing it in large chunks almost before Tatuk had time to flutter out of the way. He disappeared.

Fleet retreated from the smell of dead flesh and blinked in amazement. "Does Tatuk do that every day? No wonder he becomes exhausted."

Gemstone headed back to the lake. "No, once they've lived here for a while, they know drinking from the lake is enough to sustain them. It's only the new creatures who find it hard to accept they no longer need to eat."

"But you and I still eat, and so do the other grazers." He'd hate to give up the delicious herbs and grasses growing in this magical valley.

"We don't have to. We graze only for pleasure. The carnivores can chew on a stick and think they're eating a bone. I've told Squirrel he needn't eat either, but I think he loves berries and nuts."

Other than going for a gallop once a day to explore Gemstone's territory, Fleet and Yuma occupied themselves with their own business. Fleet spent as much time as possible with Gemstone, the most wonderful creature he'd ever met. She had related Squirrel's story, fascinating Fleet that the man looked for a mate. He'd laughed when she told him the man's name, the same as he had given him, until Gemstone said that it must be a sign from the goddess. Why did Squirrel stay? No people lived here. Then again, who'd want to leave this paradise and venture into the snow?

As Fleet and Gemstone approached the lake, Tatuk reappeared and landed on her back, his scales dim in multi-hued splotches. As he rode Gemstone, his colours brightened to full strength again. She slowed as they neared the water's edge. They drank their fill and wandered back to Gemstone's favourite oak where they rested head to tail, the stance comforting even though they needn't swish their tails against flies. Fleet thought back to the many times he had done that with Sapphire. His cheerful mood dissipated as memories flooded back.

Gemstone must have read his thoughts. "Don't grieve for what you no longer have, celebrate what you've enjoyed. Remember your dam for all she taught you and the love she shared. There's no point distressing yourself over things you can't change."

Fleet sighed. "You're right. I almost feel guilty about being happy here."

"I had to leave my dam when my horn emerged. That's when I gained the ability to communicate with my mind, which makes it difficult for two unicorns to be close. It takes a lot of effort to shield our thoughts and gain privacy."

Having magical powers wasn't as wonderful as Fleet had first imagined. He had witnessed the strain the little dragon experienced.

Gemstone continued telling him about her life. "I drifted for many seasons before I discovered this lake. When I looked in the waters and realised how ugly I am, I decided it would be a good place to hide."

"Ugly?" Fleet couldn't think of anything further from the truth.

"You don't realise, of course, my horn shouldn't be like this. It's spiralled, not smooth like other unicorns'. And look at my colouring. Unicorn mares are supposed to be white, not green as grass like me."

Fleet fidgeted in confusion. "I'd heard they're all the colours of the rainbow."

"The stallions are coloured. Tempest is azure, and Jasper is crimson, but he has a contorted horn and is always in a grumpy mood. I don't want to become like him. That's why I keep to myself and provide a haven for creatures seeking sanctuary."

"Do you mean you created Shimmering Lake?" It was difficult enough for Fleet to understand unicorns could communicate over vast distances, and dragons could turn rocks into meat, without imagining the power needed to build a haven such as this.

Gemstone flicked her tail from side to side. "The lake was here, but every time I swim, the water gains more power. I don't know how. That's one of the reasons the dragons love being near it."

Fleet had noticed many dragons flocking near the water, flying over the surface to dip their feet through the ripples, the rainbow surface and colourful dragons blending hues as if the lake rose up on waves of translucent wings. Tranquillity lapped around Fleet like the water on the sandy beach. The smell of crushed grass and the soft rays of afternoon sun warmed his soul. Birds hopped about in the branches overhead and dragons played in the air.

Overpowered by desire, Fleet walked around the tree to face

Gemstone. The artery in his throat throbbed. He flicked his forelock out of his eyes and sidled towards her, caution tensing every muscle. He breathed against her face, as light as a leaf dancing on the breeze.

Gemstone retreated, shaking, and refused to meet his eye. "What are you proposing?"

Had he approached too soon? It was too late to worry about that. Instinct drove him on. He caressed her with his muzzle. Desire rumbled deep in his throat as he drew her scent deep into his lungs. He nibbled her ear with delicate lips. Afire with need, he pressed his shoulder against hers before grasping the back of her neck.

A sigh escaped her. She nipped back. Throwing her tail over her back, she swung her rump towards him and relaxed.

He pressed against her flanks. She didn't move. Wasting no time, he lunged onto her back, grabbing her neck with his teeth and thrusting with his hind legs. Her body slipped and sagged beneath his weight as sweat lathered his neck and chest.

In sudden release, Fleet slid off her. What had he done? Would she banish him for his presumption? He hung his head and waited for a response.

I can see I'll have to teach him to slow down. I hadn't expected one so young to be ready. He'll make a superb lover given time, so big and strong.

Had Fleet heard correctly? He shook his head; Gemstone hadn't appeared to speak. *Do you really think so?*

"Oh!" Gemstone threw her head up. *It seems your lust has changed you.*

The mind communication intimidated Fleet. "How can that be? Is it the power of the lake?"

She studied him. "No. This has never happened with my other lovers. Only those with a high percentage of unicorn blood can communicate by mind. You must have more than I thought. This changes everything."

Chapter 8

Yuma strode along the lakeshore admiring the spider webs glisten-ing with pearls of spray. Unlike the flat nets used to trap insects, these were three-dimensional in the shapes of animals and plants more intricate than anything he had ever carved. One web, as high as his knees, emulated a hare, the spider a glowing topaz at its eye. Every day Yuma discovered new wonders. A unicorn! Chaytan would never believe him. He'd even doubted his own sanity when he saw her emerge from the lake in all her glorious colours.

Gemstone had told him the black stallion called him *Squirrel*, the same coming-of-age name that his clan had given him. She claimed that was no co-incidence, and that the goddess had sent him as a messenger. He didn't know about that, but how amazing that horses had names for people! And the horse was *Fleet of Foot*; the name matched his agility and speed well.

Although he had no need to hunt, Yuma wanted more flint to renew his arrowheads and tools. At some time he would have to leave. The threat foreseen by the chestnut mare worried him for his family at Waterfalls, or White Water Cliffs, as the horses called it. Again, it never occurred to him horses named their territories. How little people knew about the herds they cared for.

He chuckled at the thought of telling Winona, his sister, about their home from a horse's perspective. Always so serious, she would think he was making up another of his tales. When they walked together, she gathered herbs for healing and cooking while he collected interesting pieces of wood. In response to his description of the animals he carved, or the shapes he envisaged in cloud formations, she'd give him a lecture on how to prepare and use various infusions and poultices.

His mood sobered. Wolves could threaten the Waterfalls clan since the horses lost their lead stallion. The herd no longer gave warnings so people could light defensive fires and keep watch. Winona might need all the salves she could make. How she'd love this place. Gathering and drying herbs, he had found everything he knew, and more, close to the lake. With Gemstone explaining the properties of each, his bag bulged with ribwort for wounds, celandine for pain, and sundew for coughs.

Not finding any flints, Yuma hiked inland, his eye drawn to a solitary maple standing in splendour against the blue sky. He hadn't ventured this far before. The giant tree's leaves shone with the colours of all seasons. Nothing grew under its massive spreading limbs, the ground twinkling with stones. Crouching, he scooped up a handful and trickled them through his fingers. He gasped— emerald, amethyst, and sapphire among diamond, turquoise, and ruby. He had never seen such an abundance of colour. A few of these would make an ideal replacement for the venomous fangs. Studying the stones closer, he became even more amazed. They were all the same shape—flattened discs like fish scales, some as small as his fingernails, others the size of his palm.

A giggle overhead made him look up. He leapt back and fell on his rear, dropping the stones. Were there tiny creatures in the branches? No, of course not. It must have been an optical illusion from the multi-coloured leaves. He scooped up another handful of stones to examine. Once again, tinkling laughter greeted him. Taking care to keep his balance as well as his hold on the stones, he lifted his head. His jaw dropped. Dozens of winged creatures chattered and laughed at him.

One of the larger ones dropped to the ground and pointed his snout towards Yuma. "Do you like our scales? You can keep one if you like."

Yuma shook his head in wonder. "I'm sorry, I didn't realise they were yours. I'm Yuma Squirrel of Waterfalls."

"Yes, I know. I'm Tatuk. I've been keeping an eye on you."

"I haven't seen you before. Have you been here for long?" Yuma couldn't quite get used to the idea of talking to a flying lizard of rainbow colours. It had taken him long enough to accept the unicorn really existed and could communicate with him.

Tatuk fluttered his wings and perched on a branch near Yuma's head. "I've been with you since you and Fleet crossed into Gem's territory. I felt the veil pierced and went to see who entered without consent."

Yuma was flummoxed. "What veil?"

Tatuk explained about the protective border around Shimmering Lake. "We dragons tell Gem when creatures seek assistance, and she allows them through. For those she doesn't want, we sow delusions in their minds so they turn back of their own accord. That's what we did with the wolves chasing you. I don't know how you came in without permission, but we've never had a human visit before. Maybe it was because you were in danger."

Sitting on a fallen branch, Yuma struggled to take in the information. "Why haven't I seen you before?"

"Only those with the goddess's power, or someone touching one of our scales, can see and talk with dragons."

Testing the theory, Yuma placed the gems in his hand on the ground. All the dragons disappeared. When he picked up a single clear stone, they reappeared. "May I really have one? I don't want to take your treasures."

Tatuk giggled and flew a merry dance through the leaves. "I've said you can."

Fascinated by the rainbow creatures, Yuma burst with questions. "Where do you come from?"

The dragon dropped to the ground and nestled into a pile of gems. "Dragons were originally seahorses. Before the goddess returned to the spirit world, she created aquadragons and dragons to be friends with unicorns."

Yuma pinched himself. It hurt. Deciding he must accept the extraordinary in a unicorn's territory, he asked the dragon where to find flints.

"Follow me!" Tatuk took off, flying at head height as he guided Yuma along a rough path, the dragon's bright colours dazzling as he flitted from side to side.

Yuma marvelled at the badgers and martens lazing with voles and muskrats. A jackrabbit played tag with a wolverine and a hare entwined with a fox in the sun. Crystal waters burbled down the hillsides while slower rivers meandered along the flats, pike and trout swimming together where the waterways merged. Narrow tracks zigzagged through a carpet of flowers, thick cushions of moss grew on rocks, and straggles of lichen hung from trees.

Even a cave they entered teemed with life behind a screen of ferns—bats and newts, salamanders and crickets, all shared the space in harmony. Tatuk perched on a ledge and chattered directions. "Follow the tunnel and you'll find jade, much better than flint. You can carve it with the diamond scale."

Yuma collected a range of green stones hard enough to use as arrow tips and carried them out to the light. He settled against the smooth cliff wall and whittled with his diamond, delighted at how easily the jade carved. He created a range of tools and ornaments, losing all sense of time until the sun moved from his face. The little dragon had gone, only the scale in Yuma's hand evidence that Tatuk really existed.

Content and mellow, Yuma headed back to the lake for a swim. The surface glinted as before, but with a difference. A vast difference! With the diamond in his hand, he stared in wonder at the flocks of dragons flitting above the water. So many! They zoomed and chased each other in play, splashing their feet through the water and performing acrobatics unlike anything a bird or bat could do. All of them sparkled like rainbows; the only difference between them the colours of their legs—solid green, red, or purple.

After watching the spectacle for a while, Yuma located Fleet and Gemstone dozing under a tree. He headed in their direction to share his exciting discovery. From their close proximity, he sensed a change in their relationship. Fleet no longer looked submissive, coming alert at his approach with ears pricked and tail held high. Gemstone radiated contentment, her coat glistening emerald. Perhaps the diamond scale enhanced his perception of her too.

She greeted him as he came closer. "Tatuk tells me you've found the jade caves."

"I've made a good store of items, probably more than I can carry."

Fleet leapt sideways and stared at him. "I can understand you! Can you follow what I'm saying?"

Yuma was thrilled to understand Fleet. "Yes, Tatuk gave me one of his discarded scales." When he'd seen the dragons over the lake, he dreamed the diamond scale might enable him to understand the horse, like he could the unicorn. "What a difference this will make, my beauty."

Fleet threw up his head. "I'm not your beauty, Squirrel. Horses don't belong to people. If anything, you belong to me."

"I didn't mean to imply ownership, merely admiration." Yuma held up his hands in apology. "While we're talking of names, I'd prefer you called me Yuma. Squirrel is my maturity name that identifies me to strangers, not what my friends use."

Gemstone bowed her head to acknowledge his point. "We still have much to learn about your kind. I'm surprised, yet delighted, that Tatuk offered you one of his scales. But it isn't the scale enabling you to understand Fleet. That only gifts you the ability to see and talk with dragons. Fleet has come into his own powers."

Yuma caught the glance that passed between them. He placed the scale at his feet to test this new discovery. "You have powers like a unicorn?"

Fleet arched his neck. "It seems so."

Yuma grinned. "I thought I saw a difference in you. I can guess how you gained that."

Gemstone twitched her upper lip. "What this means is Fleet is a warmblood, a horse with unicorn ancestry."

At first, the notion surprised Yuma. Then he considered how strong and determined Fleet was. Another young stallion wouldn't have taken on the task Fleet had. "That's wonderful."

He picked up Tatuk's scale, untied the thong holding back his hair, and wrapped it around the rare gift. "I'll treasure this anyway. The dragons are beyond anything the bards sing about in even their wildest fantasies. Even unicorns!"

Gemstone stepped closer and nuzzled his shoulder. "Take care not to lose it."

Yuma hung the precious scale around his neck and stroked Fleet's neck. "Thank you for allowing me to accompany you here. I'm honoured and overawed. I'm also thrilled you have found such a beautiful and interesting mate. I wish I could do the same."

Seeing the loneliness in Yuma's eyes, Gemstone understood that beauty and riches were meaningless unless shared. Nothing she could do would assist the man find a lifemate. And the handsome black stallion intrigued her. Why had he come to her for help rather than seek it from first-generation unicorns? All she could offer was friendship. "You may both call me Gem."

Tatuk alighted on her crest. "The new fox is causing trouble. The den she's preparing for whelping belongs to another vixen."

Dreading the troubles to come as more animals sought sanctuary, Gem bid farewell to Fleet and Yuma. She cantered after the dragon, glad of the excuse to remove herself from the horse's company. The surprise at his newfound ability to communicate his thoughts troubled her, both for the implications of his heritage and the loss of her privacy. After their initial coupling, he had become intense, desiring her again. She had rebutted him, reminding him he was in her territory; she was no mare to push around.

As Tatuk had said, two vixens snapped and snarled at each other in front of the hollow. Gem whinnied. "Stop it, both of you. I won't have discord in my land. If you can't live together in harmony, you'll have to leave. As much as I'd hate to banish you to the cold winter, I will if you don't stop this nonsense."

The original owner of the den grovelled and begged forgiveness. One of her ears had been torn and dripped blood. The new arrival crouched low and apologised.

After wielding her horn and healing the injured fox in a sparkle of emerald stardust, Gem addressed the newcomer. "I'll help you create a den under the adjacent oak. That way you'll have someone to help raise your litter and teach them manners."

Using her horn and hooves while the foxes dug with their paws, she carved a shelter for the vixen between two massive roots. The smell of damp earth mingled with the moss and leaves they used to line the nest for the new family. As she departed, Gem could hear the vixens swapping stories about the horrors they had experienced at home. Although happy they would become friends, her concern for the future grew from their news.

With a heavy heart, she climbed to the ledge where she communicated with Echo.

He answered immediately, sharing her worry regarding Fleet's ancestry. *Tell me again who his parents were.*

Gem passed on the names of Fleet's sire and dam. *He believes Sapphire's dam might have been called Mist and came from west of White Water Cliffs, though he's not sure. Other than that, she shared nothing more about her ancestry with him.*

Echo was silent for a few moments. *Mist? I had a daughter by a horse mare with that name. It might be possible. Warmbloods live much longer than normal horses. That would make Fleet my great-grandson.*

His response confirmed Gem's suspicions. *Would that be enough to allow him to pierce the veil? He'd only be a noncorn with an eighth hot-blood.*

It must be, and why we must take Sapphire's vision seriously. You must contact Moonglow and seek a prophecy.

Worried what reception she might get from the First Unicorn, Gem hesitated. *Will she speak with me?*

I don't see why not. Call her now. No, wait; you'd better have Fleet with you in case she has questions. I doubt his power will be enough for him to talk with her at Tern Island.

Gem breathed deeply to calm herself. Fleet stood shoulder to shoulder with her on the ledge, his excitement at contacting another unicorn in contrast to her nervousness.

Waiting longer would achieve nothing. She directed her thoughts out to Moonglow. *Can you hear me? It's Gemstone, Diamond and Echo's daughter.*

Gemstone! I never thought to hear from you. Diamond says… Oh, never mind. Tempest tells me… What was it? You have a warmblood companion? How nice. Or maybe not. I never did hold much with the company of horses.

Relieved Moonglow sounded welcoming, albeit muddled, Gem related Fleet's arrival and his dam's vision. *Echo suggested I contact you for a prophecy. Can you help?*

Wait. If one comes, you'll know. A strong warmblood? How fascinating. But troubles? I don't know about that. Everything's fine here. Hang on.

Gem's mind went silent, as if all her thoughts drained away. None of her senses pierced the void, not the whisper of the wind, or hard stone beneath her hooves, or the warmth of Fleet's body touching hers.

She waited, not daring to move, her eyes clamped shut.

> *Golden feathers there are five*
> *Time and rock has healed*
> *Strong and straight have stayed alive*
> *Only the true can wield*

Sensation returned to Gem, the shuffle of Fleet's hooves loud on the loose stones, and the dryness of her tongue rasping against her teeth. *What does it mean?*

Did Diamond not tell you? Jasper saved Aureana's feathers. They must have regained power. From contact with Equinora. Or maybe not. Who knows?

Her dam had told her of Dewdrop's death, and the goddess being unable to revive her. But what did this mean for Equinora now? Before she could ask, her mind blanked again.

> *Hidden deep in peaks of white*
> *Guarded by a bear*
> *Transform red and black to right*
> *Horse must venture there*

Once again, sensation returned, leaving Gem dizzy. *I still don't understand what this means.*

Your horse must get the Snowhaven feathers. Then go to Obsidian Caves and use them on Shadow.

Moonglow added no more to explain her words other than that prophecies came to her only in critical situations.

Gem passed on the conversation to Fleet, who had been unable to hear Moonglow. He said nothing as they headed back to the lake, giving Gem the chance to absorb the information.

Yuma rested against the base of her favourite tree, carving a hand-sized lump of jade. The figurine had Fleet's muscled contours and thick mane and tail, as well as his heavy-boned head, unlike her own chiselled features. As much as she admired the artistry, the image troubled her. "Please don't make a unicorn. We'd rather remain unnoticed."

Yuma accepted her request. "There's so much I have to learn. I'm glad my father sent me away, even if this journey isn't quite what he had in mind."

Gem touched his shoulder gently with her horn. "I'm glad you feel that way. Fleet must go to Snowhaven and Obsidian Caves to save the herds from annihilation. I hope you'll go with him."

"Of course! I'll do anything I can to help. My people are under threat too. I should have returned to them ages ago, but I see now that my path lies elsewhere." Yuma stood and untangled Fleet's mane.

Fleet ignored him and pawed the air, squealing at Gem. "I've only just found you! I must stay. The riddles don't say I have to be the one to go."

Gem stamped her hoof. "This is not a request. You sought help from me. Moonglow's prophecy is an instruction from the goddess. She said, 'Your horse must get the Snowhaven feathers.' Of course it means you."

Fleet's skin rippled as if swarmed by biting insects. "But the snows still ravage the lands outside Shimmering Lake. At least let me wait until spring. The prophecy didn't say I had to go right away."

Yuma interrupted their argument. "Where are Snowhaven and Obsidian Caves?"

"You'll need to head east until you reach Lost Lands, a forest of bogs." Gem described Obsidian Caves to the north within spires of volcanic rock. "They smell of rotten eggs. Snowhaven is further east. Their tips are covered in snow all year round."

Yuma nodded. "I know where you mean. I've seen them only from afar. I don't know anyone who's ever been there. That's wolf country."

Gem agreed they were dangerous places. "Tatuk has offered to show you the way. He'll also report to me on your progress."

Fleet turned his back, his tail clamped tight to his buttocks. "I thought unicorns were supposed to protect the herds. Why does it have to be me to go?"

Gem struck with her foreleg, catching Fleet on the shoulder. "You have no choice. The goddess has spoken. That is how we help. Besides, I can't have you remain here now you've opened your mind, especially as you can't conceal your thoughts. Learn to do so quickly, else you may find others listening in."

"What about the wolves on your boundary? How will we get past them?" Fleet paced around the tree, kicking up puffs of dust.

Gem sighed. "Tatuk will show you another pass, further to the north. They won't be expecting anyone to leave that way. And if you do encounter wolves, you should be able to outrun them with your strength and stamina now your wounds have healed."

"But the poison remains in my veins. I'm still plagued by nightmares." He struck the ground with a hoof and snaked his head, his thick mane writhing like a tangle of black serpents. "What will you do with so many animals arriving, or if bloodwolves pierce your barrier? I should be here to defend you."

Anger brewed within Gem. Why did horses always become so argumentative once they mated? "I'll do what I always do—help in any way I can. The best way you can defend me is to stop Shadow from sending his beasts out."

Her gaze lingered on Fleet, Yuma, and Tatuk in turn. "Moonglow agrees Sapphire's vision is dire, and her prophecy tells you what you must do. There can be no delay. You must leave Shimmering Lake tomorrow."

Chapter 9

Sensing a patch of clover, Tress pawed at the snow, teasing the frozen lobes free with her lips. Her tongue numbed as she sought more, her stomach rumbling with hunger. Giving up, she studied the dark skies. "Let's see if the oats have been put out yet."

Breeze stirred under the tree, snow crusted in her flaxen mane. "They won't be. It's only just past midday."

Snows had come earlier than any horse could remember. Without hay and oats, they would have suffered many losses. Two old mares had already perished, their skeletal bodies devoured by hogs. The people had burnt what little remained, unable to save even the torn hides or hair. The clan spent a lot of time gathering fuel, collecting dried dung in addition to fallen branches. Flowering Valley had too few trees to chop down for firewood. Families trekked long distances to gather timber for new dwellings.

Tress nudged her friend's neck. "Let's go anyway. I could do with a canter to warm up."

The palomino turned her head away. "You just want to see who the delegate is who turned up yesterday. Streak won't be happy if we interfere with his negotiations."

Tress stamped her cold hooves. "You're so boring. I thought you'd be interested in where we might end up."

"Of course I am. That's why I don't want to be rude. I don't want to belong to King Flash." Breeze shifted her weight, not showing any intention of moving.

Tress huffed. "I'm going to the creek then. I can't stand around doing nothing. There's not enough grass to bother digging."

Before Tress could act, a pair of stallions approached. Lifting their knees high through the snow, they made a magnificent sight. Streak led the way. "I've been looking for you two. Why are you never with the other mares? Come and meet Wolfbane, the delegate from Oakvale."

Tress and Breeze shook the snow from their coats and trotted to meet the newcomer. They stretched their soft noses forward to blow into the bay stallion's nostrils. Not as tall as Streak, his solid frame rippled with muscle. Shaggy hair hung from his lower legs, heavy with wet snow.

Wolfbane pranced in greeting. "You're certainly worthy to be Oakvale mares. I had heard of the beauty of King Streak's offspring."

Tress arched her neck at the praise, lifted one foreleg, and squealed as she struck at the snow.

Streak barged between Wolfbane and the fillies, snapping at the delegate. "These two aren't for my brother. They're destined for country far to the east and will have to cross Flash's territory. I'm only introducing them so your warriors won't interfere with their progress."

The heavy bay stallion was obviously disappointed. Tress had heard he was Head of Warriors and likely to be the next Oakvale king. "I don't want to go far away. I like it here. Why can't I wait a few more years?"

"You'll go where you're told when you're told."

After flattening her ears at her sire, Tress pricked them towards Wolfbane. "What's so important a noble warrior is acting as delegate?"

Wolfbane stood proud. "I also come with news of serious danger. Wolves from Dark Woods have crossed River Lifeflow and are massing in Great Forest."

Stepping forward, Tress quivered all over. "Surely that's more reason for you to stay in your own territory. Do you think they'll come as far as Flowering Valley? They must be hungry. I didn't think they liked open country."

Streak nipped his daughter on the shoulder, driving her back from the visiting stallion. "These wolves are unlike any we've heard of. Bloodwolves. They're as tall as you, with crimson eyes and blood-red fur. They killed two colts before the snow made stalking impossible. And they hunt alone instead of in packs, so there's less chance we can smell them."

Wolfbane added that injured horses didn't recover. "They suffer terrible depression and don't eat, and their wounds don't heal. At least three more bachelors are likely to die before winter is over."

Streak addressed both fillies. "We must be vigilant. Do you think I order you to stay with the mares for fun? Go and join Starburst."

The risk of danger had never occurred to Tress. In her short life, no wolves had been sighted within the heart of Flowering Valley. The hogs were no threat. A shiver ran down her spine. She thought of the young stallion, Fleet, who had visited in late summer. All she knew was that he had headed northeast on a task set by her sire. At least he was heading away from the bloodwolves. He interested her, even if he was rude and ignorant. She felt a strange affinity with him being the only other black she had met. Now she doubted she would ever see him again. That troubled her.

Another nip on her neck broke in to Tress's thoughts. Streak pressed her away with his broad chest. Breeze had already headed towards the main herd. Tress obeyed and trotted after the palomino, her head buzzing.

Later that evening, content with a belly full of hay and oats, Tress and Breeze wandered to the creek for a drink. Most of the mares had drifted back to the shelter of the trees. A cool wind tugged at Tress's mane and tail. "I bet there'll be ice on the water soon."

Breeze sipped at the sparkling stream where it burbled over pebbles in the shallows. Unlike River Lifeflow marking the western border of Streak's territory, the small creeks criss-crossing the rolling grasslands were narrow enough to jump. Breeze's pale hooves glistened where tiny waves lapped over her toes. "Last winter we had the queen's milk."

Tress savoured the memory of the sweet drink she had suckled for the first nine moons of her life. "It's good she's dried up. She's definitely expecting again."

The fillies chatted on about what the future might hold for them. At least it sounded as if they would be staying together. Breeze lifted her head, water dripping from her muzzle. "Do you think Streak negotiated for you to be queen at the new territory? I wonder if the land is open like this, or forested like Oakvale."

Tress didn't answer until after a long drink, the cold water slithering into her gut like a snake of dread. "I expect there'll already be a queen. We've more chance of rising up the ranks if we work together."

They paused as Wolfbane cantered towards them. Snow sprayed as he pulled up a few horse lengths away. "I've been waiting all day to find you two alone."

Glancing around to make sure Streak was not in sight, Tress tossed her tail and pranced on the spot. "It's nice to see you again. Why do you want to talk to us?"

Wolfbane sidled closer. "I know where Streak aims to send you. It's an awful place and the queen is a bully. She'll never let you wander like you do here."

Taken aback, Tress flicked her tail in annoyance. "She'll respect me if her king has traded well for us."

The bay stallion snorted. "Once the swap is done, there's no going back. You'll be made to have a foal every year and have no say in how it's raised. I've spoken with my sisters who have gone there. They're keen to be the ones selected to come here in return. King Scar has offered six proven mares for you."

Shocked at Wolfbane's words, yet at the same time delighted the other king considered her worthy, Tress didn't like the sound of King Scar. She'd heard of mares being killed by stallions if they misbehaved. "Perhaps by spring Streak will have a better offer."

Wolfbane stepped between the two fillies. "Another reason I'm here, rather than a junior delegate, is that I've been sent to aid the black stallion on his mission to find a unicorn. Your sire sent a runner to warn King Flash of Sapphire's vision. Why don't you come with me instead of being sent east?"

Breeze moved away. "We could never go against our king's will. Even if we wanted to, he'd send warriors to chase us down." She told how, the previous year, a mare had run away with one of the bachelors. Streak had sent horses after them, killing the rogue stallion and returning with the mare. The king had mounted her until she slipped her foal and he sired her progeny.

Heedless of the dire warning, an adventure to find a unicorn appealed to Tress. "How will we be able to leave without being noticed?" Tress wavered, her inner desires tugging against her rigid upbringing. "What do we do once we find them? What if we don't?"

Wolfbane seemed to have a solution for all her arguments. He pushed his case further. "Think of the glory that would be added to your name if you returned with help from the unicorns. You'd be so valuable you could choose your own future, maybe even challenge Starburst as lead mare."

Leaving the suggestion hanging in the air, the stallion spun and galloped away, calling over his shoulder. "I'll come and find you when it's dark."

Breeze headed for their usual resting tree.

Tress ignored her and sought out Starburst. "Is it true Breeze and I are to be sent east in spring?"

Starburst continued to graze. "Don't worry, Blackfoot will escort you. You'll be safe."

"I don't want to go. What if the king is horrible? What if the queen doesn't like me?" Tress shadowed her dam, adding her desire to stay close to Flowering Valley.

The mare switched her tail in irritation. "Streak has made a good match for you. You'll go where you're told. I suggest you improve your manners if you want to be accepted. You've a lot to learn."

Seeing she wouldn't get any support from Starburst, Tress joined her friend at the solitary cottonwood on the river flats. Most of its golden leaves had fallen, mingling with old droppings and seedpods to provide a soft footing. The old trunk showed scars where horses stripped bark to chew. One twisted branch had been worn smooth where the fillies scratched their withers and rumps.

Tress pleaded with her friend to escape with Wolfbane. "Come on, it'll be fun. We'll probably be back before we come into season anyway."

Breeze tossed her flaxen mane. "Don't be ridiculous. We can't go with that stallion any more than we can refuse to go east. And what about the wolves?"

"We'll be safe with a mighty warrior like Wolfbane." She reared and pranced, gambolling like a foal. "We'll dance with the stallions, our beauty outshining even that of unicorns." She pounded her hooves in the snow and bit at wet clumps. "We'll slaughter the bloodwolves and trample them beneath our hooves." She whinnied long and loud. "All the herds will welcome us in celebration of our victory!"

Breeze sniffed in disdain. "You do what you like. I'm staying here."

Disappointed Breeze wouldn't go, Tress was torn between an adventure to meet a unicorn and the familiarity of home for the winter. The final deciding factor became the chance to meet the black stallion again.

As night closed in, Breeze still refused to accompany Wolfbane. Despite her friend's resistance, or maybe because of it, Tress became more determined to run away with the bay stallion. Adrenalin flowed through her veins, keeping her senses alert. As the bitter wind dropped, fluffy snowflakes started to fall. She tensed as she heard muffled hoofbeats.

A dark horse loomed out of the whiteness, excitement exuding from his warm body.

"Are you coming?" Wolfbane stood so close his breath melted the crystals on her mane.

Tress snatched a last look at her friend and made up her mind. As the Head of Oakvale Warriors departed, she cantered after him, their hoofprints soon covered with fresh snow.

They reached River Lifeflow before dawn, its dark waters roaring like a beast intent on devouring everything in its path, its far side out of sight. Tress perched on the bank, rigid.

Wolfbane stood behind her. "Jump. This is the narrowest spot."

She hesitated. She had never swum before. The water swirled, bottomless, hiding she knew not what.

She shied as Wolfbane bit her rump. "Get going!"

She could do this. She was a princess! Holding her breath, she leapt, her legs thrashing the air as she plunged into the unknown.

The force of water knocked her sideways. Her legs struck out in frenzy, no ground beneath her. The freezing cold numbed her to the core. She thrashed, fighting to hold her head above the surface. Chunks of ice banged her right side.

Wolfbane's presence loomed upstream. He overtook her, leaving her to the mercy of the current.

Gritting her teeth, she stretched her neck and paddled to keep up. With relief, she heard hooves clatter on gravel. Her feet touched bottom, floated, and again grounded. This time she scrambled onto the far shore, her lungs searing with every gasp. Her coat froze into icicles as soon as she emerged.

She vowed never to immerse herself higher than her knees again.

"Hurry up, running will help." Wolfbane set off without waiting for her.

Tress broke into a canter, her hooves numb, and her knees threatening to give way.

They reached a smaller river. Much to her relief, they veered away and headed towards the trees. Apparently, following the river made tracking them too easy. However, when they reached Dark Woods, Wolfbane avoided the shelter, cantering among the shadows at the edge of the forest. He called for her to stay close. "The trees can hide wolves."

She warmed, and then became hot. Sweat broke out on her chest despite the rush of frigid air. Dark shapes whizzed past her head. She dodged and skidded, every bone brittle with tension. Her breathing laboured. "Can't…we…slow…down?"

Wolfbane came abreast and snapped at her shoulder. "Not yet. Keep going."

Tress had never been so cold in her life. As she stared at the vast expanse of water ahead, her heart lurched in fear. This made River Lifeflow look like a tiny creek.

The excitement of leaving the herd for a great adventure had worn off days ago. Her stomach rumbled as Tress dreamed of the oats and hay, the women's careful grooming, and the company of Breeze back at Flowering Valley. Wolfbane never wanted to talk and drove a hard pace. If he spoke at all, it was only to chivvy her on. Although the snow had long since covered any sign of the black stallion's passing, Wolfbane claimed this was the right way.

She had no choice but to go on; she couldn't swim back across the river.

Tress peered down the hillside where the water glinted under heavy clouds. Movement caught her eye. "Look, horses! This must be Silverlake."

The stallion drove her back from the ridge. "Don't let them see you. I thought I smelled a herd close by. We must go."

"Why? They probably live with a clan. We could seek food and attention." Tress could almost taste the oats and smell the rich alfalfa.

"Attention is exactly what we don't want." Wolfbane bit her on the rump, driving her down the hill.

Tress fumed. "Will you stop doing that?" Her bruised hind-quarters stung from the many bites she had received since leaving home. Although Streak had occasionally nipped her for some transgression, he never dug his teeth in like this stallion. "The herd might have seen Fleet. They'll be able to tell us when he passed through and which way he's headed. They might even know more about a unicorn."

Wolfbane threatened her with bared teeth. "They might also try to keep you or send a runner back to Streak. Leave the decisions to me and get a move on."

Fearing how brutal the stallion could be when she crossed him, Tress set off at a canter down the rocky hillside. She ducked and weaved through scrubby trees, lashing out at scraping branches, wishing she kicked Wolfbane instead.

Once hidden behind a low range of hills, Wolfbane changed back to a northwest heading. Avoiding other horses meant ignoring the easier paths alongside creeks or the direct routes over hills and through valleys. Instead, he forced a jagged trail from copse to copse.

Tress groaned and slowed to a walk. "Can't we graze for a bit? I'm starving."

Wolfbane sniffed at the tussocks poking through the snow. "These grasses are no good. We'll keep moving until there's something better."

Tress couldn't imagine they would find anything better than they had for the last few days. As tired as she was of needlegrass, she needed to eat something. Her legs wobbled with exhaustion. She grabbed a mouthful of snow to wet her parched mouth. Only the fear of being alone kept her moving.

The sun had sunk below the horizon by the time Wolfbane called a rest. "We'll graze here. Keep close."

Too tired to care about the stallion's abruptness, Tress tore at the rough blades of tufted hairgrass that cut her tongue. Chewing, chewing, chewing, she followed the mouthfuls from one clump to the other, oblivious of her surroundings, only aware of the cold and her hunger.

A scream rang out.

Tress looked for Wolfbane. She couldn't see him. What should she do? She reared, eyes rolling. A rank smell wafted on the air.

A pack of wolves sprang from the forest. Wolfbane fought among them. The stallion struck out with teeth and hooves. Shaggy grey beasts smothered him. He knocked one down. Another leapt for his neck. He lashed his front hooves at the attacker's head before spinning and kicking out with his hind legs. Blood poured from his shoulder. In a moment of respite, he lunged forwards and pounded a downed animal, bellowing in anger.

The wolves that could still run bolted into the darkness. Those who lay maimed or stunned, Wolfbane trampled to death, striking his forelegs hard on their skulls.

Puffed, he limped to where Tress stood gaping. A streak of blood ran down his shoulder. "We'd better move on."

Stunned by the stallion's power and brutality, Tress remained silent. Not needing any more encouragement, she set off at a lope, her hunger forgotten.

The following days merged into one long bout of cold and hunger. Tress stopped thinking about where they were going or why, focusing on grabbing enough to eat to keep moving. Only when the snow became too deep to navigate in the dark did Wolfbane let them stop. If her body started to flag, she only needed to remember the wolf attack to give her new energy.

Reaching the flatter grasslands, Wolfbane allowed the pace to slow. The wide open spaces gave protection from the approach of predators. Piles of horse dung and frozen hoof prints looked old. As they headed closer to the river, the snow lessened and the quality of the feed improved. Tress caught herself falling asleep mid-bite whenever she allowed herself to relax.

Heading down to the water, she slurped before raising her dripping muzzle. "This water isn't as cold as it has been. Do you think spring is on its way?"

Wolfbane walked upstream, tasting the water in a number of places before reaching a fork in the river. He studied the smaller branch coming from the north. "We'll follow the main stream to the west."

"I thought we needed to go north. That seems to be where the better water comes from."

"We'll go west." Wolfbane trotted off with dragging hooves, his thick tail clamped against his wasting body. His head bobbed as he shortened the stride of his near fore to protect his wounded shoulder.

Tress jogged after him, her head low and toes scuffing the ground. When they next stopped to browse, she sidled up. "Are you sure we're going the right way?"

He turned his rump towards her. "Your dam must have been sloppy not to teach you any manners, like not questioning a stallion. I thought we'd find a few bachelors to join us for added protection."

Although Tress could see the sense in more horses to help in their defence, she couldn't let the insult to Starburst go unchallenged. Taking a deep breath, she braced her legs. "It's not up to you to say when and where we go. A queen finds good feed and fresh water. You should mind your own manners and consult me."

Wolfbane lashed out with one hind leg. "You're not a queen yet, not even a mare. I won't be consulting an upstart filly."

Rebuffed, Tress missed the herd back at Flowering Valley. She wished she'd never followed the Oakvale Head of Warriors to find Fleet. Not even the handsome black stallion was worth suffering the cold, hunger, and insults. She hoped they'd encounter a few bachelors soon. Maybe they'd treat her with more respect. Why did Wolfbane want to avoid the Silverlake herd, yet now sought horses to accompany them? Maybe the wolf attack had scared him, despite his success at driving them off. The cold made thinking hard and her stomach complained.

Before her hunger was satisfied, they moved on again.

The further west they travelled, the hillier the country became. The river twisted its way through rocky outcrops interspersed with flats covered in drifts. Their pace slowed as they navigated sharp rocks or made the most of the pasture where the wind had blown away the snow. In the lee of the hills they occasionally found grasses still laden with seeds. Fresh signs of other horses started to appear, yet they saw no-one. With her stomach full, Tress's mood improved, at the same time as concern arose that they had gone astray in their search for Fleet.

As they grazed their way up a wide valley, the roar of tumbling water increased. Wolfbane, for once in a good mood, strode up to Tress. "This must be White Water Cliffs. See if you can find the clan while I find out who's taken over from King Thunder."

Confused at this change of strategy, Tress did as ordered. The chance of asking people for assistance gave a spring to her step. The village would be close to water, so she followed the river to the falls. A cool spray misted her mane and formed droplets on her eyelashes as she headed along the base of the cliffs. Spotting what looked like caves, she went to investigate.

The clatter of her hooves on the loose scree echoed off the limestone walls. A cavern wide enough for several horses loomed above her. About to peer in, she shot backwards, her head raised and eyes blinking, as a bay mare lunged out with bared teeth. "What—?"

"Get away!" The horse snapped at her and struck out with her foreleg. "You don't belong here."

Tress pranced in a circle with her head high. Striking a pose with her tail slung over her back didn't have any effect on the mare's attitude. She adopted a different stance, lowering her head to appear humble. "I'm sorry. I didn't mean to startle you. I'm Princess Silken Tresses of Flowering Valley, travelling with Wolfbane, Oakvale's Head of Warriors. We haven't seen other horses for many moons."

The mare made no attempt to conduct polite greetings and didn't budge. "You can keep moving. There's nothing here for you."

"Where's your clan? Can we get something to eat, and perhaps a groom?" Tress was sure that at least the people would extend their hospitality.

A derisive snort came from the bay mare. She pointed with her nose. "Their huts are that way. Help yourself."

Tress set off in the direction indicated. Saliva burst into her mouth as she spotted the first dwellings. Her nostrils flared as she tested the air for the sweet smell of hay. Instead, a rotten odour forced her to close her mouth, her tongue dry. She slowed to a walk and looked around the cluster of buildings, calling in a low whinny. No-one responded. No women beat corn in pottery bowls. No children played, or brought baskets of nuts from the forest.

The nearer she approached, the greater the stench. She walked up to the communal building and flinched as her eyes adjusted to the gloom. Smashed skulls and broken bones imprinted on her mind. She cantered back to the open grasslands and didn't stop until she found Wolfbane.

Gasping more from fear than exertion, she pulled up. "All the people are dead! Wolves have eaten them. There's no-one here except for a cranky old mare guarding a cave."

Wolfbane pawed at the ground and sniffed the dirt. "No ordinary wolves either. Bloodwolves. We must remain in the open."

"What about the mare in the cave? Maybe that's why she's there, for protection."

He gazed across to where Tress indicated. "More likely that's where the hay is stored. I'll sort her out. Stay with me."

Tress guided Wolfbane to the large cavern. Even with his aggressive attitude, his strength and growing familiarity gave her comfort. Dropping back as they neared the cliffs, she let him challenge the mare.

The old mare rushed out with her teeth bared, as she had with Tress. Nothing Wolfbane said made any difference. She continued to resist his attempts to enter the cave. He barged her, knocking her to the ground. Pinning her neck with his good front leg, he bit off the tip of her ear. She squealed and thrashed her legs, unable to rise.

Tress had never seen punishment meted out like this. "Stop it! This is her territory. Fight her king if you must, but don't attack a mare."

Wolfbane turned his head without removing his weight from the prone horse. "I haven't found any other horses, let alone a king. That makes this territory mine, and you two are my first mares."

Tress trembled, confusion blurring her mind. "What about our quest? We can't stay here."

"Quest? My only quest was to steal you and find a new territory. Did you really believe we were searching for a stupid colt who allows a man to ride him on a mission to find a unicorn who doesn't exist? You're more naïve than I thought."

Tress backed away from the cave and fidgeted from foot to foot. Her mind reeled with the implications of Wolfbane's revelation. A desire to race back to Flowering Valley filled her head. Before she could think more about what to do, she became aware of the old mare struggling under Wolfbane's hooves.

The mare managed to stand, gasping in ragged breaths. "Don't think...you can take over...that easily. There are many...in the woods…who will challenge you."

Wolfbane snapped at her neck leaving teeth marks where he tore off her hair. "What's your name? Tell me what happened here."

The mare recovered her breath. She drew herself up, her head high. "I am Precipice. If you want to know more you'll make me queen."

Tress didn't think Precipice looked much like a queen. From her sunken back and distended belly, it was obvious she had borne many foals. Her mane hung lank and her ribs protruded. Her cracked hooves curled at the toes showing it had been a long time since she walked far. "Who became lead mare after Queen Sapphire? We heard she was killed by a wolf in Dark Woods."

Precipice cocked her head. "Was she? Hardly a surprise. There hasn't been a true herd since Thunder was murdered. This cavern is mine."

As Wolfbane made to go inside, the mare blocked him, snapping as hard as he had bitten her. "Mine, I said. Don't come any closer."

He didn't bother to reply with words, rearing and striking out, walking forward on his hind legs. He barged her over with his chest, biting and stamping as she squirmed beneath him. He continued to pound her as he had the wolves. Her squeals turned to groans and her struggles slowed. Blood smeared the ground. With a final shudder she ceased moving, her mashed head oozing gore across the stones.

Wolfbane strode into the cave before returning to Tress. "What little hay is left is stale and musty. We can't eat that. We'll leave her body for the forest creatures to clean up." Without a backward glance, he trotted off to the river.

Anger overcame Tress's terror. How dare Wolfbane kill a mare! How did he expect to build a herd if that was his attitude? Heat flooded her veins and her breathing quickened. She had no hope of returning to Flowering Valley on her own. Even if she could steal away, she despaired what her future must hold. Her only hope was that another stallion would challenge and beat Wolfbane.

Chapter 10

Away from Shimmering Lake, the winds cut through Fleet's coat and tangled his mane. He plodded through the slush, the muck dragging the warmth from his body as heavily as the distance from Gem sucked the wellbeing from his heart. Claws of stone pierced the skyline like the troubles needling his thoughts.

Grunting, Fleet heaved himself over a tangle of dead tree trunks and twisted branches. "Will we never leave those mountains behind? It feels like we're not making any progress."

Yuma struggled to stay upright by hanging on to Fleet's tail. "The way south will be longer, but the going may be easier."

Fleet clambered up a rise. Sparsely treed hills rolled to the horizon, the steeper yet more pleasant terrain alongside Silverstream a distant memory. "Let's go south for a while then. Hopefully we'll be able to go faster to make up for the extra distance."

Since mating with Gem, his senses picked up subtleties he'd never noticed before, like the way light reflected off wet leaves, the difference in pitch of bird calls, and the vast array of flower scents. Grasses tasted sweeter, or, here in the far north, bitter and rough. Could it be true he had unicorn blood? He wasn't sure he wanted to be a warmblood. He wanted to lead a normal life. Being able to use mind communication didn't seem such a great thing considering the disadvantages, like having to live alone. Was that the reason Sapphire had fled to Dark Woods? So many questions remained unanswered.

He had done as asked—warned Streak and found a unicorn. Then as soon as Moonglow announced her prophecy, Gem refused to have anything more to do with him. Why couldn't the unicorns go after these feathers? Why him, and not one of Streak's experienced warriors? When he'd promised to find the horse with twisted horns, he hadn't expected to have to do so much. He huffed as the burden of another task dragged his spirits down, taking him further away from settling with a herd.

Tatuk appeared in a flash of colour and alighted on Fleet's crest. "Cheer up. There's good pasture close by. Follow me." He darted away.

Fleet set off at a trot.

"Hey! I can't run like you." Yuma scrabbled up from where he had fallen in the squelching mud.

Fleet returned and suggested he mount. "Don't lose sight of Tatuk. He might disappear again."

"He only disappears when you're miserable."

Trying to lift his mood, Fleet hurried after the dragon. Even before he warmed up from the faster pace, they reached a meadow. He dropped his head and tore at the grass. Tired and sore, his anger festered like his nightmares that had grown worse since leaving Shimmering Lake, the bloodwolf poison seeping through his veins.

For days, they followed the same routine. Yuma rose at first light for a cold breakfast and rode all day before making camp at sunset. Occasionally, he gave Fleet a break by running alongside or going hunting.

They saw less and less of Tatuk.

Heavy clouds obscured the peaks over the northern horizon and rain lashed down, churning the earth to a quagmire. They hadn't seen the sun or stars for days, but had turned back east once into better territory, the gentle slopes lightly wooded with wide open tracks.

Fleet stumbled.

Yuma grabbed his mane, worried how tired the horse seemed.

Regaining his balance, Fleet halted and peered around. "Is something on my hindquarters?"

Yuma ran his hands over Fleet's rump, making him flinch. "The wounds have re-opened. I thought Gem healed them. There wasn't even the slightest scar when we left Shimmering—"

"Wolves!" Fleet threw up his head, his nostrils flared.

Yuma unslung his bow and reached for an arrow, his hunter's senses alert. "I can't see anything."

Fleet scanned around, his ears twitching to catch the slightest sound. In a rare clearing with no trees close by, the grass rose no higher than Fleet's knees, offering nowhere for wolves to hide.

A dark shape rose from the ground, shaggy fur streaked red. Crimson eyes glowed in a head heavy with fangs.

Yuma pulled his bowstring taut.

Fleet leapt into flight.

The arrow flew without aim, falling wide of the bloodwolf.

Spray flew from Fleet's nostrils with every stride. Foam lathered his neck. He soared across a creek, thrusting into a gallop as he touched the far bank.

Yuma clung on, the fingers of one hand tangled in Fleet's mane, his bow useless in the other. They had never galloped so fast. Fleet's head lunged with every stride, his hooves throwing up turf. The wind whistled in Yuma's ears and sucked the air from his lungs as he chanced a peek over his shoulder. "Slow down. It's gone."

Fleet didn't react.

Leaning back, Yuma braced and thrust his feet forward. "Whoa! Hold up!"

Still Fleet galloped on, every muscle straining.

Yuma slipped on the horse's sodden back, sweat soaking through his leggings. He leant forward and ran one hand down Fleet's neck to rub his ears and get his attention. "It's gone!"

Fleet slowed to a canter. His ears flicked in every direction. He stumbled to a trot.

Yuma reassured him they were safe with calm words and a stroke of his hand.

Fleet halted, his head hanging and ribs heaving. Gobs of lather dripped from his chest and shoulders.

Yuma slid off and tore up handfuls of rough grass. Rubbing Fleet down, he murmured nonsense in an attempt to soothe away the horse's fears.

Still trembling, Fleet gasped. "That bloodwolf was much bigger than the one that attacked Sapphire. No wonder Streak is worried. Are you sure we've left it behind?"

"I doubt it could keep up that pace for long. That was an impressive run. You must be as parched as I am. Let's find a drink."

By the time they found a deep creek, sweat crusted on Fleet's coat like filthy scabs. The wounds on his rump seeped pus and blood, the surrounding flesh hot to Yuma's touch. He scratched grime off with his fingernails. "I'll give you a wash."

He emptied his bladderflask over Fleet's neck and shoulders and rubbed away the muck. Why had Tatuk left them? He would have been able to see the bloodwolf from the air and warn them. Yuma fingered the dangling diamond scale before tucking it back under his jerkin. It was cold. His worry increased; the scale radiated warmth when the dragon was near.

After drinking from cupped hands, Yuma thrust his water bag below the surface to refill. A jerk almost tore it from his hands. Tugging hard, he fought to maintain his grip as something wrestled the skin beneath the water, whipping his arms back and forth. Digging in his heels, he straightened his legs and pulled.

A spray of water and slime erupted. An eel the length of his outstretched arms soared over his head, landing near Fleet.

The eel would make a good dinner. Yuma had often eaten them, though he had never seen one as massive as this. Smoked, the flesh would last for moons, a boon he couldn't ignore with meat so hard to find. As he crept towards it, the dark grey body raised like a snake. Rows of needles gnashed below red eyes. Crimson streaks ran along its writhing length. Slime oozed from its skin, scorching the ground wherever it touched, sending up wisps of acrid smoke, the stench overpowering.

Fleet stamped his forelegs in an attempt to pummel the squirming beast. The eel gnashed at his legs and escaped, wriggling across the grass and flopping into the creek. Water splashed over Fleet's legs. He shied as if stung. "What was that? It stank like the bloodwolf."

Yuma held up the wrecked bladderflask with shaking arms. "No eel I've ever seen or heard of before had teeth like that." He tossed it under a tree. "I'm in trouble now. I can't go far without water, and I'm not drinking from that creek."

He rested against a boulder and grasped his right hand. The flesh was blistered as if singed by embers. He retrieved the discarded water bag and squeezed a few drops out to wash his wounds. Where the residual slime ran to the ground, the grass shrivelled and burnt like the smoking path to the stream left by the eel, anything touched by the slime smouldering and hissing.

"If that scorching eel is another sign of what Shadow has unleashed, I need to rest and eat. Pity I don't have any meat. There's been none for days." He unwrapped the remains of his last meal.

In a brilliant blaze, Tatuk alighted on the stone near Yuma's shoulder.

Fleet whickered a greeting.

The dragon's scales pulsed like multi-coloured fireflies.

"Tatuk! I thought you'd abandoned us." The appearance of the dragon and the warming diamond against his chest lifted Yuma spirits.

The dragon fluttered in the air until he swooped down and alighted on a large stone. "I was reporting to Gem. I can make meat for you. You only had to ask." His whole body sparkled and coloured the magenta of his legs. He breathed over the rock, steam wafting around his greying body. The mineral transformed to a hunk of red flesh.

Fleet stepped back, rolling his eyes.

Yuma laughed, more from relief than humour. "Thanks, Tatuk. That looks delicious. Now all I need to do is cook it."

The dragon's scales returned to their full spectrum. He tilted his long snout to one side. "You need a red-legged dragon for that. I can't make fire."

"Don't worry, I can." Yuma wandered over to a lone pine tree and gathered cones and kindling.

Fleet followed. "What are we going to do? I don't feel safe here. I don't even know where we are."

Yuma struck his flint and tended the tiny spark with beards of lichen and dry leaves. A thin wisp of smoke rose from the kindling. "I haven't seen any animals for days, other than Shadow's beasts, let alone one big enough to make a bladderflask. I hadn't expected the route to Snowhaven to be so sparsely populated."

Tatuk's scales pulsed like oil rippling on water. "You're a long way off track if you're heading towards Snowhaven."

Tiny flames flickered around the kindling. Yuma added larger sticks to the fire. "We detoured to find easier going. We'll be back on track soon."

The dragon fluttered up onto the boulder and perched next to Yuma's shoulder. "I don't think so. You're still heading south."

"Are we? How can that be?" Yuma prodded the fire into a blaze.

Tatuk flew in circles above the heat. "The trees have been fooling you. They do that to stop creatures living among them. They twist their trunks so you can't be guided by moss on their bark. They shuffle their roots to open and close paths."

"Why didn't you tell us before?" Yuma couldn't believe they had gone astray.

Tatuk paled. "I assumed you were heading to Flowering Valley before seeking the feathers."

Suddenly weary, Yuma sagged at the wasted travel. But maybe it was for the best. "That's a good idea. I can get a new bladderflask at Bloomsvale, and Fleet can share our news with Streak."

The hubbub of many voices grew stronger as Yuma approached Bloomsvale's common shelter. People thronged around the central fire, chatting in groups or preparing food. Most were strangers to him. After a winter of having no contact with other people, Yuma hesitated to enter the throng. As much as he had looked forward to company, he couldn't face such a large crowd. He strode across to Chaytan's hut. The familiar figure sat outside his home working leather.

Yuma greeted him. "Did you save those marrow bones for me?"

"Yuma!" The stocky man stood and spluttered through the long beard he'd grown during the cold moons. "Those stock bones made it into the pot long ago. Where've you been? We've been worried about you."

Yuma smacked his friend on the shoulder and squatted next to him. "Have you any ale? I've a lot to tell."

Chaytan called to Aponi in the hut. His lifemate appeared cradling a jug in one elbow and two cups in the other. She rushed across and dropped both armfuls in Chaytan's lap before hugging Yuma. "I thought Chaytan must be drinking with Gomda again. The old chief likes to escape the visitors sometimes. I'll get another cup and join you. You owe us an explanation for disappearing like that."

"I was going to share my story with the whole clan, but the meeting place is full of strangers." Yuma outlined riding the black stallion far to the north beyond the lake where he fished each autumn, their encounters with bloodwolves, and the caves of green stone.

"What's been happening here?"

Aponi excused herself. "I'll make us some food, little as there is."

Chaytan's look of wonder at Yuma's travels changed to a frown. "It's been hard on everyone. Remember I told you some of the folk from Boasville often winter here? Well, they all came. The rivers and streams are full of vicious eels preventing them getting water. Several children died and many people suffered burns."

"I encountered one myself. It had nasty teeth and a terrible stench, as big as my leg at least. Its slime scorched anything it touched." Yuma held out his burnt hand.

"Where did you see it? Was it close to here?"

"No, in the woods to the north. The horses call the place Lost Lands." Yuma faltered as he saw Chaytan's eyebrows rise.

"The horses? How do you know what they call anything? Don't tell me you can talk to that stallion of yours."

Having said as much, Yuma pretended it was the magic stone he wore. After all, he had originally thought it was the scale that let him understand Fleet. He didn't think it wise to explain about the horse's ancestry or the existence of dragons. Not yet, anyway. Chaytan would think he'd gone mad. "I don't know how it works. I found it far from here. Since then, Fleet and I have been able to communicate."

Despite his surprised look, Chaytan didn't question Yuma's word. "Anyway, the Boasville clan moved here. The weather has been too bad to build more accommodation, so they're sharing the meeting place. Actually, it suits me, as it means I can spend my evenings here rather than listening to the gripes of everyone else."

"Has it been a severe winter?"

Chaytan stroked the ends of his beard. "The snow has been thicker than we've ever seen. The additional people have diminished our fuel so there's barely enough to cook with. Not that there's much to cook. The smaller animals have disappeared, and the last hog hunt only produced a couple of runts."

Yuma grimaced at his friend's suffering while he had been enjoying himself at Shimmering Lake. "Any news from Waterfalls or other clans?"

"A few of us are heading to Marshward now the weather is warming up. I'm not looking forward to leaving Aponi, with her pregnant again." At a call for them to come and eat, Chaytan led the way through a hide hanging over the doorway.

Yuma shivered even though he was warm; the evil the horses and unicorns feared was affecting the clans as well. As he entered the dim interior of Chaytan's home, an urgency to reach Snowhaven and then return to Waterfalls gripped him.

After greeting Chaytan's two boys and sharing a meal of vegetable broth, tiredness and worry overwhelmed Yuma. "I'll find a corner in the main shelter for tonight. Your place isn't big enough for me too."

Chaytan slapped Yuma's back and said goodnight. "Don't go disappearing again. We'll talk more in the morning."

Yuma found a niche in the communal hut to unroll his bedding before joining the crowd around the fire, greeting a few people he knew. Unlike the usual stories, the songs that night rang of strife and hardship. More than once he heard of unnatural wolves with crimson eyes and blood-streaked coats. He gave a quick account of his own adventures. Even though he suspected no-one believed he could talk with a horse, most enjoyed the unusual tale.

Jolon Fist and his brood slumped in their usual corner. The man stuck his leg out as Yuma passed to settle for the night. "How long are you here for?"

Yuma didn't bother to look at Jolon as he stepped over the attempt to block him. "Only tonight."

The miserable man grunted in response without withdrawing his leg.

Yuma took a long time to get to sleep. The whispers of families around him brought back memories of his childhood and his mother's routine at bedtime. She always talked to Winona and him about their day, weaving in lessons of how to live in harmony with the world around them. Although they had been good days, he couldn't see himself settling to such a life, especially now he'd seen wonders beyond even the most fantastic tales of the wandering bards. Perhaps that was how he should spend his life, playing his pipe and recounting his adventures rather than seeking a lifemate.

Someone else could be the next Waterfalls chief.

Rising early, Yuma found Chaytan swilling the sleep from his eyes at the creek. "How soon are you heading east?"

Chaytan ran his fingers through his long hair. "Are you thinking of coming with us? We could do with another archer."

"Sorry, I'm heading north to the snow-capped mountains."

"What on earth for? You'll have to pass through Boasville." Chaytan held up a hand to prevent interruption. "Don't tell me, the horses told you to go. It's alright, you keep your secrets. I've known you long enough to know you're not telling me everything. I only hope we're both still alive to meet at the next gathering."

Before Yuma could respond, Jolon's elder daughter, Laila, ran up. "I saw your hand last night." She held out a small pouch and showed him wax balls the size of his thumbnail. "Bumblebee nectar. I doubt you'll find much this year. Rub a little on your burns each morning and night."

Surprised at the both the gift and the giver, Yuma thanked her. "I thought it would've all been traded by now."

The girl lowered her eyes and blushed. "These are from my personal store. I wanted to become a healer, but Nina, our medicine woman, won't take me as an apprentice. Ayiana Honey, one of the elders at Oakvale, also refused to train me."

"Why ever not? It's a great vocation." A twang of homesickness stuck in Yuma's throat as he thought again of his mother and sister.

Laila twirled the long braid hanging over her shoulder. "Nina says she's too busy with her family, and Ayiana thinks I prefer caring for animals. She says I'm never where people need me, always out spinning daydreams among the trees."

Touched by the girl's sentiment, Yuma couldn't accept such a valuable gift without giving something in return. He rummaged in his pack and withdrew a carved otter. "Here, take this. It's jade."

Laila thanked him and dashed off.

Chaytan peered at Yuma. "Is that the stone you mentioned? I've never seen anything like it."

"I found it a long way from here. It can be worked smooth or sharp." He handed his friend a bag of arrowheads. "Treasure these. I expect you're short of food, but I'd appreciate a bladderflask in return."

A late frost coated Fleet's surrounds as he watched the sun rise. Dewdrops twinkled from grass blades as the shadows retreated.

He switched his tail and fidgeted as he prepared to meet Streak, wondering if he'd also see Tress. Part of him wanted to show off his success in finding the unicorn, the other part dreading meeting her, sure his satisfied lust would be obvious. His visions of sharing his life with the black filly seemed silly and immature.

Now when he thought of his future, it encompassed the pleasures at Shimmering Lake. Yet Gem had sent him away. At least he'd found her. Would Streak be surprised? Perhaps the king would let him settle with the bachelors as he'd promised, and send someone else to Snowhaven.

No. That wouldn't happen. With or without the help of other horses, he had to see his mission through, if only to find a cure for the poison in his veins. Shadow must have the solution, or maybe the goddess's feathers would cure him. Maybe that's why Gem had really sent him away. And he'd made a promise to Sapphire to save the herds. Hopefully it would be over soon and he could find one to join.

A light breeze blew across his face. Turning his rump against the cold, he spotted Yuma approaching.

The man cradled a woven bowl in both arms. "I've brought you breakfast. The clan was sure you'd be starving after I told them about our adventures. They kept me up late retelling stories of riding and talking with a horse."

Fleet lowered his head to the enticing aroma of rolled oats and savoured a mouthful before speaking. "What did the clan say about us finding a unicorn, only to have to go on another mission?"

Yuma groomed Fleet with a hog's hair brush he'd obtained through his trading. "I didn't want to tell them about Shimmering Lake or what we must do. I doubt Gem would be pleased to have a clan searching for her territory, regardless of the protective veil. I respect her desire for privacy."

"What about the unnatural wolves and eels? Surely your clan need to know about those?"

Yuma continued to massage him with long strokes, cleaning the brush with the fingers of his other hand as he worked in a sweeping rhythm. "The Boasville folk have experienced the scorcheels, and bloodwolves have been sighted in the forest."

As much as Fleet enjoyed the massage, he had to find Streak and tell him everything he'd learned. "Did you find out where I can find the herd?"

"They're over to the east. They don't need to be close to the river when the snow melts and their need for hay is dwindling. Not that I think it'll be a good year. The trees should be in leaf by now but the buds are barely open. That's another reason the horses have moved, to let the alfalfa flats grow for the hay harvest."

Fleet finished the oats and suggested Yuma accompany him. "Streak may be a day or so away. It would save time if we headed off as soon as I've shared our news."

Yuma agreed. "I enjoyed Chaytan's company, but one night is enough of listening to a crowded room full of people snoring and farting."

Streak must have seen them coming long before Fleet could make out individual horses in the herd. The grey stallion pranced up to meet them at the top of a rise, blocking the way to the mares below. "You've fared well through the hard winter. You must have found better conditions than here. But I told you not to come back unless you found a unicorn to protect the herds."

Fleet lowered his head in submission. "I did, else I wouldn't have returned."

Streak snaked his head out and snapped at Fleet. "Do you expect me to believe that? How can you achieve what none of my bachelors ever have? Prove it to me."

Yuma coughed. "What's he saying?"

Fleet translated, realising this could be the proof he needed. He held his ground against Streak. "The unicorn, Gemstone, gave me the power to talk with people."

Streak stared at Yuma, his upper lip twitching. "Ask him why there are so many more people at the village."

Although Yuma had already shared that knowledge with him, Fleet went through the process of asking Yuma. Streak added question after question, long after Fleet thought he had proved the point, the king's curiosity about people deeper than his own. "Do you believe me now?"

Streak pawed the ground and shook his thick mane. "If you found a unicorn as you say, why are bloodwolves still stalking the woods? Foaling time is approaching and the mares are nervous."

Fleet related all that had happened since leaving Flowering Valley, Moonglow's prophecy, and the interpretation Gem had made.

The king interrupted at almost every sentence. When he seemed satisfied with Fleet's tale, he advanced until his breath wrapped Fleet's face. "And what of Princess Tress? You fail to mention her and Oakvale's Head of Warriors, Wolfbane."

Fleet didn't like the look in Streak's eyes. He backed up and prepared to flee. "I haven't seen any of your herd since arriving last night."

"Not here. They left soon after you. Breeze tells me Wolfbane had some ridiculous idea to follow you."

Fleet's heart thudded against his chest. He had been looking forward to showing off to the beautiful filly. Disappointment swam through him as fear sent adrenalin trickling down his legs. He risked death if he couldn't convince Streak he had nothing to do with the princess's disappearance, regardless of his mission to save the herds.

Fleet squared his chest at Streak, prepared to do battle. "We haven't seen any sign of other horses, except very old stallion piles around Gemstone's territory."

The grey stallion stared at him hard, one foreleg raised. Then he slumped and sighed. "It's as I feared. Breeze's story is a ruse. Wolfbane has stolen my precious Tress."

Chapter 11

The hint of spring did nothing to cheer Tress. The fresh grass didn't taste as sweet as at Flowering Valley. Buds on the trees looked pale and tired. No butterflies clouded thimbleberry thickets. The only things in abundance were the annoying flies. Tress whisked them away with her tail, but no sooner had they risen from her coat, they settled back. She longed for Breeze with her idle chatter and mutual swishing. Had Streak sent her east yet? No doubt she was being feted by her new stallion.

Tress didn't even have Wolfbane's company. She wasn't sure whether she preferred the loneliness or the gruff presence of the stallion. Apart from returning to ensure she remained at White Water Cliffs, he spent his days scouring the country for other mares. So far he hadn't brought back any.

At least the spring flush of growth renewed her strength, even if she had lost her plump glossiness. Her mane hung in dirty tangles and a snagged blackberry runner in her tail scratched her hind legs at every step. It didn't make sense for Wolfbane to establish a territory where no people lived to care for them.

She climbed to the top of one of the rocky outcrops, scrambling and puffing up the steep slope, bounding from boulder to boulder. Wind whistled past her ears and eagles glided below her. To the north, range after range of hills blurred in a grey haze. To the south, dense forests blocked any chance of seeing what lay within. The river wound through towers of volcanic plugs, islands of sheer rock, their isolation a reflection of her loneliness. Despairing of seeing any other horses, she headed back down, her heart racing as her hooves slipped on the scree.

She picked her way along the river, snatching at mouthfuls of feed from habit rather than hunger. The rushing water reminded her of River Lifeflow blocking the way back to Flowering Valley. And the wolves. She daren't risk the woods on her own. Instead, she meandered aimlessly along the creek, waiting for Wolfbane to return. Maybe this time he would bring company.

The shadow of a hill loomed over her. She shivered.

Something groaned behind the shrubs.

She shied, her hooves slipping and clattering on the pebbled river bank. Her pulse raced. Snorting, she scented the air for any threat. That wasn't wolf! The pungent sweat of horse wafted on the breeze. Whickering, she took a tentative step towards the source.

The groan came again, louder.

Tress broke into a trot. "Hello? Where are you?"

The smell of fear checked her. She halted, tense, every sense alert. "Are you hurt?"

One step at a time, Tress wove between the shrubs.

A mare lay prone on flattened tussocks, her barrel heaving and legs twitching. The chestnut raised her head and glanced at Tress with pain-filled eyes before slumping back. "Go away. I don't need your help."

Tress shook her head in confusion. She couldn't see any wounds, or sense any predator. If an accident had befallen the mare, then surely she'd need assistance. "What's wrong?"

Another groan answered her.

Tress stared, uncertain what to do.

Two long forelegs poked from under the mare's tail, followed by a wet brown head resting on huge knees. A white membrane slithered out of the mare towards her hocks. The newborn struggled out of the bag and scrambled towards the mare's head. The chestnut stretched her neck to lick the damp bundle.

Tress stepped back, not wanting to interfere, yet fascinated by the birth. She had never witnessed a foaling before.

The mare heaved to her feet and shoved her baby with her nose. The foal splayed her front legs and hefted herself up, only to fall flat on her chest. She tried again. Her legs wobbled and gave way. At the third attempt, the filly remained standing. She shook her whole body and nuzzled her way to the mare's teats.

Tress stared in awe. What would it be like to have a foal? With the coming of spring she'd had urges she'd never experienced before. Sometimes she even forgot Wolfbane's rudeness and aggression when she saw him galloping, his muscles rippling, his power evident.

Visions of the black stallion came to her. Was Fleet still alive? Where was he?

Her dreams of unicorns had long since faded, survival requiring her sole attention. Many of Starburst's lessons had proved crucial, even if as a filly she'd thought them pointless, like eating broad-leafed plants as well as sweeter grasses, ensuring she drank even when she wasn't thirsty, and respecting the personal space of her elders.

Allowing mares their privacy at foaling had been a strict rule, but after so long without company she couldn't resist staying with the chestnut. "I'm Princess Silken Tresses of Flowering Valley. You have a beautiful new filly."

The mare stopped her washing long enough to bare her teeth at Tress. "If you're going to hang around, find me something to release my afterbirth."

Tress couldn't remember which herbs would work. "What do you need?"

"If you're a princess surely your dam taught you that. Yarrow and raspberry, I think." The mare turned back to her foal, who switched her tail as she suckled.

Tress hesitated. "What's your name? How much do I need to get?"

The mare blinked long lashes at Tress. "I'm Half Moon. As much as you can carry, I guess. I don't know. This is my first foal. Leave me in peace."

Tress foraged for the necessary plants, listening to the mare comforting her foal. A pang of longing for her mother twisted her gut. Starburst would know what herbs to gather. She always assisted the mares of Flowering Valley when their birthing time came, leading them to a sheltered spot away from the herd, keeping other horses away, and visiting them only to ensure they had everything they needed. After a few days, she would accompany them home and introduce the newborn to the mare herd.

She imagined Starburst doing just that now at home. Her heart thumped. Flowering Valley was no longer her home. She should never have run away.

119

But she had, so it was pointless her thinking about that. Determined to make the most of her situation, Tress carried a mouthful of flowers back to Half Moon and the new filly. The little one's nut brown coat matched her tufty mane and tail except for large white splotches on her hindquarters. A narrow strip of white ran down her face and she had long white legs to her knees and hocks.

Tress dropped the plants at Half Moon's head and reached her nose forward to greet the baby.

Half Moon bit hard on Tress's neck and spun, lashing out with a hind leg, her hoof connecting with Tress's shoulder. "Get away! She's my foal."

Tress hurried backwards. She shivered in shock. "I was only saying hello. Fine thanks for bringing you what you need."

The chestnut mare rolled her eyes and glanced at the proffered herbs. "There's no need to come near."

Disappointed at not finding a friend, Tress wandered off to graze. For the remainder of the day she kept her distance, watching as the foal became stronger on spindly legs. Before long, the filly could gallop and buck with confidence. After another drink of her dam's milk, the tiny horse folded herself in the shade and slept.

Tress day-dreamed. By next spring, she might have a foal of her own.

Half Moon tore at the grass, gradually making her way over to Tress while keeping an eye on her filly. "I'm sorry I was harsh. I've heard of newborns being stolen."

Tress turned her rump to Half Moon. "I haven't even had my first season, so I'm hardly a threat. How would I feed a newborn foal?"

The mare came closer, staying between Tress and her foal. "I've said I'm sorry."

Tress blew acceptance through her nose and turned alongside Half Moon. They grazed and shared histories, gradually opening up about how they came to be there. Tress took especial note when Half Moon mentioned the former lead mare of White Water Cliffs, Queen Sapphire.

That must be Fleet's dam. So he was a prince. She shared the news about Sapphire fleeing to Dark Woods and birthing a colt before a wolf killed her. "Fleet has been sent to seek help from the unicorns."

Half Moon curled her upper lip. "I've never seen a unicorn. I think the tales are fantasies of the bachelors who can't build themselves a herd. Don't expect any help from that quarter."

Over the next few days, Tress and Half Moon stayed together. With pleasant company at last, Tress began to enjoy spring. As the new-born filly grew stronger they ranged further afield. Eventually Tress was invited to greet the baby. "What have you called her?"

"Pebbles." Half Moon whinnied to her foal, who had taken off to explore. The filly came galloping back, kicking up her heels in play. "Her spots look like the stones in the river."

"I wonder where she gets such unusual markings." Tress nuzzled the filly's rump as if to check the white splotches were real.

Half Moon pushed her away. "Her sire is an appaloosa. We should go and find him. I doubt he'll be far."

Tress chirped up. "You mean he's near here? Why didn't you say before? Let's go!"

Anticipation lent vigour to Tress's stride as she followed her new friend at a trot. They wove through a scattering of trees and crested a rise into a glade where several other horses grazed. A young stallion whinnied when he saw them.

Half Moon broke into a lope. "That's Boldearth. Come and meet him."

Boldearth cantered to greet them, his head raised and tail high despite the ravages of a hard winter showing in his protruding ribs and hips. "Congratulations, Half Moon, a beautiful filly. And who's this?"

Tress danced over. She'd certainly be happy to have a foal by this stallion. "Hello, I'm Princess Silken Tresses of Flowering Valley."

He wiggled his lips, his eyes sparkling. "I don't think you're a princess here, nor of Flowering Valley any more, but you're welcome to run with us if you like."

Tress didn't sense any malice in his words. "Are you king of this territory? I must warn you that Wolfbane, Oakvale's former Head of Warriors, claims it too."

The young stallion reached forward to blow at her nostrils. "No-one is king here, not since King Thunder was killed. There's no structure, no warriors, no queen. A few mares run with me, others wander with my brothers. We're too busy fighting wolves to worry about squabbling among ourselves."

The lack of formality was a new concept to Tress. She wasn't sure she approved of the loose arrangements. "How do you know when to move to new grazing or where the best watering places are? Don't you need a queen to guide the youngsters and ensure they eat a balanced diet?"

Half Moon nudged Pebbles closer. "That knowledge has been lost. Finding enough to eat takes all our effort. We go where the grass is best. There's little competition."

As they talked, other mares came over and added their stories. A buckskin pony with a patchy coat spoke of the dangers. "If a bloodwolf or its drool touches you, you die. If they don't kill you straight away, your wounds become poisoned. You can't walk. You can't eat. You go mad and leap from the cliffs."

Tress threw up her head in shock. "You mean horses kill themselves?"

"Yes. That's why we live up this end of the valley, away from the bodies."

Boldearth told how the wolves had slaughtered all the people because there had been no warriors to warn of the danger. "The village is a terrible place."

About to tell them about the mare at the cavern, Tress spotted Wolfbane galloping towards them, his ears pinned to his neck, the ground shaking from his hoof beats. "Watch out! He murdered Precipice!"

Boldearth cantered off to face him. The two stallions drew close. Wolfbane reared and thrashed his hooves, challenging Boldearth.

The younger stallion ducked away.

Wolfbane pursued him, driving him with his chest, ignoring his attempts to converse.

Boldearth dodged, nimble on his feet, snapping back in defence.

The mares retreated to a safe distance. Tress quaked as Wolfbane's screams echoed against the cliffs.

The appaloosa's inexperience was no match for the heavier stallion. After receiving vicious bites to the neck, shoulders, and rump, he fled.

Wolfbane pranced up to the small gathering of mares. "You're all mine now. Get moving. We're going upstream."

Tress led the way without hesitation. Two of the other mares balked and received nasty kicks for their trouble. Even Half Moon was driven by the stallion's teeth, Pebbles sticking close to her dam's side as they trotted ahead of Wolfbane.

The small herd spent a tense night under the shelter of the cliffs near the hay cavern. The roar of the falls brought Tress bad dreams, bloodwolves with poisonous fangs leaping and snarling, and horses throwing themselves to their deaths, their bones littering the river.

When she awoke, she found Wolfbane storming in a rage.

All the other mares except Half Moon had disappeared.

Chapter 12

Despite the easy conditions north of Streak's territory, Fleet fretted, his nightmares worsening and his hindquarters stiff and sore. Worse, he'd left the company of horses behind again. Although Streak had dropped his aggressive attitude, he didn't invite him to linger. Fleet had left as soon as he'd told Streak his news. After fording the branch of River Lifeflow forming Streak's boundary, he followed the major stream northeast. He and Yuma fell into their travelling routine with long familiarity, aided by their ability to converse.

Talking with the man was interesting, though did little to assuage Fleet's need for other horses. Or Gem. The more he thought of the beautiful unicorn, their pleasures, and then her rebuff, the more he questioned why he must be the one to overcome Shadow. All he wanted was to return to Shimmering Lake, to gallop, and swim, and play. When the loneliness became too much, he even considered abandoning his promise to Sapphire, but Gem had made it clear she wouldn't welcome him back, and his suffering demanded he rid himself of the bloodwolf poison. If that meant he helped other horses in the process, so much the better. Maybe then he'd be permitted to settle with a herd.

He cantered on, Yuma's cheerful whistling in contrast to his mood. Tatuk darted in and out of view, reminding him of Gem. The ground squelched beneath his hooves, draining his energy as it sucked at his legs. "Isn't there a drier route to Watersmeet?"

Yuma pointed. "Boasville is over to our right, built on a rise. The crossing is shallowest near there too."

Fleet veered away from the marsh, relieved as his feet found firmer going. He picked up speed—the sooner this mission was over the sooner he could return—following the paths appearing through the short grass that widened as they neared the village, trampled by the feet of many generations of people.

Only the croak of frogs greeted them. Door hangings flapped in the breeze and no smoke spiralled from hearths. Dust eddies blew around the central shelter.

Yuma tensed. "Don't stop. I don't like the feel of the place with everyone gone." He directed Fleet to where the villagers accessed the river.

Fleet splashed into the shallows, alert for scorcheels. The water ruffled in the wind, the dazzle preventing him from seeing what might lie beneath the surface. Currents pulled at his legs in multiple directions, upsetting his balance.

Halfway across the wide expanse, Fleet's rump throbbed. The pain increased. Hot spikes shot down his thighs.

The water churned around his front legs. Something grabbed his left knee. Fire needled his flesh as if a swarm of biting ants were devouring him.

Fleet thrashed. A weight disconnected from his leg. He raced back to the bank.

He bounded to the village, oblivious of anything but the burning.

Yuma jumped off. "What happened? Are you hurt?"

"My leg. It's on fire!"

Yuma squatted and peered. "It's blistering. Don't move."

Remaining still took all Fleet's self-control while Yuma rinsed his leg and squeezed blobs of bumblebee nectar onto the burn. "Did you see the scorcheel?"

"No. One moment you were wading across, the next I almost came off and we were back here. No wonder people abandoned the place." Yuma rummaged in his pack and offered Fleet a handful of dried leaves. "Here, this might help the pain."

Fleet swallowed the herbs, his mind spinning with visions of horses torn apart, their carcasses devoured by bloodwolves or dragged beneath the water.

Yuma made a fire and set up camp, even though the sun still rode high in the sky. "What are we going to do?"

Tatuk arrived as if on demand. "The river narrows upstream, but it's still too wide to jump."

Fleet pushed away the pain. He had to get to the other side. "What if we go much further east?"

Yuma shook his head. "Two rivers join. One comes from the south, which will take us the wrong way. We need to cross here. If I had a spear, I might be able to defend us, but only if I can see the scorcheels before they attack."

Fleet agreed there was no point going far out of their way, only to risk finding more scorcheels anyway. "I hadn't made the connection before, but I'm sure my rump throbs whenever bloodwolves or scorcheels are near. That should give us warning."

"Great. But we'll still need to go back to the forest so I can cut a spear."

Fleet shifted his weight, his discomfort subsiding. "Can't you use your arrows?"

"No, they're too short and will bend. I need a long, heavy shaft, preferably cedar or fir."

"We'd better get going then. Those trees are a long way back."

They returned to Boasville for Yuma to fashion a branch into a weapon, hardening the tip in the fire.

Fleet watched with interest. "Won't the spear slip off the slime?"

Yuma shrugged. "I hope not. I've never tried spearing an eel before. I usually catch them on a bone hook."

Fleet paced around the fire to ease his sore muscles. "What about the tusks you took from the wolf that killed Sapphire? Could you attach one of those like you bind the stone to your arrows?"

"That's a good idea. The poison might kill the scorcheels even if I can't stab them properly. I don't fancy landing one, anyway." Yuma extracted a fang from his medicine pouch and removed the hyssop leaves. He soaked a length of bark string and bound the tooth to the tempered shaft.

When the binding dried tight, Yuma kicked out the fire and mounted. "Are you sure you're well enough to try again?"

Fleet walked towards the river. "Time won't heal me. I need a cure for the poison."

He trotted upstream of the shallows, stopping prior to where the water became murky and deepened in a narrow channel. His rump remained stiff, but didn't throb. "Are you ready?"

"As ready as I'll ever be." Yuma tightened the fingers of one hand in Fleet's mane, the other clutching his spear.

Fleet lunged into the water, splashing his legs high in an attempt to cross as fast as possible.

The riverbed dissolved beneath his feet. He swam.

Yuma was immersed to his waist. "I can't use a spear like this! Get to shallower water!"

Fleet veered and let the current wash him back to where the scorcheel had attacked. His hooves met solid ground.

His rump throbbed. "Look out! It's near!"

A long fin cut the water, winding its way towards him. Yuma twisted on Fleet's back and thrust the spear at the scorcheel.

The beast reared out of the water, rows of needle teeth gnashing, slime streaking the air.

Fleet dodged.

Yuma thrust again. The bloodwolf fang grazed the side of the scorcheel.

Its crimson eyes whirled. Already as long as Fleet, it grew. Its grey body thickened. Crimson streaks glowed down its sides. It lashed out at Yuma's leg.

Fleet lunged towards the opposite bank and burst from the water, ignoring his pain, terror blinding him. He scrambled out on the far side, galloping away from the river. Yuma clung tight.

He could run no more. He slowed to a walk and halted. "Are you alright, Yuma?"

"Yes, it missed me. But we won't be using those fangs again." He dismounted, soaked, gasping, and looking horrified.

"Why not? You did well."

Yuma coughed and spat. "The venom made the creature bigger. Whatever Shadow uses to create bloodwolf poison must be what transforms eels too."

Fleet hung his head, sucking in deep breaths. "The feathers are our only hope. We must keep going."

Peak after ragged peak cleaved the horizon. Yuma squinted into sparkling white valleys, the sun transforming the hillsides as shadows crept across them. Birds of prey circled on unseen currents, watching for the slightest movement of a snow hare or weasel. Eventually the glare became too much and the climb too demanding. Yuma stopped looking, concentrating only on placing one foot in front of the other. He longed to complete this task; the adventure had stopped being fun moons ago. He had never suffered homesickness before. Now all he wanted was to drink mulled ale around a crackling fire and listen to his family chatter about their day.

His family. Had bloodwolves reached Waterfalls? He should go home, no matter what Fleet had to do. But he didn't want to abandon the horse, and his friendship, when they might be close to saving the land.

He blinked, the white peaks in front of him dazzling, and gawped at the narrow track winding up the mountain. "Are we supposed to go up that?"

Tatuk fluttered his wings where he perched on Fleet's neck. "It's the only way in to Snowhaven."

Vapour misted from Fleet's nostrils as he scrambled up the steep slope. Yuma tagged on his tail, gasping from the high altitude, so different to the flats around Boasville. They reached a ridge.

Tatuk hovered over his head. "The bear's cave is near."

Yuma groaned at the steep descent; going down into another valley meant he would have to climb back up again. He released Fleet's tail and let gravity pull him. Stones clattered down the hillside, loosened by his stumbling on the narrow track.

"Careful! You don't want to disturb the bear." The dragon flew ahead, giggling as he disappeared, as if this quest were a merry jaunt.

Where the ground levelled out, Fleet picked up the pace. Yuma lengthened his stride to keep up, and caught his breath. How were they going to get past the bear?

A narrow brook crossed the track. They hadn't encountered scorcheels for days, but Fleet still flared his nostrils and blew at the surface before drinking.

Kneeling beside Fleet, Yuma sucked the water, the coldness numbing his tongue and making his teeth ache. They couldn't rest for long; he had already lost sensation in his fingers and toes. He struggled to his feet and strode on, the exercise barely stimulating his circulation. A layer of snow obscured the path, creaking under their footfalls, their way marked only by the level ground of a well-trodden track beneath the packed covering.

Ice balled into Fleet's hooves as if he had stones stuck to his soles, raising his feet off the ground. Yuma picked them clean with an old flint as often as he could. The sun disappeared below the horizon and a chill wind blew. He hugged his furs around him. "We need to find shelter and get a fire going."

Tatuk flitted into view and twitched his wings for them to follow. A hollow in the hillside offered a windbreak and protection from any snow that might fall in the night. Yuma cleared a place to camp, and unstrapped a bundle of dense wood and a few pieces of kindling from his pack. He soon had a soup pot bubbling. The tiny fire did little to warm him. After a hasty meal, he curled into a ball, relieved the night remained dry. He'd need all the sleep he could get to face the next day.

Early morning fog rolled through the valleys, the treetops appearing like islands in a sea of mist. Yuma ate the leftovers from the brace of ptarmigan he had downed the day before with his sling, packed up camp, and set off on the trail in Fleet's wake.

The sun chased away the last of the mist, revealing a landscape of glittering white. Once his stiff muscles unknotted, Yuma's spirits lifted, despite still having no idea how they would claim the feathers. He climbed a steep rise and gasped as the mountain fell away in sheer cliffs, the path ahead narrow and twisted. Grey-blue shale slushed beneath his feet as he trod with care, the dizzying height churning his stomach. He rested his hand on Fleet's rump for support until they reached a broader platform of trodden ice.

Tatuk perched on a jutting rock, greeting them as if they enjoyed the warmth of Shimmering Lake. "This is the cave. The feathers are deep inside. The guardian is with them."

An overpowering odour of bear wafted from the entrance. Fleet blew through distended nostrils and pawed the ground. "I'm not keen on enclosed spaces."

Yuma slipped off his pack. "I'll go. Hopefully the bear will be deeply asleep. But if not, I have my arrows. You stay here."

Creeping into the gloom, Yuma held his bow ready. He had replaced his flint arrowheads with jade in the hope they would be sharp enough to pierce a thick hide. Following the bear's spoor, he crept deeper into the mountain, peering into the shadows, the way becoming darker the further he progressed, every boulder and stalagmite taking the form of a defensive bear. He should have made a torch from the remains of his fire.

Too late now.

Roaaarrr!

Yuma tensed mid-stride and tried to gauge which passage the bellow came from. Taking care not to make any sudden movement, he pulled his bowstring taut.

An enormous beast lumbered towards him, raised claws stretching higher than Yuma's head. The bear gnashed his yellowed ivories and bellowed again, his anger echoing around the chamber.

Yuma couldn't pass by the beast. His stomach flipped as if he tottered on a precipice. His arms shook. He retreated backwards to the mouth of the cave, step by careful step.

The bear stopped.

Yuma reached daylight, leant against Fleet, and exhaled. "There's no point me trying to shoot that. There must be another way."

Tatuk alighted on Yuma's pack. "Bears like sweet things. Tempt him away."

He didn't have any corn. "Fleet, have you seen any sweetgrass?"

Fleet rolled his eyes. "If I had, I would've eaten it last night."

Yuma rested his bow on the ground and ran a hand through his hair. "Can you make something the bear will like, Tatuk?"

The dragon hopped up and down on Yuma's pack. "Sweets in here."

Scratching his head, Yuma considered what he might have, going through all the contents of his food and medicine stores. Bumblebee nectar! Only a few cells remained. If they encountered more scorcheels, he'd need every drop. He extracted the pouch, sticky from where the wax casings had burst and soaked the suede. So much for saving them for future use. A sweet aroma wafted from the leather. Would it be enough to entice the bear?

He crept back into the cave.

The bear remained where he'd stopped, standing tall and form-idable.

Yuma waved the nectar pouch in front of him.

The guardian sniffed the air and dropped onto his forelegs. His long claws raked the ground as he approached.

Yuma flung the pouch down a narrow passage.

The bear followed, almost brushing Yuma with his thick fur.

As soon as the bear passed, Yuma ran into the depths of the cave. He mustn't waste the precious moments the distraction might buy him. Light needled through a crack in the ceiling, making it easier to find his way to the bear's den. The passage ended in a small cavern. Greasy patches of old hair stuck to smooth protrusions and gouges marked the walls, the space large enough for several bears. Relieved at the lack of other residents, Yuma quickly took in his surrounds. Bones and old droppings littered one side of the shelter. A deep bed of dry grass nestled beneath a high recess in the rock. Yuma leapt across in expectation, and scrambled up to inspect the hideaway.

He gasped. Five golden feathers as long as his arms glinted on their smooth shelf, the rock carved to match their shape. He reached to grab them.

A deafening roar reverberated around the chamber.

Yuma snatched away his hand.

The bear bellowed and lumbered forward.

Yuma dropped to the ground and fired arrow after arrow. They bounced from the bear's hide. Down to the last one, Yuma dropped to one knee, steadied, and aimed at the beast's eye.

The arrow hit the bear's nose. It reared, clutching its face, roaring.

Yuma grabbed the feathers. Cradling them in both arms, surprised at their weight and solidity, he dashed past the guardian and ran for his life.

Chapter 13

Fleet didn't like Yuma entering the bear's cave alone—this was supposed to be his job—but at least the man had weapons. Hopefully, as Yuma supposed, the guardian would be hibernating and the feathers easily retrieved.

Roaaarrr!

Fleet sprang to the cave entrance. He hesitated.

Hooves clattered behind him.

A mighty unicorn burst along the trail, fury belching from his nostrils. He charged, his lowered head pointing a horn like an ancient branch from a whitebark pine, twisted and knobbly. His crimson coat dripped with sweat, in stark contrast to his black mane and tail, crusted with icicles.

Fleet's mind whirled. A horse with a twisted horn! Was this Shadow? But he was supposed to be trapped at Obsidian Caves. This equine had only one horn. That's what unicorn meant. Or was it two twisted together?

Their bodies crashed, chest to chest.

Fleet pawed the air and screamed, his eyes rolling, showing the whites.

His assailant backed off, bunching for another attack.

Fleet charged.

They smashed together. Rocks tumbled from the hillside, pelting down like hailstones.

Fleet ignored them, all his attention on his adversary, far stronger than him.

They dodged and parried and dodged. Fleet ducked sideways to avoid the brutal horn before spinning and kicking out. As quick as he made contact, he leapt back and reared, thrashing his forelegs. His opponent met each onslaught with equal vigour, crashing his hooves against Fleet's shoulders and rump.

Fleet feared for his life. Not the bloodwolf, the bog, or the scorcheel scared him like this.

He summoned his courage and fought back. He hadn't come so far to fail now. He must get the feathers. He wouldn't let Sapphire down. He reared and struck.

His enemy lashed back.

The contorted horn struck Fleet's shoulder. A blast of pain coursed through his body. He stepped backwards towards the edge of the cliff. Stones clattered as his hooves scrambled. He teetered on the edge.

Yuma rushed from the cave, ears tuned to any pursuit.

Fleet tottered on the edge of the path, his hind legs scrabbling at the cliff, stones flying from his front hooves as they sought purchase on the rock.

A massive crimson horse was trotting away down the narrow trail; it turned, preparing to charge, aiming straight at Fleet.

Yuma leapt forward and dropped the feathers, waving his arms and shouting.

The horse—no—*unicorn*, showed no sign of slowing.

Yuma dashed out of the way. How could he stop it? He had no arrows left. He whipped his slingshot from his waistband and grabbed a handful of stones.

The missiles made no impact on the advancing unicorn.

Fleet continued to scramble, panic in his eyes.

Yuma grabbed a golden feather and hefted it in one hand. Could he throw it like a spear? The rigid vanes ran smooth along the shaft. Unslinging his bow, he loaded the feather and pulled the bowstring taut.

The unicorn sprinted towards Fleet.

Yuma let the feather fly. Brilliant gold shimmered as it flew straight at the unicorn's chest.

Fleet threw his weight forward. Every sinew in his legs screamed. Sweat erupted from every pore. He lurched over the lip of the hillside, grazing his muzzle on the sharp rocks, and clambered to his feet.

The smell of blood permeated the air. He must have damaged his foe. This was his chance! He gathered himself to renew his attack, searching for his opponent's weak spot.

A golden shaft protruded from the crimson chest. Ichor oozed from the wound. The horned horse shuddered and retreated, head sagging and lungs pumping. Skin rippled along his neck, across his flanks, and over his rump. Within moments, his whole body quaked on splayed legs.

Fleet stared in amazement, exhausted from the confrontation and by the scramble that had saved him from a fatal fall over the cliff's edge.

Yuma stood nearby, bow in hand, gaping.

Groans sounded from the cave.

Yuma hastened to retrieve his pack and raced towards Fleet, four golden feathers clutched underneath one arm. "We need to get out of here before the bear recovers."

Fleet quivered under Yuma's touch. "We can't go yet. I must know who he is. Look, his horn is straightening."

The unicorn convulsed with a final shudder. Sweat mingled with his blood, streaking and matting his coat. The golden feather tinkled as its fronds shivered. Black streaks ran up the shaft to accumulate in the tip. As the gold dispersed, the unicorn stood taller with his ears pricked. The blackened feather dropped from his chest and fizzled into ash. The wound closed, leaving no scar.

No-one moved or spoke. Even the air stilled.

A flock of geese honking overhead broke the spell.

The unicorn tottered forwards.

Fleet blocked his progress, ready to attack.

The unicorn veered and bowed to Yuma, his soft nose scraping the rocky track as he bent one foreleg. "I must thank you. I've never been free of pain before."

Yuma grasped Fleet's mane to mount. "We really need to go. The bear is very angry."

The unicorn tilted his head towards Fleet before returning his attention to Yuma. "I'm Jasper. Who are you? How did you get past the guardian? Why do you want the feathers?"

Fleet straightened to his full height and arched his neck. "I'm Fleet of Foot and this is Yuma Squirrel. We're on a mission to save Equinora from bloodwolves and scorcheels. Moonglow's prophecy says I must use the goddess's feathers on Shadow."

Yuma glanced towards the cave. "Fleet, we must go. I used all my arrows on the bear. We need to move before it recovers and attacks us."

Jasper flattened his ears. "You shot him? I must help him. Kodi won't attack me. Give me one of the feathers." He snatched one in his teeth and disappeared inside the cave.

Yuma headed off down the track at a jog. "I'm not hanging around for an angry bear."

Fleet hesitated. "Perhaps we should wait. Jasper might be able to tell us more about Shadow."

"And risk being torn to shreds when he heals the bear?" Yuma continued on, breaking into a run.

Fleet couldn't risk parting from Yuma and the three remaining feathers. He clattered after him on the treacherous track.

They reached the stream and both guzzled the icy water.

Tatuk flickered into view and hovered in front of Fleet. "Jasper wants to speak with you. He promises the bear won't harm anyone."

Fleet dropped to a halt. "Do you trust him?"

The dragon alighted on a boulder and folded his wings. "He's a unicorn! They're all friends of dragons. Please, he begs you to wait."

Torn between the need to keep going and the desire to understand what had transpired, Fleet sniffed the grass. "We're not going back to the cave. I'll graze for a while if he wants to come here. But if I smell bear, we're off."

He nudged Yuma. "You'd better rest. That was a hard run. I'll keep watch."

Yuma removed his pack and cleared the snow around a boulder. "I guess we have to trust Tatuk. I could do with a breather. If you're going to eat, I may as well too."

Fleet kept one eye on the path as he picked at the little vegetation free of snow along the waterway.

Yuma finished his meal and stretched out on his bedroll, his hands clasped behind his head. Tatuk flittered down and landed on his chest. The little dragon's colours brightened as he nestled above the diamond hung around Yuma's neck. He curled into a ball, tucked his snout under one wing, and fell asleep.

Fleet relaxed.

Before long, Jasper arrived and bowed from a respectful distance. "You have nothing to fear from me or Kodi."

Fleet nickered to Yuma, who stirred and joined him.

Jasper greeted him too. "The guardian forgives your attack in return for straightening my horn. I was unable to heal his wounds with the feather. I guess it needs to penetrate the skin, and I couldn't make it do that, but he'll be alright. He's one of the goddess's creatures."

Not reassured, Fleet remained a distance away. "I'm glad you're cured, but I suspect we needed all the feathers. I don't know if three will be enough."

"Tell me more about this mission of yours."

Fleet shared the story from when his dam had been killed. "Sapphire's vision seems to be true."

At the mention of the chestnut mare's name, Jasper gasped in surprise. "Your dam was Queen Sapphire?"

Fleet coughed. "Yes, she was originally from White Water Cliffs."

The unicorn blew a spray of mist from his nostrils. "So, I was right, she was a warmblood."

"You knew her?" Fleet couldn't imagine his dam meeting this strange and powerful unicorn. She'd certainly never said anything. Yet she hadn't told him about many things.

Jasper made his way towards the creek. He took a long drink before answering. "Now I understand how you entered my territory. You're more than half hotblood. No wonder the unicorns entrusted this task to you."

Fleet was tired of mysteries. "Echo believes he's my great-grand-sire."

A look of surprise glinted in the unicorn's eye. "So that's where Sapphire got her hot blood. That makes her Gemstone's niece."

Fleet couldn't take in all these family trees. "How do you know my dam? What does it mean? She and I are warmbloods, if what you say is true. And how can I be more than half hotblood? Are you saying my sire was also a noncorn?"

Jasper took a deep breath and led Fleet to a sunny spot. "It's a delight to revel in the warmth after a lifetime of seeking the cold to alleviate my pain. Forgive me this luxury before I tell you what's going to be difficult to relate."

Fleet flicked his tail in impatience. "We can't linger here. It's a long way to Obsidian Caves and every moment sees bloodwolves and scorcheels wreak havoc."

Jasper acknowledged the threat. "I'll try to make it short. You have to understand I've wandered this land for many horse generations. I've never been free of pain. Like any male, I have urges. When the lust builds to a point I can no longer ignore, I go in search of a mare, preferably one with warm blood."

Understanding how powerful a force lust could be, Fleet remained quiet. His daydreams of Gem stirred his loins making him shuffle his back feet.

Jasper appraised him. "I hadn't picked up that before!"

Embarrassed Jasper had heard his thoughts, Fleet stepped away. "Isn't it rude to read my mind?"

"Sorry, you need to learn to shield yourself. Didn't Gemstone teach you?"

"No. There wasn't time." Fleet wasn't sure being a warmblood had any benefits.

The unicorn returned to his story. "In my travels, I came across a mare with deep blue eyes, a sign of hot blood. She ran with King Thunder."

Fleet threw up his head and half-reared. "That's my sire. Was it you who murdered him?" Shocked at the revelation, Fleet retreated, scared the familiarity was part of a ruse to lull him into security.

"Wait, wait, wait. I've promised I'm no threat. How could I hurt a horse of my blood? Thunder wasn't your sire."

"What? Sapphire never mentioned unicorns to me until just before she died. You lie!" His head spinning, Fleet galloped off, throwing up stones as he tore alongside the creek, his hooves pounding like the implications of what Jasper had said. It couldn't be true. Could it? Maybe that was why, unlike other horses, he could fight the bloodwolf poison and enter Gem's territory without her knowledge. Those abilities had surprised her even after discovering Echo was his great-grandsire. And what of Cirrus, the old stallion at Silverlake? This would mean he hadn't found his grandsire after all.

Fleet slowed. The bitter chill froze the sweat on his chest and neck. Nobody pursued him. Hatred for Jasper killing Thunder bubbled deep in his gut. Even so, he was desperate to hear the full story.

He returned to find Jasper grazing in the same spot. "Is it true? I'm more than half unicorn?"

Jasper continued as if nothing had happened. "It would seem so. I admit your dam wasn't willing. Thunder fought valiantly to protect her. But I was convinced if she was no longer a maiden, she would come into healing powers and help me manage my pain. As it happens, she wasn't a maiden anyway, and her power was of sight, not healing, so I needn't have forced her to mate with me."

"You raped her! How dare you?" Fleet thought back to the many moons he had wandered with Sapphire. No wonder she'd never told him about Jasper. "She would have helped you without that. She knew a lot about plants and their special purposes."

"Maybe so, but it was power I needed, not herbs. Eventually she disappeared into Dark Woods and I didn't pursue her. It never occurred to me she would be in foal."

Fleet's emotions roiled. "Did you kill the unicorn enabling Gem to be conceived?"

"No!" Jasper trembled in rage. "It was the one you seek, Shadow, who murdered Dewdrop. Not even in my wildest pain would I harm a unicorn mare, especially her."

"So it's okay to rape a warmblood mare, but you wouldn't touch one of your own. I hate you! I wish we hadn't cured your horn. Why don't you go and stop Shadow instead of me? Maybe that's what the goddess intended, why the prophecy sent me here."

Jasper blocked Fleet's path. "Wait. Please. There's more you need to know. Stay with me tonight and let me explain."

A cold shadow fell across the resting spot as the sun sank behind the peak. Yuma tried to calm Fleet with a stroke to his neck. "Fleet, we need to find shelter. I don't want to sleep out under snow."

Fleet fought his indecision. Part of him wanted to leave Jasper and this place far behind. Another part wanted to hear more, no matter how painful. In the end, Yuma's needs swayed him. He wouldn't let down a friend.

"Alright, we'll stay one night. I trust Tatuk to warn us of any threat." Relieved for the excuse to do something normal, Fleet waited for Yuma to pack his bag and mount. Although Jasper suggested they go back to the bear's cave, promising Kodi would welcome them, Fleet didn't find that comforting and knew Yuma would prefer somewhere safer. Instead, they agreed to follow Jasper to a spot he recommended. As they meandered along a narrow track, the valley opened up. Pockets of white flowers nestled in lush pasture. An area large enough for a whole herd of horses bloomed amid a ring of snowdrifts.

Jasper led them to an overhang large enough to shelter them all. "This is my home. Here I can enjoy good grazing yet still have the cold numb my pain. Not that I need the cold any more. I can't thank you enough for what you've done."

Yuma gazed around. "How does this valley stay so lush when the surrounds are cloaked in snow? Is that your power?"

Jasper shrank, his eyes half-closed. "No. This is where Dewdrop died." He straightened up and turned to Fleet. "I must avenge her death! I believe your quest for the goddess's feathers may in fact have been a mission to save me, not to fight Shadow. I doubt the feathers will be of any use against him. Aureana tried to use her wings many times to overcome his powers. She couldn't eliminate his evil, which is why she locked him at Obsidian Caves."

Fleet's anger grew. He stamped his hoof. "I'll do what I came for. I must get rid of the poison in my veins. Maybe the feathers are different now. Maybe it needs Yuma's bow to force the feathers through his skin, like he did with you. I only hope three are enough."

Yuma rubbed Fleet's ears. "Do you think I should try one on you to rid you of the poison? Is that why we're really here?"

The idea had occurred to Fleet. "Not yet. If I can overcome Shadow, his beasts and their poison may disappear. We can't risk losing another feather until we find him."

Feelings Fleet didn't understand bubbled beneath his skin like boils threatening to erupt. Why did he feel so compelled to save Equinora? All he wanted was to settle with a herd, and one day have his own territory and breed strong foals. If the goddess couldn't change Shadow, what chance did he have? He'd be better off returning to Dark Woods and risking his life with the bloodwolves. But if no-one saved his world, no safe place to live would remain.

Tatuk drooped on his perch and his eyes glazed over. Yuma straightened Fleet's forelock and pointed out the effect his anger was having on the dragon.

Fleet struggled to calm down. He needed time to sort out this new knowledge. "I'll head to Obsidian Caves tomorrow. Maybe I'll learn something useful along the way."

Jasper studied each of the three companions in turn. "It'll take more than determination to overcome his evil, and I have a score to settle. I'm going with you."

"No!" Fleet shuddered. Jasper had murdered Thunder, raped and crippled Sapphire, and sent her into exile. His crimson coat and black points reminded Fleet of bloodwolves and scorcheels. Red and black, like in the prophecy. Dread slithered down Fleet's spine. Maybe *Jasper* was the one who threatened Equinora.

Chapter 14

Serrated peaks gnawed the horizon. Cold winds swept from the north. The mountains that had never seemed to disappear when Fleet journeyed towards Snowhaven, looming in the background like thunderheads, now never seemed to get any closer, remaining the same size, elusive in the distance. As the terrain became more rugged, animal corpses littered the trail, from tiny mice to massive deer, their eyes glazed and guts spilled, reeking of poison. Fleet's rage at their cruel deaths simmered beneath his skin, heating his resolve to find Shadow and make him pay—or lose his life in the effort.

Only the hope that many other creatures might have reached the safety of Shimmering Lake helped him control his anger. The nearer they approached Obsidian Caves, the more the wound on his rump throbbed. His dark moods increased. For Tatuk's sake, he tempered his attitude towards Jasper, needing the dragon to improve the richness of the alpine tundra for him and create nourishment for Yuma. Even with the pain, he welcomed the warmth of Yuma on his back—a companion he had come to rely on. At least Sapphire had been right that he could trust the man.

Despite Tatuk's reassurance that Fleet could also trust Jasper, his guts squirmed whenever he looked at his sire. *His sire.* The notion weighed like a boulder. Would letting the unicorn accompany him prove unwise? At least he had taught Fleet to shield his thoughts. He also shared stories of the places they passed through, regaling them with the antics of the goddess and her creations in far more colour than Tress had shared. Often, Yuma asked for clarification of some fact or other for the songs he was developing to share with his people. Absorbed in the conversations, Fleet could almost forget the urgency of their mission, and who Jasper was.

With the lengthening days giving them more time to travel, and the constant pain, Fleet wearied and paid little attention to where they were going, letting Tatuk and Jasper guide him. He had no idea where to go anyway. On and on they cantered, only trotting or walking where the terrain demanded a safer pace. Each night they stopped for Yuma to cook and sleep. Fleet alternated dozing and grazing while Jasper disappeared into the dark, claiming he wanted to enjoy the land in his new pain-free state and talk with any animals left alive. Too tired to question his sire's motives, Fleet pushed away worries of what Jasper might really be doing.

After a night of fitful dozing, he woke to a blood-red sunrise. Foothills loomed as if they had crept closer while he slept. Soon after they set off, the track ahead wound between two narrow pillars into a desolate land of basalt crags. The stone towers loomed like guardians of a different world, dark and sinister. Thunderheads roiled, blocking the meagre light from the interior of the rock forest. A sulphurous odour drifted on the wind. Dread prickled Fleet's coat like sticky burrs needling him at every step.

Tatuk alighted on his crest. "I can't go any further. Eat well before you pass the Sentinels."

Fleet halted. "I'm sorry my mood is upsetting you."

The dragon flitted to the branch of a dead tree. "It isn't you."

Fleet dithered. They had arrived at Obsidian Caves. Now that a confrontation with Shadow loomed, he wasn't sure what to do. He didn't want to go further without the dragon's help. What was he doing here? Why must he be the one to save Equinora, not the unicorns?

Jasper trotted in circles. "I thought dragons could cross veils the same as any of the goddess's creatures."

Tatuk folded his wings and refused to budge. "There's too much evil. I'll wait here."

His stomach rumbling, Fleet cajoled and begged to no effect. "You must come! I demand it!"

The dragon disappeared in a flash.

Jasper nudged Fleet on the neck. "Don't worry, I suspect it won't take long to find Shadow. We'll either defeat him or be destroyed ourselves soon enough. Either way there's little need for food."

Fleet inhaled deeply. Poison thrummed through his veins. Images of rotting corpses flashed through his brain. A picture of Sapphire lying beneath the bloodwolf stabbed his heart. He would avenge her death. He would find a cure for his sickness. He would do all he could to save Equinora—if he lived.

He strode between the Sentinels.

His guts roiled in waves of nausea as he crossed the boundary. Rain slashed his face and crimson torrents ran down pillars of black rock like the wet fur of a bloodwolf. Fleet bowed into the wind, Yuma shivering on his back. Icy rivulets streamed off the man's clothes and down Fleet's sides as he splashed along the zigzag trail.

The lack of light made it impossible to discern how long they trekked through the jagged peaks. With only one path, no decisions about which way to go were needed. Every so often Jasper sniffed at huge dung piles and confirmed they belonged to Shadow. "He can't be far. We must take care."

Step after step, Fleet plodded on. He missed Tatuk's cheerful chatter. His rump throbbed and his head threatened to split. If he'd had the energy to climb one of the peaks, he'd throw himself off— no, the depression came from the poison in his bloodstream. Being within Shadow's territory must be exacerbating the effect. He must fight it. He tucked his nose in behind Jasper's tail. Let *him* lead for a while.

Lost in his misery, Fleet bumped into Jasper where he had stopped in front of a narrow passage, his horn pointing upwards.

Fleet searched the mountain tops, blinking against the rain. Silhouetted by lightning against the stormclouds, an enormous black horse reared, his hooves flashing as he pawed the air, his crimson mane and tail flowing like blood. Two thick horns curved backwards from between the stallion's ears, circling round level with his eyes. He neighed deep reverberations of thunder.

The ground trembled. A rumble resounded from the hillside.

Jasper barged back past Fleet and lunged into a gallop. "Run!"

Fleet bolted. Sharp rocks lacerated his soles. A cascade of stone plummeted from the mountain and wedged in the pass. Black dust billowed.

Gasping, Fleet pulled up next to Jasper under an overhang, out of the way of the rocks showering down the mountain. "Did Shadow do that?"

Jasper squeezed under a protective ledge. "An avalanche is easy to create. He must have wanted to trap us in the canyon to prevent us from reaching him."

Fleet raged. He hadn't come this far to confront only a pile of stones. "He'll have to do more than that to stop us."

"We'll have to go back to the Sentinels and find another way." Jasper set off back along the trail.

"Wait! I didn't see any other tracks on the way in, and Tatuk would have told us if there was another entry, surely. We need to think this through. We've come so far."

Yuma slid from Fleet's back. "I'll start a fire to warm us while we plan what to do."

Fleet agreed a fire would be good. "You have rope. We could haul the stones away."

Spray flew from Jasper's coat as he shook himself. "That will take even longer."

Yuma extracted a twist of dry grasses from his pack and rubbed Fleet down. "We need a powerful tool like the one that carved the ledge for the feathers. What could have done that?"

Jasper fidgeted. "You have sharp eyes. I did that with my horn."

Excited at the news, Fleet nudged Jasper in the shoulder. "So you could carve a way through the rock-fall."

"That was a long time ago. I haven't had much need to carve rock since. I don't even know if I can now my horn has been straightened."

"You must try!" Fleet shoved Jasper in the ribs.

"What if it twists again? I can't go back to a life of pain." He walked away.

Fleet bit him on the rump. "We're so close! Do it for Sapphire, if not for me. You owe her!"

Jasper halted and stared him in the eye. "Alright, I'll try. Pray to the goddess I've retained my powers."

As Fleet and Yuma warmed themselves, Jasper headed back to the rockfall. Each time he returned to rest he looked more fatigued. Flecks of rock specked his face and chest. A thin trickle of blood ran down one foreleg where a shard had sliced his skin. "I can't do any more. There's so little energy to draw on here. I can't cut down to the path."

Fleet wouldn't be defeated. "We'll have to scramble over."

Yuma poked the remnants of the fire. "Isn't that dangerous? The rocks could give way and crush us. And think of your feet. They're already badly cut."

Jasper threw Fleet a quizzical glance. "I don't understand why you're suffering so much."

"I'm only a horse, remember? Not a unicorn." Envisioning Sapphire's rape, Fleet's ire boiled. He paced in the confined space, blowing hard.

Jasper watched him without moving. "Maybe it's time we sought help from the other unicorns."

"*Now* you suggest that! How long will it take them to get here?"

"I have no idea. I don't know where they are. Or what they could do. None of us could beat Shadow before Aureana locked him up."

Fleet stopped and held himself tall. "Call them if you will, but animals are dying and Equinora is being ruined as we delay. I'm going on, with or without you."

The rain froze to sleet as Fleet scrambled over the tumbled rocks, Jasper on his tail, the passage barely wide enough to squeeze through.

No sound or movement gave any sign of Shadow being near.

Once through, with more scrapes and cuts driving his anger, Fleet broke into a trot alongside Jasper, ignoring the pain in his soles. "Any idea how far we have to go?"

Jasper didn't slow. "No. Perhaps we'd better find a safe place for the night."

Needing to regain his strength, Fleet agreed with reluctance. "We should take turns at standing guard. I'll go first."

His watch was uneventful, but the remainder of his night passed in fits of shivering interspersed with nightmares of bloodwolves and his dam's screams. When it was time to move, he was more tired than when he had stopped. Hunger gnawed at his innards. In desperation, he ate the grass wisp Yuma had used to groom him. The quicker he ended this mission, one way or another, the better.

As soon as Yuma had packed up, Fleet urged him to mount and stumbled into a trot. He pushed on, the wind chasing them through canyons and pelting them as they crossed barren ridges. Swirling floodwaters threatened to wash them off stone bridges or coated them with icy spray as they leapt from bank to bank. Scant vegetation clung to crevices in the cliffs—he ignored his hunger pangs, trotting on, on, on.

Drenched, sore, and depressed, he struggled to maintain speed, envious of Jasper's floating trot. The track opened onto a field of boulders, the wide expanse bleak through the lashing rain. Walls of basalt bordered the valley, with no sign of an exit. At the end of the canyon the circular mouth of a cave hunkered at the base of a sheer cliff. Fleet lumbered alongside Jasper, tripping over rocks with heavy hooves.

A howl echoed from the cliffs.

Fleet halted, head raised, and scanned the walls of rock. "It's probably a trick of the wind." With visibility almost nil, he picked his way across the sharp stones.

Yuma's knees tightened on Fleet's sides. "It might be a trap."

Doubts clung in Fleet's mind like briars in his mane. He had seen Shadow, his black and crimson colouring mirroring Jasper's in reverse. Was that significant, or merely a reflection of the goddess's creation? He paused. "Shadow will have to come out to eat and drink eventually. We can wait for him here."

Jasper paced around. "He'll know these lava tubes well. No doubt there's another exit. Besides, he has no need to go anywhere. Do you think Aureana would have caged him here if he needed to eat? He'll draw power from the storm."

"In that case we have no choice." He would have to go into the tunnel. With every muscle on edge, Fleet led the way. His hooves clopped on the ice-slick cave floor, echoing off the walls that enclosed him as he traipsed into the dark.

Yuma released his hands from Fleet's mane. "Why don't I light a torch? I have a small amount of fat left."

The tiny light barely illuminated one horse length ahead, adding flickering shadows to the menace. Fleet feared his bones would crack from tension. Placing each hoof with care, he advanced. He stopped and held his breath to listen. Only the trickle of water broke the stillness, the cave walls dampening any other sounds.

A glow drew Fleet on. He entered a large chamber. Lava oozed in bubbles of orange and red like a giant deformed caterpillar crawling across the floor, the air thick with heat and fumes, the walls rippling in the wavering light like a waterfall of rock.

Fleet halted, nostrils flared. He pricked his ears, sensing another presence. Every hair stood erect as his eyes adjusted to the cavern's tricks. He threw his head up in alarm.

Shadow stood proud on a platform, declaring dominion over his territory. "So, you have come, a trio of misfits. To what do I owe the pleasure?"

All Fleet's anger surged in a rush of adrenalin. He leapt to the edge of molten rock and lashed out with a front hoof, striking the ground in a burst of agony, the radiant heat keeping him at bay. "Stop destroying Equinora! In the name of the goddess I demand you call back your beasts!"

Shadow leapt over the lava stream to stand opposite Fleet and Jasper. "And who's going to make me? A crippled unicorn, a desperate noncorn, and a wandering human? You may entertain me with your attempts, but don't think I'll play with you for long. I tire of creatures once their spirit is broken."

Fleet arched his neck and stood four-square. "Moonglow foresaw your doom!" Although the Spirit Unicorn's prophecy had no such conclusion, the declaration made him feel stronger.

Shadow paraded in front of them. "Oh, I'm so scared. An exiled unicorn has brought his son to teach him about good and evil. How touching. This may be amusing after all."

Jasper advanced and screamed a challenge. "What makes you think he's my son?"

Shadow tossed his head. "Surely you can't believe I don't have mind communication? I'm stronger than all six of you! Just because I've chosen to block you from my thoughts doesn't mean I can't hear your puerile chatter. I've been listening since Gemstone first sought help."

Shock drove Fleet back. What else had this evil creature heard? "You'll know, then, that we won't stop until you're defeated!"

Shadow's lip curled in a sneer. "Spoken just like your grandsire. I'm almost proud of you, Prince Fleet of Foot of Dark Woods."

Fleet's eyes narrowed. "What do you mean? If Jasper sired me, Cirrus can't be my grandsire. Jasper was created by the goddess."

"But what about your dam? Where do you think your colour comes from? How do you think you've resisted the bloodwolf poison? Any other creature would be dead and rotting by now. Your resistance proves your bloodline."

Fleet trembled. "My dam was a good mare, Echo's granddaughter."

"Ah yes, so I heard. But I mated Mist before I was locked up here, your dam's dam and Echo's daughter." Shadow's crimson eyes glinted and his scarlet nostrils flared. "I always preferred a mare with unicorn blood, a small revenge. Even that's denied me now."

Fleet's bottled-up anger and despair found an outlet. "You lie! I'll kill you!"

He charged.

Shadow leapt forward, eyes rolling and teeth bared.

Jasper flung himself between them, thrusting Fleet aside and striking at Shadow with his horn. The stallions reared and locked heads, their horns clashing as they writhed. Hooves struck and drew blood. Teeth gnashed and tore flesh. Their bodies entwined and writhed, black on red and red on black, like the molten rock creeping over the cavern floor.

Fleet ran at Shadow.

Jasper blocked his way.

Again, Fleet launched in to attack, unable to make contact.

Ripples of power emanated from the two stallions, intensifying as their bodies clashed.

Fleet screamed in frustration. "Yuma! The feathers!"

Remaining astride, Yuma extracted the golden feathers from his quiver. One after the other they flew and struck Shadow, hitting his rump, chest and neck before clanging to the floor. Not even a scratch marked the black hide.

The two hotbloods fought on. Lightning flashed from their horns. Sweat and blood streaked their coats. The smell of sizzling hair and burnt flesh hung in the air.

Fleet stood rigid in silence, helpless, his mind a whirl. Was this really his sire and grandsire? The notion was harder than the rock surrounding him. At least the intensity of the fight reassured him Jasper was not the threat to Equinora. Tatuk's belief in the good of unicorns was deserved. Hope rose in Fleet's heart. Perhaps the goddess's plan was for him to save Jasper after all.

Desire to know his sire better fought with his pain and anger. He wanted to fight alongside him and destroy Shadow. He had to do something. But he was no match against their power. And Jasper had raped Sapphire! His indecision bubbled like the lava encroaching across the floor. Perhaps it was better to let them kill each other.

The fight raged. One moment Shadow looked to be flagging, the next Jasper floundered to his knees. The battle of wills as well as bodies was palpable. Shadow grew in strength whenever the fight neared the lava. Jasper did his best to keep away from the seeping rock. The stallions' hooves slipped on the smooth floor as they thrust chest against chest.

Fleet could only watch, transfixed by the spectacle, frustrated and confused.

A wild scream echoed around the chamber. Jasper struck the wall of the cavern with his horn. A shower of rocks became a torrent. He blocked Shadow and screamed at Fleet. "Get out! The roof's collapsing!"

Obsidian shards knifed from the ceiling.

Fleet raced away, Yuma clinging to his mane. He dashed back towards the entrance, struggling to maintain his balance on the slippery rock, weaving around bends in the narrow tunnel.

Escape!

Fleet had no sense of a new danger until he spied a silver net across the entrance. A great white orb as large as his body glistened at its centre. He braked and skidded, his hooves unable to gain purchase on the smooth wet surface.

Eight long legs detached from the web and beckoned him.

Fleet fell onto his side, still moving.

Yuma catapulted off.

Riderless, Fleet slid to the embrace of the giant spider.

Yuma came to with a splitting headache and shook his head to clear his vision. He blinked in an attempt to make sense of the scene. Fleet hung suspended by silver strands across the entrance of the lava tube, immobilised by gossamer threads, unable to even twitch his ears. A giant pearl perched on his rump.

Struggling to sit, Yuma pushed against the walls. Flakes of obsidian peeled off and cut his hands. He picked the sharp stone from his flesh and waited for the vision to dissipate.

"Get away, Yuma. Find another exit." Fleet's muffled plea whispered through fine gauze.

Pain threatened to drop Yuma to the ground as he jumped to his feet. His right arm hung crooked. Ignoring the break, he advanced another step.

Two snowy mandibles raised in response. "Stop. Mine. You. Next."

The croaky voice sent a cold trickle through his veins. He had no idea how to tackle the spider. Although he'd replenished his arrows, he couldn't draw his bow with a broken arm. And if he killed it and the strands were magic, he might not be able to free Fleet. What if the spider had already injected Fleet with its venom? He must do something, and quickly. "Don't hurt the horse! He's on a mission from the goddess. She won't be happy if you hinder him."

"Hungry. Winter. Long." The spider skittered over Fleet's back, sparkling like sunlight on snow crystals. Her long legs wrapped more silk around Fleet's head and neck.

"Stop! I can hunt for you. You needn't feed on Fleet. There are many creatures in the valleys." Yuma gabbled on, saying anything to hold the monster's attention. He introduced himself and gave Fleet's full title, hoping to impress the spider with the horse's lineage. "What's your name?"

"Snag."

"You're very beautiful. Please let me help you catch something else." Yuma maintained a wary distance from the spider's reach.

"How?"

Yuma explained how he could play his pipe to attract animals.

"Give."

He rummaged in his pack with his good arm and played a series of warbling tunes one-handed. Birds gathered outside the cave.

Snag spun a fine net and, after easing to the other side of the web, cast it in the air. The sticky material snared a snowy owl.

"No!" Yuma couldn't bear to see the magnificent bird of prey fall victim to the spider. His mind churned to come up with a solution.

Snag wrapped and stored the owl on the edge of her web before preparing another net.

Yuma waved his pipe. "Now you've seen how it works, I'll give you this in return for releasing Fleet. You'll be able to call all the food you want."

Snag returned to Yuma's side of the web and stared at him with eight crimson eyes. The hair on her legs bristled. "Eat. You. Have. Pipe."

"I'll break it if you don't let us go. Please, it's a good gift." Knowing spiders didn't breathe through their mouth parts, he also knew she should be unable to play music. *But she could talk!* Or was it Tatuk's scale enabling him to understand her? No, a spider that large had to be another of Shadow's creations.

He played a few more notes.

"Good. Gift."

Yuma's heart raced. Was Snag agreeing, or repeating his words? He held out the pipe, ready to retreat if the spider tried to trick him. "Release him first, then I'll give you the pipe."

Snag didn't move.

"Okay. I'll put the pipe down here. You can retrieve it when we're free." Yuma placed the musical instrument on a protruding rock and walked with his back to the wall, his spear in his left hand.

"You. Tear. Permit." Snag extricated herself from the web and scuttled a staccato patter towards the pipe.

Yuma leapt towards Fleet and grabbed handfuls of silk. The softness rather than stickiness surprised him. The threads wouldn't tear. He grabbed a shard of obsidian, slashed at the fibres, and tore them away from Fleet's head, worried he might suffocate.

Fleet had sunk into a stupor. As his face came clear, he sighed and shuddered. "Leave me. It's better I die. I'm Shadow's grandson. Black like him. Evil."

Yuma grabbed one of Fleet's ears and twisted. "Don't talk like that! Quick, kick through the silk as I cut it."

Snag picked up the pipe and inspected it with her mandibles. The only sound came from her clacking legs.

Yuma hacked at the fine strands, amazed at their strength. They came free, the strands sticking only to themselves, not his hands. Hurrying before Snag changed her mind, he cut Fleet free.

Fleet's head drooped. "Go without me. The feathers are lost. Jasper is dead. I've failed."

Angry at Fleet's tone, Yuma stuffed the obsidian shard in a pouch in his jerkin. "If Jasper is dead then so is Shadow. Stop feeling sorry for yourself. It's the poison."

Not knowing how quickly Snag could make more silk, he rolled it into a small bundle and stowed it on top of his pack, worried the spider might be able to re-use it. He leant against Fleet to steady himself. Adrenalin tingled in his chest as he struggled to mount from the offside, unable to use his right arm. He swung his left leg over and hugged his arm to his chest. "Let's get out of here."

Fleet didn't move.

Snag waved her hind legs and started spinning a net.

"Run, Fleet! For Sapphire's sake!" He booted Fleet in the ribs, something he'd never done before.

Fleet sprang out of the entrance and galloped down the track. The sound of drumming followed them as Snag rebuilt the web across the cave's entrance.

The pain in Yuma's arm became too intense for the fast pace. "Slow down, I think we're safe."

Fleet dropped to a walk. "Why did you save me?"

"You'll feel better once we're away from this place. Tatuk will be waiting for us."

Away from danger, sadness swamped Yuma at the loss of Jasper. But with Shadow's death, at least their mission was over.

Hooves pounded from a side valley. Fleet pricked his ears towards the sound.

Yuma stared. No-one could have survived the collapse of the mountain.

Jasper thundered along a narrow cliff edge, blood from numerous wounds streaking his neck and chest.

Yuma remained astride as they waited for Jasper, in too much pain to dismount.

Jasper arrived, puffing hard. "Get moving. Shadow's following. Cross the barrier!"

With renewed haste, Fleet set off for the Sentinels. Yuma rode in silence, the speed jolting his broken arm.

Jasper slowed, his muscles quivering.

Relieved, Yuma burst with questions. "How did you get away? Did you encounter Snag?"

"No. I tunnelled out a side wall where I could sense it was thin. The effort was almost too much for me. I can't use the source of power Shadow feeds on. He escaped via another route. I don't know how long it'll take him to catch up." Jasper plodded on.

The basalt pillars at the edge of Shadow's territory came into sight.

Fleet trembled as they passed through the Sentinels, nausea rising in his throat and shudders racking his skeleton.

Tatuk remained perched on a ledge, a tiny jewelled dot on a sea of rock.

Yuma winced as they jolted to a halt. "Tatuk! Thank the Mother you're still here. We could all do with some of your food, please. Then we'll tell you what happened."

Tatuk fluttered in the air and flapped his wings. "Jasper is stuck! He can't get past the barrier."

The possibility of Jasper being restricted by the Goddess's cage had never occurred to any of them. Yuma urged Fleet back to where Jasper fought the invisible wall, lathered in panic. "We'll find another way out."

Jasper swished his tail, shivering with fear, pain, and exertion. "If another path existed, Shadow would have found it. But if the veil bars all hotbloods, how did Fleet get through? He's seven-eighths hotblood."

Yuma thought back to Gem's reactions when they first met her. She had believed Fleet evil due to the poison in his veins. "Shadow's bloodwolves get through. Maybe their poison is a shield."

He rummaged in his pack and unwrapped the parcel of maple leaves. "I still have the fangs from the one that killed Sapphire. Try carrying these."

Jasper backed up, snorting at the foul smell. "Tangle them in my mane. Be quick or Shadow will be here."

Yuma struggled to attach the venomous teeth one-handed, finally getting them to stay in the long hair.

Jasper leapt to cross the barrier. It tossed him back like a leaf in a gale.

Yuma growled. "They lose contact when you move."

"Then get on and hold them against my neck." Jasper sidled next to Fleet to let Yuma slide over onto his back. "Hurry!"

If he hadn't been in agony in a dire predicament, Yuma would have believed he'd gone mad. Ride a unicorn! Only a few seasons ago he didn't even know they existed. He heaved himself across onto the crimson back, gritting his teeth to bite back a scream.

Jasper trotted towards the border. Still the veil rebuffed him.

A piercing neigh shook the air.

Shadow galloped towards them, his mane and tail flowing like lava, rain pouring from his slick coat. His crimson eyes glared and steam puffed from his flared nostrils. The ground shook and rocks careened from the hillsides.

Yuma raised his good arm and slashed it down, thrusting the bloodwolf fangs deep into Jasper's neck. "Go!"

Fleet bounded at the Sentinels. Nausea clogged his throat. Convulsions rippled along his spine. His legs thrashed the air as if swimming across River Lifeflow in full torrent.

Again he broke through. This time Jasper followed.

Shadow raged on the far side of the barrier.

Tatuk flew high, giggling at their escape. Safe outside the veil, they sought shelter from the foul weather and Shadow's screams.

Jasper shook from head to tail, spraying water in an arc of rainbows. "We must rest and work out what to do. There must be a way to overcome him."

Sweat dried cold on Fleet's trembling coat. "We're no better off than when I first found King Streak. The feathers were no good. I can't fight Shadow. I can't save Equinora. I've failed."

Tatuk turned pale. "You need to eat." He flitted outside and blew on the meagre grasses.

Yuma stroked his nose. "Tatuk's right. The poison will be clouding your mind. Eat his sustenance and we'll work out what to do."

More from a lack of will to argue rather than agreement, Fleet tottered into the rain. Steam wafted around his legs. He had no appetite. Wandering away from the Sentinels and the omnipresent sense of doom, he nibbled the feed in the hope it would settle his nausea.

Yuma followed and leant against a boulder. "I need to fix your and Jasper's wounds. Have you seen any comfrey for a poultice?" He glanced about for the large soft leaves. "Does it grow this far north?"

"No idea. Ask Tatuk." As Yuma went to find the dragon, Fleet swallowed another mouthful. Strength returned to his legs and warmth permeated his body, but the pain in his neck and rump, plus the despair at Equinora's fate, kept him from feeling better.

Yuma yelled.

Fleet raced to where he crouched. "What?"

"It's Tatuk. He's gone grey. I think he's dying." He lifted the dragon with his good arm and cradled the limp form.

Fleet inhaled the scent of the wasted body. His heart tore—first Sapphire, then Cirrus, and now Tatuk. "He's worn out from fending off Shadow's evil. You must send him love. I'm exhausted and more likely to kill him."

Ill ease squirmed through Fleet's veins like the poison. Was everyone linked to him destined to suffer? Evil slithered after him like a scorcheel. Why had the goddess chosen him, Shadow's grandson? Perhaps they were both meant to perish. She never intended him to find a cure, only destroy them. With his colouring, he should have realised he wasn't like any other horse he'd met… apart from Tress.

Fleet trembled. Perhaps Tress was also Shadow's progeny. She certainly had the arrogance of his grandsire. But she was too beautiful to be evil. Memories tore at his heart. Tress wasn't as glorious as Gem. Yet the arrogant princess had a presence about her that attracted him. And Gem had sent him away as soon as his hot blood became evident. Perhaps she'd detected his foulness and been afraid to tell him. It would be better if he died, too.

Yuma smacked him on the nose. "Fleet. Stop feeling sorry for yourself. You're killing Tatuk."

Concern for the dragon drove away Fleet's horrors. His love for his dam and the need to fulfil her dying request warmed his veins. A glimmer of colour seeped into Tatuk's scales as Fleet remembered Sapphire with love.

His rump throbbed. What would it be like to live forever with pain? The agony of Jasper's contorted horn drove him to act as he did. His sire had never meant to harm Sapphire. He'd only been seeking help. Yuma was right: the poison clouded his mind. His heart softened. As he forgave Jasper, the ailing dragon's colours returned.

"He's coming round." Yuma clutched Tatuk to his chest.

Fleet's concern turned to Yuma. "You must do something for your arm."

Fully recovered, Tatuk flew up to perch on Yuma's shoulder. "Make a sling with the spider silk."

Yuma unravelled the tangle from his pack and tried to separate the threads. "I can't do it on my own."

Fleet grabbed a strand in his teeth. Under Tatuk's direction, they wound the silk around Yuma's arm in a cocoon. The threads set hard.

Yuma ran his fingertips over Jasper's neck. "The salve I used on Fleet's wounds is finished. I left the anise hyssop on the other side of the barrier. And the goddess's feathers. I wasn't able to retrieve them when the roof collapsed."

Jasper nuzzled him. "I know. Don't worry, they're buried deep. I sensed their power. And as I've said before, I believe Moonglow's prophecy brought Fleet to cure me. The feathers were never going to change Shadow."

Fleet's heart thudded. His breath roared through his nostrils. Every raindrop splashed against the rocks like a waterfall. He couldn't stop now. He had to find a cure for the poison or die. He had to avenge Sapphire's death and do whatever he could to save the herds. "Can you contact Moonglow and seek a new prophecy?"

"Don't forget Shadow will hear."

Fleet sighed, his legs heavy with dread. "Then we must go to her." Another trek before he could settle.

Chapter 15

The grasses had barely had a chance to fatten their seed heads before the cold weather returned. A flurry of amber leaves settled around Tress. She twitched and stamped. "Isn't it ever quiet? If it's not the wind in the trees or the rushing river, it's the howl of wolves."

Half Moon grazed closer, one eye as always on her filly. "Don't mention those beasts. They give me the shivers."

The mares had remained at White Water Cliffs despite Wolfbane's bullying. Tress had nowhere safe to go and Half Moon didn't want to travel with her foal. Even though Wolfbane occasionally brought back other mares, they never stayed long, sneaking away when the stallion dozed or ventured afield.

Tress watched Pebbles gambol after a cloud of butterflies with yearning, but her feelings for the young horse were mingled with sadness. The poor pasture meant the filly had not grown tall and Half Moon was reluctant to wean her. The scent of unknown horses drifted on the wind. Tress pricked her ears and looked to see who came.

A ragtag mob trotted over the rise. A skewbald mare led two chestnuts and a red roan. Their ribs protruded and their coats were dull. Wolfbane herded them towards Tress and Half Moon with snaking neck and bared teeth. As they cantered up, he broke away and headed to the river.

Tress welcomed the newcomers. "I'm Queen Silken Tresses of White Water Cliffs. How far have you travelled?"

The skewbald gave a sultry greeting. "I'm Patches of Maple Woods, beautiful country to the west. Bloodwolves have broken the herds and killed our lead mare. Your stallion stole us before we could regroup."

The other mares didn't bother to introduce themselves and wandered off a short distance to graze. Tress had no idea how to reprimand their rudeness.

Patches looked around with a sour expression. "Where can we get morels? I could do with a pick-me-up after the long journey."

"I don't know. What are they?"

The new mare scratched her face on her knee. "Fungi. Very good to eat and they lift your spirits. There must be some here. They're always abundant after fires, and the trees here are scorched."

Tress arched her neck. "Well, maybe in your territory, but I haven't seen any."

Half Moon motioned to the edge of the forest with her nose. "There are a few behind the old village. I wasn't sure whether to eat them while suckling Pebbles."

Patches stared at Half Moon. "You're right to avoid them. If that's your filly, she should be weaned. Try eating sage to help dry up your milk."

Half Moon thanked her and asked questions about what the herb looked like. Patches shared her knowledge before turning back to Tress. "How come you don't know the medicinal plants?"

"My sire is King Streak and my dam Queen Starburst of Flowering Valley, so I grew up in open grasslands. I only moved here recently." Tress paraded around the skewbald, her tail held high.

"It doesn't look as if you've had your first foal yet." Patches called to the other new mares and headed to where Half Moon indicated they might find morels.

Tress nudged Half Moon. "Let's go to the river. I don't like these newcomers."

Half Moon hesitated and cocked an ear to check Wolfbane hadn't returned. "If they leave, we should go with them. Pebbles is old enough to travel."

"They're likely to return to Maple Woods. I'd rather go home, but I don't know how to get there. Do you have any idea where Boldearth will have gone? Perhaps we could find him."

"No. Anyway, I suspect you don't really want to leave Wolfbane. I've seen you mating with him. You didn't look too upset." The chestnut mare drifted away as she grazed.

Tress followed. "I can't help my urges, and he's a big strong stallion, worthy to sire my foal. But I'm carrying now and don't need him." She flushed at the thought of the new life growing within her. Wanting the company of an experienced mare when her time came, she longed to return to Flowering Valley and Starburst.

Tress missed the deep friendship she'd shared with Breeze. Was the palomino also in foal? What was her new country like? She feared for her half sister; Wolfbane had been sure King Scar would be a hard task master. The bay stallion had tricked her into leaving without intending to locate Fleet. Where was the handsome black stallion? Not that she'd ever see him again, but sometimes when the nights were long and the wind tore through the valley, she dreamt of him challenging Wolfbane and becoming king.

Daylight always brought back reality. She had chosen to run away and deserved her harsh life. Only her swelling belly gave her any satisfaction.

Tress stole a glance at Pebbles who lay nearby, curled up asleep in a sunny spot beside a boulder. None of the mares Wolfbane brought back had foals at foot, so she never had a playmate, but the filly became prettier with age. Even Wolfbane was proud of her, though he probably thought of her more as a future mate than a youngster. Maybe that's why Half Moon wanted to leave.

The newcomers came back in sight, with Wolfbane chivvying them towards Tress and Half Moon before driving them all towards the falls. He neighed to get their attention. "I'm going for another trip before snow makes it too hard to travel. Stay near the cavern in case of danger."

Tress hated the old hay cave where Precipice had been killed. The tumultuous waterfalls with the bones of dead horses jutting from half submerged rocks gave her nightmares. The village where the people had lived also gave her the spooks. Little feed remained at that end of the valley. But she didn't argue; predators would be growing hungry too.

A clear sky indicated a cold night. As Tress suspected, the new mares used the opportunity to sneak away. Returning to foal at Flowering Valley to enjoy her dam's support overpowered Tress's need for safety. She'd worry about crossing the river when she reached it. Hopefully it would still be low after the dry summer.

She whickered to Half Moon. "This might be our last chance to run."

The other mare didn't hesitate, calling her foal to join them. "Do you want to follow Patches?"

"No." Guessing Wolfbane would search west, Tress suggested east, hoping her dislike of the older mare didn't show. "If we don't meet up with Boldearth, we'll eventually reach Silverlake. There were many horses there."

The full moon cast ominous shadows as the three of them set off. The two mares settled into a rolling canter with Pebbles cavorting at their sides. The further they headed east, the more assured Tress became. Even without seeing fresh signs of other horses, her spirits were as high as when she'd left home. Sometimes she raced with Half Moon and Pebbles for the sheer joy of galloping, kicking up her heels and throwing in an occasional buck. Their companionship grew with each decision made—which direction to head, when to stop, and the safest place to rest. Tress enjoyed being in control of her life for the first time. She tried to make out landmarks as they followed the myriad tracks networking the country.

Nothing looked familiar. "Let's rest here. Wolfbane won't find us gone for days."

The mares huddled under a giant spruce, the filly between them. Apart from an owl startling Tress when it landed on the mossy trunk to feast on insects, she felt at peace. Now they had made the break she wondered why she hadn't done so before.

As the sun rose, a mix of deciduous and evergreen trees blazed yellow, orange and green on the horizon. Tress recognised the border of the forest she had trekked alongside with Wolfbane, remembering the clearings with fresh springs and swards of duckweed. Thistles would likely be still flowering too. The change in diet would be welcome.

She headed into the woods. A cacophony from jays, larks, and warblers filled the cool interior. Squirrels scampered up and down trunks gathering nuts. She avoided a chattering porcupine thumping its hind feet and swinging its tail. Pebbles pranced from tree to shrub, shrub to flower, as she explored the new environment, a chorus of frogs accompanying her excited whinnies.

Half Moon neighed.

Tress lifted her head. A patch of beargrass had distracted her from noticing a change in the direction of the breeze, now blowing from the south. She scented wolf.

Half Moon raced towards her filly.

A crimson-streaked wolf leapt at Pebbles.

Tress bounded to help Half Moon. A rank smell repelled her as she reached to sink her teeth through thick fur. She spun on her forelegs and lashed out with her hind feet.

Pebbles screamed. She went down.

Half Moon thrashed the bloodwolf with her forelegs.

Tress charged the beast. Sharp claws raked her sides. She barged over the stricken filly, galloping to the edge of the clearing, her sides heaving in fear.

The bloodwolf grasped Pebbles and dragged the limp body into the forest.

Half Moon lunged and screamed in its wake.

Bewildered, Tress wavered as pain tore her flank. She wanted to follow but her legs wouldn't move. Her mind filled with flames. She collapsed with a thud.

Night had settled when Tress regained consciousness. Only the sound of chirruping crickets reached her. Her side, swollen and throbbing, had stiffened with dried blood. The blood-stained grass where the bloodwolf had attacked Pebbles was the only sign of Half Moon and the filly.

Wolfbane's punishments seemed inconsequential in comparison to the pain racking her body. Visions of crimson beasts amid a roaring fire swamped her as the sun rose and set.

A raging thirst demanded she seek water. Tress struggled to her feet. She was born a princess and wouldn't be beaten by a lone wolf, no matter how evil. She dragged herself from the clearing and followed the trail left by Pebbles' dragged body.

Before long she found the remains of the chewed carcass, the dotted hide torn and empty. Heartache split Tress as she sniffed the ground. A short distance away, she found Half Moon's body disembowelled in the bushes. The mare's broken neck lay twisted and disjointed, her delicate lips pulled back over her teeth, her eye sockets empty.

Not bearing to look any further, Tress shuffled into a trot. She had no choice—she must return to Wolfbane, her only concern to protect her unborn foal.

Chapter 16

old and amber aspens broke the monotony of the evergreens as
Fleet and his companions headed south. When they paused to
graze, rippling grasses fat with seed heads offered the best feed Fleet
had tasted since Shimmering Lake. He caught up with Jasper at a
creek. The darker forests of Lost Lands loomed ahead.

Jasper blocked his path. "My neck hurts. There are scorcheels
here."

Fleet's rump throbbed. A crimson-streaked grey fin cut the
muddy water. "Have you seen Tatuk? Maybe he can locate a safe
pool. And we'll need him to lead us through the trees."

Jasper backed away from the water. "Tatuk's returned to Shimmering Lake."

"What?" A pang of loss changed to guilt. Had his grumpy mood
chased their guide away? "He didn't even say goodbye."

"Dragons don't like haste. I can find the way. But as there's no
reliable water, we'll need to keep our pace up." Jasper cantered off.

Not reassured, Fleet followed. He and Yuma hadn't been short
of water when they crossed Lost Lands earlier; Tatuk had created
sustenance for them both. Now what would they do?

The further south they travelled, the warmer and drier the
country became. Jasper slowed. "We'll have to travel at night and
rest in the day to help Yuma conserve his fluids."

"What about us? How much further is it to River Lifeflow?"

Jasper's coat was crusted with sweat. "Your warm blood should
cope without water for moons. Absorb Equinora's energy through
your hooves, inhale the wind, and soak up the sun's rays through
your coat. Being black should make it easy."

The reminder about his origins didn't help quench Fleet's thirst. "I don't know how to do that."

"Then learn. Open your mind to your powers."

Fleet struggled to quash the anger boiling inside him. "I thought I was supposing to be shielding my thoughts."

"Your thoughts, yes. Your imagination, no." Jasper laid back his ears. "Embrace your gifts rather than pining to be a normal horse. I can't imagine why any noncorn would want to dissociate themselves from their hot blood."

Biting back a comment about his blood being a quarter duocorn, Fleet cantered along, stretching his senses to detect the energy swarming around him. Even though he could sense the life of the forest, he failed to connect to any elemental power. Perhaps the poison in his veins prevented him from accessing it.

He struggled to keep up with Jasper, needing help from him, not a reminder of his ancestry. Ever since Yuma had stabbed the bloodwolf fangs into Jasper's neck, his moods had grown darker.

They went on in silence.

Fleet's tongue thickened and his skin pulled taught over his tired muscles. Sweat stopped pouring down his neck and flanks. He dropped to a walk and hung his head in exhaustion. "I must have water soon."

Yuma slid from his back and opened his pack. "You can have what's left in my bladderflask."

Fleet refused. "You need it more than me."

"I'm riding. You're the one doing all the work. Have it." Yuma inserted the neck of the flask into the side of Fleet's mouth and tipped it up.

Grateful for the tepid drink, Fleet ignored the taint of the hog container. What had his life come to, that he couldn't even drink by himself?

As they continued, the pace and his dry mouth prevented conversation. Fleet trotted behind Jasper, focusing only on each stride. His mind numbed as they plodded on until the scent of water perked him up. His rump ached but didn't throb. The water ran fast and clear. "It's safe."

Yuma dismounted and hurried over.

Fleet staggered to the bank and stretched down to the river, letting the moisture soften his lips and fill his stomach. Desperate to cool his parched flesh, he waded into deeper water and pawed the surface, sending a shower over his back.

Jasper splashed in the shallows further downstream, his horn and hooves glistening like the obsidian of Shadow's caves, his body sparkling with droplets like fresh blood. "Thank the goddess for cold water. All those years I yearned to be hot. Now I think Snowhaven wasn't such a bad place."

"We should go via Flowering Valley to let Streak know what's happening. Is it far?"

Jasper scrambled up the bank. "We haven't got time to chat. We must push on."

Fleet had no desire to share his failure, anyway. "In that case he'll have to wait for news." His rump throbbed. He jumped back from the river. "Look out! Scorcheels are near!"

Yuma leapt clear. The water flowed uninterrupted by the tell-tale churn of mud.

The pain in Fleet's rump intensified. He sniffed the air. "Blood-wolf!"

As Fleet galloped in panic, Yuma clung tight, wind tears streaming from his eyes, his right arm cradled to his chest. Jasper streaked in a crimson blur, first one side then the other, laying a zigzag trail in the hope of delaying the bloodwolf.

Fleet's breathing came in ragged gasps.

Jasper ran alongside. "You can slow down. It's gone."

They continued at a steady canter, every muscle of Fleet's back tense beneath Yuma's seat, mirroring the tension in his own. With his arm still in a cast, he couldn't use his bow, and he'd had to abandon his spear long ago. The far bank of the river stretched beyond sight as they sped over the rough ground. Stones flew as they maintained their speed, Fleet's hooves tough and hardened from the dry going.

A rocky outcrop drove them into the damp interior of the forest. Yuma, having never ventured south of Oaktown, felt dwarfed by the hemlock, larch and maples that stretched taller than any forest he'd ever seen.

Fleet slowed to a trot, winding between trees where sunlight struggled to penetrate the thick canopy. Trails of tiny scavengers wove through the tree litter. Nurse logs carried saplings on their rotting trunks, the roots of the young trees reaching down among the ferns and fungi. Beetles of every shape, size, and colour scurried among the shed needles, and flying insects pestered Yuma's exposed skin.

Jasper flicked his tail at the annoying bugs. "Let's get back to the river so we can pick up speed."

With relief, they broke out into open ground and raced down the bank. Yuma welcomed the chance to refill his bladderflask, almost falling off Fleet, his legs cramped from riding for so long. They didn't even set up camp each night; he lived off whatever he could forage along the way. He slid his pack from his aching shoulders and headed to the river.

The cast on his arm made descending the steep bank a challenge. The break should be mended by now and the itchiness drove him mad. Using an obsidian shard, he cut the silk cocoon and peeled back the casing like the shell of a nut. Pink flesh shone with no sign of any injury. Impressed by the clean healing, he flexed his fingers without pain.

Fleet bounded chest deep into the roiling current, mirroring Yuma's relief.

Yuma rinsed his clothes for the first time since breaking his arm, but the strong current prevented him from enjoying a full bath. He splashed handfuls of cool water on his face, blinked the sweat out of his eyes, and settled on the bank above where Jasper waded. He still couldn't quite believe this adventure was real. "What's the sea like? I've only heard tales."

Jasper had said little on their journey south. "You'll find out. We'll be there soon."

Fleet clambered out of the river and shook. "That's better. Let's go."

Yuma scrambled back onto Fleet, weariness making his pack feel like it was full of stones rather than its true depleted state. They may have access to water now, but his food stores were almost gone.

They trekked on, ascending above sheer cliffs. The ground became stonier and the trees thinned away from the river. From high on the ridge, Yuma peered across to where he had tracked Fleet through the bog. That seemed a lifetime ago. Unable to climb down the steep cliff, the need to find water drove them inland again through dense forest. Tannin-rich creeks trickled through hummocks of moss.

Jasper called a rest at a rare clearing.

Fleet dropped his head to drink and eat as soon as Yuma dismounted. Glad of an opportunity to stretch his legs, he unslung his bow on the chance of encountering game. He wandered from the grazing horses, gathering what he could for the onward journey. Handfuls of tree lichen from the lodgepole pines would store well. Creeping woodsorrel made a tasty snack of fresh leaves. He tucked a long root of ginger inside his medicine pouch, enough for him to enjoy as tea if only they would stop long enough for him to light a fire. Meat would be welcome but he'd seen nothing to shoot, accentuating the lack of Tatuk's cheerful presence.

As he meandered through the forest, the smell of wet ash and cooking attracted his attention, as if someone had roasted a hog. He advanced with caution, not knowing of any clans living this far south; he didn't want to surprise a band of hunters.

He dodged from tree to tree, taking care not to sound like a foraging hog. He reached charred ground and balked—hog carcasses lay scattered over an area larger than his village, their bellies ripped open, and their entrails gone. Neither the flesh nor the skins had been touched. Burnt trails snaked from shallow pools to the remains. He hastened back to the clearing to fetch Fleet and Jasper.

Jasper snorted as he paced around the devastation. "This place reeks of stale bloodwolf scent. They're killing for the sake of it, not to eat."

Fleet joined them and sniffed the ground. "Yuma, mount up. These trails are from scorcheels. They're leaving the water to feed."

Days and nights blurred together. The mass slaughter of hogs became a familiar sight. Yuma had no stomach for shooting meat on the rare occasion they encountered a scurrying squirrel or woodrat. The berries, nuts, and greens he recognised provided just enough to eat. Tatuk's diamond scale lay cold against his chest. The absence of the dragon's chittering and teasing was magnified by Fleet's and Jasper's solemness. Neither of them spoke, other than essential communication.

With longing, Yuma imagined Gem and Tatuk playing and swimming at Shimmering Lake, such a contrast to the world around him.

He tried to conjure the image of jewelled dragons skimming the water into a song, but the words wouldn't come, and the new pipe he had whittled had yet to feel comfortable in his hands.

Pine sharpened the air as they crushed a carpet of needles on a downward slope. Fleet's step picked up as a fresh breeze beckoned. The trees gave way to sandy soils and clumps of tufted hairgrass. Dazzling sunshine warmed their spirits. Yuma squinted as they trotted across the rolling hummocks, arriving on top of a high dune, a blue vista stretching from their feet to an indistinct horizon.

He blinked as glinting waves crashed in mesmeric rhythm against the shore. "The songs don't do justice to the sea. How far does it stretch?"

Jasper led them down to the water's edge and halted. Salt spray dusted his eyelashes and the tips of his muzzle hairs. "I don't know. I've never been to the other side."

Fleet lowered his head to drink, and leapt back as if a scorcheel loomed beneath the surface. "It's salty. Disgusting."

Jasper tossed his head and curled his lip. "There's fresh water up the beach. Come on."

Yuma clung to Fleet as they raced along the firm sand. He had never seen Jasper so joyous, the wind streaming his tail behind him and his powerful muscles rippling. He reached a creek running into a rocky inlet, reared, and neighed to the wind.

Fleet joined in.

Yuma delighted in the sweet water. As Fleet and Jasper strolled away to roll in the sand, he unpacked the last of his food. Tired of dried vegetables and shrivelled fruit, he wandered along the seashore to find mussels or other shellfish in the rock pools. A bed of large clams, similar to the smaller freshwater ones he loved, tempted him to gather an armful of driftwood and light a fire.

He enjoyed his feast and settled against a warm rock. Worries for his family at Waterfalls tussled with the excitement of reaching the ocean. How could he return to village life after experiencing these adventures? But the clans were under threat and he had a duty to share all he'd learned.

A shrill whinny woke him. He leapt to his feet and shook the grogginess from his head.

A short distance away, Fleet stood rigid behind Jasper, facing a sapphire unicorn.

The new arrival's white mane and tail draped along the sand, his glistening white horn thrust towards Jasper's chest. "How dare you violate my territory? Begone!"

Jasper backed up a step, bumping into Fleet. "Tempest, don't you remember me? I'm Jasper. This is my son, Prince Fleet of Foot of Dark Woods. His friend cured my contorted horn. We need to cross to Tern Island and see Moonglow."

Tempest advanced and struck the ground with a black hoof. Spume blew from his nostrils. "I'll not listen to your lies. Do you think I can't smell your evil? Do you think I don't know what occurs outside Seashore? You're one of Shadow's creations, mimicking Jasper."

Yuma approached with an outstretched hand, hoping to calm the situation. "I'm Yuma of Waterfalls. We've travelled far to seek help. I—"

Tempest charged Jasper. Waves crashed in a flood of foam around their hooves. Wind blasted sand against their bodies.

Fleet reared and screamed as Jasper clashed his horn against Tempest's.

Yuma waved his arms at the unicorns' heads in an attempt to distract them. "Stop! This is madness!"

Jasper and Tempest locked shoulders to shove each other backwards. Lightning sizzled from Tempest's horn and bolts of energy sparkled from Jasper's. Fleet dashed in and bit Tempest on the neck before thudding his heels against the blue ribs.

The unicorn didn't flinch.

Yuma had to stop the fight. "Fleet, you're not helping! We need him!"

Fleet backed off and drew a deep breath. "You try to stop them, then."

Yuma grabbed a double handful of sand and threw it at their heads.

Blinking, they broke apart. Jasper cantered off a short distance and shook.

Tempest glared at Yuma, his black eyes glinting. "It's a sad day when a man interferes in the business of unicorns. Why are you here?"

"Fleet's dam had a vision. We found the goddess's feathers and cured Jasper. Shadow chased us through the barrier. We must find a way to defeat him."

As he explained in more detail, Tempest relaxed. The wind died down and the waves calmed. The sand settled into drifts.

Jasper waited for Yuma to finish before adding his own tale. "It's Aureana's will we're here. My son and his friend saved me from a life of agony and hiding."

Doubt lingered in Tempest's eyes. "So, why didn't you contact me before you arrived?"

Jasper explained that, despite what they'd always believed, Shadow could listen in to the unicorns' mind communication. "We witnessed awful ravages across Great Forest. We must seek a prophecy advising what to do."

Tempest still held his ears back. "Why is there a man with you? Aureana made them to care for coldblood horses, not to aid unicorns."

Yuma edged closer to Fleet. "Gem asked me to come, and sent Tatuk, one of her dragons, too."

Tempest checked the skies. "Where is he? Let him relate what's been happening. Dragons can't lie."

Keeping a hand on Fleet's withers in case he needed to mount in a hurry, Yuma regretted mentioning Tatuk. "He returned to Shimmering Lake, where Gem resides. But he gave me one of his scales."

Tempest strutted over and inhaled Yuma's scent. "You don't have the same evil about you as the other two. Show me."

Yuma extracted the diamond from where it hung beneath his jerkin.

Tempest sniffed the scale. "Come with me. The aquadragons will know whether it was given or stolen."

Unsure what Tempest intended, Yuma followed him to the sea's edge.

"You must go in."

The waves calmed and lapped at Yuma's feet. Not wanting to drench his clothing, he stripped and paddled in, the cool water welcoming after the long journey. The shifting sands and pull of the current made him wary. "I don't like the feel of this. Can the aquadragons come to me?"

Tempest dipped his horn into the water. "You won't drown. They're near." He trotted into the surf and disappeared beneath the waves.

Determined not to go deeper than his knees, Yuma waded into the sea. The sensation of the salt water caressing his legs tempted him further. He plunged into the water, swimming with powerful strokes parallel to the beach. He dived like an otter, relishing the silkiness of the buoyant ocean.

Aquadragons, similar to those he'd swum with at Shimmering Lake, surged around him, blowing bubbles from their long snouts, their leafy appendages wafting as they swam circles. They flowed over his skin like the kelp forest, stroking his arms and legs. The diamond sparkled on its thong around his neck. As he rose for air, a life force flooded through his veins as if he had indulged in Chaytan's best ale.

Fleet paced on the shore. "I feared you'd been sucked away."

Yuma grinned. "You should come in!"

Tempest erupted from the water and shook a spray of rainbows from his coat, his mane and tail flowing like spuming waterfalls. The sea flattened to a sheet of blue. "The aquadragons recognise the scale is a gift. We will go to Tern Island tonight, as you request."

Chapter 17

Tempest led them to the base of towering granite cliffs where the low tide revealed a tumble of jagged rocks. Barnacles clung among the tidal pools and crabs scurried in the moonlight. He pointed out to sea with his horn. "We can be there by morning."

He lowered his head and swirled the waves. Tendrils of light crept like roots across the surface. Beds of kelp wafted together in the current. He whinnied. "Malila, I need your help."

A school of aquadragons bubbled through the surf. The lead one grabbed an end of the kelp in her snout. The others did the same. Diving around each other, they wove the strands into a tangled web to form a roadway to the island.

Tempest strode onto the living bridge. "Don't be afraid to gallop hard." He leapt across the water.

Jasper followed, the moon casting bloody shadows across the sea from his reflected coat. They galloped away, leaving only indentations in the kelp that filled with seawater, obscuring their passage.

Fleet hesitated and nuzzled Yuma's foot where he sat astride. "Do you think it's safe?"

"Having come so far, there seems little point in stopping now."

Reassured, Fleet walked onto the bridge. Water lapped over his hooves. He halted, legs splayed. He sniffed the surface. Aquadragons giggled and zoomed on either side of him. He stepped forward. The bridge wavered, but didn't sink. Taking a deep breath, he sprang into a trot. The platform bent beneath his weight, but held.

He broke into a canter, the sensation of moving over water and the spongy kelp upsetting his balance, the horizon blurring with the night sky. Only the turquoise sheen from the aquadragons gave any sense of perspective, their glittering forms keeping pace with ease, maintaining the tangle of kelp a few strides ahead, letting it drift apart behind him. The only sounds came from the gentle splash of his hooves and the wind in his ears, no lapping of waves or cries of night birds. Aromas of salt and seaweed and fish came and went.

He galloped on.

A glimmer of violet delineated the eastern horizon. Cliffs rose to the south, their faces streaked grey and white. Cries of gulls and terns competed with the wind.

The kelp gave way.

Water sucked at Fleet's legs.

He floundered and thrashed, and then stumbled onto shifting pebbles. The rocky beach had a few patches of sand barely large enough for a horse to roll. Sea otters played with aquadragons in the surf, or floated on their backs and cracked clams on their stomachs. His hooves gained purchase as he cantered up the beach to join Jasper and Tempest. He hung his head, blowing hard, glad the ordeal was over. "I'm starving."

Tempest peered down his nose and sniffed Fleet's neck. "You should be refreshed after being surrounded by the sea's power. Didn't you absorb the energy of the ocean?"

"It was all I could do to stay upright."

"Never mind, it'll come with practice. Moonglow's island has good grazing at the top of the cliffs. You can eat while I locate her." He led the way along a narrow track winding up the cliff.

Jasper bounced along in a springy trot. "I'm sorry I didn't think to help you with the crossing. I was having too much fun. I haven't felt this good in all my life. If it weren't for the nightmares, I would think I'd joined Aureana in the spirit world."

Irritated by Jasper's buoyant mood, Fleet dragged himself up the trail. As promised, a vast meadow of lush grass and sweet flowers cloaked the island.

Yuma gathered leaves and blooms by the armful. "Why are the plants still in flower? Is this place like Shimmering Lake?"

Tempest tested the wind with flared nostrils. "I've not been there. But I keep the weather temperate all along this coast. Aureana may have liked four seasons, but I prefer everything to remain the same. It's bad enough I have to contend with the moon changes and tides without having seasons to worry about." He galloped off.

What was wrong with seasons? Fleet loved the spring freshness after a cold winter and the cool autumn after the hot days of summer. It had been rare enough to see any variation in Dark Woods without the weather always being the same. The succulent feed reminded him of Gem. Seasons had passed since he'd mated with her. His longings brought back memories of the two fillies at Flowering Valley. They'd be far away with their new stallions by now. He should have stolen Tress instead of seeking a unicorn. Although he'd learnt much and had companions, he still yearned to belong to a herd and live in one place, somewhere with lush grass and clean streams, shady trees and singing birds.

Instead, he had horrific dreams and encounters with terrifying beasts, always on the move. Pushing aside his frustrations, he drank from a spring of fresh water and settled beneath a giant maple to doze.

The scent of an unknown horse woke Fleet. He opened his eyes. A snow-white unicorn stood next to Tempest, her gold points glinting, a flock of dragons flitting around her head in a rainbow cloud. Her deep blue eyes flooded him with memories of Sapphire.

Moonglow stretched forward to sniff his nose.

He blew back into her nostrils. "I'm Fleet of Foot of Dark Woods."

Jasper also greeted her and shared their story. "Your prophecy must have related to curing me, not overcoming Shadow."

Moonglow strolled about the meadow. "Prophecies can lead or confuse. You must follow your instinct."

Fleet trailed behind her. "Does that mean you can't help us further?"

"Help how? Oh, you mean you seek another prophecy. I can't promise. And if one comes, you have to interpret it yourself."

She wandered away and lifted her horn to the sky. Sparks like fireflies glittered from the tip, floating away in a twinkling shower.

"His black red and two curved horns
Needs him from bears den
Join together unicorns
Bring her from Goose Fen"

Fleet hadn't known what to expect, but it wasn't this riddle. He was none the wiser. "What does it mean?"

Tempest didn't seem perturbed by the strange conversation. "So, Echo is still at Bearsden. That's west of Rattlesnake Ranges. Goose Fen is east of Dragonspine Mountains. I wondered where Diamond was. It won't take her long to get here, but for Echo it's a different matter. What about Gemstone?"

Moonglow didn't respond.

As she drifted away, Tempest stamped a hoof and followed her. "Come on, tell us more. What do you suggest once we're all here? We know Shadow is a threat. How do we deal with him?"

A flock of gulls cawed overhead as they wheeled and hovered on the updraughts. The regular crash of surf far below added to the sense of a strange land. Fleet had never felt as exposed as he did on this clifftop, so unlike his home in Dark Woods. Even the bleak high plains between Snowhaven and Obsidian Caves hadn't felt this open. Dizziness and despair threatened to overwhelm him.

Moonglow halted and her horn flared again.

> "Six hotbloods come together
> Solstice embolden
> Eat death caps control weather
> Call who flies golden"

She wandered away.

Tempest ignored her departure. "So, the others need to be here in time for the solstice."

Fleet didn't understand the prophecy. "What then? How does any of this help us defeat Shadow?"

Jasper nuzzled his neck. "Have patience. I believe Moonglow is saying all six unicorns must gather and hold a ceremony to call Aureana. We can receive instructions from her."

While everyone on Tern Island waited for the arrival of the other unicorns, Yuma rested and replenished his medicines and food. An abundant supply of roots, leaves, and fruits kept him busy. Moonglow had asked him not to kill any animals.

The mild weather belied the shortening of the days as the winter solstice approached. Tempest left to meet Echo and Diamond. Apart from Moonglow gathering what looked to Yuma like poisonous mushrooms, he rarely saw her. When she did drift to their end of the island, she rarely spoke, her glazed eyes blind to all bar her dragons.

Fleet spent most of his time grazing or dozing. Although at times he jumped awake with sweat running down his neck, he appeared more settled. Yuma suspected that sharing his experience with the ancient unicorns helped him shoulder his burden.

Tempest had asked Yuma to build a great bonfire on a high outcrop of rock away from the cliffs. He struggled to find any wood on the exposed pasture and went to find Fleet. "How large a fire do they need?"

Fleet continued chewing a mouthful of grass and flowers. "No idea. I could carry driftwood from the beach if you want help."

Relieved he hadn't abandoned their partnership, Yuma accepted. Several trips up and down the winding trail later, they had a pile of timber higher than Yuma's head. "I guess that'll do until Tempest returns."

Taking the opportunity to groom Fleet, Yuma wisped his coat until it gleamed. The horse's rump showed no evidence of his former wounds. "Do you still have nightmares?"

Fleet's bottom lip quivered. "I imagine I see Shadow leaping out of flames, but I can't quite picture him. It's like something you see out of the corner of your eye, but when you turn to look, there's nothing there."

Yuma teased the tangles out of Fleet's mane and checked his hooves, now trimmed and hard, composing songs of his adventures as he worked. He still couldn't believe they'd travelled over water held up only by a net of seaweed. Seeing the otters earlier in the day reminded him of Laila and the jade figurine he had given her. Her gift of bumblebee nectar had saved his life and enabled Jasper to be cured. He must thank her again at the next gathering; he had already missed this year's at the summer solstice. How many more would he miss before he could return home?

He turned around at the clatter of many hooves. A white unicorn with a flashing silver mane and tail followed Tempest. Alongside her came another unicorn, the colour of rich earth, with a blazing emerald mane. Jasper cantered behind. If it weren't for Fleet's solid presence next to him, Yuma would have believed he was hallucinating.

Fleet whinnied in response to the newcomers' greetings. "Echo, thank you for answering Gem's call when I was at Shimmering Lake. Diamond, your daughter will be pleased to know you're well."

Diamond blew in his nostrils. She backed up as if stung. "There remains a taint about you like Jasper. Hopefully Aureana will rid you both of the poison."

Jasper introduced Yuma. "Without him I'd still be in terrible pain and Fleet would have died. It's time to consider accepting people as more than servants of horses."

Tempest snorted and stared at the bonfire. "Of course we're delighted your horn is straightened, but we've more important matters to attend to than discussing coldbloods and humans. We must prepare for tonight. I only hope we have time."

Confused, Yuma looked at them all. "Doesn't Gem need to be here? I thought all six of you must be present for the ceremony."

Tempest glanced at Fleet. "We haven't heard from her. I asked Malila to leave the kelp bridge intact in the hope Gemstone reaches us in time, but if she doesn't—"

Diamond interjected. "She's maintained silence with us ever since her horn came through. It was only because she made contact about Fleet that I believed the severity of the situation, otherwise I wouldn't have translocated across both Dragonspine Mountains and Rattlesnake Ranges to bring Echo so quickly. I fear the effort has cost me so much I won't be ready for tonight. We need Gemstone's strength. She had the least distance to travel, and I can't fetch her if I don't know how far she's come. We must trust that she'll arrive in time."

Chapter 18

Bare branches pointed at Gem as if accusing her of neglect as she trudged through the forest. She had never known the seasons to affect her territory. Now the bitter winds from the north swept through the valleys and browned the grasses. Dung lay in frozen heaps as the earthworms retreated to warmer soil. The creeks fouled with mud as too many paws churned the banks.

Tatuk landed on her crest. "There's a racoon fighting a skunk over by the alder pond. I can't get them to stop."

Gem changed direction. "I'm tired of all these squabbles. There are so many animals here I can't keep up with all the disputes."

The dragon paled. "I don't have the strength to feed them, and the lake's waters aren't providing the nourishment they need. You should close the veil."

"If I do that, those outside will perish." Summoning up energy from the last of her reserves, Gem cantered down the slope to the arguing mammals.

The cramped conditions had taken a toll on everyone, their skin hanging in loose folds with matted fur. Even the chipmunks had ceased their chittering and guarded their stores of hard-won nuts.

At Gem's approach, the racoon raced to her feet. "He stole a snail right from my paws!"

"It was mine first." The skunk raised his striped tail. "This is my burrow. You're trespassing."

Gem struck the ground with her hoof. "Stop it, you two. If you can't get on, I'll banish you both. Everyone is finding it hard to locate enough to eat. Nobody should be eating the snails. I've told you before to drink from the lake. I can't waste more energy sorting out your differences."

Other animals came to listen. As a squirrel scampered up with an acorn, the racoon snatched it from the smaller creature. The skunk jabbered and hissed.

"Enough!" Gem lashed out at the racoon with a hind leg. Her hoof caught him in the ribs and bowled him over. She whinnied in horror and checked he was unhurt. "I'm sorry. I don't know what came over me."

The racoon scampered up a tree and eyed her through his striped visage. "The lake doesn't satisfy our hunger anymore."

She had to do something. She looked for Tatuk, who'd flown off when the skunk raised his tail. He was nowhere in sight. She called for him as she headed back to the lake.

He settled on a rock near her favourite resting tree. The once-mighty oak was almost devoid of leaves, and dead branches scattered the ground. She swished away a fly as it sucked blood through her dull coat. "You're right. I have to close the veil. What will the creatures do who are stranded outside? I've failed them."

The dragon's colours no longer pulsed with vigour. "We must save those who are already here. They'll be needed to repopulate the land. I'll inform the dragons on the borders that no more animals are to be permitted through."

Gem sank to the ground. "What sort of guardian am I that I can't look after those who seek refuge? Who knows how long it will be before Equinora is safe?"

Tatuk flew off without answering. Gem flopped down her head, ignoring the ants crawling into her ears and the flies drinking from her running eyes. As she lay prone, her mind filled with words.

Come to Tern Island. You're needed here for the solstice.

The voice was one she hadn't heard often until recently. Tempest rarely communicated with the other unicorns. For him to send out a summons must mean the threat had spread wider than she'd feared. She'd been optimistic when Tatuk had returned and told her that the golden feather had cured Jasper's horn, and then saddened that the same power hadn't worked on Shadow. Tatuk had also shared that Shadow could hear the unicorns' mind messages. She'd had no news since—the dragon had refused to leave her with all the troubles at Shimmering Lake—but the lack of recovery of the land could only mean Fleet and Jasper hadn't found a way to overcome Shadow.

The summons came again. Diamond and Echo were already there. Good, let her parents deal with the troubles, they were stronger and wiser than her. She would only add to their woes. It might even be her twisted horn corrupting Shimmering Lake— the more she tried to help, the worse the situation became—and everything around her was dying. But why now? Nothing made sense.

Plunged into misery, Gem dragged herself to the lake, failing to feel any invigoration as she waded into the crystal waters. Diving deep, she searched for aquadragons. The underwater channels they loved to frequent were empty. She rose to the surface and struck out for the far shore. A few dragons skimmed the water, their normal giggles absent.

She scrambled up the marshy bank and stopped in horror. Grey, lifeless forms tangled among the reeds. The dead aquadragons' bodies had shrunk to bare bones. Their sparkling skin had shed and shattered, fragments of turquoise and aquamarine forming a layer of grit at the water's edge.

Gem climbed onto dry land, her heart bursting with sorrow. One by one, she carried the corpses to a pile of driftwood. A small flock of dragons hovered nearby. A couple had red legs, denoting their mastery over fire. She called them down. "Please give the aquadragons a ritual farewell. I can't bear for them to be eaten by the other animals, no matter how starving everyone is."

The largest of the flame dragons landed near the bodies. "We'll need your help."

Summoning her love for her lost friends, Gem sent energy to the dragons to light the pyre. Flames licked the tiny bodies that shrivelled and crackled. A wisp of smoke wafted skywards as each body was consumed. She stared at the last remains, her despair deepening like the purple clouds billowing overhead, a sight she'd never seen at Shimmering Lake. Rumbling thunder echoed her pain. She tried to cheer herself up by remembering the aquadragons riding her bubbles, at how thankful she'd been for their laughter and play.

Attracted by her love, Tatuk appeared. "Maybe you need to go to Tern Island."

"How can I? I don't have the strength to help my charges, let alone travel. And what would happen here if I were away?"

Chapter 19

The swollen sun on the horizon cast ripples of orange across the sea. The five unicorns waited in array around the bonfire on top of the cliff, fidgeting and pensive, the tension in the air setting Fleet's hair on edge.

Tempest strode over to him. "There's still no sign of Gemstone. We can't proceed without her."

"You must! I've come all this way for help. And it's the solstice tonight. Isn't that when Moonglow's prophecy said you should call the goddess?" Fleet trotted around the pile of firewood, watching the expressions of the other unicorns. None of them would meet his eyes.

Tempest remained calm. "Moonglow is adamant we need six hotbloods."

Fleet's temper built. "Did she tell you that? Or is that your interpretation of her riddles? She could mean anything! I can't make out her nonsense."

Diamond joined them. "It's not nonsense. That's her power. It's why she doesn't often speak, and why she says confusing things. But she's never been wrong. We must listen to her, even if she's off with the dragons most of the time."

Fleet gnashed his teeth and lashed out with a hind leg in frustration and anger. "I promised Sapphire I would do whatever I could to stop horses being destroyed and avenge her death. I found King Streak and he sent me to find a unicorn. I found Gem only to be sent away again. I found the goddess's feathers. I confronted Shadow and barely escaped with my life. I discovered more about my ancestry and Sapphire's life than I wanted to know. I came all the way here, when all I want is to settle somewhere safe and be part of a herd. And now you're refusing to help! I'm sick of being pushed around. Don't you care about horses? Don't you care about Equinora?"

Jasper wandered up. "Calm down. Of course we care. We'll do everything we can, but if we need six hotbloods, there's no point starting without Gemstone."

"Has she come before when you've needed to call the goddess? Is it always at the solstice or will there be another time?" Why were the unicorns being so complacent?

Echo clustered with the others, only Moonglow holding her place at the fire. "We've never called Aureana before."

Fleet reared, neighing long and loud. He dropped back to the ground and confronted Tempest. "I'll take Gem's place. Then there'll be six of us."

Tempest backed up a step.

Diamond leant forward and stretched her nose to Fleet's. "You're very brave, but you don't have a horn to deflect the power. You're not a full hotblood. The ceremony might kill you."

"How do you know, if you've never done this before?"

Jasper closed in, too. "Aureana told us how to call her before she left for the spirit world. It's bad enough I'll have to counteract the poison in my blood, but you won't have the strength."

Tempest stamped the ground. "And whose fault is that? You should take more care of your progeny."

Yuma walked over and rested a hand on Fleet's mane. "Take care what you do. You're still weak from your wounds and the arduous travel, and the fungus Moonglow collected is very potent."

Echo flicked his ears. "Why was Fleet sent on this quest if he wasn't meant to take part? Moonglow isn't worried about Gemstone not coming. We must trust her prophecy."

Glad one of the unicorns supported him, Fleet thanked him. "And I'm seven-eighths hotblood. I may not have a horn, but maybe the ceremony will cure me. Aren't poisonous fungi sometimes used as medicine?"

Moonglow walked over to the pile of mushrooms she had collected and carried a mouthful to each of them. "I think I've picked the right ones. The yellows and oranges look so similar, then I remembered they had to have white spots."

Fleet sniffed at the pile in front of him. "Do I have to consume them all?"

Moonglow tilted her head. "I don't know. Eat until you feel the effect, I suppose." She ate her share and took up a stance close to the stack of driftwood.

Tempest snorted at the mushrooms in front of him. "It seems Moonglow believes you are the sixth, Fleet. So, let us commence."

Fleet stared at the fungi, disliking their smell. Sapphire would never have allowed him to eat these.

Diamond chewed her mouthful, her coat darkening with sweat as she resumed her place at the pile of wood. Her horn sparkled. "We must join horns over the flames. How can Fleet do that? We must try with only five of us."

Tempest shuffled her over to make more space around the fire. "No. There must be six of us. Fleet must take Gemstone's place."

Jasper looked at each of them in turn. "I'll help him. If he holds his head against mine, he can share my horn."

At Tempest's instruction, Yuma lit the fire, placing coals from his hearth at close intervals around the base where he had stashed piles of kindling. The driftwood crackled without smoke as the unicorns resumed their places. The two mares stood like the peaks of Snowhaven, their white coats reflecting the flickering light. The stallions glinted like the dragons perching a safe distance away among the trees.

With no other option, Fleet consumed the mushrooms. They tasted as foul as they smelled. Not wanting to risk spoiling the ceremony, he ate the entire pile Moonglow had given him. He took up his position around the fire, his head in contact with Jasper's with his rump pointing to the sea. Sparks danced in the air, spiralling up into the moonlit night.

The unicorns' horns pointed towards the centre of the fire, flames licking their tips. They held their bodies rigid, tails over their backs and necks arched. Saliva slid from their lips as they mumbled words Fleet didn't understand. Stars drifted across the heavens and sank into the ocean.

The flames grew and enveloped them. He experienced no pain. Was that the mushrooms numbing him, or the power of the goddess? Wind whipped his mane and tail into tangles. Thunderous clouds scudded above the island. A dry storm lashed waves against the cliffs.

Lightning struck the heart of the circle.

Fleet twitched and trembled. His mind swirled, full of golden flames.

The bonfire flared and roared, engulfing their heads and necks.

Why have you called me?

He almost jumped, almost broke the unity of the circle.

Moonglow raised her head. "We need your help. Equinora is in danger."

The bonfire flared and roared, roiling about their heads, their necks. Though there was no sensation, Fleet could see that the flames reached almost down to Echo's powerful shoulders, and realised that to the unicorns, he must seem similarly half-swallowed in the conflagration.

You are the protectors of Equinora. You are ignoring your roles. Why should I help you?

Moonglow, you offer your prophecies yet stay on Tern Island instead of sharing your powers with those in need to the north, east, and west.

Echo, you ignore the creatures in your territory when floods, fire, or storms destroy their food, or when deep snows cover the land and waters turn to ice.

Tempest, you prevent the seasons renewing the land at Seashore, yet allow storms to rage elsewhere without tempering their fury. You allow the rivers to silt up and gales to tear down forests.

Diamond, you wander at will for your own pleasure, never aiding those you encounter, staying hidden, and avoiding your duties. You haven't even taught your daughter her role. No wonder she isn't here.

Jasper, as pleased as I am you are finally free of pain, you continue to mope over Dewdrop when you could be using your power to create caves for bats and bears, or ledges for roosting birds.

You must all use the powers I granted you to protect Equinora.

In the centre of the flames, a prancing unicorn appeared. She radiated beauty, golden feathers from her wings sweeping the ground. Her voice moderated, now trilling with birdsong, burbling creeks and rustling grasses. Fleet smelled lupins and lilies.

Fleet of Foot, only you endeavour to counteract Shadow's harm. You will henceforth live up to your full name, drawing power from the earth, wind, and sun, to become the fastest horse in all creation. Use your speed wisely, and save my land. Return to Obsidian Caves and confront Shadow.

Acrid smoke smothered the sinking moon in a blood-red haze.

Fleet's heart pounded and his skull threatened to burst. He heaved in deep breaths, relieved that Aureana's anger hadn't been directed at him. Yet how was he to confront Shadow?

He blacked out.

The rising sun shone straight into Fleet's eyes. Yuma crouched by his side and stroked his mane. He blinked, raised his head, and rolled onto his chest. Warmth suffused his veins as if he had drunk from a steaming pool. His body glowed with nourishment. "What happened?"

Jasper blew into Fleet's nostrils. "Thank goodness you're alright. Can you stand?"

Fleet braced his legs and shoved to his feet. His heart glowed with love for those around him. "I saw the goddess!"

Tempest walked around the burnt remains of the bonfire and greeted him. "Yes, she came, for all the good it did us."

The smell of singed hair lingered in the air. Fleet could still taste the powerful mushrooms on his tongue. Each single hair of his mane tickled against his neck as Yuma untangled the sweat-drenched knots. Moonglow's dragons glimmered brighter than any he had met at Shimmering Lake. The sounds of lapping waves carried up from far below.

Echo shook himself and stretched his hind legs. "It's been a long night, and we're no better off. It seems Aureana won't help."

Jasper snorted. "That's not quite true. My neck is healed and the poison has gone from my veins. I no longer suffer depression." He addressed Yuma with a bow. "I understand why you stabbed me with the fangs to escape Obsidian Caves. Without you, I wouldn't be here. Now I'm fully cured. I will forever be in your debt."

Diamond added her thanks for his wellbeing. "But Echo is right. We're no nearer to overcoming Shadow. How can Fleet fight him?"

Fleet nibbled at a patch of clover. The leaves had never tasted so sweet. He relished his new extraordinary senses in direct contrast to the fear that racked his guts.

Moonglow drifted over and stared at him. She gasped as if startled. Sparks flared from her horn.

"Death and poison cross the land
Entwined destiny
Shoot and dust green stone in hand
For their dynasty"

Echo waved his horn. "Green shoots and dust? Does she mean my power? Or Jasper's over stone? Or is the green stone emerald, like my horn?"

Diamond nudged Moonglow's shoulder. "Or does the prophecy mean Gemstone? Her whole body is emerald. Is that it?"

Echo paced around the dead fire. "Maybe our daughter did have to be here."

Tempest grumbled. "Indeed, what's the use of having a cohort of six unicorns if one can't even be bothered to turn up?"

Diamond jumped to Gemstone's defence. "We don't know why she didn't answer our calls. Maybe she can't leave her territory because of the threat. And we don't even know if the prophecy means emerald. There are other green stones."

Fleet had no answer. He no longer believed, like he had before the ceremony, that Gem hadn't turned up because of him. That would be ridiculous. There must be another reason she wasn't here, part of the goddess's plan. *Gem.* His last memory of her was when she sent him away, when Yuma was carving the image of him. "Yuma! The green stones Tatuk showed you. Do you still have any?"

Yuma retrieved the last two arrowheads of jade from his pack. "You mean these?"

"Yes!" Understanding clicked. "The goddess must intend us to hunt the beasts down like horses and people do with hogs."

None of the unicorns had ever witnessed a hog hunt. Fleet and Yuma described how herds and clans lived together, the horses driving the hogs to slaughter in return for oats and hay.

The idea horrified and fascinated the unicorns at the same time. Diamond shivered. "I can't imagine participating in anything so brutal as killing creatures like that, no matter how evil. There must be another way."

Echo agreed. "Aureana wouldn't want anyone murdered. If the prophecy refers to jade, it must be to change the animals somehow."

Moonglow backed up and faced Fleet, the multi-hued dragons settling along her spine. Her sapphire eyes glazed as she scented the air around his withers and along his back. Again her horn sparked.

> "He of unhorned black no white
> Red and black bubble
> Challenge death to put things right
> End of the trouble"

Fleet shivered. What did it mean?

Moonglow said no more. The four other unicorns discussed the prophecy. Obviously, Fleet was meant to put things right as Aureana demanded. But how? And how did this latest riddle link to the previous one?

Jasper ended the speculation. "Whatever is meant, it's obvious we can't remain here. We must locate Shadow's beasts. When the time is right, Aureana will guide us."

The return journey to the mainland flew as if Fleet travelled like this every day. Gone was the strangeness of galloping over water. Gone was the struggle to maintain his balance against an invisible horizon. Gone was the exhaustion of forcing his poisoned body to keep up with the unicorns.

The sun delineated the beckoning waves with glistening rays. The power of the sea thrummed through his legs and swelled his body. With every stride he grew stronger, his breathing slow and deep, his heart a gentle pulse. He revelled in his newfound power, energy coursing through his veins. So this is what Jasper meant about drawing on Equinora's elements! No wonder unicorns could live for generations.

As they made land, Fleet wanted to keep on galloping up the beach and buck and rear with joy. Only Yuma on his back made him contain his exuberance. The unicorns had also absorbed the energy—Diamond sparkled like Yuma's dragon scale and Jasper glowed like hot embers. Tempest surged like a massive wave rolling up the beach, deep blue crested with white foam. Even Echo's form became a moving forest, his dark brown trunk topped with his verdant mane and tail. They raced along the dunes, spraying sand over the crests.

Fleet sped up, absorbing the sun through his black coat. Five abreast, they surged up the grassy hillside, Moonglow having refused to leave the island in spite of the goddess's recrimination. Clouds of hovering gulls marked their path as they raced with the wind to the summit. Wintering terns rose from their cliff perches, their warning cries filling the air.

They neared the top.

Fleet's rump throbbed. He propped to a halt in sudden pain. The stench of bloodwolves filled the air.

The others skidded to a stop beside him.

Five bloodwolves, standing abreast, growled at them from the highest point of the hill, their fangs bared, their shoulders hunched, their fur matted with crimson streaks.

Fleet stood motionless, despair returning. The poison remained in his veins. He could draw on Equinora's energy, but the goddess's fire hadn't cured him like it had Jasper. Why was he still suffering? Did Shadow's blood taint him? What more did he have to do to rid himself of the curse?

The bloodwolves launched down the slope.

Yuma readied his bow.

Echo and Jasper leapt to meet them. Diamond and Tempest headed in different directions.

The bloodwolf pack divided.

One closed on Diamond.

Fleet raced after her, faster than he had ever galloped.

Diamond disappeared in a flash, only to appear further up the hill.

Fleet circled behind the confused bloodwolf to give Yuma a clear shot.

The bloodwolf veered. The arrow missed.

Fleet spun on his hindquarters to allow Yuma another try.

Again, the arrow missed. Yuma snatched another from his quiver. "They were the only jade heads! I'll have to use flint!"

His next shot struck home, wounding the bloodwolf in one leg. It ignored the arrow, leaping at Fleet, black drool swinging from its jowls.

Fleet kicked at the shaggy head. His hooves connected with bone. The bloodwolf fell. He bolted after another closing on Tempest.

Clouds roiled in what had been a blue sky. A bitter wind howled over the hill. Lightning sheeted across the ocean.

Tempest galloped into the sea, his horn to the sky, foam frothing around his legs.

The bloodwolf hesitated on the shore.

Fleet caught up.

Yuma released another arrow, wounding the bloodwolf in the shoulder, the wind deflecting his aim.

The beast snarled and leapt into the waves.

Tempest whinnied and galloped parallel to the beach. Waves reared and crashed. Lightning streaked to earth with a crack.

Diamond continued to elude the bloodwolves by translocating. Echo and Jasper raced towards each other, dodging at the last moment, their pursuers slowing to avoid crashing into each other. Then they split up, with Jasper heading for the cliffs.

Bloodwolves streaked after them both.

Unsure which to chase, Fleet recoiled as lightning struck the one pursuing Tempest, the smell of burnt fur drenching out the rank stench of bloodwolf.

Another strike on the hill lit the scene. This one missed, spurring a bloodwolf closer to Jasper.

Fleet took off after it.

Jasper faltered and smashed forward, piercing the clifftop with his horn. A burst of power flashed from the tip as it hit the ground.

A tremble ran through Fleet's hooves, rattling his bones.

Cracks appeared in the ground, snaking out from where Jasper was now staggering to his feet. He turned, readied for attack. A slab of clifftop broke away, the rumble of sliding, falling rock reaching a crescendo. More rocks tumbled to the sea. Jasper scrambled to maintain his footing.

In vain. The ground collapsed. He disappeared over the edge.

The bloodwolf scrambled back and fled, the remaining two following, one limping, all three with their tails clamped between their legs.

Open air gaped where Jasper had stood a moment before.

Fleet stared at the cliff edge, unable to move. Should he chase the fleeing bloodwolves or help Jasper?

A cry from Diamond unfroze his limbs.

Fleet raced to the edge, Yuma still clinging to his back. Far below in the surging foam lay a crimson body, twisting and tossing in the waves.

"Yuma, slide off! I must get down there." Fleet neighed long and loud, his rump hammering despite the disappearance of the bloodwolves.

A foul stench rose from the water. The waves churned brown. Crimson-streaked fins broke the surface. When had scorcheels reached the ocean? They must have followed them down the river.

The water boiled red.

A flash of gold blinded Fleet. Heat seared his body.

Diamond screamed and shuddered beside him where he stood transfixed, looking over the crumbling edge. She stepped back. "He doesn't need us now."

Jasper's body was gone. Fleet could see no scrap of hide, no bones, not even hairs from his mane and tail. "What do you mean?"

Diamond nuzzled him. "Didn't you see the gold flash? He's joined Dewdrop and Aureana."

Fleet trembled, the pain in his head overwhelming, his heart breaking. He'd only just started to get to know Jasper—the hole in the cliff was nothing to the hole in his heart.

Between them, Diamond and Echo shepherded Fleet and Yuma back down the dunes to the beach, all of them silent.

Tempest lay exhausted in the sand. He rose on stiff legs and arched his neck as they approached. "Killing a unicorn is unforgiveable! First Dewdrop, now Jasper. Shadow must pay!"

Fleet pawed the ground. Why had the goddess helped them cure Jasper, only to snatch him away? Nothing made sense. He vaguely heard Tempest say something about returning to Tern Island to find Moonglow. "Do you think this will bring on another prophecy? Do we all need to go?"

Diamond avoided Fleet's gaze and swapped intimate looks with Echo. "There must always be six unicorns. With Jasper dead, one pair must mate and produce another. We created Gemstone when Dewdrop was killed."

Fleet shook his head in exasperation. Is that why Tempest was going to Tern Island? How could Tempest think of mating at a time like this? "Isn't it more important to defeat Shadow's beasts first?"

Diamond attempted to explain. "I can't fight those beasts. All I can do is move out of their way."

Fleet railed at the calm unicorns. His nostrils flared and his breath quickened. "You must do something to avenge Jasper's death!"

Tempest butted his shoulder. "No. This is not for us to do. We must look after Equinora. You and Yuma must pursue Shadow's beasts and follow Aureana's plan. You are the chosen one."

Chapter 20

The snow muffled all sound as Yuma rode towards Oaktown, following the river to Oakstream in an attempt to avoid whatever dark creatures lurked in Great Forest. Their journey had been uneventful though tiring, the weight of Jasper's death and the importance of their mission a double burden, limiting their conversation to essentials. Neither of them found solace in galloping with the wind.

Yuma ran one hand through his beard. He should take time to tidy up if he was to see people again.

Fleet halted on the crest of the final ridge before the rolling grasslands thickened with forest. "Are you sure you want to go down? We'd be better off going to Flowering Valley."

Yuma stared at the barren trees that reflected his mood. "There are more people here. It's a hub for all the clans. We'd better inform them before seeking our friends."

Fleet didn't agree. "The last time I came to King Flash's territory, he threatened to kill me."

Those early days of their friendship were a distant memory. "Remember Streak sent a runner to Flash to tell him of our mission? I expect news of us finding Gem will have reached him too. And Wolfbane headed west."

Yuma encouraged him forward with a squeeze of his legs. He had no doubt Fleet could defeat the king with ease these days if they were not welcome. They neared the bare oaks delineating King Flash's territory.

Fleet stopped again. "I think I should find the herd on my own.

Why don't you go to the village and deliver our news? We'll meet here at the new moon."

The idea of being separated from Fleet battled with Yuma's desire to see other people. Fleet had become more than a companion, no longer a mere horse. They had travelled far and helped each other through troubles he couldn't have dreamt of before he left Waterfalls. They had shared many pleasures too, racing across meadows or sunning on grassy slopes, discovering new places and meeting the unicorns.

Yuma slid to the ground and adjusted his pack and quiver. "Take care, my friend. Come to the town earlier if you want."

As Fleet trotted away, Yuma washed and shaved before striding along the riverbank. Soon he was puffing and loosening the ties of his furs. So much for cleaning up. Since their need for haste after leaving Tern Island, he had spent most of the time riding, hunting only when Fleet wanted to graze, which was rare; having been granted the power to draw on Equinora's energy, Fleet ate little. Or was that from grief?

Back on his own, Yuma fell into his old habits of munching nuts and berries as he discovered them, collecting greens and herbs to dry, and selecting interesting wood to carve. The physical exercise also took his mind off his loneliness.

Food became scarce nearer to Oaktown, with not even the tracks or droppings of small game. The woods always became depleted after the annual gathering, even though visiting clans brought their own supplies. Carrying his bow at the ready, he kept alert for bloodwolves.

He ascended a rise and paused, his breath misting in the frigid air. Burnt scars marred the landscape, and an odour of rot rose from the damp ground. The snow had thinned among the trees and mud caked his leggings. Wishing he were astride Fleet, Yuma looked for signs of horses. A few bachelors picked at brown grass on the far side of the valley, their coats thick and dull.

He headed towards the village down a well-worn track. With his eyes on the ground, he almost failed to see the barricade in the dusk. Spiked logs had been rammed into the earth. A narrow gateway gave access to the compound.

A growling voice hailed him. "Lost your horse, Waterfalls man?"

Surprised to see Jolon Fist, Yuma greeted the burly hunter with caution. "What brings you to Oaktown late winter?"

Jolon barred the entry with his bulk. "Begone before I send an arrow through your heart. That's the only way to deal with evil like yours, bringing unnatural beasts among us."

"What makes you think I'm responsible for the foul creatures? I've come to share news of how we may fight them." The surprise at seeing Jolon here was nothing to Yuma's shock at being considered the cause of Equinora's problems.

Legs apart, Jolon swung a club at his side as he glowered. "The bloodwolves appeared soon after you rode in on that black stallion, showing off killing hogs on your own, and disappearing before the plagues came to haunt us. Now anyone left alive shelters here, in fear of the nightmares that follow even a minor scratch."

Not knowing how to counteract the accusations, Yuma slid off his pack and used it as a stool. "What of Waterfalls? Are any of my clan here?"

"Only folk from east of the river. If it weren't for the high death rate, we wouldn't all fit. Even so, it's against the Mother the way we live locked in this fort. Now begone before I cull you as you deserve." He rushed at Yuma.

Yuma rose, arms wide and hands open.

Jolon thudded into his chest.

Yuma held his ground. The hard seasons had taken their toll on the Bloomsvale man. In contrast, the constant travel had made Yuma lean and tough, and the sustenance provided by Tatuk had strengthened his body. He side-stepped a renewed attack from Jolon and shoved him to the ground. "This is ridiculous. I've come to help."

Jolon scrambled onto his knees and charged, head down, grunting like a stuck boar. Again Yuma avoided the attack, tripping Jolon into the dirt. The commotion attracted men inside the gateway. They loitered in silence, parting for a stooped and wrinkled elder.

"Cease! Jolon, what are you thinking? We need every man we can gather." His command spoke of authority. He hobbled over to Yuma and peered through one eye, the other socket scarred and empty. "Yuma Squirrel of Waterfalls, take no heed of this ignoramus. Come to my hearth and share your news. It's a long time since anyone reached us."

With a plentiful supply of timber available, the buildings of Oak-town were sturdier than those in other villages. The main meeting house dominated the central gathering place. Flat stones from the riverbed provided a dry walkway between the rows of huts clustered among the towering oaks.

Ituha Tanner, Chief of Oaktown, gathered the other elders. They sat cross-legged in the dim hut, the cramped quarters warm with their bodies and the small fire.

Over a bowl of thin gruel, Yuma recounted his tale. He explained his strategy for other men to learn to ride the bachelor stallions in order to hunt bloodwolves.

A mutter rippled through the men.

Ituha held up his hand for silence. "How do we know the horses will let us?"

Yuma coughed. "Fleet is talking to them now."

People raised their voices, some in doubt, others in excitement. This time, Ituha let them talk themselves out. When a hush fell, he added a log to the glowing embers. "We can't spare people to learn to ride horses. We need to defend the barricades."

Gomda Hunter, the chief of Bloomsvale, added his agreement. "The horses haven't even been able to give us warnings of attacks like they do with grey wolves. How will being on their backs help?"

The same problem had occurred to Yuma. The elders threw question after question at him. He gave up insisting they learn to ride, not knowing if the horses would even agree. To be proficient hunters on horseback would take a lot of practice. He'd worry about that part of the plan later. "At least change your arrow tips for jade. The stone is strong and sharp, and doesn't flake like flint."

Ituha conceded the jade, at least, sounded like a good idea. "Is there nowhere else we can collect this green stone? I can't spare men to travel to this place of the emerald unicorn."

Yuma had resisted sharing his knowledge of Shimmering Lake, not wanting other people to venture into Gem's territory. However, his tale made no sense until he explained about the magical land, though his instinct made him keep the existence of dragons to himself. "I don't know of anywhere else. Anyway, it'll be quicker for me to travel alone as I'll be on horseback. I left some jade arrows with my friend, Chaytan Strong of Bloomsvale. Is he with you?"

"Yes, a good man." Ituha sent his son to fetch Chaytan.

When Yuma's friend arrived they gave little time to sharing welcomes. Chaytan confirmed he still had several of the sharp arrowheads. "They're too large for small prey so I reserved them for hogs. It's been a long time since we've had the opportunity to use them."

The pleasure of the reunion was tainted by the drawn lines on Chaytan's face. Yuma sensed more than malnutrition in his friend's subdued demeanour. After the meeting closed, he accompanied Chaytan to his small dwelling.

Chaytan stopped outside the door. "There are only two of us. Aponi and the baby died in childbirth, and my eldest son perished from the bloodwolf curse. He suffered a lot. Do whatever you can to rid us of those beasts."

The new hut was devoid of decoration. Chaytan's Bloomsvale home had been filled with bunches of drying herbs and sacks of grain. Worked leather and intricate weaving had brightened the simple interior. Here, only two grass pallets covered in worn skins huddled near a circle of stones containing smouldering coals. A few clay pots and wooden utensils huddled against the doorframe. Chaytan's son lay curled in one of the beds.

Yuma unrolled his sleeping skins. "Has there been any news from Waterfalls?"

Pouring a mug of ale, Chaytan shook his head. "No-one I'm aware of has crossed the river in either direction. When I saw you last, we were heading to Marshward. The clan there has been almost wiped out. The few who could travel accompanied us back."

The pain evident on his friend's face tore at Yuma's heart. Should he be pleased or worried at the lack of news from Waterfalls? Had the clan perished, or were they locked in the shelter of the valleys, safe yet unable to go far? He tried not to dwell on the calm voice of his mother or the nagging of his sister. The demand of his father to find a lifemate seemed trivial and irrelevant now.

By the next morning, Yuma's news had spread among the entire population. He couldn't even relieve himself without people quizzing him about jade arrows and magical unicorns. Some accused him of being mad to suggest they ride horses. Others, particularly the young, sounded interested in having a try, though few liked the idea of hunting down bloodwolves. And the problem of how to tackle the scorcheels remained unsolved.

His throat ached from talking. Against Chaytan's protests, he retreated alone to the woods with a flask of mead. He would be expected to regale the entire community with his stories that night around the communal fire. Hoping to bring cheer rather than alarm, he climbed into the safety of the branches and rehearsed the songs he had composed.

"Your voice is as pleasing as your rhymes." Laila stood at the base of the trunk, her arms wrapped around a bundle of corms.

Yuma slid down the rough bark and greeted her. "Should you be wandering out here?"

Laila placed the lily bulbs down and settled on a mossy log. "People fear their shadows these days. I prefer to be out gathering than shrouded with their misery."

After briefly relating his adventures, Yuma explained how the cave bear had been distracted with the bumblebee nectar. "Without your gift I doubt I'd be alive, and Jasper would never have escorted us to Seashore. Your kind act may well result in saving the clans from the bloodwolves. I don't know how to thank you."

Laila fingered the jade otter hanging around her neck. "You already have. You've given me a name. I'm now Laila Otter."

Surprised the girl had come of age, Yuma acknowledged the appropriateness of the name for one who immersed herself in nature. "What of your apprenticeship? There must be great need for a trained healer these days."

Laila shook her head while keeping hold of the otter. "There are still those who think I'm unsuitable. I learn what I can, but my father keeps me busy. I should have left for the women's hut but he demands I remain at his hearth. I think he plans to send me to a distant clan in return for some favour, but no-one is travelling far these days. And I have no desire to be anyone's partner."

Laila's eyes glittered. "There must be a need for a wandering healer, like the roaming minstrels or adventurers like you. Maybe there are people stranded in their villages that I can assist. I hate remaining in one place."

Yuma had always believed he was unusual in his need to explore.

He had never considered other people might be constrained by society, especially a girl. "These aren't the times for needless risk. I advise against you venturing out until we've overcome Shadow's beasts."

Laila grasped his arm. "I can't stand another season here. Please, when you leave, take me with you."

Chapter 21

King Flash stood guard as Fleet descended toward a herd of mares. The large mob raised their heads in unison as he approached, ears flicking in all directions.

The buckskin stallion galloped to meet him, snorting his disapproval. "Keep your distance, Fleet of Foot of Dark Woods. Your mission doesn't give you access here."

Fleet drew on the strength of the land to fill him with confidence. His coat glistened with power and his muscles rippled as he strode forward. "I'm not after your mares. I've come to share news."

Flash snorted in derision before leading the way to a stand of fir trees, keeping a distance from Fleet. "Tell me what you must and be on your way. There's too little food here for strangers. It's bad enough my brother has brought his own herd to my territory."

Surprised two herds could graze in one area, Fleet quizzed the king of Oakvale. "Streak is here? Why has he left Flowering Valley?"

"The people came south, for protection from the bloodwolves we presume. The horses followed. They'd starve without the harvest." Flash's ribs protruded and his hip bones jutted above his flanks. His coat was patchy and dull, even though his mane and tail were well groomed.

Knowing the king of Flowering Valley was nearby, Fleet didn't want to inform the buckskin of his news. He still held to his promise to Sapphire and her command to warn King Streak. "We need to meet with the other leaders to save me telling my story more than once. Where will I find them?"

Flash gave several loud whinnies, the calls echoing through the trees and rolling across the open spaces. "Let's go to the creek."

Although Fleet had no desire to drink, he assumed the king was trying to keep him away from the mares. He trotted alongside as they crossed the clearings to a shallow brook. The water tasted bitter and muddy. "Why don't you drink from Oakstream? Isn't it cleaner and sweeter than this?"

Flash rolled his eyes and curled his upper lip. "The deeper water can hide the burning eels. I've no evidence they've come this far, but we won't take the risk. One of the women was taken only a moon ago. It's not a nice way to die."

Blackfoot galloped up.

Flash tasked him to gather Streak and the queens.

Curiosity roused in Fleet. "How do two herds live in the same territory?"

Looking towards the large mob of mares, Flash tossed his head. "I told my brother he is a guest here, not a leader. I don't want to fight him, especially not in our current condition. We agreed to guard as equals until the evil is overcome. The herds run together, but there's no harmony between the lead mares. Starburst doesn't know this territory but insists on making the decisions. My queen is much younger and lets herself be bullied."

Fleet had the impression that Flash would prefer the entire herd to be his own. He dreaded to think what would happen when the mares and fillies came into season.

Four horses cantered towards them—Streak and Blackfoot, accompanying Starburst and a delicate liver chestnut mare.

Flash nickered as they slid to a halt. "This is my lead mare, Queen Acorn of Oakvale."

Fleet blew into each of their nostrils and thanked them for coming. "Much has happened since I was at Flowering Valley. The unicorns believe we have a solution to the beasts that are harming horses and people."

While Fleet regaled the leaders with the events that led to his vision of the goddess, the horses paid him full attention, interrupting only to clarify some point. When he explained they needed to fight the bloodwolves with people like a hog hunt, all five fidgeted in alarm.

Blackfoot lashed out a hind leg at an invisible enemy. "We're not like you, so desperate for company we'll carry a man. Besides, my warriors don't have the skills to do battle with those creatures."

Streak interjected. "Wait, we need to consider this seriously. As you say, we can't fight the bloodwolves on our own. Yet the herds are being decimated." He faced Fleet. "Will the unicorns aid us? How would the men kill such beasts?"

Fleet described the jade arrow tips and the prophecy's reference to green stone. "We think it means jade. Yuma only has two weapons left. We must go to Shimmering Lake for more. When we return, we'll build an army."

Streak glanced at Flash. "Who will lead this army? Where will it go?"

Flash snorted. "What of the mares and foals while the warriors are off fighting? Who will keep them safe?"

Fleet looked from one stallion to the other. "You must decide for yourselves. As much as I long to settle in a herd, I must travel Equinora and share this strategy. Echo has gone over Rattlesnake Ranges to see the situation there. Diamond has returned east of Dragonspine Mountains. The bloodwolves hadn't reached that far before they left their homes, but there's no telling how fast the foul creatures can travel."

Starburst stepped forward. "We haven't had any news from afar since the mare transfer in spring. The delegates from Hawk Plains had no experience of the terrors we face here. You've experienced a lot. Thank you for the news."

Blackfoot shoved in front of her. "Without Wolfbane, all the bachelors are under my control. You haven't said what's happened to the mastermind behind this evil. What can we do against Shadow?"

Fleet reassured the horses that Shadow couldn't escape Obsidian Caves. "Hopefully, once he knows we can defeat his bloodwolves, he'll stop creating them."

The lead stallions conversed among themselves.

Fleet took the opportunity to speak with Queen Starburst. "Is there any news of Princess Tress?"

The chestnut mare looked about as if hoping to see the black filly appear from the trees. "We fear she's gone for good. There haven't been any horses arrive from across River Lifeflow."

The news saddened Fleet. "Can't one of the bachelors look for her?"

Starburst's head lowered in anguish. "She made her choices. We need them here." She hesitated and snatched a peek at the stallions. "Golden Breeze was heartbroken when she had to leave without my daughter. They'd been together every day since birth, which was why Streak negotiated for them to travel together. Blackfoot was supposed to go with them and start a herd with Breeze, but without Tress we had to send Breeze to King Socks and Blackfoot returned."

Fleet had never heard of Socks. "Where's his territory?"

A wistful look came into Starburst's eye. "Hawk Plains is far away over Dragonspine Mountains. Tress would have loved it there, wide open spaces and plenty of grass. Streak and Socks ran together as bachelors and were great friends. Queen Meadowlark is getting frail and Socks wanted fresh blood to replace her."

The fate of the black filly weighed on Fleet's mind. There had been a time when he had dreamt of building a herd with her. Then he had met Gem, making a coldblood horse appear dull in comparison. Had he been wrong to abandon Tress to her fate? Even though he hadn't known of his warm blood at the time, perhaps that was part of what drove him to seek the unicorn. What did Gem think of him? From travelling with Jasper, he knew how naïve he must have seemed. Had she taken another lover? Although his mission forced him to return to Shimmering Lake, Fleet dreaded the reaction he'd receive.

Streak interrupted his thoughts. "You'll have to talk with the men for us. If we're going to fight together, we'll need to work out a method. It won't be as easy as hunting hogs."

The depressing confines of the village and the despondency of the people drained Yuma's energy. His head throbbed from Chaytan's ale and he had tired of being the centre of attention. Although the horses' strategy to fight the bloodwolves had given the clans hope, many people still doubted their ability to succeed. Killing driven hogs was one thing, hunting and attacking venomous beasts another.

Winter had started to lose its grip and buds struggled to open. A hint of green crept across the meadows with the promise of new life. Yuma hoped the coming summer would be more fruitful than the last. He doubted many of the old or frail would last another lean year.

He met Fleet in their usual place, as had become their routine through the negotiations with the horses. Today was different; it was time to head to Shimmering Lake. After brushing Fleet, he gathered his possessions and mounted. They headed away from the village.

Fleet turned his head and then halted. "There's a woman following. Did you forget something?"

Yuma peered into the glare of the sun, shielding his eyes. "It's Laila. She's the one who gave me the bumblebee nectar."

"She seems in a hurry." Fleet strode back down the hill towards the panting girl.

Yuma dismounted. "What brings you out so early?"

Laila kept her head down. "I want to go with you."

Yuma threw out his arms. "I've told you. That's not possible. We must travel fast and are likely to encounter many dangers. Besides, what would your father think? Neither of us has a lifemate."

Brushing the hair from her face, the young woman pleaded with her eyes. "I can't remain at Oaktown. I don't care what people say. I'm of age and entitled to go where I please."

The bruise across Laila's face shocked Yuma. Even though he knew Jolon had a temper, he'd never thought the brute would hit a girl. "I'm sorry, it's impossible. I'll be riding and you won't be able to keep up. Can't you enter the women's hut? The council of elders will defend you against your father."

Laila ignored Yuma and approached Fleet with her hand held out. "Prince Fleet of Foot of Dark Woods, I am Laila Otter of Bloomsvale. I've heard how good and strong you are. May I accompany you? I bring skills of healing and can gather you nutritious foods."

Before Yuma could intervene, Fleet nuzzled the woman's hand. "Greetings, Laila. Thank you for the bumblebee nectar that enabled my sire to be cured."

"You really can speak!" Laila stepped back before advancing again and stroking Fleet's neck.

Fleet snuffled her hair. "You're welcome to join us."

Yuma threw up his hands. "It's too dangerous! And she can't ride."

Fleet pinned back his ears. "It's not for you to say who may or may not ride me. I'm strong enough to carry you both."

"You don't understand. There'll be trouble among our people if we go together. It would be like you stealing another stallion's mare."

Fleet nibbled at Laila's fingertips. "I may not understand your clan rules, but I can see it's dangerous for her to stay. It sounds as if you're making excuses because you don't want her along."

This stubborn streak in Fleet was new to Yuma. He confronted Laila. "Please, return to Oaktown. I can't be responsible for you. We've no idea what we'll encounter."

Straightening tall next to Fleet, Laila stroked his neck. "I'm not asking you to look after me. I only wish to join you and help. You're not the only ones who care about the land. If I can't be of help at home, I'll assist somewhere else."

A sharp wind grew as the sun rose above the trees. Fleet flared his nostrils. "It's time to move. If you don't accept this woman's company, I'll take her to Shimmering Lake instead of you."

Taken aback by the threat, Yuma could think of no more arguments. Believing the escapade a mistake, he gave Laila a leg up onto Fleet before vaulting on behind. The stallion's broad back was spacious enough for them both, even with Laila clutching her sack in front of her. "We'd better go fast. Once Jolon knows his daughter is missing, he's likely to raise trouble."

Laila steadied herself with her hands on Fleet's neck. "I didn't leave without telling anyone. Delsin, my younger brother, knows my intentions."

The girl's warmth seeped through Yuma's leggings. He squirmed. "And what do you think your father will do to him for not stopping you? It's not too late for us to take you back."

Fleet didn't wait. He broke into a rolling canter. "Tell me if you need to dismount and rest. It took Yuma a while to get the hang of riding."

Despite their need for haste, Fleet paced himself to Laila's comfort. The girl quickly found her seat and rode well. When they camped, she lit a fire and prepared a meal as Yuma tended to Fleet. Having another person along had its advantages.

His fears of what the villagers would make of the situation faded the further they travelled; he had never been one to follow etiquette. Laila was pleasant company and they shared an interest in plants and animals. He was sure his mother or Winona would accept her as an apprentice. He imagined his father's surprise at him returning with a horse and a medicine woman rather than a mate. No doubt the clan would be glad of an extra healer with the troubles. That idea soured his mood and increased his worry.

The trio lingered only long enough at Silverlake for Fleet to search for any bachelors. He returned looking grim, saying many horses had perished from either their wounds or the poison.

Setting up camp on the outskirts of the forest, Laila snapped off branches from the fir trees to make a bed near the fire. Finished, she shivered and crouched to hold her hands to the flames.

Yuma laid his arm over her shoulders. "You're welcome to share my furs."

She shrugged off his embrace, keeping her eyes averted. "I didn't leave Oaktown to replace my father with a bed mate. I don't need men in my life. I know you didn't want me to come along, but I'm sure I can be of assistance. I had a dream I must venture to far lands."

Yuma retreated to his own side of the fire. She was still a girl, regardless of having been through her naming ceremony, more of a sister than a possible lover. That thought reminded him of Winona, and he laughed to himself. He couldn't think of two more different women—Winona with her forthrightness and bossy ways, and Laila with her quiet determination. Or maybe they weren't so different; both were stubborn and shared a love of all the Mother's creations.

When they reached the fork of Silverstream, Yuma called a halt. "I know it'll take us out of our way, but I must see my family. The Waterfalls clan need to know how to fight this terror too. I doubt Echo will have journeyed this far north before crossing Rattlesnake Ranges."

Neither Fleet nor Laila disagreed. Yuma sensed Fleet was happy to delay their mission, even though he would have thought the young stallion would have been eager to return to Gem. But his experience on Tern Island had changed him. His friend no longer revelled in simple pleasures.

They made quick time to Yuma's homeland, the territory Fleet called White Water Cliffs. The eerie peace of Waterfalls was the first sign all was not right. Not even the tumbling cascades crashed as they normally would. Yuma failed to see any sign of horses or other animals as they approached the head of the valley. No bands of hunters or foragers met them along the way. Sticks and leaves littered the trails that used to be worn clean. Yuma's heart sank as they drew nearer the village. The clan must have moved to safer country.

He dismounted and walked away from Fleet and Laila as they settled for the night. Following the familiar paths through the trees, he kept his bow ready in case wolves lurked. The unkempt village was abandoned—cold hearths all that remained of some homes.

Yuma entered the central shelter. He froze in horror. Twisted skeletons stared out of empty eye sockets. One bore the formal headdress of the chief. By his side, a bleached neck still wore a wooden carving of a mink. Yuma choked back a sob. He had carved the amulet for his mother.

Fleet picked at the scant grass while Yuma and Laila worked in silence to build a pyre. The lines of anguish on Yuma's face excluded any communication. With the loss of Jasper fresh in his mind, and the constant reminders of his dam's demise, Fleet shared Yuma's suffering. What he didn't understand was the need to burn the remains of all the dwellings as well as the corpses.

When Yuma started to lug the heavy timbers from the huts, Fleet queried his purpose. "Why waste what's still strong?"

Yuma growled and shooed him out of the way. "I need it to cremate the bodies. No-one will want the taint of death and bloodwolves soaked into their homes anyway. If anyone ever comes to rebuild."

Laila helped lay out the dead and covered them with dry grasses while Yuma destroyed what was left of the village.

The rank scent of the bloodwolves lingered, but Fleet's rump didn't throb. He decided to investigate the land where his dam had ruled with King Thunder. He could see why Sapphire hated Dark Woods so much. Here the light sparkled from the tumbling waterfall like dragon scales, and kingfishers dived into crystal pools. The river wound between steep hills and verdant meadows, the clearings overrun with golden dandelions and buttercups.

As smoke billowed from the village, Fleet trotted deeper into the hills to avoid the overpowering stench. The breeze shifted, carrying a faint whiff of horse to his nostrils. He dropped back to a walk and whinnied to announce his presence. "I'm Fleet of Foot on a mission for the goddess. Whose territory am I visiting?"

"Fleet!" A shrill neigh preceded an uneven clatter of hooves as a bedraggled mare raced into the open, heavy in foal. Her spine protruded in a bony ridge and her dull eyes were crusted with gunk. Her long hooves were cracked and her patchy coat revealed weeping sores. She moved with a pronounced limp, her near fore swollen and crooked above the knee.

Fleet backed up in alarm. "Where's your stallion? Have the bloodwolves killed your herd?"

"Fleet, it's me, Tress. It's so good to see you. I thought you must be dead or gone far away. You look magnificent. Where have you been to grow so much in these hard times?"

Snorting in bewilderment, Fleet stared. "Tress? No. The princess has a snow-white mane and tail with a glossy black coat. You're trying to trick me. I can smell the evil on you. Are you another of Shadow's offspring?"

Tress stepped closer and reached forward with her nose. "Truly, it's me, formerly Princess Silken Tresses of Flowering Valley, now one and only mare of Wolfbane of White Water Cliffs. I haven't had any people to groom me for many seasons. What you smell is bloodwolf poison in my veins. I would throw myself off the cliffs if it wasn't for my unborn foal."

Fleet found it hard to believe this wreck of a mare was the once proud princess. His heart fluttered, and sorrow at her ruin fired his anger at Shadow. He must protect her! Then he accepted the truth of her swollen belly; she belonged to another. Regardless, he felt bound to aid her. "You must come to Shimmering Lake with me. Gem can cure your lameness and make you well."

"Gem? Who is she?"

"A unicorn, the daughter of Echo and Diamond."

"You found one! I knew they were real!" The bedraggled mare faced away. "I'm in no fit state to travel, and it wouldn't be safe for my foal."

She was probably right. It was a long way, and he didn't need the complication of fighting the former head of Oakvale warriors. Grazing on the spring growth, he swapped stories with Tress. Before he could ask about Wolfbane's whereabouts, the bay stallion charged down the hillside.

Fleet prepared to greet him, whinnying a welcome.

Instead of answering politely, the stallion screamed a challenge as he raced along a stony track, shards flying as his hooves churned the ground.

Tress showed the whites of her eyes and sweat broke out on her neck. She fled to a copse of spruce for shelter.

Without giving him a chance to explain his presence, Wolfbane attacked.

A deep bite stung Fleet's neck. He spun round and struck out with his hind feet.

Wolfbane barged into him.

Fleet staggered. The old warrior was strong and experienced. Fleet had only ever fought Jasper, and that struggle had been over almost before it had begun. He stumbled backwards, reeling. Wolfbane's onslaught didn't give him time to breathe, let alone talk.

Determined not to be beaten, he called on the energy beneath his feet.

With renewed strength, he thrust his chest at the bay stallion and drove him backwards. Wolfbane lashed out with both hind legs, catching Fleet on the shoulder. Pain lanced his sides as another double blow caught him in the ribs.

A vision of crimson wolf smothering his fallen dam flooded Fleet. A rage at the world and its unfairness brewed in his heart. He lunged forward and pummelled Wolfbane.

The stallion staggered before rearing and retaliating with bared teeth.

Fleet drew power from the sun and strengthened his assault. He slammed his head against Wolfbane and crashed his hooves onto the stallion's spine, driving him to the ground. He reared, ready to deliver the death blow to the horse's skull.

"Stop!"

The cry from the trees penetrated the killing rage that had overcome Fleet.

Tress cantered over and begged the stallions to cease fighting. She whickered in distress. "There are so few of us. There's no need to fight."

Fleet backed off from the fallen warrior and shook himself, guilty at his aggression. "I would have murdered him if you hadn't stopped me."

Wolfbane lumbered to his feet, dripping with sweat. His sides heaved. He gasped for air. "I submit... You have Tress...and this territory... I'm tired...of trying...to build a herd."

All of Fleet's desires flooded back. In defeating the lead stallion, he had become the new king. But king of what? A poisoned land with a crippled mare, pregnant by another. He should vanquish or kill Wolfbane.

He couldn't bring himself to inflict more suffering. "I must take Tress to Shimmering Lake. You're a good warrior. Become Wolfbane, Head of Warriors of White Water Cliffs, if you will. Gather all the stallions you can find and build an army. On my return, we have a war to fight."

Chapter 22

The sharp pain in Tress's foreleg crept up her shoulder and along her spine, and her hindquarters ached from compensating for her weak front end. Fleet maintained a hard pace, desperate to reach Shimmering Lake.

The banks of Silverstream offered the freshest pick Tress had tasted since leaving Flowering Valley. The scent of the crushed grass beneath her hooves sucked her head down. She nibbled at the sweet shoots. "Can't we rest here?"

Fleet refused to permit a break. "Yuma and Laila will want to camp at sunset. You can rest then."

Tress found it hard to get accustomed to travelling all day and sleeping at night. She preferred short bouts of grazing, moving, and resting, driven by the need for warmth or shelter, hunger or thirst, rather than where the sun or moon lay in the sky. Although the woman had made her feel better by washing and brushing her tangled mane and tail, her muscles screamed at the enforced exercise. Hot prickles like blackberry thorns tortured her neck with every stride. Her heavy belly dragged at her attempts to pick up speed. "I can't. I must stop. I'm worried I'll lose my foal."

Fleet hesitated and peered into the thick forest of mixed deciduous trees. "We should at least move into open country. Keep going a bit longer."

Disobeying a stallion went against all Tress's upbringing. Look what happened when she had defied Streak and run away with Wolfbane. After Fleet had defeated him, she'd been surprised he hadn't forced her to mate to abort her foal. He must have some compassion.

The survival of the life within her remained her sole concern. Her time drew close. "I've struggled this far. I can't go on."

The man approached and mumbled something. She wished she could talk with people like Fleet. He had explained that his warm blood enabled him to communicate with other creatures. Tress had thought his stories fanciful until she saw firsthand how he could even talk with squirrels.

Fleet ignored her protestations and kept going.

At times, the possibility of meeting a unicorn had been the only thing to keep her taking one stride after another. Ever since Starburst had shared the legends of creation, Tress had dreamed of meeting one of the magical creatures. Now she was on a journey to do just that, all she wanted was to go home and forget she had ever heard of horned horses. "Please, let's stop for at least a short while. Remember what the poison was like in your veins before the goddess gave you strength, and I don't have warm blood to help me fight it."

Fleet finally relented and stopped. "Don't wander far. At least it'll give Yuma time to hunt. He says there are many animal tracks through these woods."

With a bit of sustenance in her belly, Tress started to improve. Nibbling at clumps of grass, she edged nearer the denser forest where the moister ground offered sweeter pick. A rank smell drifted on the slight breeze. She lifted her head in alarm. Dappled light filtered through the branches.

The shadows moved.

She fled towards the river, screaming a warning. A yowl echoed back. The stench grew. Pain lanced her shoulder wound. Heavy paws thumped behind her.

Fleet charged to meet the bloodwolf bounding close on her heels.

She reached the riverbank. She could go no further. She was doomed. She propped and turned to face the enemy, prepared to go down fighting.

Something flashed by. A pole appeared in the side of the blood-wolf. It slid on its nose towards her, the stench overpowering.

Fleet arrived and reared to pummel the creature into the ground.

The man ran from the forest, shouting and waving his bow.

Fleet paused mid-air, his raised hooves hovering.

Tress gawped. The crimson beast shook where it lay prone. Its hunched back withered and lost its bloodied streaks. Its shaggy coat shrank to short grey fur. Its long fangs receded to those of a normal timber wolf. The wolf leapt to its feet and bolted for the darkness of the trees, an arrow still embedded in its side.

Tress trembled all over. "What happened? Why didn't you kill it?"

Fleet conversed with the man and then sniffed the place where the wolf had lain. "The jade arrow removed the poison! The green stone worked!"

He danced around her, tail held high. "Yuma didn't want me to damage the arrow tip. He has only one left."

He settled and nuzzled her face. "This makes our mission all the more urgent. We must get as much stone as I can carry and return to the herds."

Up until now, Tress had focused on reaching Gemstone for a cure for herself in order to save her foal. Now she realised that once healed, Fleet must seek all the affected animals and rid them of poison. As the magnitude of his task dawned, exhaustion overcame her. Although she had known they were headed to Shimmering Lake to gather stones, she hadn't fully appreciated the relevance of their journey. Why had Fleet bothered to drag her along? She slowed them down and he didn't desire her. Why would he, with an emerald unicorn waiting for him?

Tress was a burden to their trek. "You must go on without me. Leave me signs to follow and I'll catch up when I can."

Fleet nudged her neck. "There are sure to be many more bloodwolves. You won't stand a chance on your own."

"You can travel faster without me. The fate of Equinora is more important than one mare." Tress shifted her weight as the foal moved within her. Despite her brave words, being at the mercy of poisonous beasts terrified her. At the same time, she desired to be alone when her time came.

"I'm not leaving you. You're my responsibility now." Not allowing any further argument, Fleet drove her along, encouraging her with a shove of his nose.

Feeling slightly refreshed after the break and still spooked from the close encounter with the bloodwolf, Tress managed a steady trot, her swollen barrel swinging from side to side. As their track wove between rolling foothills, she began to sense they were going round in circles. "Are you sure you know the way?"

Fleet cantered alongside, keeping his stride short to match her heavy trot. He whickered in reassurance. "We haven't left the stream. This is the path Yuma and I followed."

Not convinced, Tress watched for familiar landmarks, sure they would see these same trees and rocks in a few days' time. The belief they were going astray consumed her mind more than the hunger gnarling her guts. Thunder rumbled to the northeast. Obsidian spires pierced the skyline like rows of fangs. "Where are you leading me? I thought we were headed for Shimmering Lake. We're going towards the dark mountains."

"We'll turn soon. What you're sensing is the confusion the unicorns use to protect their territory. Trust me." Fleet loped on, aglow with energy and vigour.

The weaker Tress grew, the stronger Fleet appeared. He floated over the ground, even carrying two people and their gear. Tress could hardly believe he was the same young stallion who had come to Flowering Valley all those seasons ago. The memory made her long for those peaceful days gossiping with Breeze under the protection of King Streak. How could she have considered her old life tedious? She had dreamt of adventure and found it, only to wish she was safe at home. With gritted teeth, she slogged on.

When they reached a split in the river, Fleet turned away from the massing storm and headed towards blue sky. With relief, Tress drank the warm water and tried to follow. Her legs felt as if she were pulling them through a lake of mud. With every stride, the effort to lift her feet became harder. She dropped to a trot. Unable to keep up even that pace, she slowed to a walk. Soon she came to a halt. Every effort she made to go forward was like pressing into a bramble thicket.

Fleet came back to chase her along. "It's not much further. Soon we'll be safe."

Tress rolled her eyes. "I'm trying to keep up, but my body won't work."

She tried again, and again. It was as if a thornbush straddled the path, blocking her way, prickling her skin, demanding she retreat. In desperation, she trotted back the way they had come, feeling the relief of being able to move freely.

"There's nothing wrong with you. Hurry up."

Tress attempted to rejoin Fleet. "Every time I try, my body goes rigid. My mind screams we're going the wrong way. But when I turn back, I can move with ease."

Fleet stepped forward and walked to and fro. "This must the edge of Gem's protective barrier, but I can't feel anything."

Panic at being alone overrode Tress's earlier objections. "I've come this far. Please don't abandon me."

It had never occurred to Fleet that Tress wouldn't be able to cross the veil. *Gem, can you hear me? I'm on your border. I have a mare with me who can't cross. She needs your help. Can you lower your shield?*

Knowing Shadow would also hear, Fleet hesitated to send too much information. The only answer was an increase in the wind. The clouds they had been avoiding built like mushrooms sprouting after heavy dew. A chill fluffed Fleet's coat. This didn't feel right. When he'd visited Shimmering Lake before, the weather had been mild, even this far from the sustaining waters.

Increasing the intensity of his call, he messaged Gem again. To no avail.

He found Yuma gathering a large pile of firewood. "It looks like you want to camp here. Do you have any idea how we can get Tress across?"

Yuma shrugged. "She carries the poison in her veins. Maybe that's the problem."

Fleet pawed the ground. "So did I when we first came."

Yuma stroked his chin as he looked across to the mare. "She doesn't have your unicorn blood. Maybe I should use the last arrow and see if it'll cure her?"

"No!" Horrified at the suggestion, Fleet flattened back his ears. "She's too weak. Another injury could kill her or make her lose her foal."

"I don't want to hurt her any more than you, but I can't think of anything else. Let me know if you change your mind. Gem doesn't seem to want to help, and we must get the jade." Yuma returned to his gathering.

No means of crossing the veil occurred to Fleet. He wished he could have spent more time with the unicorns on Tern Island, learning how to use all his powers. Too soon, he had been thrust into yet another mission. Where were the unicorns now? The goddess had castigated them for not helping, yet he was doing this alone, a noncorn with no training.

All through the night, Fleet kept trying to contact Gem. At one point he had called Echo in the hope her sire might be able to get a response. Neither of them received an answer.

Tracking through the heavy dew, Fleet approached Tress where she grazed along a creek. "Are you sure you can't get through? Try thinking positive thoughts; don't be afraid of meeting a unicorn."

The mare blew through her nostrils and swung her rump towards Fleet. "I'm not afraid of meeting your lover, or any other magical creature. If I could pass into her territory I would. Don't you think I've tried everything I can? I haven't suffered this journey to wait here while you cavort at Shimmering Lake. I'll do anything to keep my foal safe."

Stung by the harsh words, Fleet backed off. He found fresh grazing in a small clearing away from the others and chewed without tasting what he ate.

A flash of colour flew close to his face.

He shied, and then relaxed when he recognised the jewelled dragon.

Tatuk hovered, whistling through his quivering snout in panic. "Come quick! Gem is dying!"

Chapter 23

Gem lay in anguish under her favourite tree, the branches barren, rattling as they clashed together in the wind. Her coat bore large bare patches, and scabs on her joints bled when she moved. Closing her eyes to the torment of the plants and creatures around her, she settled her head on the hard ground, the soft carpet of moss and leaves consumed by her charges long ago. The receding waters of the lake chopped into slate as a storm brewed. Since the winter solstice, the clouds sparred like the equines of her nightmares without bringing rain.

She had struggled to patrol her territory, the weight of concern a heavy burden. Experiencing the death of a unicorn was something she hoped to never feel again. Who had gone to the spirit world to be with the goddess? She only wished it could be her. She sank back and let sorrow engulf her. Too many had died. She could do no more. Perhaps she should summon her last reserves and throw herself off the jade cliffs. She groaned and sank into a heavy slumber.

An insistent tugging on her mane woke her from a dream of soaring with the goddess. Tatuk. Was her faithful dragon dying too? She opened her eyes and blinked—his scales glistened with renewed vigour. "What's happened?"

Tatuk flapped and fluttered around her head. "Fleet is here."

Sighing, Gem rested her head and stretched out her legs. "It's too late for me. Let me join the goddess."

A horse snorted. "Don't be ridiculous. We'll beat the foulness. Don't give up."

Gem couldn't find the energy to rise. "Prince Fleet of Foot of Dark Woods, please, do everyone a favour and strike this awful horn from my head. Let my blood feed the land as recompense for my corruption. Forgive me for harming Equinora. I tried my best."

Fleet stamped his hoof, kicking dust in her face. "It's not you! Shadow is behind the terrors, you know that. You must be strong and fight."

Gem flinched at a sharp nip on her neck. The onslaught of bites continued. She staggered to her feet. "Punish me if you must, but help me reach the cliffs so I can end my sorry life."

Fleet backed off. "I don't want to hurt you. I need you. Equinora needs you. Can't you absorb the energy from this gale? There's a lot to be done."

"What do you mean? How can I regain strength from the wind?"

Fleet described what Aureana had shown him about sharing the energy running through all nature. "When I learnt how to draw on the power, I assumed that was how you created this paradise. Don't tell me you've been using your own resources. No wonder you're almost dead."

This new information was too much for Gem. "You forget I left my dam when my horn emerged. I hadn't been taught any more than you. Shimmering Lake just grew more beautiful every day. The dragons said it came from me, but I didn't know how."

As Fleet described how to draw life from the elements, Gem followed his directions. Nothing worked. Drained of the will to live, she staggered towards the path leading to the hills.

Fleet cut in front of her and shoved her around. He drove her back to the lake. "Remember how you send love to Tatuk? Do that now, but listen to the beauty of the birdsong, inhale the power of the breeze, and smell the flowers near the fresh water. Channel the energy through your body rather than giving your own strength."

Gem followed his instructions. A tingle prickled her nostrils and vibrations strummed her ears.

Tatuk pulsed with brightness.

Her coat quivered, the hairs twitching from her neck to her tail in warm ripples. The stronger she became, the more power she could draw until her body hummed with energy. "It's a miracle! The goddess has sent me new life."

She trotted down to the foreshore, the grass growing in her wake, the shrubs thickening with leaves. Marsh violets and water speedwell bloomed. She bounded into the water. The lake's surface calmed and the clouds dissipated. Dragons swarmed down to the surface and skimmed their feet in rainbow showers. Swans, heads bobbing, trumpeted and splashed with outstretched wings. The "yak yak yak" of the magpies drowned out Tatuk's giggles as colour and wellbeing returned to Shimmering Lake.

Gem emerged and shook her glowing mane, her coat glimmering emerald, and her sores healed. "I feel wonderful! Thank you."

"You're beautiful. Don't ever think you're bad." Fleet stepped forward and nuzzled her neck. "Let's explore and help your territory recover."

They sprang into a gallop, covering the ground with ease, their escort of dragons sparkling with love. As they careened through copses and meadows, trees and shrubs burst into leaf, and grasses thrust seed heads high. The faster Gem sprinted, the stronger she became. The more she revelled in the effects of the healing powers, the greater the improvement in her territory. The animals who had slunk in hunger now scurried around gathering food.

At the far side of the lake, she veered towards the shore and plunged in, diving among the eelgrass beds. She swam down to the dim channels of the lakebed, effervescence streaming from her tail as she paddled among submerged timbers. Flashes of turquoise shot by her head before a small procession of baby aquadragons rode her wake, escorting her to shore—her friends had hatched a brood before their demise.

Fleet delighted in watching Gem cavort with the aquadragons. He had been shocked when Tatuk had found him near the boundary and told him Gem was dying. Fearing he wouldn't be in time to help, he'd galloped hard, abandoning Tress, Yuma, and Laila. Now, with Gem's recovery, the need to help Tress and save Equinora pressed on his mind. "Yuma needs more jade to fight the bloodwolves and scorcheels. He's remained on the border with Princess Silken Tresses of Flowering Valley who's desperate for your help, but she can't cross the barrier."

Gem exited the water and trotted back and forth, her tail slung over her back and her head high. "I don't permit mares into my territory, no matter their status or problems. Fetch Yuma, but hurry back. I want to hear all about your travels."

"Don't you find it hard to have a noncorn nearby? I've discovered a lot more about my ancestry. I'm nearly a full hotblood." Fleet avoided explaining Shadow was his grandsire.

Gem sidled close. "You've grown into a magnificent stallion and learnt to shield your thoughts. You're welcome to live in my territory. There are many creatures to care for, and I could do with help."

Finding it hard to tear himself away from Gem, Fleet recounted some of what had occurred. Being with her was bliss, but he had a duty to fulfil. He stopped.

Gem nuzzled him. "Go on. Tell me who died. I must know."

Fleet choked. "Jasper. I can't talk about that now."

Gem whickered in sympathy. "I never knew him. I've never met my sire either, but I feel for you." She paused. "Tell me how the ceremony on Tern Island worked."

Fleet fidgeted. "That story will have to wait. I must fetch Yuma."

"No, please, I've waited all my life to learn. Don't deny me now you're here." Gem sidled up and raised her tail, swinging her rump invitingly towards him.

Why shouldn't he stay? The other unicorns and the horse herds could help people destroy Shadow's beasts. He'd done enough. It would be wonderful to remain here with Gem. The sun warmed him as the last of the clouds dispersed. With Shimmering Lake returning to its former glory, it was hard to think of the troubles outside the thriving hills. As they rested under her tree, he regaled her with all he'd done since leaving Shimmering Lake.

Tatuk landed on Gem's neck and clawed her mane. "This is no time for tales. With your new strength and Fleet's help, you can reopen the veil. There are still animals trying to escape the horrors."

The dragon was right. Fleet couldn't abandon Tress, especially in her current condition. "I'll fetch Yuma. Please let Tress in, too. She's very sick, and heavily in foal."

Gem blew her nose in a glittering spray. "Alright. As you taught me to summon Equinora's power, I'll heal your mare, but I won't share you. First I must visit the guardian dragons and open the barrier."

She cantered off up the beach. Her voice carried back on the breeze. "Choose a life with me. There's room for us both."

Fleet galloped along the riverbank, keen to fetch Yuma and Tress and end his mission. Once healed, Tress could head back to

Wolfbane. Yuma could take the jade back to Oakvale with Laila. He would stay here with Gem and spend his days grazing, mating, and cavorting with the dragons. By aiding the creatures in the sanctuary, he would be helping Equinora on its recovery while others fought the last of Shadow's beasts.

Yet he longed for his own territory and many offspring. What was the point of being king of a distant land, one he didn't rule, with no chance of siring progeny here? The poison remained in his veins, even if the boundless source of energy helped him overcome his weakness. But it didn't stop his nightmares. If anything, they were worse, filled with images of him fighting Shadow among boiling lava, bloodwolves tearing at his throat.

By the time Fleet met up with his fellow travellers, the veil had lifted. Tress hobbled towards him, her head low. Yuma and Laila walked on either side of her, encouraging her with handfuls of herbs and clover.

Yuma strode ahead when he saw Fleet. "You might have told us you were leaving. We've been worried."

Fleet explained about Tatuk finding him and Gem being near death. "Things had become so dire Gem closed her sanctuary. She's busy reopening the borders and encouraging creatures back. Many have died. It'll take time for the land to fully recover."

Yuma stroked Fleet's neck and plucked a twig from his mane. "We've tried to encourage Tress to walk faster. Without being able to talk to her, it's hard keeping her going at all."

Fleet nuzzled the mare and explained Gem had agreed to help. "Can you go quicker? The nearer we get to the lake, the better you'll feel."

"I'll go as fast as I can." Tress's sides heaved with the effort of talking. As Yuma and Laila mounted Fleet, she shuffled into a stumbling trot.

Worried Tress might not reach help in time, Fleet tried to send her love like Gem did with her charges. He didn't see any difference in Tress's movements. Sensing instead the poison flowing in her veins, he gave up the effort. For all his warm blood he didn't know how to wield unicorn power. And of course he had no horn. He was foolish to think that, just because he could draw on Equinora's energy, he could wield other powers.

By the time they reached Shimmering Lake, the territory had almost returned to its former glory. Gem dozed under her tree with Tatuk on her crest. The serene setting teased Fleet to forget the horrors still ravaging the land. At their approach, Gem stood proud with her opal horn and hooves dazzling in the sun and her coat flashing emerald. She tossed her mane and tail in a ruby fountain.

Tress gasped behind him. He had forgotten she'd never met a unicorn. He introduced her to Gem.

Tress bowed as low as her bad leg would permit. "Thank you for allowing me to visit your territory. You're even more beautiful than I imagined. But I'm no longer a princess from Flowering Valley. I'm Queen Silken Tresses of White Water Cliffs. I wish my friend Breeze was here to see you!"

Gem stepped forward and blew through distended nostrils. "You stink of the poison Fleet carried when I first met him. I can't cure you of that."

Worried he had forced Tress to come all this way for nothing, Fleet cajoled Gem. "Remember how you healed my rump with your horn? You can draw on even more power now. Can you straighten Tress's leg?"

"Of course, but as soon as I have, she must leave. I'll not have that darkness in my land. At least you can suppress the effects of the poison. Have you decided what you'll do?"

Fleet had not expected to be asked to make a decision so soon. "I'll go with Yuma to get the stones. We'll return before sunset."

Gem tossed her head and pawed the ground. "Take the woman, too. You take too many liberties bringing people here. I didn't detect her because of Yuma."

Laila stood beside Tress, stroking the mare's neck. She approached Gem and bowed, and then held out both hands. "Lady Gemstone, I thank you for your help and am glad you've recovered from your illness. I'm Laila Otter, originally of Bloomsvale. I can't tell you how awed I am at your presence, more magnificent than Yuma told me, more wonderful than the legends! And you're not a myth!"

Gem snorted. "No, I'm real. Why are you here?"

Laila held out her hands. "I wish to become a healer, but have much to learn, and the healers of the clans won't teach me. May I please stay and see how you work? In return I can gather plants or make salves."

Gem walked a circle around the company, peering at each of them before answering Laila. "The goddess works in mysterious ways. I could certainly do with your help. There are many animals still sick. You may stay while Fleet and Yuma go to the caves."

Tress trembled at the close proximity of Gemstone. She had never imagined a unicorn would be so stunning, gleaming like the coloured stones on the bed of the shallow creek they had jumped on their way here. In comparison, she must look shocking with her swollen belly and dull coat. Although the woman had untangled her mane and tail, they hadn't recovered their brilliant white. "Thank you for agreeing to heal me."

Gemstone strutted around Tress. "You introduced yourself as a queen. I see little in you that's regal."

Determined not to cower, Tress stood erect and held her head high. "I'm sorry I present myself in this condition, but as you know, there's much evil in Equinora at the moment."

"I do not refer to your poor condition. Beauty doesn't make a queen. Is your foal Fleet's?"

"No. I was running with Wolfbane, formerly Head of Warriors of Oakvale, before Fleet won the kingship of White Water Cliffs in a mighty fight." Tress couldn't see the relevance of this conversation and had expected a unicorn to speak in magic riddles.

"Good. Fleet is mine and will remain here. You must return to this Wolfbane or your sire. You look too young to be a queen."

Not surprised at Gemstone's claim, Tress didn't doubt Fleet would prefer a unicorn to a plain black mare. Until today she had always considered herself special, but how could she compete with such beauty and power? She dreaded the long trip south on her own. Would the people go with her? At least the man and his arrows could protect her and her foal from bloodwolves.

Gemstone laid the tip of her spiral horn on Tress's shoulder. Colours flashed behind Tress's eyes and dizziness overcame her. Stars filled her head and hot tingles ran down her leg. She toppled to the ground with a thud, her hooves twitching as if she galloped in a dream. Thrashing her legs, she scrambled to rise away from the sensation of drowning. A swarm of wasps stung her body and ants crawled over her skin. Gasping, Tress struggled to her feet, sweat dripping from her neck and chest.

Gemstone stood a short distance away. "I'm sorry if I hurt you. There was a lot of damage and the poison fought me. Your cold blood is more susceptible than Fleet's warm blood. Let's refresh ourselves." She cantered to the lake and plunged into the water.

Tress tested her healed leg with a single step. After limping for so long, her atrophied muscles pulled tight. Forcing herself to walk soundly, she struggled after Gemstone. By the time she reached the foreshore, her limbs moved with more grace. She quenched her thirst and waded fetlock-deep into the water. The warmth surprised and pleased her. This was nothing like crossing River Lifeflow. The firm bottom gave her confidence as she ventured further. As the water reached her chest, the gravel beneath her hooves slipped away; she was out of her depth. She panicked for a brief moment before relaxing; Gemstone wouldn't have healed her to let her drown.

Keeping parallel to the shore, Tress stretched her legs and paddled. The more she swam, the more energy pumped in her veins. The buoyancy of the water relieved her of the foal's drag on her belly. With ease, she followed Gemstone to deeper waters. As the unicorn disappeared beneath the surface, Tress's panic returned. No way was she diving like that! She splashed her way back to shore, lifting her legs high, and scrambled up the bank, torrents of water pouring from her head and neck.

Far out in the lake, Gemstone surfaced and rolled as if scratching in a bed of sand.

Tress re-entered the water, swimming deeper than before, a sensation of peace flooding over her. She let the soothing silk cover her neck and ducked her head into the ripples, enjoying herself for the first time since leaving home.

When Gemstone returned to the beach, Tress hesitated to follow until the unicorn called her. She joined her where she conversed with the woman. "I wish I could talk with people like you and Fleet."

Gemstone snorted. "You're not a noncorn. I don't know why Fleet bothered to bring you all this way."

Tress wandered back to the lake, wishing Gemstone would be friendlier. She'd imagined all unicorns would be graceful and loving.

But she shouldn't have been surprised; Gem wanted Fleet. Not that Tress posed a threat. Peering at her reflection, all she could see was a heavily pregnant mare with a spine that would make a short-horned lizard proud. At least her mane had cleansed to its former snow-white. She didn't want to return to Wolfbane alone. Would Streak still be able to send her after Breeze? Remembering what Wolfbane had said about Scar, her proposed king, that future didn't look bright either. Then again, Wolfbane had lied about following Fleet.

Thoughts scudded through her head like autumn leaves in a storm. What did it matter? She doubted she'd make it back to either territory. Maybe if she could foal here, her son or daughter might be raised at Shimmering Lake. The bloodwolves could take her, if only her foal was safe.

Fleet cantered back to the lake, Yuma and the sack of jade barely noticeable on his back, still undecided about what to do. Duty demanded he escort Yuma and Laila back to Oakvale, and Tress to White Water Cliffs. And he couldn't forget his pledge to Sapphire. How much more did he need to do?

Here he could forget his worries and spend his days with Gem. Maybe he was never destined to live in a herd. They could be happy, the two of them, caring for everyone who sought refuge at Shimmering Lake. Did being a warmblood mean he'd live as long as a unicorn, the equivalent of many generations of horses? If he returned to White Water Cliffs, he'd outlive his own progeny.

The desire to sire foals added to his quandary. What impact would his warm blood have on his offspring? Would they be able to talk with other species? If he stayed with Gem, he'd never have young. There'd never be fillies or colts playing in the meadows or carrying on his bloodline. His mind continued to whirl as they made their way back to the mares. He didn't understand why Gem refused to produce warmbloods.

Reaching the lake, Fleet delighted in the renewed strength he sensed in Tress. Freshly groomed, her black coat shone as it had when he first met her, her snowy mane and tail flowing like a waterfall. Only a tiny scar remained on her shoulder from the bloodwolf wound. "How do you feel?"

Tress stretched her head towards Fleet. "I'm no longer lame, thanks to Gemstone, and the waters were invigorating."

Gem strutted over and spoke to Yuma. "You must leave soon. The mare's poison makes me unsettled. It'll take you longer than before as you won't be able to ride. She's too heavy with foal to carry you or the jade."

Yuma slid from Fleet's back and stroked his head. "Is this really goodbye? I thought we'd see this war to the end together. You've been through a lot, but Equinora still needs you. I need you. Who knows what else Shadow might get up to?"

Fleet backed away from Yuma's hand and wandered away. He didn't want to make this decision now. He'd rather rest for a moon or two and deal with the fate of the world later.

While Yuma remained talking with Gem, Laila followed Fleet to the lake. The young woman knelt down and trickled pebbles through her fingers. "This land is a miracle. I can imagine why you want to stay. I feel the same."

A neigh rent the air.

Tress galloped by as if her tail was on fire. Fresh blood streamed from the scar on her shoulder. Fleet's instinct told him to flee alongside her. Then his need to defend Gem came to the fore. Had bloodwolves breached the barrier? He raced up the bank.

Gem stood under the tree where he had left her, chatting to Tatuk and Yuma.

Fleet slid to a halt, stones flying around his knees and hocks, unable to comprehend the relaxed stance of his friends. "Why has Tress bolted? She was bleeding. I thought you must be under attack."

Flicking her tail and stomping a hoof, Gem looked away. "The jade is a cure against the poison. I suggested Yuma apply it to the mare's wound. When he did, she took off."

Yuma held out the green shard. "Touching the scar didn't help. I had to thrust it into the bloodwolf wound."

Fleet's heart thumped as if he had been the one harmed. He'd told Yuma it was too risky to try the jade, especially with her so heavily in foal. Hadn't Tress been through enough? "You idiot! If she comes to any harm, I'll never forgive you!"

He galloped after the bolting mare.

Broken twigs and chopped ground made her trail easy to follow. Fleet slowed as he twisted through outcrops of rocks. Shrubs smothered with new growth scratched his sides as he barged onwards. He broke out into a clearing and skidded to a stop.

Tress lay on her side, blood soaking the stony ground. She didn't move.

Fleet approached one step at a time, every hair on edge. A tangle of legs massed in a thick membrane near Tress's tail. Fleet sniffed the stillborn filly. It stank of bloodwolf poison. He moved away and nickered in grief, and then blew love into Tress's face. A slight rise of her ribs gave him hope. He licked her neck to wash away the sweat and nuzzled her nose.

She lifted her head. "You're too late. My baby's dead. Leave me."

Fleet's heart tore at the anguish in her eyes. "Gem can heal your wound again. I can't smell the poison anymore. The jade has worked. You'll be alright."

Fleet encouraged Tress with gentle shoves of his muzzle. She rose on wobbly legs and tottered round to sniff at the dead filly.

Yuma and Laila ran up, puffing hard. The woman tore up handfuls of greens and offered them to Tress. "These herbs will cleanse you of any remaining afterbirth."

Tress refused to eat, even after Fleet translated Laila's words.

Fleet stood by, feeling useless as Yuma buried the dead foal and Laila washed Tress's wound.

Tress drooped with exhaustion. She nuzzled Fleet. "Don't be cross with the man. I suspect my foal died from the poison anyway."

Even accepting she spoke the truth, Fleet still couldn't believe Yuma had attacked a pregnant mare. Sapphire had said to trust him, yet he had deliberately hurt a sick horse. The seasons of friendship crumbled. Yet, despite his anger with Yuma, Fleet thought the result might be for the best. A newborn foal couldn't escape bloodwolves. At least Tress should recover. "As soon as you feel strong enough, we'll leave. I'll escort you wherever you want."

Tress sighed and nibbled Fleet's wither. "I think it best if I return to my dam and learn how to be a queen, if Streak will have me back. He won't be happy I ran away with Wolfbane. If he can no longer make a good trade for me, perhaps one day you'll come and find me."

Fleet shuffled from foot to foot. "Surely he'll be delighted to have you back. At least you've proved you can carry a foal."

Tress didn't answer, only glancing at the fresh earth where her foal lay buried.

Regretting his choice of words, Fleet left the blood-soaked area. He joined the people, barely able to look at Yuma in his fury. "We're going to Flowering Valley. Gem can heal Tress's shoulder while you both pack up the jade."

Laila shook her head. "I'm not going with you. Gemstone has invited me to stay."

Yuma's mouth dropped open.

Before the man could say anything, Fleet poked him. "Don't argue with her. She doesn't belong to you, and my patience is thin. I'm only taking you for Equinora's sake. Tress may be able to forgive you for stabbing her, but I can't."

Chapter 24

An old sentry welcomed Yuma at the barricade. "Chief Ituha will be pleased to see you. He's in the central hut."

The village sounded quiet compared to his previous visit, reminding him of the desolation at Waterfalls and the loss of his whole family, his whole clan. He must find and kill the bloodwolves! All of them.

Striding to the communal area, he slipped off his quiver and pack, the latter lighter without the jade he'd stashed beneath a pile of rocks when starting out on foot. It had been a tense journey back, with Fleet talking to him only when necessary. He didn't understand why Fleet was angry. He hadn't been upset when Yuma stabbed Jasper with poison to save him at Obsidian Caves. And the jade worked! They'd seen that from the recovery of the wolf. Tress's foal had reeked of foulness, and wasn't Fleet's anyway.

The full implications of losing Fleet's friendship drove another stake like the poles of the barricade through his heart. Not only would he be alone again, he'd no longer have the thrill of riding. And now he had no home to go to.

He pushed his worries aside and found the clan leader working leather with three old women weaving baskets. After greeting each of them, he accepted a mug of tea. "Where is everyone? Are they out gathering?"

Ituha threw his hands in the air. "You'd think so with our hunger. But no. Where are they, you ask? Off riding horses! Since the young stallions came to start practicing tactics to fight the bloodwolves, we haven't seen our young people while there's light in the day. It's been left to us old ones to feed everyone."

Yuma thrilled to hear the horses and clan had accepted the challenge to work together. "With the Mother's bounty this spring, the horses must be in good condition. It sounds like we'll have a fit and able army."

The clan elder smacked his knee with one hand. "If you can get them to stop playing games. The horses seem to delight in racing and jumping obstacles as much as the men and women do."

Raising his eyebrows, Yuma sipped at the hot brew. "Women too? I've no doubt they make good riders, but will they participate in the hunt?"

Ayiana, the elderly healer, harrumphed. "Most of the girls are a better shot from horseback than the boys. They're more balanced and supple than the heavier men."

Yuma didn't like the idea of women involved in battle. "Are they strong enough to draw a bow?"

A bellow rang across the clearing.

Jolon Fist barged up and dragged Yuma to his feet by his jerkin. "Where's my daughter? What have you done with her?"

Yuma thrust the man away and braced for a fight. "I didn't steal her. She ran away from *you*. Don't blame me."

Ituha eased between them and held up both hands. "This is no way to solve disputes. Jolon, I've told you many times, bring a complaint before the elders if you wish to seek redress for Laila's choice of partner."

Yuma couldn't let the old man believe the girl had become his mate. "I tried to prevent her from leaving, but the horse overruled me."

Jolon launched himself at Yuma, knocking Ituha aside. "The horse! You expect me to believe that?"

Yuma's head wrenched back as Jolon's fist connected with his jaw. He retaliated with a punch, bowling Jolon over. "Believe what you will, but I haven't touched her."

The old women who had been weaving steadied the chief as he pointed a shaky hand at Jolon. "If you can't behave with civility, you must leave Oaktown." Turning to Yuma, he wagged his finger. "I know you were provoked, but we won't have fighting here. Bring Laila Otter to us so she can tell her story."

Yuma cradled his right hand where it had connected with Jolon's head. "She didn't return with me. She chose to stay with the unicorn."

A small crowd of elderly people had gathered during the fracas.

Their murmurs increased as they debated among themselves whether to believe this tale. A female voice rose above the group. "We have only your word unicorns even exist. Are you sure she wasn't taken by a bloodwolf and you're too scared to admit it? Or maybe you tired of her and abandoned her."

Fury boiled inside Yuma. He had travelled for many moons to aid these people while bloodwolves slaughtered his own clan. He hadn't invited, or even wanted, Laila to accompany him. He had lost Fleet's friendship while trying to help Tress. Now Ayiana accused him of being a woman snatcher. He stomped out of the central hut, whispers trailing after him.

After dumping his gear in Chaytan's hut, he jogged out of the village. Would the elders believe Fleet if the horse talked to them? But Fleet wouldn't enter the stockade. And would he help Yuma? No matter their differences, he'd have to arrange a meeting between Fleet and the elders.

Yuma settled against a sturdy oak and whittled at a rough stick in an effort to distract himself from the injustices of life. Realising he'd carved the figure of a young woman, he cast it aside. He selected another piece of wood and turned it this way and that to see what animal resided in the curved outline.

Heavy footsteps crunched on sticks.

He sprang to his guard.

Chaytan waved a flagon of ale. "I thought you might need some of this. I heard you were back. Travel makes a man thirsty."

Yuma slumped back against the trunk. "You're a welcome sight. I was beginning to think I might get thrown out."

Chaytan seated himself next to Yuma and swigged from the flask. "I heard about the altercation. Don't worry about the elders. They have to be seen to listen to both sides."

They enjoyed their ale in silent companionship. Yuma sensed that losing Aponi was still a raw wound in his friend's heart. A flock of crested jays scolded each other, hopping across the ground for seeds or grubs. The vociferous birds would make a good carving. At least birds still flew here. The scant signs of mammals or reptiles worried him. It was a long way from Shimmering Lake for animals to return and repopulate the region.

Chaytan handed over the ale flask. "Where is Laila, anyway? Don't tell me she couldn't make the return journey because she's heavy with child."

Yuma sighed in exasperation. "I haven't touched her. She wants to be a healer, not my mate. It's true what I told Jolon: she's remained at Shimmering Lake. Gem took her on as some kind of apprentice."

Chaytan swallowed another mouthful of beer. "Ah, that won't help with Ayiana; she feels guilty about not taking Laila on years ago, though being a student of a unicorn is a new one on me. Are you sure you didn't find those magic mushrooms we used to enjoy at the annual meets?"

The memory of the hallucinations he and Chaytan had experienced broke the tension. Yuma chuckled. "No. And I've not had any smoke either. I've witnessed enough magic without needing to imagine more."

"Did you get the jade?"

Chaytan listened with patience as Yuma described all that had transpired. As the friends devoured the remainder of the ale, Chaytan informed Yuma of the young people's progress with the horses. "They're ready to fight the bloodwolves as soon as we've made the arrows."

Fleet left Tress with Queen Starburst, the young mare happy to be back with her dam to learn all she needed to know, relieved Streak accepted her return with pleasure rather than admonishing her for running away, both parents only delighted that she had survived. Her experiences with Wolfbane and the terrors of the poison had matured her manner and body, and she had recovered from her physical wounds and rebuilt her strength on the journey. Maybe the jade had done more than rid her of the poison.

Nothing, however, could cure her sorrow at losing her firstborn foal.

Fleet could understand that. Seeing the foals and yearlings run with the mare herd, he wished he and Gem could have offspring.

Cantering at dawn to where Blackfoot waited with the bachelors, Fleet spotted Yuma among the gathered people. Away from Gem, and seeing Tress happy, Fleet's ire abated, and his resolve to see this through to the end renewed. He'd have to carry Yuma to fight before he could return to Shimmering Lake. Having spoken with some of the stallions, he was surprised at their joy at being ridden. Remembering how hard it had been before he could talk with Yuma, he had translated between the two groups to develop new signs.

Fleet halted next to Blackfoot. "Are your warriors ready?"

Blackfoot signalled for the young men and women to mount. "The colts who are too young to be ridden are scouting the forests. They'll whinny if a bloodwolf is detected."

Ignoring Yuma's greeting, Fleet stood still as his former friend mounted, and then accompanied Blackfoot into the forest at the head of the army. "I hope you only sent the fastest and nimblest if they're to act as bait. Even a dribble of venom will drive them insane."

The grey stallion bobbed his head. "They're all volunteers."

Fleet itched to get moving. "I'll head west where I know the land better."

Rocky, the stocky skewbald who had befriended him before he'd gone to seek Gem, wandered over, welcoming him back and congratulating him on finding a unicorn. "We're to remain in pairs. I'll accompany you if you like."

Blackfoot gave out final instructions to the mounted teams. "Remember, if a bloodwolf takes chase, split up so the other rider can use the arrows. Travel safe and hunt well."

Mist drifted through the valleys as the sun rose above the trees. The morning chorus burst into full song as Fleet trotted between the towering oaks, splendid in their summer green. With each step, the earth shared its energy through his hooves, buoying his spirits and flowing power through his limbs. Grateful that he and Yuma had been together so long they had no need to converse, the warm contact on Fleet's back became an extension of his body.

Rocky trotted by his side, refraining from chatter, his pricked ears swivelling and his nostrils distended. By the time the sun reached its zenith, he dripped with sweat. His rider, a teenage boy, flushed red.

With no indication of bloodwolves, Fleet called a halt at a stream. "Refresh yourselves here while I climb the hill and listen for calls."

The boy slid from the horse's back. "I thought we had to stay together. What if you're attacked?"

With his powers, Fleet could outrun any bloodwolf. The same couldn't be said for Rocky. "I'll leave Yuma with you. I'll be quicker on my own without needing to avoid low- hanging limbs."

Yuma grasped an overhead branch and swung into the tree. "I don't fancy being caught on the ground by a bloodwolf."

The sight of Yuma in the foliage with his bow at hand brought back the moment when Fleet had first seen him. They'd travelled so far since, and been through so much, each task leading to another. His heart softened, before hardening again. Here he was, still seeking to destroy the bloodwolves, never staying in one place long, never having a chance to make friends with other horses, his mission dragging on season after season.

He wanted it to end.

But it wasn't Yuma's fault.

With determination driving him hard, Fleet galloped to a vantage point where an outcrop of rocks broke the tree cover.

Muffled screams of fear and rage drifted up through the forest. Horses whinnied and people yelled, interspersed with yowls of pain.

Frustrated the action happened elsewhere, Fleet hastened back to Rocky, intent on joining the fight. He needed to wreak vengeance on the beasts that had thwarted his plans of a settled existence for more than half his life.

He cantered through the oaks. His rump throbbed. He gagged on the rank scent of bloodwolf. Charging faster, he pounded down the narrow trail to where he had left Yuma and the other pair. He sensed a bloodwolf close in front. Reaching the stream, he caught a glimpse of crimson fur flash through the trees.

The skewbald stallion was nowhere in sight.

"Fleet! Here!" Yuma swung from a branch.

He dropped onto Fleet's back as he cantered beneath. Without breaking stride, they tore after the bloodwolf, the track easy to follow from both the smell and the snapped twigs where Rocky had bolted.

Fleet broke into a clearing.

The bloodwolf bunched its hindquarters.

He spurted forward. An arrow whizzed past his ears, bowling over the bloodwolf as it launched its attack. The beast's momentum carried it forward, knocking Rocky down, his rider trapped beneath him.

Yuma leapt to the ground before Fleet had even halted. "Delsin! Talk to me!"

Rocky scrambled to his feet.

The boy groaned and waved a hand. "I'm okay. Just stunned."

Yuma retrieved his arrow from the neck of the bloodwolf.

Fleet trotted around the corpse, the stench keeping him back.

The bloodwolf heaved and lurched to its feet, shaking its jowls and spraying saliva in a wide arc.

Fleet leapt to attack. Before he had time to bring his front hooves down, the massive beast shuddered and crashed over. He gaped at the enormous carcass, crusted with gore and reeking of poison. "I thought it was dead."

Yuma kicked the body. "It is now. Any other creature would have died instantly with a shot like that to the throat. It was too dangerous to try and cure it by shooting it in the rump."

The boy shrieked.

They rushed to his side.

Yuma knelt beside him. "What's the matter? Is something broken?"

Clasping one arm, Delsin shook his head. "It's only a graze. But I think poison splashed me. It sears like fire."

Fleet nudged Yuma. "You must stab him with an arrow like you did Tress."

"No! I can't do that to Delsin."

Fleet tossed his head and flared his nostrils. "So it's okay to risk my mare, but not okay to do the same to one of your clan? And you wonder why I'm angry."

Yuma led Fleet out of Delsin's hearing. "He isn't as strong as a horse, not even as strong as a normal man. Can't you see he's crippled? An illness when he was young bowed his legs. I can't risk injuring him further. And this is Laila's brother. Imagine their father's wrath if I return to Jolon having murdered his youngest son." Yuma rummaged in his emergency medicine pouch. "I'll try a goldenrod poultice, but I'll need more water to wash the wound."

Fleet snuffled the bag. "Give me something to fetch it in."

When Fleet returned, the boy's eyes had glazed over and he refused to speak. Curled up in the shade, he rocked back and forth, his arms hugged around his belly. The moans emanating from his contorted body didn't sound human.

Fleet carried the suede pouch to Yuma. "Next time, don't give me hog hide to hold in my teeth."

Yuma retrieved the container. "I didn't exactly have time to braid a grass handle." He crouched next to the boy. "The wound looks clean, but the poison has taken hold."

Still believing Yuma should stab Delsin with the jade, Fleet walked over to where Rocky grazed nearby. "If any poison touched you, we must wash it off."

The stallion raised his head and checked his sides. "I'm fine. People are very vulnerable with their bare skin."

He returned to where Yuma ministered to the boy. "He's recovering! Your poultice worked. It's a pity you didn't use that with Tress."

Yuma sat back on his haunches. "I haven't tried it yet. The water you brought sizzled when I poured it on his skin. Where did you get it? It's a miracle. The wound is almost closed."

Delsin coughed. "I saw flames and dark creatures. They were all over me. I thought I was dead."

Yuma explained to him how the poison had entered his system.

The boy straightened and brushed down his arms and legs. "What did you use to heal me?"

Fleet stepped closer and sniffed the boy's arm. He had been careful to check for scorcheels before dunking the container. He didn't believe the stream water was any different from that in Yuma's bladderflask, and the water hadn't emitted the same essence as the healing waters of Shimmering Lake. "What do you normally carry in the pouch?"

Yuma looked up, his eyebrows raised. "The jade arrow tips. There must have been flakes or dust in the bag."

By the time Fleet led his team back to Blackfoot's warriors, all the bloodwolves lay dead or transformed. Those that had reverted to grey wolves had disappeared into the forest as if they'd never been there.

Fleet congratulated the stallions and their riders, but refused to follow them back to the village.

Yuma tried to coax him on. "I must tell the elders about Delsin's recovery, and get him home to rest. You don't have to go all the way."

"Rocky will take him. It's time I let you apply the jade to my wound."

Yuma dismounted and unlashed the pouch from his waistband. "I doubt there's any dust left. I can find stones and grind some more from one of the arrow tips if you give me a while."

Fleet didn't want to wait. "No. Shoot me. I'm strong, and can draw energy from the land to help."

"Why don't I just pierce the wound like I did with Tress?"

"The poison has been in my veins a very long time. Can you hit the wound accurately from a distance so the head buries deep?"

Yuma weighed an arrow in his hand. "Yes, especially if you don't move. Stand over there by that oak. I'll climb this one so I get a better angle. Are you sure you want to do this? I only pricked Tress, I didn't shoot her."

Fleet trotted to where Yuma indicated and pointed his rump back to him. "You've wanted to do this since you changed the first bloodwolf. Get on with it."

Taking his time to aim, Yuma stretched his bow taut.

Fleet held his breath in anticipation of the pain.

The arrow struck deep, right in the heart of his wound, the shaft pointing out at an angle. Waves of nausea racked his body. He stood firm.

Yuma raced over and extracted the arrow, adding to the excruciation. "Can you feel anything?"

Flames roared in his head. Green clouds covered his eyes. Every artery pumped, every vein sucked, his pulse roaring in his ears. The green morphed to red like a fire-dragon readying to huff flame. His legs gave way.

A black torrent flowed into his bloodstream like a river in flood. Visions from his nightmares leapt around him: Shadow rising out of pits of lava, rearing and spewing fire, bloodwolves leaping at his throat, howling and slavering. Sapphire screamed and told him to run, and rotted into a mass of bloody gore. Jasper charged him, his horn contorted, striking him in the chest, knocking him over the edge of the cliff, stone crashing around his head, falling, falling …

"Fleet! Fleet! Come round! What's happening?" Yuma sat on his neck, pinning him to the ground.

The poison retreated, leaving him drained as if a great tide ebbed away his life. "The poison won. Shadow's obsidian overpowered the jade."

"How can you say that? Did Tress tell you what she felt? Maybe this is how the green stone works." Reassured Fleet had recovered from his fit, Yuma rose and let him stand.

Fleet staggered about the woods. "I didn't ask her, but I saw how the boy recovered. And I can feel the poison, stronger than ever. It's made of the stone where Shadow lives."

Yuma walked alongside. "Give it time. As you say, the poison has been in you a long time. Tress didn't recover straight away, either."

Fleet halted, his head drooping almost to the ground. "That was from foaling." He looked north. "Call together your elders. I'll talk to them, as you asked."

Yuma hadn't expected so many people to meet Fleet in the woods. The stallion shortened his stride, jittery and nervous, as Yuma accompanied him into the clearing. Ituha and Ayiana sat in a semi-circle with the rest of the council of elders, plus Gomda Hunter and Mojag Carol, the chief and spirit-man from Bloomsvale, on whatever stumps or logs they could find. Chaytan, Jolon, and the other older clan members stood behind them. None of the young people attended, having met Fleet to refine the signals with their mounts, and Ituha had promised to keep numbers to a minimum.

The chief opened the meeting. "The first battle has been a success. Three bloodwolves were killed and six escaped after reverting to grey wolf form. Our only injuries are minor, with one broken arm from a fall and the odd laceration from galloping through branches. I thank Yuma Squirrel of Waterfalls for showing us how to defeat this enemy."

A loud beat of drums reflected the acknowledgement as a murmur of gratitude ran among the attendees.

Yuma held up his hand for silence. "I'm glad we found a way to fight this terror. But if thanks are due, they are for King Fleet of Foot of White Water Cliffs, not me. Without his knowledge, strength, and determination, we would still be cowering behind our barricade."

This time the murmur contained a mix of dissention. Jolon stepped forward and punched the air. "We would have overcome the beasts without your intervention. We still have no proof it wasn't your horse that brought the bloodwolves in the first place. And what about the poisonous fish lurking in the waters? What do we do about them? People want to return home. How do we know next winter won't bring more hardship? I think the pestilence is far from eradicated."

Sensing Fleet wouldn't remain if Jolon continued his tirade, Yuma held back from mentioning Delsin's recovery from the poison. "I agree the scorcheels are still a problem. That's partly why Fleet is here, to discuss what we do next. He's also offered to tell you about Laila. Isn't that what you wanted? I suggest you give him a chance to speak."

People shuffled on their seats and the murmuring grew.

Ituha signalled for them to settle. "I add our thanks to King Fleet of Foot of White Water Cliffs and welcome him to speak of his travels. We're keen to know how we might work more with horses, and hear about unicorns."

Quiet descended.

Fleet stepped forward. At first hesitant, he told how he had been born in Dark Woods, of Sapphire's death, and meeting Yuma. Many of the people had never heard the full tale. No-one interrupted. Fleet became more animated as the story progressed, prancing around the clearing as he spoke of finding Gem, fighting Jasper, and escaping Shadow's territory. He skimmed over the ceremony on Tern Island and Jasper's death, expounded on Gem's healing powers and her befriending of Laila, and ended with Delsin's miraculous cure.

When he finished, multiple conversations erupted. Everyone babbled about a horse who could talk and whether or not to believe the fantastic story. How could they not have known such magic abounded? Why had they never encountered unicorns? What if Shadow escaped and came south?

Yuma didn't want to lose the focus of the meeting. He borrowed one of the drums and beat a tattoo.

A hush fell.

Yuma placed a hand on Fleet's neck. "Without the horses, we would never have overcome Shadow's foul beasts. Even though we've had a small victory with the nearby bloodwolves, many more must roam the land. We need to seek them out, and cure or destroy them. We need to tackle the scorcheels in the waters. Without doing all this, we are still at war. And then we need animals to return to our country and re-establish the food chain."

Fleet side-stepped away from Yuma. "It's time the unicorns helped. The goddess created them to protect Equinora. I'll call them to join us."

At noon the next day, Yuma returned with Ituha to the clearing at Fleet's summons. He refused to permit a large number of people like before, only relenting to allow Ayiana when she insisted someone needed to represent the women. Yuma suspected she desired to meet the fabled unicorns as much as not wanting the men colluding. She walked between them, her head held high, a heavy necklace of hog tusks and ermine tails overlying her ceremonial suede dress, her braided hair heavy with freshwater shells.

They reached the agreed meeting place and waited in silence while Fleet disappeared into the woods.

He returned in moments, Diamond and Echo striding out beside him, sunlight sparkling on their coats.

Ayiana drew in a sharp breath.

Ituha leapt forward with his hands outstretched.

Carrying over a large bowl of oats in both arms, Yuma greeted Diamond. "Are the others not coming?"

Small and delicate next to Fleet—he had grown a lot since Yuma first met him—Diamond's white coat contrasted his glowing black, her namesake eyes sparkling more than usual. "Tempest is still trying to get Moonglow interested in mating. He won't leave the island."

Fleet hung his head. "Gem answered me, but said she was helping Equinora by looking after her charges. She wouldn't come."

Ituha offered Echo another bowl of oats. He had also dressed for the occasion with a headdress of eagle feathers and his best fringed leggings. "Lord Echo and Lady Diamond, thank you for coming. I never imagined the myths were true, let alone that the Mother would grant the delight of your appearance in my lifetime. I'm only sorry it's the threats we face that brought us together."

Ayiana trembled at Yuma's side. "Lady Diamond, you are magnificent, more beautiful even than the legends describe! Is there anything else we can get for you?"

Diamond snuffled Ayiana's hand. "No, thank you, we have no

need of anything. Only, like you, to get rid of Shadow's beasts. What is it you need from us? Fleet tells us the jade worked against the bloodwolves."

The healer bowed her head. "Yes, but they are only part of the problem. Do you know how we can overcome the scorcheels? I'm sure there is much you could teach us. We have no experience of fighting water creatures, and the burning slime makes fish traps or nets impractical."

Diamond paced the clearing. "Tell me again how the water cured the young man where poison splashed his wound."

Yuma added his thoughts about the jade fragments entering Delsin's bloodstream. "Although it didn't help Fleet, we've tried feeding it to people suffering from the poison. It works for them. If only there were a way we could feed it to the scorcheels."

Fleet fidgeted. "What if you dropped jade in every stream? The scorcheels might eat some."

Ituha frowned. "That would take an enormous amount of stone. Do we have that much?"

Not being put off, and seeing merit in the idea, Yuma explored the possibility further. "We have many fragments too small to use as arrow tips. We could grind them to dust to make it go further. Dust! That's it! Remember the prophecy?"

Excitement bubbled out of him. "It didn't take much to cure Delsin. But how would we get the scorcheels to consume it? Do you think it would filter through their gills?"

Echo swallowed his mouthful of oats. "I could enhance the stone to make it appealing. After all, that's my power, to change stone into food and medication."

Fleet looked from Echo to Diamond. "How would we reach every creek and waterhole?"

Diamond twitched her upper lip while thinking. "It wouldn't need every pond and stream to be seeded, only the source of each river. By depositing the dust there, it will find its way downstream. I can certainly locate all the waterways. But I'd need a lot, and would have to carry it with me rather than repeatedly returning. I don't know how I'd do that."

Yuma's eyes lit up as another idea developed. "Perhaps I could ride you and carry the dust."

Diamond rolled her eyes and backed away. "I believe you sat on

Jasper to save him at Obsidian Caves, but I couldn't allow a man on my back. I'd feel every movement, maybe even your emotions. I doubt I could translocate like that."

Ayiana had been quiet for a while, a thoughtful look on her face. Now she spread her arms to measure Diamond. "We can weave grass ropes for you to carry leaf pouches all over your body. That would be different from having a rider. When you reach each destination, all you need to do is bite through the grass. The packages will come free and release the dust."

"I don't like the idea of being harnessed any more than carrying another living creature. What if I can't release the ropes? There must be another way."

Echo nuzzled her. "Take me with you, like we did to get to Tern Island and here. Then I can free the packages. The effort will cost you, of course, but I can also help by feeding any animals we meet. They'll need all the help they can get."

Ituha clapped Yuma on the back. "I thank the day you met Fleet. You are both mighty warriors. Now, while Lady Diamond and Lord Echo dust the rivers, you and our young people must seek and destroy the rest of the bloodwolves."

Ayiana joined in with her thanks and praise. "Our older people should return to their villages and restart their lives. There is much to be done."

Yuma stroked Diamond's neck. "Will you go back to Goose Fen after you've visited all the waterways?"

She looked at Fleet. "No. I'll go to Shimmering Lake. It's been too long since I've seen my daughter. I can help relocate the animals to repopulate the territories where the slaughter has been worst."

Fleet avoided her gaze. "I don't think Gem will want to see you. She believes she's ugly, which is why she ran away from you."

"Of course she isn't!" Diamond threw up her head, tossing her silver forelock out of her eyes. "She's the most beautiful creation I've ever seen."

Yuma calmed her with another stroke. "We agree, but she believes unicorn mares must be white and that her spiral horn is disfigured. You must have told her tales of Jasper and his temper when he had a contorted horn. She believes she carries the same bad blood, which is why she works so hard to care for all the animals."

Echo pawed the ground. "Is this why she never answers our calls?"

Diamond cried in anguish. "All this time she's been under a misapprehension! Aureana decreed each generation of unicorn would be more powerful than the previous. My daughter's colouring shows great strength, and a spiral horn is the sign of the second generation. I must go to her. It's well past time I taught her all she needs to know."

Yuma held out a handful of oats to Fleet. "What about you? Will you return to Gem when our work is done?"

Fleet arched his neck and raised his tail. "No. I must get rid of the poison in my veins, and stop Shadow from creating more of his beasts. You'll have to find another horse to ride. I'm going back to Obsidian Caves as the goddess demanded."

Chapter 25

The grass blurred beneath Fleet as he galloped north through Streak's territory, Echo thundering alongside him, each lost in his thoughts. With no need to pause to eat or stop for the night for Yuma to camp, they made good time. They expected Diamond to translocate to Watersmeet after the women completed her harness and the men had loaded parcels with jade dust.

The journey so far had been mainly uneventful. Only once had Fleet's rump warned of a nearby bloodwolf. He'd outrun it with ease, the crimson beast giving up the chase after a short sprint, its ribs protruding and eyes dull from starvation. Few animals remained in the rolling pastures; even birds were scarce, with any nests on the ground raided before the young had a chance to hatch.

They found a shallow crossing over the river coming east from Greenslopes, taking care to step only in clear water. A fresh flow from rainfall burbled over the stones of the broad causeway, but no silver fingerlings flashed in the sun, no reeds held croaking frogs, and no flycatchers darted to sweep up the clouds of hovering insects.

The village of Boasville lay deserted as before, the cluster of buildings fallen into disrepair, the same looming sense of doom emanating from the empty huts. Fleet stepped carefully to the river's edge and called Echo over from inspecting the people's abandoned homes. "This is where Yuma and I encountered the scorcheel."

Echo joined him and sniffed the muddy water. "I agree, this is a good place to test the dust. There's something foul in there."

"Don't get too close. Remember I told you Jasper and I found evidence of the scorcheels crossing land in Great Forest." Mentioning his sire's name renewed Fleet's pain. With his worries of Tress, and Gem, and the bloodwolves, he'd pushed away thoughts of the cliff breaking under Jasper. Now he had too much time to dwell on the past: the loss of Sapphire who had been his one true companion, Cirrus who he'd barely met, and Thunder who he'd known only in stories.

"Our timing has been good. Diamond messaged to say she's being loaded now." Echo trotted away from the river and rolled in a sandy hollow.

Fleet didn't have the heart for such pleasures. He stood on the edge of the forlorn village, waiting, thinking, and stewing.

The air shimmered, silver fireflies dancing in a beam of light. Diamond appeared, gradually becoming more solid, her familiar shape deformed by leafy packages hanging from her neck and shoulders, across her back, and down her flanks. "Is this the right place? Let's hurry up and get this over with. I hate feeling trapped."

Fleet led her closer to the water's edge. "Hold still while we bite the ropes."

Freeing a parcel took longer than any of them had anticipated. Finally, the last strand gave way, dropping its burden to the ground with a soft thud.

Echo picked it up with his teeth and stepped to the shore.

Fleet's rump throbbed. The water boiled. "No! Stop!"

They scattered, Fleet close on Diamond's heels.

A giant scorcheel slithered and hissed after Echo, the ground burning, trails of acid devouring everything in its wake, pungent smoke coiling above the path it had taken.

Fleet froze with indecision. If Yuma were here, he'd stab it like before. But Fleet had insisted he stay behind; this was his fight. He cut between Echo and the scorcheel, rearing over the slimy beast, bringing his hooves down on its writhing back. Rows of needle-like fangs gnashed at his legs. He dodged, quick as a snake, and attacked again.

And missed.

The scorcheel reared to the height of his chest, slime oozing down its crimson-streaked body, its stench overpowering.

He retreated before it could strike again.

Instead, it squirmed back to the river, its skin peeling and flaking off in rotting slabs where the sun dried the slime. It disappeared without a splash.

Diamond gasped. "We can't get near enough to shake the dust in the water with that thing there."

Echo paced back and forth. "This is madness. We'll never overcome Shadow's beasts like this."

Fleet stamped a hoof. "There must be a way. Echo, can you fling the package into the water from here with your horn, like Yuma uses his slingshot? He can bring down a flying bird."

"I'll try." Echo retrieved the fallen package near the river, keeping well clear of the slime trail, and hurried back with the tied leaves in his mouth. After placing the parcel on the ground, he stabbed it with his horn and tossed his head.

The package fell short.

Fleet fetched the parcel back. "Try again."

On the third go, the laden leaves fell into the river with a plop.

They waited.

Nothing happened.

Diamond peered downstream. "I don't think the parcel burst open. The jade won't—"

A spray of mud and blood erupted from the surface of the water. A twist of crimson and grey bodies burst out in a frenzied thrashing.

A single drop of acid burned Fleet's nose. He leapt away. "Keep clear!"

The three of them watched from a distance. The water churned and swirled like a whirlpool, streaked with slime and blood. A grey mass of flesh washed onto the bank, meat peeling from the bones, fins separating from the skin. Another dead scorcheel writhed its last on the gravel, and another. Bodies cloaked a sandy bank downstream.

Fleet snorted from his vantage on dry land. "I thought they'd revert to normal eels and swim away, like jade transformed the bloodwolves."

Diamond winced beside him. "I can't believe we did this to Aureana's creatures."

Echo nuzzled her. "Not Aureana's. Shadow's. I don't know how he created them, and don't care. Good riddance. Now that we know it works, let's get on and dust the source of all the rivers."

Fleet gawped at the pile of corpses building up on the sand: images of Jasper being torn to shreds left him no sympathy for the tortured creatures. The jade had transformed the bloodwolves. It killed the scorcheels. It healed the poisoned people. Why didn't it work on him? The only difference was his tainted blood. Shadow's blood.

As on Fleet's first visit to Shadow's territory, the same sense of nausea flooded him when he passed between the Sentinels. Again the rain poured, but the cold didn't affect him with Equinora's power pumping through his body. He tapped into the storm, drawing energy from the clash of clouds, sucking in the force of the wind.

This time Jasper wasn't here to guide him. This time Yuma wasn't there to light the way. This time Tatuk wasn't waiting to aid him on his return. The sooner the confrontation was over the better, one way or another. He broke into a gallop and zoomed along the slippery trail, his hooves gripping the stone with ease, the obsidian no longer cutting his soft soles. Nothing stopped his passage to the entrance where Yuma had lit the way with his meagre torch.

Except that entrance no longer existed.

A wall of black rock faced Fleet, the result of the cave-in caused by Jasper's power. The only other way in Fleet knew of went past Snag's web. He trotted around the mountain until he reached the mouth of the cave, hoping the giant spider had moved on.

A silver web stretched across the opening. At his approach, Snag scuttled round to the front. "You. Man. Trick."

Fleet halted a short distance away. "I need to see Shadow. Will you let me by?"

"Hungry. Eat. You." Her legs clattered as she wove an intricate net.

Retreating out of throwing range, Fleet considered his options. The spider wouldn't be tricked again, even if he had a plan. *Shadow! Your beasts are destroyed! Come out and meet me!*

Why? What have I to say to you? If you want to see me, come in here where it's warm and dry.

Pacing a distance from the entrance, Fleet snorted in frustration. He couldn't risk Snag's trap, no matter how much strength he could draw from the elements. She was one of Shadow's creations; the sticky strands might be imbued with power. And the tunnel mouth was small, black like the maw of a gaping bloodwolf.

At least the rain had stopped. Clouds scudded over the ragged mountain tops, ripped to pieces by their peaks. A shaft of sunlight hit his black coat, swelling his sense of well-being. The beam shifted as the break overhead moved, tracing a path towards the lava tube. Fleet watched, entranced, as a spot of light danced over the puddles, growing in size and strength until a perfect circle of gold rose up the wall.

It crossed to Snag's web, illuminating the tunnel behind in a blaze.

Snag disappeared, her staccato footfalls receding.

The goddess had cleared the way. He had come too far to let his fears overcome him. This was his chance! He raced to the entrance, building speed and increasing his power with every hoof-beat.

Fleet shut his eyes and hit the web at a run, his ears pinned back and his nostrils pinched closed. The web stretched and engulfed him. Threads cloyed at his throat, tightening like they had around Yuma's broken arm. He choked. Blackness filled his head. He must go back!

But it was too late; he must trust the goddess. He thrust his feet against the stone floor, thoughts of Sapphire, and Jasper, and all the savaged creatures driving him on.

The web tore. The strands fell free.

Fleet's propulsion flung him against the wall. Ignoring the raw scrape down his side, he charged forwards, towards Shadow's lair.

Fleet slowed down as darkness closed in. Then, as he neared the large cavern, the glow of lava relit the rock, ominous shadows climbing over protrusions, deep recesses sinister and threatening.

He advanced with care. The stillness after the roar of the wind outside smothered him as if all the air had been sucked away, the only sound the muffled *clop clop clop* of his hooves on stone. The musty smell of old bat dung penetrated his nostrils, his tongue furred with dread.

Clop clop clop.

He halted at the edge of the cavern, no longer as vast, fresh rock piles strewn across the floor. A trickle of light ran down to the giant rubble heap from what was presumably Jasper's escape route.

As before, Shadow perched on a broad ledge on the other side of the lava slinking along its channel. "Why have you come?"

PAULA BOER

Fleet strode to the edge of the burning rocks. "Your beasts are dead or vanquished. You've lost. Stop creating bloodwolves and scorcheels. They'll only be killed."

Shadow reared. "Lost? I have nothing to lose! Nothing!"

"Then why are you destroying all the goddess created? Why are you poisoning us?"

"Why shouldn't I? Those useless unicorns can't even perform their role as protectors. Why should they enjoy life in the sun and warmth when I am incarcerated here in the dark and cold?" He strutted around his platform, his blackness melding with the obsidian around him, his crimson mane and tail outlining his movements like blood smeared on the walls.

Fleet kept abreast of him, matching his strides one for one. "They are protecting Equinora! Who do you think is transporting jade to all the river sources even now?"

"Jade? Is that how you've overcome the obsidian? But it didn't work for *you*, did it?" He curled his lip and stopped, staring down at Fleet.

"No. No doubt it's your rotten blood in my veins preventing—"

Shadow leapt across the lava.

Fleet had no time to evade him. His neck stung from a deep bite. His ribs broke from a kick. He saw black and red, smelled ash and fire, tasted rock and blood. He whirled, defending himself with teeth and hooves, dodging and darting, escaping and attacking.

Fury drove him hard. His rump throbbed. A bloodwolf bounded down the spill of light and leapt at his throat. He threw up his head and ran backwards. The molten rock flared. His tail burst into flame, singeing his legs, burning his buttocks.

His nightmares came alive. Had they been a vision? Was that how Sapphire saw the future? Memories of his dam renewed his strength. He increased his attack, oblivious now to the pain.

Shadow didn't waver. His onslaught continued unabated.

Fleet weakened. He couldn't draw as much power from the hot rocks as Shadow could. He must do something! He had no breath or thought for words, only for fighting, to survive.

But did he want to survive? His job was done. The herds were safe. He couldn't rid himself of the poison, his blood. His blood was the poison! Always had been.

256

Only one solution would save the land forever. Shadow had to die!

Fleet gathered all his remaining strength and barged into Shadow's chest. He didn't relent. He pushed and shoved.

Shadow's hooves slipped on the rock, back towards the creeping lava. He reared, his forelegs locked with Fleet's.

Dragged vertical, Fleet neighed, his scream echoing around the cavern.

They tottered on their hind legs, front legs entwined, gnashing at each other's necks. Side-on to where the land's core oozed from the surface, they hovered.

Fleet glimpsed the madness in Shadow's eye. He had to end this. No matter what it cost him. He toppled to his side, towards the lava, taking Shadow with him, falling through eternity, through all creation, through all life.

Unimaginable heat consumed him. His lungs seared. He lost all feeling in his limbs. His spine melted, only his head left in the sulphurous fumes. "Sapphire! Jasper!"

The molten rock carried him along, as River Lifeflow had when he saved Yuma. So long ago. He swam. He gasped. He thought of Tress, and Gem, and dragons. He thought of Diamond, and Echo, and Tempest. He thought of Yuma, and Laila, and Delsin.

Almost submerged except for his head and neck, he cast his eyes around. He could see no sign of Shadow. The hot rock carried Fleet without burning him, his body intact. No pain assailed him. The only light came from the roiling lava.

Had he died? Was this how he'd be forever?

The world trembled. A huge fissure opened above him. The rock split to the sky. Beneath him, the land tilted. A great power flung him up into the void.

Fleet came to on a grassy slope, morning dew clinging to his coat. He blinked to get his bearings. Far in the distance, the Sentinels stood guard—he had landed outside Shadow's territory.

Shadow! Had he survived too?

Shoving himself to his feet, Fleet tested his legs. No broken bones. No pain. No dark clouds inside his head! The earthquake had saved him, throwing him beyond Obsidian Caves' barrier. The lava had healed him. Did his ancestral blood from Jasper give him power over fire? Or had the goddess kept him alive?

He didn't care which. Alive! And free!

Memories of Gem and Shimmering Lake sprang to his mind. His loins heated and his hair tingled as he imagined mating and then swimming in the healing waters. His hooves longed to gallop as he remembered playing with the dragons.

But he was a horse, not a unicorn, no matter his ancestry. What should he do?

Wolfbane may already have gathered many war horses. He had a duty to them, and he desired foals of his blood. He wanted to see youngsters chasing butterflies and bounding over streams. He wanted to protect mares, and spend time dozing and grazing with friends. With Gem, he'd lead a solitary life, meeting only when it suited her. He'd be a consort only.

He made his decision with conviction. He'd take Tress to White Water Cliffs, Sapphire's original home, and rebuild the herd as king.

Epilogue

Fleet stood sentry on top of a grassy knoll. It had been a long time since any sign of bloodwolves had been seen near White Water Cliffs, but grey wolf packs could still be a threat to the newborn foals. Since becoming Head of Warriors, Wolfbane had been successful in gathering the mares and stallions roaming the hills. When Fleet and Tress returned, a sizeable herd had awaited their leadership.

Watching the fillies and colts gambol in the sweet meadows, Fleet thought of Gem at Shimmering Lake. He had no regrets. A number of the young stallions who fought in the bloodwolf war had talked about trying to find the protected territory. Gem would have another companion by now. Hopefully, Tatuk had introduced himself to Laila too. Yuma had agreed not to mention dragons to anyone. Some magic must be protected.

Fleet gazed down on the young horses growing strong on the lush feed. Tress instructed the mares about which herbs they should eat to make their milk rich, and led the foals to patches of nettles and garlic to aid their bone development. His eyes lingered on her colt. They had expected him to be black like themselves. Instead, his silver coat sparkled. His hooves, mane, and tail shone like the copper that threaded the basalt cliffs. His light build and dished face belied his heritage; hence they had named him Mystery.

As he surveyed his territory, Fleet spotted a trio of humans trekking along the river. It wasn't unusual for people to join the growing Waterfalls clan. The first settlers had remained after exterminating the bloodwolves last summer, finding the meandering river protected by hills to their liking. Diamond and Echo had been true to their word and visited every water source twice, once to deposit the jade dust and later to ensure all the scorcheels had been vanquished.

The three people far below all looked to be men. A pity, as more women were needed for them to build their numbers. Although Fleet still didn't enjoy the company of children, with their screams and sudden movements, he understood the need to establish a larger clan. The people groomed the mares and sometimes rode out to hunt hogs, but with such a small clan, they couldn't grow sufficient oats and hay for the herds. Maybe more men were a good thing after all. They could help at the forthcoming harvest.

Fleet studied the newcomers. The walk of the lead man looked familiar. A ray of sunshine caught in the man's orange hair. "Yuma!" Fleet's heart quickened as he remembered the seasons of travel and the hardships they had overcome. He had missed their friendship.

Leaving his post, he galloped to greet the people.

He pulled up in a cloud of dust.

Yuma threw his arms around Fleet's neck and buried his face in his mane. "Greetings, old friend. I see you've been busy."

"Why aren't you riding?" Fleet would have welcomed more warriors to his domain. No coldblood was a threat to his rule. After a fateful challenge from a former king, the rest of the stallions had treated him with respect.

After introducing his companions as Chaytan and his son, Yuma explained he had no desire to ride a horse he couldn't talk with. "You've spoilt me, my friend."

Fleet nibbled Yuma's hair and then accompanied the men to the village, sharing their news along the way. No-one else was around, as most people had returned to their homes even though plenty of daylight remained. With only a small population, food was plentiful despite the slow return of animals. A reduction in the number of wolves meant the hogs' offspring had survived in vast numbers.

Pleased as he was to be reunited with Yuma, Fleet didn't understand why his friend had returned, especially making the long trek on foot. "So why are you here?"

"I want to rebuild the village. I owe that to my parents. Not that I want to be chief. But it's too good a site to waste, and many people have no wish to remain in their old homes with the memories of those they've lost." Yuma stopped on the outskirts of the huts, the new timber bright and strong where once there had been only charred remains. "It looks as if some people have arrived already."

"You'll be surprised how many are here."

The village buzzed with activity. Fleet escorted Yuma and his friends to the central hut. "You must meet the healer. She's very different from Laila, but she helps with difficult foalings, and tends to horses and people alike."

When Fleet called her, a tall slim woman ducked out of one of the huts. Before he could introduce her, she ran across the clearing.

Yuma ran towards her and threw his arms around her. "Winona! I thought you were dead. How did you survive?"

After wiping away her tears, Winona told how she had been gathering far afield when the bloodwolves attacked the clan. "I lived rough in the forest for many seasons. One day I saw a huge blaze. When I investigated, the Mother had purified the site. Any trace of poison or destruction was burnt. Since then I've been rebuilding what I can."

When Yuma had built the pyre to cremate his parents and the other dead, and had burned the huts, neither Fleet nor Yuma had thought anyone had survived. Fleet was pleased his friend's sister still lived. It was bad enough to lose one's parents, let alone a sibling as well. A twinge of regret pricked him as he thought of Shadow. He was the goddess's most powerful creation. Was he still alive? If so, where? Pushing his doubts away, the recovery of the land was all the proof Fleet needed that he had done the right thing.

As Yuma and Winona shared their stories, Tress galloped up in a panic. "Fleet, I need the healer! Mystery is in great pain. Come quickly!"

They huddled around the colt. Fleet was shocked to see Mystery's forehead swollen. Sweat poured from around his ears. His copper forelock tangled in a wet mass, the hair underneath falling off in clumps.

Winona opened her medicine pouch and extracted a wad of maple leaves. She ordered Yuma to sit on the colt's neck and applied a poultice over the boil. "I may need to lance it. Perhaps it's an allergic reaction to a sting. I've never seen anything grow so quickly."

Tress paced around her colt. His flanks heaved.

Fleet shuffled from hoof to hoof, powerless to help.

Chaytan sent his son to fetch water and held the colt's forelegs to stop him thrashing and injuring any of them. A spray of ichor gushed from Mystery's forehead.

Winona jumped back.

A copper snake erupted from the wound. It straightened, hardening into a spiralled horn as long as Mystery's leg below the knee. The colt blinked away the moisture. "I'm alright. Let me up. Give me space."

Yuma and Chaytan immediately leapt up and joined Winona.

They had understood Fleet's son! Mystery was almost half warm-blood but hadn't mated. How could he be heard by people? Fleet blinked as he realised the truth: he wasn't a noncorn like his sire.

Mystery had become a unicorn.

Yuma congratulated Tress and Fleet. "Moonglow must have foreseen this, which is why she wouldn't mate. A pity she didn't think to explain so we could have been prepared."

Fleet couldn't help thinking Tempest would be unimpressed. He shared his amusement with Tress.

She ignored him and nuzzled her colt's neck as he leapt to his feet. "Does it still hurt? Maybe we can travel to Shimmering Lake to seek help from Gemstone."

Mystery shook himself before bounding over to the creek to splash in the shallows. "No, I feel wonderful. I could gallop forever."

Dismayed, Fleet watched as Mystery cavorted. It seemed he could already draw energy from the land. How much more powerful would he become?

Tress stood by Fleet's side. "How will I rear a unicorn? I can't teach him to use his powers."

The other horses cantered over to investigate Mystery's new status.

Fleet acknowledged their son needed more guidance than either of them could give. "He must be sent to one of the other unicorns. It's time he was weaned anyway. You need to rebuild your strength ready for your next foal. But I can't leave the herd. I'll see if one of them will come here."

Yuma glanced at Winona. "I was bringing Chaytan here before heading to Shimmering Lake. I can take Mystery to Gem."

Fleet blinked. "I thought you'd returned to rebuild the village. Why would you travel so far now you've come home and your sister is here?"

"I'll be back. But we've very little jade left and I fear, as you do, that Shadow may not be dead."

Slapping his friend on the back, Chaytan winked at Winona. "More likely there's a certain young woman he'd like to see again."

Yuma shrugged and addressed Winona. "I'm sorry I have to leave so soon. We had to abandon the goddess's feathers at Obsidian Caves. If he's alive, Shadow might be able to use them."

Fleet agreed, and glanced toward his son. "Shimmering Lake is a good place for Mystery to grow up. I think Diamond may still be there too, even after all this time. I'll tell them you're on your way."

Bursting with pride, Fleet galloped to the crest of the nearest ridge. Tress and their colt raced after him. As the sun shone on their son's copper horn, Fleet reared and whinnied. He absorbed the energy of the wind and sent a message to the far corners of Equinora.

Welcome Mystery, the new Fire Unicorn!

Fleet's Ancestry

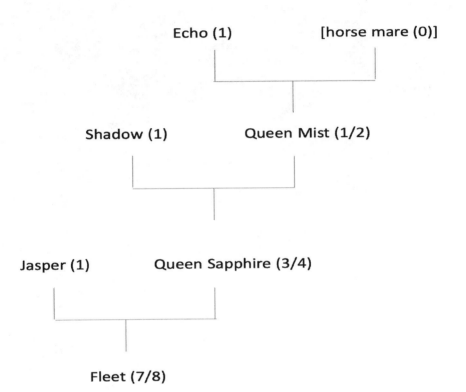

Echo (1)   [horse mare (0)]

Shadow (1)   Queen Mist (1/2)

Jasper (1)   Queen Sapphire (3/4)

Fleet (7/8)